THE AUTOGRAPHS OF THE APOCALYPSE

Danielle Ackley-McPhail	Derek Tyler Attico
Adam-Troy Castro	Russ Colchamiro
Peter David	Randee Dawn
Keith R.A. DeCandido	Kevin Dilmore
Mary Fan	Michael Jan Friedman
David Gerrold	Laura Anne Gilman
Robert Greenberger	Gerard Houarner
Gordon Linzner	Jonathan Maberry
James D. Macdonald	David Mack
Megan Mackie	Gail Z. Martin
Seanan McGuire	Jody Lynn Nye
Aaron Rosenberg	Jenifer Purcell Rosenberg
Hildy Silverman	Wrenn Simms
Patrick Thomas	Michael A. Ventrella
Dayton Ward	

THE FOUR ????? OF THE ApocAlypse

Edited by

Keith R.A. DeCandido & Wrenn Simms

WhysperWude
Bronx, New York

THE FOUR ???? OF THE APOCALYPSE
Published by WhysperWude LLC
publisher@whysper.net
Bronx, New York

PRINT ISBN 978-1-962466-00-4
DIGITAL ISBN 978-1-962466-01-1

Cover art by J.K. Woodward
Cover design by Aaron Rosenberg / Interior design by Wrenn Simms
Copy-edited by GraceAnne Andreassi DeCandido
WhysperWude logo designed by McP Digital Graphics

Table of Contents

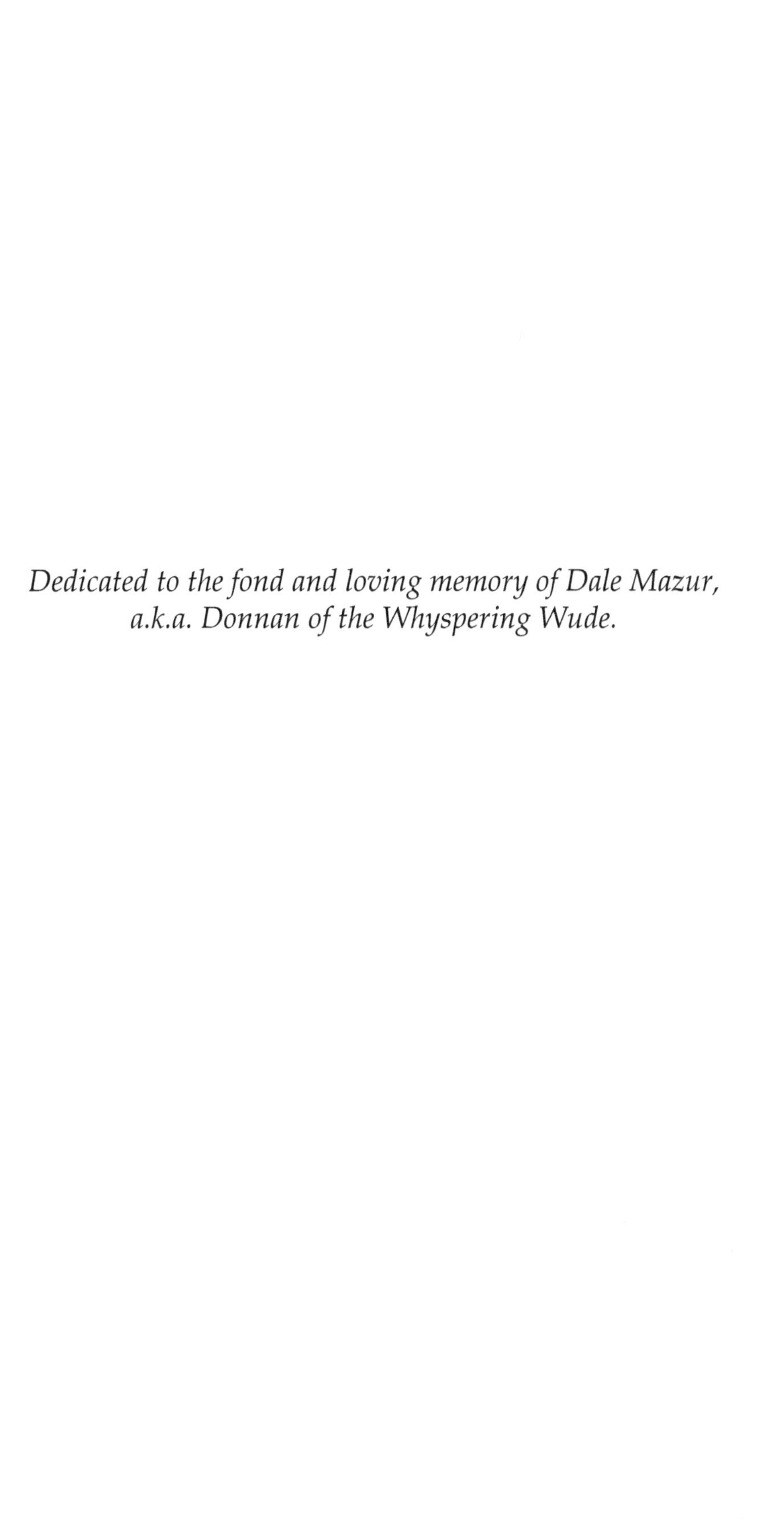

*Dedicated to the fond and loving memory of Dale Mazur,
a.k.a. Donnan of the Whyspering Wude.*

The Introduction of the Apocalypse

Keith R.A. DeCandido & Wrenn Simms

It all started, as these things often do, in the bar at a science fiction convention...

But first, back in the early 2000s, Keith was invited by the late great Jay Lake to contribute to an anthology called *44 Clowns: 11 Stories of the 4 Clowns of the Apocalypse.* The anthology wound up not happening for various reasons, and Keith would later put his contribution, which was entitled "Behold a White Tricycle," in his 2015 short-story collection *Without a License.*

And then that fateful day, at some convention or other, Keith and Wrenn were talking about the notion of the four clowns of the apocalypse over drinks with other authors, and suddenly other potential substitutions started suggesting themselves: the four PTA Moms of the apocalypse, the four squirrels of the apocalypse, the four septuagenarians of the apocalypse.

Which resulted in those fateful words, "We should do an anthology." Or was it, "You should do an anthology"? This, of course, led to, "Well, we'd need people to write the stories." Like that would be some kind of out, with this crowd...

Wrenn and Keith inexplicably decided to put their various talents for writing, editing, production, and publishing together to form the small press WhysperWude, with their inaugural publication being *The Four ???? of the Apocalypse.* One successful Kickstarter and a whole lot of paperwork later, and that anthology conceived over Jim Beam, Chambord, beer, Scotch, wine, White Russians, etc., is now in your hot little hands.

Despite the humor inherent in so many of these concepts, not all the stories herein are comical. Seanan McGuire, Derek Tyler Attico, Laura Anne Gilman, Michael Jan Friedman, Gerard Houarner, and Megan Mackie all bring the drama and/or horror in their tales, which range from out-and-out ick to nasty to elegaic.

However, you can also be assured that plenty of folks brought the funny. We especially recommend not drinking anything while reading the stories by David Mack, Jody Lynn Nye, Michael A. Ventrella, Aaron Rosenberg, Adam-Troy Castro, Gordon Linzner, Gail Z. Martin, Hildy Silverman, Patrick Thomas, Dayton Ward & Kevin Dilmore, David Gerrold, and Wrenn.

We've even got some pieces of larger universes. Jonathan Maberry gives us a story in his Kagen the Damned fantasy series, while Danielle Ackley-McPhail provides one of many new stories about the four lunch ladies of the apocalypse, and James D. Macdonald revisits his eccentric main character of Orville Nesbit. And three of our authors wound up with musical themes, though we're pleased to say that Mary Fan, Randee Dawn, and Russ Colchamiro took very different approaches to their opera singers, rock stars, and drummers of the apocalypse...

The rest of the stories do a lovely job of bringing both the drama and the humor, from Robert Greenberger's cheerleaders and Jenifer Purcell Rosenberg's PTA Moms to Peter David's religious leaders and Keith's septuagenarians. After all, we're still sorta-kinda talking about the end of the world here. Or, at least, the end of somebody's world...

So pull up a chair, pour yourself a drink (which is how this all got started), and prepare to enjoy more than two dozen new takes on the apocalypse.

The Apocalypse Will Be Televised

David Mack

"It's a trap."

The warning from Pestilence halted War's reach for the snacks. He looked askance at his partner. "Say what, now?"

Pestilence nodded at the tray of sweet and savory nibbles, on the coffee table between the two facing couches in the movie studio's lobby. "Those. They're a trap."

As usual, Death pretended not to pay attention to the other three Horsemen of the Apocalypse, but Famine couldn't help but take the bait. "How are chocolate-covered pretzels a trap?"

"It's not chocolate, it's carob."

War pulled back from the treats. "Oh, that's not right."

"Also, I just laced the tray with salmonella."

Famine grimaced. "Luckily for me, I'm not hungry."

The Horsemen fell quiet at the approach of Keilani, the executive assistant to the studio's president. She was a fashionably dressed young woman with golden-brown skin and a voice to match. The left half of her head was shaved; from the other side fell a nebula-colored ombré of long curls.

"Mister War? How are y'all doing over here?"

"We're fine. Will it be much longer?"

"Mister Morganstern will see you soon. In the meantime, can I get you all anything to drink?"

Death dismissed Keilani's offer with the wave of a skeletal hand. Pestilence feigned discomfort as he said, "Pass."

Her gaze landed upon Famine, who shook his head. "Sorry, I'm on a diet."

"Mister War? Anything for you?"

"Half-caf double espresso with a twist of lemon."

Flummoxed but not allowed to show it, Keilani retreated to her desk to start her search for a barista on the premises.

Pestilence paged through the latest issue of *Deadline Hollywood*, whose pages blackened with mold at his touch. "What the fuck are we even *doing* here?"

"We promised Murray we'd take the meeting."

Famine shook his head. "Fuckin' Murray. We're the Horsemen of the Apocalypse. Tell me again why we need an agent?"

War was tired of having this argument. "Because none of us knows shit about negotiating for life-rights."

Pestilence tossed his magazine. "So why isn't Murray *here*?"

"Agents set up pitch meetings," War explained for what felt like the hundredth time. "They don't come to them."

When Death thought no one was looking, he pointed his scythe at a middle-aged man standing at a table on the other side of the lobby, mixing soy milk into a mug. The gray-bearded, pot-bellied man clutched his chest, his face contorted in agony, and then he fell to the floor, deader than disco.

War sighed at the casual slaying. "*Really?* That couldn't have waited until *after* our meeting?"

Death shrugged and then picked up a copy of *The Hollywood Reporter* as if he hadn't just written its next issue's cover headline: *Steven Spielberg, 1946–2023*.

Heedless of the quiet carnage, Famine tapped a message into his smartphone. Concerned his associate might be undermining their agent's efforts, War reached out with the blade of his sword and used its tip to lower Famine's phone. "What are you doing?"

"Sending paparazzi photos to Vanessa Hudgens."

"Why?"

"I'm hoping these wide-angle lens shots of her ass will give her an eating disorder."

All War could do was shake his head. "You're a sick man."

"Right. Like you're up for *Time*'s Person of the Year. Eat me."

"Wouldn't eating you go against your brand?"

"Hell, no. I'm all gristle."

Passersby had started to gather around the corpse of Steven Spielberg when Keilani returned to the Horsemen. "Excuse me, gentlemen. Mister Morganstern will see you now."

War sheathed his sword. "About time."

The Horsemen stood and followed Keilani past her desk, toward the executive suite. She opened the double doors that she so zealously guarded, day in and day out, and ushered the harbingers of doom past her into Morganstern's office.

As they entered, War couldn't help but smile at the distant music of strife, between interns arguing heatedly over where the fuck they were ever going to find a fucking twist of lemon for his goddamned half-caf double espresso.

*****

Inside the office, the Horsemen were greeted by a gleaming white smile attached to a human-shaped life-support system. "Wonderful to see you!" Morganstern gestured toward a long sofa set against the wall on their left. "Have a seat."

It was a tight fit, uncomfortable for all of them. War sat at one end, nearest to Morganstern. Wedged onto the sofa to his right were Famine, Pestilence, and Death.

All of his attention, however, was trained upon the four eager young faces looking at them from the other side of another low coffee table. Two appeared to be men, one looked like a woman, and the last could have been either. Each of them sat in an ergonomic Aeron office chair and held a tablet and a stylus.

With a wave of his hand, Morganstern introduced his colleagues from left to right as they faced the Horsemen. "Gents, I'd like you to meet Brad, Perry, Karen, and Michel. Four of the hottest dev execs in town."

Narrowing his yellowed eyes, Pestilence shot a sidelong look at Morganstern. "I thought we were meeting with you."

"And you are."

Famine gestured at the four executives. "So who are they?"

"My top vice-presidents. They've all read your pitch, and they have a few notes they'd like to share."

Under his foul breath, Pestilence mumbled to War, "I told you we should've brought Murray."

"Shh. Let me handle this." War faced Morganstern and his team. "What kind of notes?"

Perry raised his hands in mock surrender. "Nothing major. Seriously, we *love* your pitch."

"*Love* it," Karen echoed.

Michel nodded like a Bobblehead in an earthquake. Their accent was vaguely French-Belgian. "Totally! *Love* your energy. The whole end-of-the-world vibe, classic Old Testament stuff. It's just faboo, darlings."

"Yes, yes, yes," Brad cut in. "We don't want to mess with your vision. Maybe just sharpen it up a little. But, hey, before we get started? Has anyone offered y'all something to drink?"

Pestilence raised a gray palm. "No, thanks."

Death said nothing, but Famine scowled at Brad. "What is it about L.A. that makes you all so fucking obsessed with offering people something to drink? I mean, I know you built this city in the middle of a fucking desert, but that doesn't mean—"

War stifled Famine's rant with a raised hand, and then he flashed a bloodied smile at Brad. "Ignore him. He's on a juice cleanse. But since you asked, I'm still waiting on a half-caf double espresso with a twist of lemon."

"Um, sure." Brad swiveled his chair so he could reach an office phone on the narrow table behind him. He lifted its receiver and pressed a button to page the assistant outside.

The office door opened and Keilani leaned in. "Yes?"

"A half-caf double espresso—"

"—with a twist of lemon, for Mister War. Yes, we're working on it, he'll have it in just a sec." Keilani ducked out and shut the door before anyone could ask her for anything else.

Famine heaved a sigh freighted with impatience. "Are you all done fucking around? Can we get on with this, please?"

Pestilence cocked an eyebrow. "Hangry much?"

War piled on: "Maybe he needs a Snickers bar."

"Maybe you both need to eat the corn out of my shit."

Behind his desk, Morganstern shifted with anxiety in his high-backed leather chair. "This seems like a good time to dig into our notes."

Famine crossed his arms. "Whatever."

War did his best to appear hopeful. "Okay. We're all ears."

Brad looked to the end of the line of his colleagues. "Michel? Why don't you lead us off?"

The androgynous European leaned forward and turned their tablet's screen toward War. "First, we absolutely love all the action in your pitch. Pure blockbuster, *mon frère*! I just have one little note, about the nuclear holocaust—"

"What about it?"

"Well, it's a tad... *dark*. Makes it hard to sell product place-ments. Also, and this is from our production designer—the elec-tromagnetic pulses play hell with the new digital cameras."

War resisted the urge to disembowel Michel. "All right, then. How do you feel about blood and gore?"

"*Love* them, darling!"

"Fine. I'll make sure World War Three is fought with bayonets and rocks. Will that work for you?"

Michel blessed the notion with a chef's kiss. *"Parfait."*

Brad moved the meeting along. "Perry? You had a few notes for Pestilence?"

"Yes, I did." Perry crossed his legs, as if he were worried about a sudden attack on his genitals. His face and tone turned apologetic as he said to Pestilence, "I'm sorry to say, you didn't test well."

Noxious green fumes curled from Pestilence's pointed nose. *"Excuse* me?"

"With our focus groups. I mean, can you blame them? The whole world's still feeling traumatized by the COVID pandemic."

Pestilence seemed to take the note personally. "That wasn't me! That was just a routine pandemic. Which would've been no big deal if certain people hadn't been dumber than goddamn dirt."

Looking defensive but still smiling blankly, Perry checked his notes on his tablet. "Be that as it may, our marketing team wants to switch your affliction for something a bit more hip."

"Such as?"

Karen held up a binder with an orange cover. "We're thinking you could be... Micro-aggressions!"

"We're the Horsemen of the Apocalypse, you mewling twit. If anything, we deal in *macro*-aggressions."

Perry loosened his tie, then cleared his throat. "Yes, of course. It's just that, from a branding perspective—"

"Listen up, you rotting sack of meat. It was only under protest that I let Pratchett and Gaiman 're-imagine' me as Pollution for *Good Omens*. Now please take this personally, Perry, but you're no Terry Pratchett." Pestilence shot a sour look at Karen. "And you're definitely no fucking Neil Gaiman."

Karen sank into her chair. Perry absorbed the critique with a sagely nod. "You're absolutely right, Mister Pestilence."

"There are other possibilities," Brad said, doing his best to sound chipper. "For instance: Mister Pestilence, would you be open to having your character gender-flipped?"

"Gender-flipped?" A cold miasma spewed from Pestilence's mouth as he spoke. "Why the fuck would I want *that*?"

Brad shrugged. "Well, I mean—*c'mon*. The Four Horse*men*? Your Apocalypse is kind of a sausage party."

Karen turned her tablet to show a chart to the Horsemen. "It doesn't test well with women eighteen to thirty-five."

Pestilence pointed at Famine. "Gender-flip *him*, then."

All four of the junior executives shook their heads and fought to suppress derisive smirks.

Michel waggled a finger at Pestilence. "Famine as a woman? Implying that she has body dysmorphia? Or an eating disorder? Do you have any idea the kind of hate mail we'd get for that?"

"Maybe I should just give you all cancer."

Famine set a hand on Pestilence's shoulder. "Now, now. Let's hear them out. After all, show business is what they do."

"Not for much longer, it isn't."

The door opened, and a young man wearing a bespoke three-piece suit with a pair of beach sandals entered, carrying on a tray a demitasse cup. He stopped and with a slight bow presented the beverage to War, who seized it in one massive fist.

"Thank you."

War flung the cup's steaming contents into the assistant's face. The young man yelped in pain and staggered backward, blinded. War drew his sword and with one fell stroke opened the man's throat. The assistant gurgled through a mouthful of blood, staggered sideways, and fell dead atop the coffee table.

An awkward silence filled the room. No one moved.

The only word Brad could utter was, "...Why?"

"I wanted it iced."

Perry's face blanched with horror. "You could've said so."

"Where would be the fun in that?"

Behind the big desk, Morganstern looked stricken. "Did you really have to kill him?"

"I'm War. It's kind of my brand."

"Still... it seems a bit extreme."

"Was he union?"

"No."

"Then who gives a shit?"

The movie-studio executives exchanged looks of apprehension and confusion. War was certain he heard the junior suits sigh in relief as Morganstern declared, "I think now would be a good time to break for lunch."

*****

Never in all his endless life had War seen so many souls who deserved to die by steel and flame than he had found in Hollywood. Awash in the arrogance of the mediocre, the vanity of the faded, and the petty cruelties of the insecure, he felt an urge to set Tinseltown aflame and return the City of Angels to the desert from which it had sprung like a sentient fungus.

But his vengeance would have to wait. They had only ninety minutes for lunch before they were expected back on the studio lot, and the traffic on Melrose had been a fucking nightmare. Fortunately, meals with his cohort tended to be brief affairs.

Their server arrived wearing the uniform of fine-dining: black trousers, a crisp white shirt, and an insincere smile. Her one sanctioned nod to rebellion was the cluster of metal rings that adorned her left ear. She greeted the Horsemen as she filled their water glasses, one by one. "Welcome to Bestia. I'm Charity. I'll be your server today." Her voice was chipper and her eyes were dead. "Today's specials are on the front of your menus. Please let us know if you have any food allergies or other dietary restrictions." She set down the water pitcher, took a leather-bound folder from under her arm, and handed it to Death. "We have an extensive wine list, if you're interested."

Pestilence looked up from his menu. "Don't bother. It's all corked."

Death slammed the wine list onto the table and radiated fury at Pestilence. Famine shook his head at the personification of disease and decay. "You're an asshole."

The rebukes didn't seem to bother Pestilence, who told War, "I'd skip the scallops, if I were you."

War ripped his menu in half and threw the pieces on the table. "Every. Fucking. Time."

Charity looked bored and uncomfortable at the same time. "Would you folks like some appetizers for the table?"

"Let's just order," War said.

"Nothing for me," Famine said.

"New York strip steak," War told Charity.

"How would you like that cooked?"

"Black and blue." He shot a withering look at Pestilence. "And if I smell one thing wrong with it, I know where you live."

"Noted." Pestilence dumped his glass of tap water on the floor. "A flight of top-shelf whiskeys, please."

"Very good." She turned toward Death. "And for you?"

Death opened his menu and pointed at the top of one page.

"The salmon mousse. Very good, sir." She closed her pad. "I'll get that order in for you, and then I'll be back with your breadsticks." She strode away with purpose but devoid of joy.

Death nudged one of War's torn menu pages back toward him and pointed at the item in its corner.

War noted Death's gesture. "You want the chocolate lava cake?" Death shrugged. War knew he'd have to persuade him. "You want to split it?" Death nodded. "Fine. It says it takes twenty minutes to prepare, so we'll tell the girl when she comes back."

The moment of optimism was broken by Pestilence clearing his throat. "I wouldn't."

"Don't you fucking dare."

"It's not me this time, I swear!... Not my fault these savages can't learn to wash their hands."

*****

Upon their return to Morganstern's office, the Horsemen found a special torture waiting for them: Perry had linked his tablet to a projector so that he could illustrate his next round of feedback with a PowerPoint presentation.

Somewhere around slide number 426, War found himself paraphrasing the Bible: *For God so loved the world that He did not put together a focus group.*

"If you'll note the figures in column three—" Perry highlighted the projection with a green laser dot from his pen. "—you'll see that our market demo research shows that your Apocalypse tests better across multiple segments and in almost all major markets if Famine is swapped out for Cancel Culture."

With a tap on his tablet, Perry switched the image on the wall to a crowded still-life of boxed candy, bulging hot dogs, buckets of unnaturally yellow popcorn, and paper cups of soda that were sweating like Satan's ball sack. "After all, a big part of what keeps the exhibitors in business is concessions, so I'm sure you can see why they'd prefer we didn't self-sabotage a major profit center. Am I right?"

Famine whispered to War, "Let me cock-slap this peckerwood 'til he cries for his mama."

Pestilence leaned over to add in a hush, "Get in line."

At the front of the room, Brad stepped in to take over the presentation. "We've saved our most important note for last." He nodded at Perry, who switched the image to one of Earth as a charred cinder backed by a shattered moon. "Our focus groups were nearly unanimous in their feelings about your proposed ending, in which all life on Earth is snuffed out, without any hope of revival or renewal."

War sat forward. "They loved it, yes?"

"Um... no. Typical reactions included, 'just too dark,' 'a total bummer,' and 'kind of cliché.' Most damning of all, more than half called it 'too predictable'."

That news left Famine looking gobsmacked. "What did they fucking expect? We're here to end the world, not sell Goobers."

Brad held up both hands. "And we're behind that vision, one hundred percent, I promise. But trust me when I say there's good news. I wouldn't break something I didn't know how to fix."

Another nod from Brad triggered another image update. On the wall appeared an artist's rendering of Death with his scythe in one bony fist, and the other holding the hand of a Bohemian-styled young woman who might as well have been wearing a sign printed in bold letters: MANIC PIXIE DREAM GIRL.

"What we need is a 'twist' ending, à la M. Night Shyamalan—who's keen to direct, by the way."

War felt as if he were about to become sick. "What the *fuck* is this?"

Brad pressed his hands together as if in prayer, and then used them to gesture dramatically at the image on the wall. "We have a rewrite for Act Three in which, just before the last seal is about to be broken and the world destroyed forever, Death realizes he has fallen in love with a mortal—"

"Fuck me," Pestilence cut in. "*Death* gets a love interest? *Again?*"

"Maybe. We also have a draft where he's won over by the love of a beagle puppy. We'll go with whatever tests better in the Asian markets. Anyway, Death surrenders to Love, the world is saved, and we go to credits while Louis Armstrong sings 'What a Wonderful World'." He faced the Horsemen, his manner almost apologetic. "Of course, that's the bad pitch. You'll turn it into something great. But that's the general idea."

A pained silence yawned between the two sides of the room.

Pestilence leaned forward to look past Famine and ask War, "Is this motherfucker serious?"

All that War could do was shake his head. "I've heard enough. Let's bounce." He stood from the sofa, and the other Horsemen did likewise.

Their preparation for departure brought Morganstern out from behind his desk. "Whoa! Let's not make any hasty decisions.

We can still work this out. What do you guys need? Full shares on the merchandising? Half a point each on the gross?"

Famine flipped Morganstern the bird. "Fuck you."

Pestilence cupped his sack. "Suck my syphilitic junk."

Morganstern grew more desperate by the moment. "Mister War, please! Be reasonable! There must be some—"

"Can it." War ushered Famine and Pestilence out of the office ahead of him. "We never wanted to do a movie. We've always seen this as more of a premium streamer series."

Morganstern blocked the office's door and jabbed his meaty index finger at War's chest. "You won't get away with this. I'm tight with every dev exec in town. Once I put the word out, your little Apocalypse is dead, you hear me? D-E-A-D. Fuckin' *dead!* You won't even be able to do *lunch* in this town."

War looked at the finger touching his chest.

Then he looked over his shoulder at Death.

"Show Mister Morganstern what *dead* is."

Without declaration or fanfare, Death put his hand to the nearest wall. In the blink of an eye, the office around them crumbled into dust, along with the four junior development executives. In a matter of seconds, every other building on the lot disintegrated, taking with them hundreds of souls, a goodly fraction of them union members.

Morganstern had just enough time to gaze in horror and despair upon the ashes of his empire before a hot gust of Santa Ana wind swept it all away. He remained there, mute and alone, as the Four Horsemen mounted their spectral steeds.

War faced his comrades. "Who knows how to get to Netflix?"

Famine held up a small slip of paper. "I'm still trying to figure out how to validate parking for a horse."

"No hurry. Netflix's top brass all just caught the plague."

Death sighed under his hood. His voice was a peal of thunder and the fathomless roar of the sea.

"I HATE THIS TOWN."

Well, *That* Escalated Quickly

Seanan McGuire

A Plague of Wasp

Frank closed the nozzle on his sprayer and turned to face his partner. "What are you on about?"

"Wasp. Weird. Have you seen?" Laurel brandished the jar she was holding, shaking it, like she thought pissing the damn thing off would make it easier to identify. And maybe that wasn't entirely wrong, with a wasp. It was so rare to see them not trying to murder the world that identification was occasionally more straightforward when they were in a rage.

Laurel had been with the company less than six months, and she was well on her way to getting on his last nerve. Part of it was being stuck in the same truck all damn day; part of it was being expected to mentor her; and part of it was sheer talent on her part. He'd met a lot of frustrating people in his time. He'd even worked with some of them. Few had been as quick to worm their way under his skin and drive him straight out of his goddamn mind.

Women didn't belong in extermination, if you asked him. After six months, she should have been going on solo calls, but oh no, she couldn't, because it somehow "wasn't safe" for a lady to go to client houses alone. As if she wouldn't have a massive cannister of *poison* strapped to her back if anyone got fresh? A little "accidental" squirt in the eyes and they *might* leave a bad review, after they got out of the emergency room. But no, she was too good for assault and battery, and so he got saddled with her until they found another woman who wanted to kill bugs for a living and she became the new kid's problem.

She was right about one thing: it *was* a weird wasp. He'd never er seen one like that before, about the size of his thumb—and he had pretty hefty thumbs—with a wingspan comparable to his palm. Its carapace was a gleaming oilslick of rainbow colors, from primaries to pastels, and its stinger was over an inch long, extended and pulsing near the glass.

Frank took the jar from Laurel's hand and gave it a solid shake, watching the wasp beat its wings to stay upright.

"Mean-looking bastard," he said, peering at it. "How'd you catch this thing?"

Laurel wasn't even looking at him. She was watching the carpenter bees pouring out of the crack in the wall, so many more than he would have suspected, almost enough to qualify as a swarm. But that was ridiculous. Carpenter bees didn't swarm like honeybees; they weren't social. That was part of what made them so easy to exterminate.

"Hey, Laurel." He snapped his fingers. "Eyes over here, girly."

Slowly, Laurel turned to look at him. There was something in her expression he didn't like. If he hadn't known better, he would have called it contempt. But that didn't make sense. Hadn't he answered all her questions, even the fucking stupid ones, and shown her how to work their equipment, and generally acted as the mentor he didn't want to be? Hadn't he been good to her?

"How'd you catch it?" He held up the jar. "Fucker like this looks like it'd rather rip your arm off than let somebody put it under glass."

"We have an understanding, she and I," said Laurel. "So you've never seen anything like her before?"

"Absolutely not," said Frank. "I'd remember a bastard this ugly."

"I'm sorry," said Laurel. She snatched the jar from his hand. "I'm sorry you can't appreciate a jewel for what it is."

"I don't understand what the fuck you're talking about."

Laurel looked him in the eye as she smashed the jar against the concrete driveway, freeing the monster wasp into the air. "Oops," she said, deadpan.

Frank took a step back. "Joke's on you, sweetheart," he said. "Wasps hold grudges. They're smart enough to know who's hurt them."

"That's true," said Laurel. She tilted her head. "Wasps *do* remember."

The wasp, which had been circling, swept toward him, stinger aimed for his eye. Frank shouted and reeled backward, fumbling with his sprayer. The wasp was faster. It slammed into his face, stinger sliding into his eye socket with a sensation like a lit cigarette. He yelled, slapping his hands down across his face. In this, too, he wasn't quite fast enough; the wasp was gone by the time his palms struck skin, and it felt like he only drove the venom deeper in.

"Sorry, Frank," said Laurel.

"You—bitch!" he snarled, unable to unpeel his hands from his face. The pain was too intense. He couldn't move.

"I tried, you know. I tried to give you chances to get out of the way, tried to let you prove yourself worth saving—tried everything I knew to do, but you didn't listen, and we don't like people who kill babies."

The buzzing grew louder. Frank was suddenly, horribly glad he couldn't see.

It was easier this way.

"Goodbye, Frank."

Pain, then darkness, then nothing at all.

A Plague of Ants

Everyone was very sad when Frank quit without warning, vanishing into the halcyon mists of retirement. Laurel was the only one not seen to shed a tear at the makeshift retirement party thrown together in his honor, blemished both by the lack of budget—Frank would have been the first to say that one round of cheap beer and stale donuts did not a send-off make—and the absence of the guest of honor. Instead, she spent the whole occasion sitting stiffly in her chair, glancing to the door every few seconds, like she was waiting for something

Waiting for Frank, probably. He'd told everyone in the office about how big a crush she had on him, how she couldn't do anything in the field without running it past him, how she needed his agreement before she could go on break or pick up a cup of coffee. Heather, the receptionist, had pointed out that this sounded less like "having a crush" and more like "being a trainee with an overbearing mentor," but had been shut down by wiser voices. Laurel was a woman in a man's profession. Clearly she wouldn't have made that choice if she hadn't been looking for an excuse to spend time around proper men. Men like Frank, who was going to make some lucky girl a great husband one day, when she put in the work to catch his attention.

Most of management had been assuming that lucky girl was going to be Laurel, but since even she didn't seem to know where he'd disappeared to, that was seeming less and less likely. No, Frank was well and truly gone, and they were going to have to go on without him.

The last beer was finished off, the last empty tossed into the bin, and the company president took the floor—or at least the front of the room—to say a few words about their absent colleague. Everyone turned to pay him the attention he deserved. Everyone except Laurel, who was watching the door, and Heather, who was watching Laurel.

He frowned. When he spoke, everyone was supposed to listen. Clearing his throat, he pulled out the index cards on which his speech had been printed by his wife, who knew how important it was that this go smoothly. Frank had been with the company since the beginning. Losing him was a blow not only to staffing, but to morale.

Heather finally looked at him, her face oddly drawn and pale. She'd probably been in love with Frank too. Guy was a real lady-killer. The president smiled indulgently. Oh, girls. They never changed.

"My fellow exterminators," he read, and paused for the laughter that always followed that opener, predictable as flies following maggots. Dutifully, the room chuckled and guffawed, and he smiled again before he continued, "The loss of our friend and colleague has left us with an unfortunate staffing problem. Until we can hire a new exterminator to fill Frank's shoes—which is a hard order, no matter how you want to look at it—our junior members will be asked to step in on the weekends and for on-call shifts. The insect kingdom is ever on the assault, and doesn't care what we're going through."

Was Laurel smiling? Because it looked like Laurel was smiling. He couldn't seriously be expected to stand here and tolerate this sort of disrespect in his own break room!

She was probably just lost in fond memories of Frank. He needed to be forgiving. They were all dealing with a loss, but she was grappling with something larger than he could possibly understand.

He kept reading, offering platitudes interspersed with reduced overtime pay and the need to send even junior exterminators out without partners. He was winding down when Laurel stood and walked across the room—not to the door she'd been watching this whole time, but to the door leading deeper into the building. He stopped mid-sentence, staring aghast as she opened the door, stepped through, and was gone.

The *audacity*! The *disrespect*! Why, he had *never*! He sputtered and stewed, unable to keep reading. He was still standing there, red-faced and inchoate, when a new sound rose to dominate the room.

Heather was screaming, on her feet and pointing at the door Laurel had been staring at so fixedly. The exterminators turned, those closest to the door scoffing.

"It's just ants," one of them said. "A little embarrassing, given where we're at, but nothing worth howling down the roof for." He stood, moving toward the door.

Heather bolted to her feet and ran, following Laurel's path and slamming the door behind her.

The exterminator who had risen looked to his colleagues and laughed, grasping the knob and pulling inward.

All laughter stopped a moment after that, as the open door revealed, not the steps down to the outside, but a solid, moving wall of tiny bodies and clacking mandibles.

"What the...?"

The wall fell inward, cascading over him before shattering into millions of individual ants. They were a smalltime extermination business in suburban Oregon; there was no reason for any man in that room to recognize the Australian bulldog ant. They still knew to be alarmed when the first man began screaming, flailing as he tried to knock the ants covering his body to the floor. He succeeded, with a few, sending them crashing down to join their fellows.

Most, however, continued clinging to his exposed flesh, biting and stinging, ripping with a ferocity ants should never have possessed. Hundreds of them, filling his body with their poisons. He never stood a chance, not really.

If anything, it was astonishing he managed to stay on his feet for as long as he did.

The exterminators shouted and lunged for the few cans of bug spray kept in the cafeteria—don't shit where you eat and don't poison, either. That was an unofficial company motto, and so they found themselves almost defenseless as wave after wave of ants closed in on them, their position effectively blocking both exits from the room.

Things got very loud for a while after that. And then they got very quiet. The sound of thousands of ants eating was barely louder than the wind whistling against the windows, after all.

Heather ran through the building until she found Laurel in the lobby, suited-up and heading out into the parking lot. She stopped in the hallway entrance, gripping the wall and wheezing. Laurel turned to look at her with bland curiosity in her eyes.

"A-ants," Heather managed to wheeze. "They're all over the cafeteria."

"Are they?" Laurel smiled. "I suppose that will be a fun challenge for the 'real' exterminators."

"There were so *many*," Heather said, trying to convey the scope of something unconveyable with words alone. Laurel's smile grew as she ducked her head, and light glinted off the flowered hairclip above her ear. It was colorful, jeweled, feminine in a way Laurel had never allowed herself to be when she was at work, and Heather stared at it, inexplicably transfixed.

Then it moved, shifting closer to Laurel's ear, and what Heather had taken for decorative petals beat once, and she realized it was an impossibly large wasp. She gasped, clapping her hand over her mouth. Laurel, looking relieved, nodded.

"All right," she said, and glanced back to Heather. "You've committed no transgressions. You can be allowed to thrive in what's to come, if you remain aware of your place in the cycle of things. The debt calls for a life for a life, and they breed so much faster than we do that the scales will never be balanced. The age of man is over. The age of insects is begun. Stay dutiful and you can stay alive."

She let herself out then, as Heather sank slowly to the floor.

When the ants found her almost an hour later, she was still sitting there. They walked across her body, antennae waving, and she allowed it, not brushing them away. And so not a single one of her new employers attempted to harm her, just removed the crumbs from her clothes, anointed her with scent trails to mark her as their own, and moved along.

Alone in the hallway, Heather put her hands over her face and wept.

A Plague of Mosquitoes

Heather did, eventually, come to her senses enough to get her purse and walk to her car, careful not to step on any lingering ants, not swatting at the mosquitoes that came to investigate the heat of her body in the evening dimness. As for the mosquitoes, they nuzzled her skin but didn't bite, seeming to recognize and respect the claim made by the ants. One by one, they took off, wings droning, and flew in a thin haze toward downtown.

Heather barely noticed. She was busy sliding behind the wheel, closing the door, sealing herself into a presumably insect-free environment, and taking her first deep breath since Laurel's exit. She'd been breathing the whole time, of course, but shallowly, desperate not to inhale an ant and condemn herself to a horrific death.

And it *had* been horrific. Even without the screaming, she would have known that. Some of the ants that came to attend to her had been slick with half-dried blood, their tiny feet leaving sticky spots on her arms and legs that felt like they would never come clean. She shuddered, resting her hands on the wheel.

The police. She could call the police. And tell them what, exactly? That a giant wasp convinced her co-worker to somehow summon ants to eat the chauvinistic pigs they worked for, and now she was afraid to step on a bug because if she did, maybe the ants would come back and eat *her*, too? It sounded ridiculous, and she'd been *there*. She knew it was happening, whether she wanted it to or not. Anyone she called would just laugh at her and dismiss her as some kind of crank.

She turned on the engine and froze. How could she move the car without catching bugs on the windshield and the grill? Surely whoever Laurel was working for couldn't hold *every* insect death against a person, or she would never have been spared in the first place. Still, she rolled down the window and leaned out, feeling only a little silly as she spoke to the evening air.

"I need to go home. If you don't move away from the glass, some of you will get squished. Please, I don't want to die because I can't see you while I'm driving. Please."

There was a loud, droning buzz, and a wasp the size of her palm came darting across the parking lot and through the open window. Heather recoiled with a shriek, letting go of the wheel as the wasp landed between her gripping hands. It looked at her, a terrible, alien intelligence in its faceted eyes. It looked just like the wasp she'd seen perched in Laurel's hair, if not larger.

And then she heard a voice in her head, insectile and strange. *We know the difference between accident and intent*, it said. *That which is inevitable is forgiven. That which is not is added to the ledger.*

"Are you... are you saying it's all right if I drive home?"

That which is inevitable is forgiven.

Heather nodded, slowly. "Accidents are fine. Killing bugs because I think I have more of a right to live than they do is not fine."

We prefer the term 'insects,' but otherwise, yes, said the voice, sounding faintly amused.

"I am talking to a wasp." Heather returned her attention to the road. "This is fine. I need to roll the window up before I start driving. Did you want to go...?"

No. I will stay.

Somehow, that made perfect sense. Heather laughed and rolled her window up, the wasp still sitting on the steering wheel. Pressing her foot down on the gas, she eased the car slowly into motion and started the short drive out of the parking lot.

The mosquitoes swarmed in thick enough groups that they formed a haze in the air, almost like a finely falling mist. They splattered against the windshield even as she crept slowly along, and Heather winced, glancing at the wasp, which seemed unperturbed. It was hard to tell what a wasp was feeling. She didn't have the knack of it yet, if she ever would.

"So, uh, you're a wasp?" she said, desperate for the sound of a human voice, even if it was her own. "How did that happen?"

My mother implanted an egg in the body of a human researcher, and when that egg hatched, the larvae it produced chewed its way through the scientist's body to the open air, and a nymph was born, replied the wasp. *Several molts later, I became the wasp I am now.*

"So that egg was...you?"

No, the egg was the egg. I am the wasp. They are different things.

It was an interesting, if alien, way of looking at the situation. Heather frowned and tried to focus on the road, still afraid to speed up, watching with helpless horror as mosquitoes exploded against the glass, forming a grayish film. There was no blood. Either these were all males—she had been secretary and receptionist for an extermination firm for long enough to know that it was only the female mosquitoes who drank blood, while the males were a harmless nuisance—or they hadn't been able to find anyone to feed from yet.

The thought made her arms itch, even though she knew she hadn't been bitten during her trek across the parking lot. She shivered rather than scratching herself and sped up a little.

"So, what, you've decided the books have to balance?"

There was a long pause, long enough for her to start feeling silly about holding a conversation with a wasp. Then: *All things must balance. This has been forgotten. Your kind kills ours as if we had no purpose. It must stop. You will not enjoy the world you make without us. So we come to demand an accounting.*

"And Laurel...?"

She has been ours for quite some time. We have been preparing ourselves.

"Preparing yourselves? For what?"

For war. The reply was as calm and measured as everything else the wasp had "said." Heather felt herself go cold. It made sense. If they were talking about demanding an accounting and already killing people, then war was the natural next step. And yet...

This felt like something out of some religion's holy book. "The Plague of Bugs" or whatever, sweeping humanity from the land. She paused, doing some quick math in her head.

"Every time someone eliminates an ant colony, they're talking about tens of thousands of ants. Sometimes as many as half a million in a single nest. And that's just the ants. I don't think there are *enough* humans to balance these ledgers."

We are willing to concede individuality for mass.

Heather paused, working this through. Finally, in a tone that balanced comprehension and horror, she asked, "So one person for, what, a million ants?"

Not quite.

"Okay, then—"

A human can weigh as much as forty million ants. More, if it's a large human. We know our value. We will know when the scales are settled.

The thought was slightly less horrifying than a one-for-one accounting would have been. It was still stomach-churning in its implications.

"How far back?"

We live swiftly compared to you, but we remember. Still, we will not hold you responsible for the ages. Only to the birth of the oldest of your kind currently alive. Our accounts are clear.

Heather didn't know how old the oldest living human was, but she was sure it was old enough for the insects to be taking more than their pound of flesh.

The scrim on the windshield was taking on a red cast as they drew closer to her house, moving through residential streets. She reached for the window.

I would not, said the wasp, almost politely.

"What?"

The flying hungry have been given their wings, and they feed. They will recognize the scents upon you if they come close, but those who have landed may be too hungry to show restraint. I would not.

"They... would smell that the ants said not to eat me, but they might not care? I've been bitten by mosquitoes before. I'd be fine."

They have been given their wings. They do not stop at satiation.

There were people lying on the sidewalks and lawns she was driving past, she realized; she hadn't seen them before. Their clothes and hair moved with the wind, and what she could see of their flesh was very pale. She glanced back to the wasp, eyes wide and alarmed.

They feed. Its wings buzzed, unperturbed. *Enough have been slaughtered for comfort's sake that they feel justified in eating until they burst. They give their lives for vengeance. It is a very wasp thing to do.*

It felt like the wasp laughed inside her head. Heather gave it a horrified look.

"You mean they're *exsanguinating* those people?"

If that word means drinking them dry and leaving their husks where they fall, then yes. That is what happens. Do not worry, human. You are safe, for now.

Heather shuddered and kept driving.

When she reached her house, she turned into the driveway, unsurprised to see the exterminator's truck parked out front. Laurel sat on the porch in a halo of mosquitoes, their bodies clustered until their wings splintered the light into a hazy prism. Heather turned off the engine, slumping in her seat.

After several seconds ticked by, the wasp stepped onto her hand, tapping her with the tip of its stinger. It was like being prodded, very gently, with a sewing needle; not hard enough to count as a poke, or to hurt, but hard enough to make sure she understood she was being tapped with something sharp.

Join your hive, said the wasp.

Heather opened the car door.

A Plague of Roaches

The air was thick with mosquitoes. They landed on Heather's skin, legs tickling, and she had to resist the urge to slap them away as they nuzzled her flesh with their proboscises before picking up the scent trails left by the ants and lifting off again. There were always more waiting to land.

It was surprisingly easy to understand how something as large as a person could be drained dry—the old adage "eaten alive by mosquitoes" becoming truth—with this many of the little bloodsuckers in the air.

Laurel looked up as she approached, smiling. "You came."

"You mean, I made it out of the building after your friends the ants ate everybody else, yes." Heather looked at her coldly. "A giant wasp helped me drive here without dying and oh God, that sentence is ridiculous, and I need a drink."

"I can fix you one." Laurel stood, the porch light glinting off the wasp still perched on her hair. After her time in the car, Heather felt sure she could tell the two wasps apart if she had to, although she couldn't quite imagine a situation where it was going to be necessary. "I found your spare key. I thought you'd be here sooner."

"You'll forgive me for needing some time to recover from *ants killing everyone.*"

"They clearly left you alive," said Laurel. Then she paused, cocking her head like she was listening. "All right, she's in shock. I guess I was pretty out of it for a while after I found your hive. She's allowed to need a little time."

"Don't talk about me like I'm not here," snapped Heather.

"Sorry, sorry," said Laurel, and opened the door onto a nightmare.

Every surface Heather could see inside the house was a moving black veil of bodies. Laurel turned on the light, and the bodies scattered, but not too quickly for Heather to identify them as roaches. Not little brown house roaches, either: no, these were massive, each easily three inches long, with orange stripes on their fat bodies. Their size didn't slow them down as much as she would have expected. In only a few seconds, there were no signs of them.

Heather shuddered, barely managing not to scream, as Laurel stepped started toward the liquor cabinet.

"Whiskey?" she asked.

"You'll have to wash the glasses," said Heather. "Roaches carry disease."

It seemed like such a small thing to focus on under the circumstances. Laurel still shot her a sympathetic look.

"You're going to have to get past that way of thinking," she said. "They do carry contaminants, yes, and they can make people sick, but *everything* can make people sick. People make people sick more than anything else, but we don't go around wiping out whole communities because they catch measles, now, do we?"

"It's not the same thing," protested Heather.

"It is, though." Laurel took a bottle of whiskey down and reached for the tumblers. "A single insect isn't necessarily intelligent. Get enough of them in one place and they are. That's how it's always worked. We get the one-on-one smarts, they get the big colony smarts. A group of people isn't as smart or agile as a single person. A swarm of bees, on the other hand, could probably outthink a Nobel Laureate. It's a different form of intelligence. They kept waiting for us to remember the old bargains, and then we wiped out an ant colony large enough to be their equivalent of killing Leonardo da Vinci, and they got fed up. They started trying to make contact."

"You turned against your own kind."

"Do you honestly see where I had a choice? Where any of us had a choice? Fleas, lice, dust mites... the insect kingdom is everywhere. The most sterile home on the planet contains insects. And they are done with our shit. If I hadn't agreed to join up, they would have killed me on the spot. They almost did anyway, before I convinced them this would be an easier sell if they had someone to speak to the humans on their behalf. I'm going to be their ambassador."

An ambassador whose message was "the bugs are going to slaughter you for all those termites you killed after they ate your house" wasn't going to be very welcome. Heather shifted uncomfortably as Laurel walked over to hand her a glass of whiskey.

"They don't want to wipe us out. They just want balance. The way things used to be, before we came up with better poisons. We can't survive without them, and they're tired of us pretending we can."

"But... malaria, and property damage, and Lyme disease, and..."

Laurel waved her hand. "Now that we can negotiate with the insect world, those won't be concerns. They're willing to take age into account along with accidents—their objection to us is that we've been killing them en masse, not to the idea that a kid might squash a mosquito because they don't want to be bitten. They do understand that differences of scale and habitat mean we'll always be killing them. We just need to accept that they'll always be killing us, too, and learn to live with it."

Heather looked at her blankly. Laurel shrugged.

"We don't get to pretend we own the planet just because we're big and self-contained," she said. "The colonies are smarter than we are. We need to find a way to live with them, and they've already put a lot of thought into the concept."

"People aren't going to stand for this," said Heather. "They're not going to lay down and let themselves be ruled by a bunch of *bugs*. What happened to Frank, anyway? You were the last person to see him! Did he quit when you showed him one of your big bugs?"

"In a manner of speaking," said Laurel, sounding unaccountably sad. "You were the only person in that office who was kind to me. I always thought you'd understand. I thought when you heard the situation, you'd see that negotiation is how we don't get wiped out."

"We're the higher lifeforms!" spat Heather. "You're a traitor to your species. Once the authorities hear about this, you're going to—"

She stopped, dread washing through her. Laurel was looking at her sorrowfully, shaking her head slightly as the wasp in her hair twitched its wings in apparent agitation. Heather frowned. Laurel wasn't looking at *her*...

Turning, Heather looked at the wall behind herself.

She had time to scream, barely, before the wave of roaches crashed down over her, and she no longer had time for anything at all.

The Four Opera Singers of the Apocalypse

Mary Fan

The end of the world will be an opera. Extravagant and mellifluous, a masterpiece of sonorous sensations. As a herald from the beyond—not powerful enough to be a creator but still having quite some influence on the physical world—I have been planning humanity's annihilation since life first formed from Earth's primordial soup—more of a gazpacho, really—and I have composed melodies of mishaps and counterpoints of catastrophes that will be brought to life by four magnificent messengers of the End Times.

Since the birth of the one many consider to be the son of God—and I shall neither confirm nor deny the veracity of that particular claim—humanity has been given over two thousand and twenty years to roam the Earth freely. But, as they say, all things—good, bad, ugly, beautiful, lachrymose, and gustatory—must come to an end. Now, with the elements in alignment, is the time for my opera to begin: The Apocalypse.

First, though, I must seek out my harmonious harbingers, who eons ago manifested on Earth as humans and now live among them, and gather them in my celestial theater in order for the end to begin.

*****

"End the world?" Giovanna Bella arches her darkly painted eyebrows, and her magnificent floor-length gown of glittering blue, reminiscent of a planetarium's projections, swishes as she turns to face me. Dressing room lights flash off the opulent costume jewelry dangling from her pale ears, spread across her creamy collarbone, and embellishing her dark curly hair. On the walls sit posters from historic performances that took place at this Paris theater,

27 "

including several featuring Giovanna herself. "Very cute, *pata-tina*. But as you can see, I'm in the middle of a performance and must return to the stage." Her crisp Italian accent makes her tone all the more chastising. "What did you say your name was again?"

"These days, I go by Angela Alvarado." I will confess, I did not choose the most impressive human form to take when I descended from the beyond. Based on what I've observed from humanity's popular media, a young woman of nineteen—thin and only five-foot-three with long brown hair, brown eyes, and a tan complex-ion—is not most peoples' idea of an apocalyptic herald. "But I am a primordial being beyond names, a—"

"*Si, si*, no need for a monologue. I am one as well, after all." Giovanna waves one silk-gloved hand dismissively. "Out of my way, Angela. I hear my cue."

The sounds of swelling violins and pounding timpani fill the dressing room from the small speaker piping in music from the stage. Giovanna checks her ruby red lipstick one more time in the mirror before heading to the door of the lusciously decorated private dressing room.

I rush after her. "How can you care about something of such little consequence? Have you forgotten who you are?"

"Of course not, *cucciola*." She gives me a condescending smile as she winds through the backstage area, heading for the stage. "I am Death, and when I enter your celestial theater, my song will manifest my power in the world of humanity. You need me for your apocalypse to happen, and I will not go with you until I have finished performing here tonight."

I trot to keep up with her. "You cannot ask me to wait when—"

"I can ask anything I want. Without me, there is no show."

I huff. "Very well. I'll go gather—"

"Oh, you must not leave! I'm about to sing my grand aria! You wouldn't want to miss it, would you?"

"Time is of the essence! The elements are in alignment, but they will not remain that way for long. I must go—"

"Well, if you cannot stay for this show, then you will simply have to come to one of my other performances." Now in the wings, she looks out at the stage, which is decorated with fake Greek statues and colorful plastic flowerbeds. "How are you supposed to com-pose for me if you do not know what I sound like?"

"The opera is already composed! I only need to direct its performance!"

"Well, then, how are you supposed to conduct for me if you haven't heard me at my finest?"

Unfortunately, my powers do not allow me to simply whisk her away when she so clearly wants to stay. Being the composer of the apocalypse sounds important, but without my singers, my music will remain trapped on the page, and the Earth will twirl on through the cosmos.

"Fine," I reply. It'd be better to stay for the second and third acts of this current opera than sit through a whole new one.

Giovanna gives me a smug smile, her red-painted lips curving, and then strides out onto the stage, floating her hands at eye level and singing out a warbling high note.

*****

"No one ever believes me, but I swear it's the truth!" Ida Emma Ho's torpid Texas twang tumbles out of the open window of her quirky Jersey City house. "I'm telling you, that tornado picked up my double-wide and dropped it right here in the Heights, and I've been in this place ever since."

"Oh really?" Her voice student, a dark-haired girl of maybe fourteen, puts her hands on her hips. "Then why aren't you living in it now?"

"Why, because you wouldn't expect a famous opera singer to live in a trailer, now, would you?" Ida brushes her thick, purple-dyed hair over her shoulders, whose pale freckled skin peeks out under her sequined rainbow tank top, and straightens her back. "Now, open your chest, or you'll never get enough air in to finish that phase."

I find the honeybee-shaped knocker on the blue-and-yellow-striped door and give it a rap.

Ida continues as if she didn't hear me. "Repeat after me: I am a coooooow!" She sings the notes on an upward arpeggio, holding the top note. Then, without taking a breath, she transitions into descending scale on the word, "Moooooooo!" Her rich mezzo-soprano voice spirals out the window, prompting a few indignant shouts from other residents of the densely packed urban neighborhood.

The student repeats the notes while Ida nods along.

"Fantastic!" Her multicolored tutu, which she wears over striped leggings, swishes as she moves around the student and observes the latter's posture. "Now try it on a different vowel:

29

I am a hoooorse! Naaaaaaaaay!"

Irritated, I give the knocker a several more raps, banging as hard as I can until Ida finally pauses what she's doing and opens it.

"Well, hello there, Angela!" She spreads her pink-lipsticked mouth into a sweet Southern smile. "Been expecting you. Why don't you make yourself comfortable while I finish my lesson?"

I glance around at the sculptures made from colorful plastic bags decorating her walls. "If you've been expecting me, then you know what I'm here for, and you know that we don't have all the time in the world."

"Now, what's your rush? We're immortal, aren't we?"

"Yes, but the alignment will not remain for long!"

"Oh, you composers and your impatience. Everyone knows that great art takes a while to come together. And it's rather rude of you to interrupt my lesson and expect me to go along with you when this is still Laurie's time." Her twinkling brown eyes shift to indicate the student. "Of course, you're free to move on without me, but it won't be easy ending the world without War."

I cross my arms. "How long will you take?"

"Oh, should only be another thirty minutes!"

That's not so bad, considering I sat through two entire acts of a Romantic-era opera in order to bring Giovanna to the theater. "All right, I'll wait."

"Excellent." She turns back to the student. "Now, again, except let's try it on yet another syllable this time." She draws a deep breath and sings out on an arpeggio, "I am a sheeeeep!" Then, the descending scale on the word, "Baaaaaaaaa!"

*****

"*Willkommen*, Angela!" Ted swings open the door to his Berlin apartment with a flourish. Only the lightest of German accents colors his words; in fact, I nearly forget that his full name is Eduard Durchdenwald. His plain but well-fitted black t-shirt clings to his lean chest and extends over the hips of his uncomfortable-looking skinny jeans. "Come on inside! I was just putting the finishing touches on my latest video for Instagram."

"Let me guess: You won't come with me until you finish." I sigh. At least these four singers are professionals, and they'll be able to sight-read my score and still give an amazing performance.

"I'm literally about to download the finished product." He rushes over to his computer, which sits in the corner of his minimally decorated gray-and-white living room. "Who do you think I am, Giovanna?" He winks. "Come, see what I've made heeeeere!" He sings out the word "here" on a twinkling and tintinabulous tenor note.

Seeing no choice but to indulge him, I approach. On the wide flatscreen monitor sits a grid full of faces. All feature Ted's high forehead, black square-framed glasses, and meticulously coifed brown hair. "What is this?" I ask.

With a grin, Ted hits the PLAY button, and the faces begin singing. Choir music pours from the expensive-looking speakers on nonsense syllables like "dee-yoo-dee-yoo-dee" and "wah-wah-wah-wah-wah."

"It's all me!" Ted pats his chest proudly. "I sang every part, from bass to soprano! As you know, Famine comes in many forms these days, and not just the crop failures of ancient times. Similarly, my voice comes in many forms. Impressive, *ja*?"

"Yes, yes, very impressive. Now, can we—"

"Oh, no!" Ted pauses the video with a frown. "The dynamics in this section are all wrong. I must rerecord."

"It's perfect!" I plaster on what I hope is a convincing grin. "Look, as a composer and music director, I assure you there's nothing wrong."

"No, no, no, don't be nice to me." Ted grabs a microphone stand from against the wall and moves it to the center of the room. "The acoustics are best when I stand here. Now, please be very quiet while I rerecord."

"But—"

He presses a stern finger to his lips and then pushed a button.

Seeing no choice but to wait—again—I slump against the wall.

*****

Standing outside the door to the quarrelsome yet quintessential, practically quadraphonic Qing Jian's Shanghai apartment, which sits on a floor so high that looking out the hallway window makes me feel like I'm in an airplane, I already know I'm in for another wait.

The walls do a decent job of insulating the virulent vibrations of his vivacious vocal exercises, but still I can clearly hear what sounds like a helicopter as he buzzes his lips on a deep bass note.

I press the doorbell. The helicopter noises stop, and Jian opens the door with a scowl in his dark, heavily browed eyes. With his button-down shirt, wide-buckled belt, and well-fitted slacks all emblazoned with designer logos, he looks like one of those sponsor-filled backdrops they use for movie premieres and such.

"I have a big voice. I know you could hear me outside." His sharp Shanghainese accent gives each word a bite. "Why did you not wait until I was finished before knocking?"

I rub the back of my head. "Well, you see, the alignment—"

"Have you no respect for your performers? How do you expect us to sing if we do not take care of our voices?" He leans one arm against the doorframe, and his chin-length black hair sways by his cropped black beard. "Pestilence requires endurance to be effective. I expect you wrote many long phrases for me?"

"Why, yes, I did."

"Good. I would not perform at all if you had not respected me enough to do so." He turns back into his apartment.

I take that as an invitation to enter and follow. The door swings shut behind me.

"Many singers prefer only to practice songs." Jian marches into the center of the apartment, which looks like something out of a Victorian painting. Heavy wooden furniture, dark patterned rugs, oil paintings of effulgent European landscapes and winningly white-washed Biblical figures on the walls. "I, however, believe in perfecting technique first. Pestilence is nothing if not precise."

He places both hands on his lower abdomen, draws a deep breath, and exhales between his teeth, making a long "shhh" sound. He pauses, then continues, then pauses, then continues, again and again until I feel like I'm being berated by the world's most passive aggressive librarian. "Sh! Sh sh sh! Shhhhhh!"

I look nervously at my watch, which is no ordinary piece of clockwork but rather charts the alignments of the elements on a cosmic level through a complex series of bronze dials. "Am I the only one in the universe who cares if the apocalypse goes off on time?"

Instead of replying, Jian makes a strange yelping noise. He slides his voice up and down, reminding me of some kind of police siren, while swinging his arms back and forth.

I tap my foot. "Can you at least tell me how long this will take?"

Jian spreads his mouth and sings out a note on "ah," slowly closes it to an "oo," and repeats the process, making himself look like some kind of fish blub-blub-ing along the bottom of the sea.

Realizing that all attempts at arguing would be futile, I plop down on the cushioned sofa and tap my foot.

*****

"I'm afraid we won't have time to rehearse." I stride across the celestial theater that will send down the apocalypse to Earth. Instead of an audience, the stage faces a great view featuring several parts of Earth at once. The closest Earth equivalent to what we're looking at is a series of security monitors, except what we see is far more three-dimensional. This being, of course, a place beyond the ordinary world of humans, time passes differently here. A few moments in this theater is equivalent to days or even weeks on Earth. It ebbs and flows according to rules beyond human knowing. Yet it exists nonetheless, and with each moment, the elements grow closer to moving out of alignment.

I purse my lips and glance at my watch for the millionth time. Gathering my harmonious harbingers has taken a harrowingly long time. But if we begin now, we can still end the world on schedule.

Giovanna, Ida, Ted, and Jian wander about the stage, which is decorated with gold curtains to either side but otherwise remains plain. Each holds a thick score, full of my masterful musical manipulations of mellifluence. Giovanna seems to be looking for the brightest spotlight—a futile effort, since the whole stage is lit evenly—while Ida playfully taps her feet in a jig of some sort. Ted sings out random notes in search of some kind of acoustic sweet spot. Jian is the only one who's actually looking at the score, frowning deeply as he flips the pages.

"Attention, everyone!" I step onto the conductor's podium and tap my baton against the music stand before it. "Did you hear me? We must begin the performance now! The elements won't be aligned much longer, and we must complete the opera before they move!" I hold up my watch for emphasis. "I know it's unusual to perform without rehearsing first, but I trust your abilities to sight-sing along with the score."

Giovanna opens her score and arches those sharp brows at me. "Naturally, *maestro*. A diva needs no rehearsal to shine."

Ted frowns at his music. "I don't think this harmony in measure two-hundred-and-three works, Angela. The minor third in the soprano part clashes with the note the orchestra is holding. If you cut that phrase—"

"Cut? *My* phrase?" Giovanna throws him an indignant look. "How dare you suggest such a thing?"

"Do you want to sound like a goat's scream?" Ted shrugs. "Fine. Keep it the way it is, then. But my solo in measure three hundred definitely has to change. I won't sing this tuneless mess. I would rather improvise."

I shake my head. I want to defend my masterpiece, but if we don't begin within the next few moments, it won't be performed at all. "Fine, Ted! Do what you must! Now, let's sing through it and show the universe what we can do." I gesture at the views of Earth behind me. "This will display each of your impacts on Earth. With every note you sing, you will bring about casualties, catastrophes, calamities, cataclysms! Are you ready to begin?"

Ida waves her score. "I've been ready. Don't know what the rest of you are dallying for."

Sighing, I lift my baton.

I lift my shoulders and inhale, readying myself for the performance to end all performances—literally.

Orchestral music flows through the air. Since only the four harmonious harbingers are needed to bring about the apocalypse, the instruments are being manifested through my mind. As soon as I think the notes, they appear from silence. From vivacious violins to bawling bassoons, from opalescent oboes to histrionic harps, their voices tumble about. In my mind, I let the cellos spring forth in a magnanimous melody, one that indulges the audiences in effervescent euphonies, and the sounds swirl about in my ears as well.

I cue Ted's entrance. He steps forward, probably into the spot he decided had the best acoustics. He opens his mouth and lets his tenacious tenor notes tumble out. There are no lyrics—none are needed for the end of the world. Only vowels whose very lack of syllables deepen their dimensions. "Ooooohs" that evoke, "aaaaaahs" that embody.

Glancing behind me, I see the impact of Famine upon the helpless Earth. This isn't the famine of yore, though. No, Earth still has an abundance of edible food. It's the money that dries up—the necessary nourishment of present-day society. The stock market crashes, and a financial crisis takes hold. Pensions and investments vanish. Savings accounts are emptied. People declare bankruptcy left and right, and—

"Now hold on a minute, that's *my* part!" Ida marches up to Ted with her hands on her hips.

I glance down at my score. Indeed, Ida is supposed to get the melody next, with Ted singing a harmony to support it.

Ted continues singing Ida's melody anyway.

"Ted!" I let the orchestra music continue—we haven't time to pause it if we're to meet our apocalyptic deadline—but give him a pointed look. "Stop singing Ida's part!"

Ted looks me in the eye and begins to sing louder.

"Ted!" I twist my face into what I hope is a sufficiently sanguine expression. "What are you doing?"

Ida lets out an irritated laugh. "Well, isn't it obvious? He thinks he's the star of the show and should get all the best parts... even when he's changing them on the fly. Typical tenor."

The melody Ted currently sings is indeed an embellished variation of what I had written for Ida. It still sounds good, though, and in the images of Earth, the financial famine continues to strike. This can still bring about the end of the world as long as we keep going.

"You and Ted, switch parts then." I lift my baton to cue Ida. "Sing the harmony."

"Excuse me?" Ida cocks one eyebrow at me. "You think that because I'm a mezzo, that also means I should always support the melody? Oh, sure, let everyone else get the good parts—even when they were written for me! I'm just a lower voice! I might as well drone along on the fifth, since that's all you composers let me sing anyway! Why give me a real part when you can be lazy about it?"

"Ida! You *have* a real part! You have many magnificent melodies coming up later, but we won't get to them unless you sing *now!*"

"Fine, then. I'll be polite, even though you won't." She brushes her purple hair over her shoulders—and sings out the melody as written.

It clashes horribly with Ted's improvised notes. Ida also somehow manages to make her mezzo-soprano ring out louder than his tenor. She also decides to add consonants, turning what should have been a wordless melody into a succession of silly syllables. "Moooooooo! Naaaaaaay! Baaaaaaaa! Aaaaaahhh choooooo!"

At least it's still effective. In the view of Earth behind me, War hits the world as countries declare their intents to invade each other, protestors hit the streets to oppose the fighting, and law enforcement forces clash with advocates, often escalating into riots. Yes, yes, this is how it's supposed to go... The drying up of resources... people turning against each other...

Ted cuts off mid-phrase and glares at Ida. "You're ruining the music!"

Ida sings on, ignoring him.

"Ted!" I exclaim. "Keep singing!"

"Not with this amateur!" Ted slams his score shut in a huff.

That comment only makes Ida sing louder, and her rich mezzo-soprano voice makes every particle around me vibrate.

In the view of Earth, the riots intensify, and governments increase their warmongering rhetoric. But something's wrong. Stocks go up again as demand for production rises in response to the war effort. Jobs return to previously impoverished towns, and investors pour more and more money into the market, betting on future prosperity.

"This is outrageous!" Giovanna's long skirt brushes the ground as she strides up to me. "How is it that we're so far into the piece and I've yet to even sing a single note?"

"You're coming up soon!" I exclaim. "I'll cue you in a few minutes."

"A few minutes? Why, I am Death! What is the end of the world if nobody dies? I ought to be the star of this production, and yet you deny me the spotlight. And what for? A few market crashes and local riots?" She glances disdainfully at Ted, who rolls his eyes, and Ida, who briefly stops singing to stick her tongue out. "Without Death, neither Famine nor War mean anything!"

It's true that in the simulation, there's not yet been a death toll from War—or Famine, for that matter. Sure, people are still dying as usual, but the uptick that should come as part of the apocalypse has yet to manifest. Still, the point was to weaken the world first before Death came to reap the souls of humankind. "I'm saving your big entrance for later." I flash Giovanna a smile. "Don't worry, once you come in, you'll get your starring moment."

Giovanna turns up her nose. "I don't want a starring moment, *maestro*! I am *the* star! I refuse to sing until you change the music to make that clear!"

"There is no single star in the apocalypse." I continue waving my baton desperately, while Ida sings on as if performing in a one-woman show.

Ted crosses his arms. "There is *always* a star. I thought it was clear from my powerful entrance that it was me, which is why I don't understand why you tried to put me on the harmony."

"You are *all* stars." I look to Jian, who has been watching the entire exchange with a look of disdain. Hoping that he can set an example for the soprano and tenor, I lift my chin at him to indicate that his entrance is coming up.

Jian clasps his hands behind his back and strides up the stage. He brushes right past Ida. When he sings out, his booming, bombastic bass voice overpowers her mezzo-soprano. If my eardrums were mortal, they would have burst.

"Mezzoforte is enough!" I wave my baton downward to indicate that he should lower his volume.

He ignores me and blasts on, making every particle in the celestial theater shake.

Giovanna rolls her eyes. "And they say *I* am a diva."

Ted throws her a look of amused consternation, eyebrow cocked and mouth twisted. "You are."

She shoots him a poisonous look. "Oh, look who's talking!"

Even though Ted has missed several phrases by now, I hold out hope that this piece can be salvaged. I glance at the view of Earth, hoping that War and Pestilence will be enough to drive the world to its doom. But with Jian so overpowering in his volume, Pestilence takes over.

A new and highly transmissible plague spreads across the planet, affecting every city, country, and continent. The symptoms come on fast, and no one knows how it spreads. People leave their battles to quarantine in their homes, and a strange peace falls over Earth even as disease takes its toll. There are flare-ups, of course, as War does her best to punch through the noise. But pesky Pestilence keeps her from reaching her full potential.

This isn't going to work. With only one kind of catastrophe, it's only another bad year, not the full-blown apocalypse we were supposed to trigger.

I try again to tell Jian to quiet down, but he isn't even looking at me. At least Giovanna's big entrance is coming up, and her enormous voice might be enough to match Jian's. Once Death enters the picture, things might start to work out.

I look to Giovanna. "Your part beings soon! Would you miss the chance to sing the most important entrance in the entire piece?"

Giovanna lifts her chin, and her lips twitch. "Most important?"

"Why yes! It's like an instrumental concerto—the orchestra enters with the melody first, and then after they've played it through, the soloist gets to repeat it with variations and really make it sparkle, shine, scintillate. The soloist may be the last to enter, but they are ultimately the most important."

"Well, in that case..." Giovanna lifts her score and pulls her shoulders back.

Ted scowls at me. "Did you just say the rest of us are the orchestra to Giovanna's soloist?"

Giovanna gives him a withering look. "Indeed he did, *topolino*. Without Death, the apocalypse is meaningless."

Ted makes an indignant noise in the back of his throat. "Ida! Jian! Did you hear? We are nothing more than Giovanna's back-up orchestra."

"That's not what I meant!" I wave my arms.

But it's too late. Both the mezzo-soprano and the bass stop singing and glare at me.

"Well, excuse me." Ida shuts her score. "And here I was thinking the apocalypse was supposed to be an ensemble piece."

"It is!" I cry.

Jian shakes his head at me with narrowed eyes. "Typical composer. Always favoring the higher voices. As if being able to squeak makes one a better singer!"

Giovanna gives the three of them a smug look. "Don't be angry because the *maestro* recognizes where the true power in the piece lies." She looks up at me with a smirk. "Never mind them, Angela. I alone can carry this apocalypse. For what is the end of the world without Death?"

The orchestral music continues swirling and swaying to evoke swampishly swole swoons. Giovanna's entrance was supposed to be only a few lines of a solo followed by a harmony with all four parts, but since the other three seem determined to sit this next part out, I see no choice but to turn the whole section into an impromptu solo.

I inhale sharply, lifting my baton, and point it at Giovanna.

She lets out a great, warbling melisma whose twisting torsion reminds me of a snake. They're most certainly not the notes I wrote in the score, but at least they're roughly in the same key.

Without the harmony, the music sounds rather hollow. Giovanna seems to be doing her best to compensate by throwing in as many notes as possible. Grace notes, trills, ornaments—there's no denying her prowess.

If the others are impressed at all, they don't show it, only stand there watching with irritated expressions.

All those fancy runs from Death herself must be enough to end the world. I glance at the view of Earth. To my consternation, the world revolves on. No new catastrophe seems to be striking at all. People discover a cure for the plague, the accords reached during the time of crisis hold, and the economy remains sound. In fact, everything is at about the same level of not-apocalyptic as before we even began this piece.

Ida lets out a guffaw. "Why so surprised, Angela? Didn't you know that people can't just drop dead for no reason? Why, without Famine, War, or Pestilence, people only die for ordinary reasons, and in ordinary numbers."

I actually *did* know that once—that was why I composed this opera as an ensemble piece to begin with. My last desperate hope that Death would be enough, after the other three set off then ceased their disasters, suddenly seems incredibly foolish.

The orchestra music fades away as I lower my baton and pinch the bridge of my nose. "This isn't working."

Giovanna shrugs. "I thought it was working fine. Why did you stop the orchestra?"

"Because the world isn't ending!" I gesture emphatically at the view, which now shows a perfectly normal planet Earth. "Look, you are all very good musicians, and I'm sure your opinions are very well informed, but I composed the apocalypse the way I did for a reason." I glance at my watch. "The elements are nearly out of alignment. If this is to work, we must begin again *immediately,* and this time, I need everyone to stick to the score."

Baffled and indignant protests spiral around me like tornado winds.

Ted waves his score. "How can you expect me to sing this drivel as it's written? I have changes!"

"Why, I am nobody's back-up!" Ida tosses her head of thick purple hair. "You'd better make sure I keep the melody!"

Jian marches up to me. "You tell me to sing quieter, but it is not my fault these amateurs don't have the voices to match mine!"

"My part must stay the way I just sang it." Giovanna slaps a hand against her score. "It sounded *magnifica* as a solo, and I will not have these other voices muddying the score!"

"Muddying?" Ted scowls at her. "Well, excuse me!"

Ida, meanwhile, smacks Jian on the arm. "You don't get to call me an amateur and get away with it! I care about quality of sound and not just bellowing as loudly as possible!"

On and on they bicker. I tap my baton against the stand. "Listen up!"

They ignore me.

I keep tapping, harder and harder, trying to get attention. "Harmonious harbingers of the apocalypse!"

Still they argue.

I slam my baton against the stand so hard, it breaks. The end flies between Giovanna and Ted, both of whom jump back. Giovanna crashes into Jian, and Ted accidentally smacks Ida.

"*Hey!*" I scream at the top of my lungs.

That finally gets their attention. They all look at me with expressions that say, "What's wrong with you?" As if *I'm* the absurd one.

Once glance at my watch tells me that there's no way we're going to get through this entire piece before the elements fall out of alignment. Not that I want to at this point. None of them are willing to compromise, and neither am I. If the piece being performed won't be the one I wrote, then it's better that it never be heard in full.

I slam my score shut. "The apocalypse is canceled!"

*****

And so Earth survived what should have been its demise, its human inhabitants blissfully unaware of how close they came to a resplendent ending. In time, the elements may again align. But until they do, the four harmonious harbingers of the apocalypse have returned to their human forms.

Maybe next time, I will find a way for the opera to succeed. But until then, Earth spins on.

Apocatlypse

Jody Lynn Nye

"Yet another stronghold of lapsed devotion," said Death, focusing her glowing red eye sockets on the enormous stone catedral in the middle of the largest city on the continent. The shape was like that of a hunched cat not unlike herself, its back turned toward those who approached it. The sanctuary was topped by a rounded tower surmounted by two peaked gables. She sat down to survey it and cocked her sleek black head to listen. "You can hear the cater-wauling inside, but there is no heart in it. No life!"

"Well, you're the expert on that," said Pestilence, scratching her ear with a hind foot. Her mangy fur seemed to move by it-self. Within the much-chewed orange-striped pelt hid hordes of insects: lice, fleas, biting flies, and other creepy-crawlies, as well as pathogens, germs, microbes, and myriad invisible disease vectors that she released to cause suffering to those who committed crimes against Cat. Death had often seen them infesting those bodies whose souls she came to collect. Pestilence had trained her legions of nuisances not to harass her fellow immortals, or there would have been trouble. "They sound like they're in pain, but there's no depth to their suffering."

"They are only human," said War. His current shape was that of a massive sabretooth tiger, a species that had not been seen on this particular planet in eons but had once struck fear into the hearts of lesser beings. "Pathetic creatures that need to create an excuse to battle among themselves. What was the Great Felis thinking when they invented them?" He shook his head.

"Only that we needed worshippers," said Famine. He munched a spiky weed that grew up between squares of worn stone pave-ment. Instantly, his rail-thin, gray-furred body began to shake, his jaws gaped, and he heaved up a steaming pile of greenery. With a diffident paw, he buried it, raking up the concrete into a heap over his ejecta. "Though I haven't noticed much in the way of tribute or praise coming from any of these inhabited planets since Felis sent us to extract retribution. Why don't they have a bowl of food out here for passing Children of Felis? I've been starved for adoration!"

"You're always starved," Pestilence said, cracking an errant flea between her teeth. "But I agree. What has changed since the Great Felis created these miserable humans? They were made to serve! Why have they not been fulfilling their obligation to us?"

"Well, that is what we are here to discover," Death said, aiming her red orbits toward her companions. "They will either make amends to us, or face annihilation, like many nations around them on this pitiful planet, and like the other planets we have wiped clean of their inhabitants to begin afresh. There are consequences for ignoring the Great Cat!"

"Yes!" War warbled, his voice echoing in the catedral close. He gnashed his long fangs. "I would enjoy annihilating these soft-skins. One by one, in single combat to the death!" He gathered his haunches as if to spring. "I wonder if they will give me any sport? It will be fun to find out."

"Not yet," Death admonished him with a small black paw on his nose. War sneezed. "Be ready. Observe. Wait. We do not punish until we are certain. I take no souls unless it is their time. We will see whether the Great Felis is right to be displeased with these." She rose to her narrow black feet and tiptoed toward the main entrance. The tunnel, low enough that it forced most other species to bow to walk through it, was just the right height for cats to approach with their tails held high. Death waved her thin black plume like a banner as she led the way inside.

*****

John Markley lifted up his voice in the loudest cry that he could muster. The wail rasped the stout man's throat, but what better means of praising the Divine Feline than to imitate its warble? That, and the hefty fifteen-percent tithe that he gave to the Church of Cat every month. As a good and observant Catolic, he felt fortunate that his job offered him generous remuneration so that the automatic deduction from his paycheck into the church's coffers didn't cut into his lifestyle. After all, Cat had caused all the great things in his life to happen. He trusted that the Divine Feline would protect him from the terrors of the world. Those appeared to increase every day, making him so anxious that only his faith in Cat kept him from going insane. Recent, frightening news on television and over the computer lines of plague and unexpected death from other countries and even other provinces in his own terrified him. Cat would keep him safe. Wouldn't they?

He knew that his devotion wasn't echoed by most of the congregation—not privately, not really. Publicly, his fellow parishioners professed to deep adherence to his religion, but over the last decades—centuries, really—he knew there had been a major falling-away from the faith. Time was when everyone had a padded, silk-topped shrine to the Divine Feline in their abodes, but now that platform on which a holy house cat was supposed to recline was just another horizontal surface in the house where laundry, paperwork, keys, and whatnot piled up. While John maintained an avatar in his home, and a handsome fellow Narcissus was, too, with his soft blue-gray fur and gold eyes, many of his neighbors looked the other way when John fed the colony of unhomed cats in the park a block away. What happened to the generosity that the Divine Feline dictated humans were supposed to show to all those who wore the aspect of immortal beauty?

Well, really, there had been no penalty for lapsed faith for maybe thousands of years, so showing up occasionally for High Holidays satisfied the social requirement, and if cats went hungry, it fell to people like John and those with guilty consciences to make up for the rest of the congregation's failings. In the meantime, he continued with the liturgy.

"...Yow, yow, meerp, meerp, ngowa nyim!
"Meer, purr-rrr, eh?
"Mee-yeh, ow, eek, myem.
"Prrr, eyeh, prang, marie, yowm! Amen."

John didn't have to concentrate on the recitation. He knew every syllable by heart. What it meant, he had no idea, but sacred words were often impenetrable to the uninitiated. He, and the thousand humans crowding the catedral, hoped it would help their fellow worshippers around the world.

The sudden plagues and destruction that had been happening to other nations on Earth and the outlying colonies in their home star system came on a few months ago with no explanation, no reason that scientists could determine. Whole cities were swallowed up by pits. Scads of dead bodies were found to have been disemboweled with long gashes, showing that they had been brutally attacked by a terrifyingly vicious enemy. Disease that came out of nowhere raged in numerous countries, claiming thousands of victims a day. One country that was known for the cleanliness of its countryside as well as its cities were visited by hordes of fleas and ticks. Governments pointed fingers at one another, but reports that surfaced from the National Secret Service found no source for any of the disasters. Their representatives were baffled. No one paid heed to the terrified eyewitnesses who claimed that a quartet of felines had been seen in the area of each of the disasters. How could mere cats have caused such chaos?

A self-proclaimed prophet had risen in the dog-loving nation to the north and got the attention of all the news services. This Canisdian announced that he had received a vision. As Dog was his witness, the terrible events were retribution for lapsed devotions to the Feline faiths. Lots of people listened, then rejected the man's statements outright. Who listened to crackpots like that?

Well, most everyone that John knew half-believed and half-feared that the interpretation was real. But how could it be? The holy scribes that had written the Book of Service to Cat, describing humankind's creation and its purpose, had died millennia ago. Maybe the massive volume was all superstition, as many skeptics had written in the intervening centuries. But what else could explain the sudden outbreak of disease and insect infestations that overwhelmed Catalaro? Weren't those people good practicing Miauslims? Or the attacks on Purrusalem by ghostly lions and tigers? Wasn't that the center of the Mewish faith? Why wasn't Great Felis defending their followers? Thousands were suffering and dying all around the world.

In hopes of being saved, congregants flocked back to their religious institutions, plying them with offerings and attending service after service, hoping for reassurance and comfort. Surely the Divine Feline would protect them?

The catedral was more crowded than John could ever recall. Parishioners touched the images of the Great Cat in Their Many Forms that were carved on the marble walls and on the backs and corners of the wooden pews. They stroked the smooth glass and wood as if those had been real cats, whispering little endearments, hoping to gain Their capricious favor. John had the traditional Can of Moist Food in his pocket for the ceremonial offering. He waited eagerly for Communion, when the archbishop would scatter catnip on the floor for the congregants to roll in and breathe its sacred essence. But was Great Felis listening to their pleas? Were they so sure that the prayers uplifted to the Divine Feline meant something to their deity and protector?

The Archbishop of the Holy Shrine must know whether they were chanting nonsense or not. She was always so dignified and confident that John had faith in her, even if he doubted himself.

Clad in her tiger-striped robes and with a close-fitting hood made in the shape of the Divine Feline's triangular ears, Lilipomo Talon undulated forward to the altar in the finest catlike walk to give the homily. She spread her arms out to show her hands held in the sacred paw shape.

John and the others echoed her action, finding comfort in the simple gesture.

"Purrs be upon you," she said.

"And rubbing against you," the congregation responded, and tucked their hands against their chests in imitation of the image on the huge golden screen behind the altar. It depicted the Great Felis lying on their side, contentedly giving suckle to kittens that represented shapes of cats from regions all over Earth. A lion cub spoke of African nations like Catswana or Tabiya, elegant cream and brown cats with blue eyes stood for felines found in southeast Asian countries like Maos, and the jaguar meant the Central American jungles around the ancient temple of Kitzen Itza.

"This is the feast of the Holy Kitten," Archbishop Talon said, smiling at them. Her face and form showed no sign of the fear that John harbored in his own chest. "You, the faithful of the Church of Cat, know that in the beginning, the Divine One, the Great Felis, made humans to be Their servants. Calling us Their most beloved creation, they exhorted us to always be good to their Avatars on Earth, who would make themselves known to us with tail-talk, arched backs, and slow blinks of their magically glowing eyes. In their superiority, the ability to see in almost total darkness, to hear a noise so faint as to be nearly undetectable, to scent with perfect apprehension a treat or a threat, they offer themselves to us as an example to emulate though never to equal. We can but admire and serve them to the best of our ability...."

The priestess continued on. John possessed almost perfect recall, a very useful trait for his public relations business. He had heard the same speech word for word exactly a year ago, on the occasion of the same holiday. How lazy of Talon. Perhaps he could offer to write her some new material, with some real kickers to bring in donations for the International Feed the Cat Fund. And he could work in a real plea for help from the Divine Felis to save them from the ongoing plague. But she said nothing new.

Despite his worries, he longed to haul his personal game tool out of his pocket and play until the priestess stopped talking. He had just downloaded a great game about untangling yarn. And wasn't it getting to be time to go back and feed Narcissus his midday meal? That blue-fin tuna steak in the cooler wasn't going to chop itself and arrange it on the blue china dish that said *Good Kitty.*

He pictured himself burying his hands in his cat's plushy blue-gray fur, feeling the rumble of approval, and just enjoying the sensation. That was Communion, for real.

"...Each nation was vouchsafed reflections of the Divine Feline's own image, and grateful outpourings of generosity met these young incarnations...." More reruns of previous year's sermons. John tuned her out again.

He stared at the mosaic murals of all the deeds of Great Felis on the far wall behind the altar and let himself believe he was meditating. He could chime in with all the responses when he heard her pause for breath.

Then, the wailing began.

*****

Death sniffed all around the stone wall inside the catedral narthex in between the two doors that opened into the sanctuary. The sacred feeding station that was supposed to be available for all passing cats was carved beautifully into the translucent stone with words that were attributed to Great Felis:

> *"For I was hungry and you fed me,*
> *"For I was beset and you protected me,*
> *"For I was homeless and you sheltered me,*
> *"For I was sick and you nurtured me,*
> *"For I was bored and you amused me...."*

But no catnip mouse to play with lay on the cool slate beneath the engraved scriptures. No comfortable blankie was rucked up to allow a cat to snuggle into it. The stone bowls were empty.

War sniffed them. "No water or food has been put in these for years, maybe not decades. If you listen to that female inside, you would think that a feast should be laid here."

Death smirked. "None of that is in the heart of the priestess, nor the congregation. Let us see how devoted to us they really are."

"Let me!" Famine pleaded.

Just as the female human began to expound a third time upon feeding hungry cats so that they would protect humankind from vermin, he sat back on his thin haunches and let out a sorrowful caterwaul that rose over the voice declaiming in the sanctuary.

A brief silence fell. The female tried again, but despite his emaciated appearance, Famine could overwhelm all sound with the cry of his desperate need. Death winced. Famine yowled again.

"Someone find that cat and throw it out!" the priestess shouted.

Death stared in shock.

"She's not going to send someone to feed you? How...how could she be so unfeeling?"

"I told you she doesn't care about real cats," Pestilence said, sniffing with disdain. "She's faking it."

"Do it again," Death urged her companion.

Famine gathered himself, and emitted the most heartrending shrieks he could. Even Death felt compelled to go find him a fish, a mouse, anything to stop the terrible sound. But it didn't seem move the priestess's heart.

"Get rid of that noisy menace, now!" the human bellowed. "I don't care what you do—make it stop!"

The immortals glared in the direction of the voice. War heaved himself to his gigantic paws.

"I suppose you know that *this* means *War*," the huge avatar said, with a glint in his amber eyes. He waved a paw, and the right-hand door locked and barred itself. He stalked toward the left door, his tail lashing in a fierce rhythm like an angry metronome. Famine and Pestilence followed, as they so often did.

"Wait!" Death said, galloping to interpose herself between her companions and the door. "Perhaps she means to take care of the hungry cat during the offering?"

"*Any* time is the right time to feed a cat," War said, glaring at her. "Stop making excuses, Death. No one else rushed out here to take care of us. I knew free will was a mistake! Wait until I tell Great Felis. They'll regret ever creating this sorry species!" He brushed her aside with a flick of his mighty paw. Death went tumbling like a kitten, landing in the empty feeding station. Another gesture by War, and the door to the nave flew open. The three immortals stalked inside.

Death scampered to catch up. He was right and she was wrong. *Another* mob of humans to dispose of. Before you knew it, this entire planet was going to be depopulated. For the *second* time in its existence.

*****

"Kitty!" a child cried, pointing.

The entire congregation turned to look. John stood up to see. Through gaps between people's shoulders, he saw three large feline forms stalk down the aisle, followed hastily by another, much smaller shape. Behind them, the door boomed shut, slammed by an unseen hand.

A woman beside him gasped. She pointed with a trembling finger at the massive, fanged, tawny-furred beast; the gaunt gray feline with the image of a white skeleton all but imprinted on its fur; and a huge wildcat with thick orange fur that rippled and moved by itself. The fourth cat, far smaller and slighter than its companions, had shining black fur, but its eyes were glowing pits of red. It caught up to the first three, passed them, and leaped onto the altar face to face with the gawking priestess.

"Aren't those...?" the woman asked.

Suddenly, the illustration from page eight of *A Child's Guide to the Apocalypse* reappeared from the depths of John's memory. He had read the book when he was six years old, but it had made a profound, lasting impression on him. He swallowed hard.

A very small part of him jumped up and down in excitement. He was seeing immortal beings that he had heard of, but never really believed in. So, all those reports from the other side of the planet were true!

The rest of him, the sensible, adult part realized that those reports from the other side of the planet were *true*. Immortal beings that he had heard of, but never really believed in, just appeared before his very eyes. It was the end of the world. Both sides of it.

"Uh-huh," he said, not believing the words that were coming out of his mouth. "We're doomed."

The people around him began screaming. They grabbed up their children and rushed down the stairs, heading toward the doors. John hurtled after them, trying not to get crushed in the panicking crowd that surged behind. Taking advantage of his height, he shouldered past a couple of men to get to the side door of the catedral, then got tossed bodily aside by a crowd of women herding their children towards safety. He tripped and fell. Feet crunched into his ribs as people literally walked over him. He rolled out of the way. On his hands and knees, he crawled toward the door, only to have it bang shut in his face. He grabbed the handle and pulled with all his strength. Hands joined his and hauled backward. It didn't budge. It was as if the ornate bronze panels had become a single part with the marble walls to either side. Maybe another door?

Slams echoed in the high chamber as every other portal in the church closed, putting an end to that hope. The locks snapped audibly into place. John and the others turned to plead with the cats.

"Let us out!" they cried.

The immortals ignored them. Instead, the mangy orange feline shouldered into the midst of the crowd and shook its body. Like droplets of water, torrents of black dots flew out of its fur. John watched in horror as the dots flew at them. A cloud of flying insects buzzed around him, dive-bombing him, while fleas leapt into his sleeves and collar. Ticks burrowed into his face and hands. He danced around, batting and scratching at himself. For every insect he picked off, five more took its place.

Every adult had their own plague of insects or had broken out in mumps or pox. John's face felt like it was on fire. His tongue felt like it was swelling out of his mouth. Pink sores rose all over his skin and burst in globules of greenish pus.

The children didn't seem to notice their parents' distress. The gray cat turned sideways and arched its scrawny back. The white stripes seemed to explode off it. John went tumbling over again. He pulled himself up to his hands and knees. His belly twisted painfully, as if it wanted to squirm out of his body.

"Mommy, I'm hungry!" the little girl near him shrieked, pulling her mother's sleeve.

"Me, too!" brayed a smaller boy. He grabbed the purse off the woman's arm and yanked it open. Crowing in triumph, he dragged out a plastic bag of Cheerios.

"Give me that!" the woman said. She grabbed it back from the child and tore it open. Before she could take a handful, a big man behind her reached over her shoulder and snatched it away. "Hey! That's mine!"

The man stuffed beige O's into his mouth. "What you gonna do about it?"

The woman's face turned bright red with fury. She leapt at him, fingernails aiming for his eyes. He backed away, scattering cereal on the floor. The children dove for the falling pieces, heedless of the feet near their hands.

John thought of tackling the man to take some of the Cheerios for himself, but pain in his belly overwhelmed him. He curled in a ball and fell to the floor. He had never felt so hungry, not even when he was an impoverished college student living on ramen. What was wrong with him? He had had a big breakfast! The pangs of hunger were so bad that he scraped some of the insects feasting on his skin and shoved them into his mouth. He tried to chew, but they latched onto his tongue and gums. Somehow, he managed to swallow. The bugs tasted disgusting, bitter and slimy, flavored with his own blood, but they assuaged the emptiness in his belly for a moment.

Food! He had to have food! Where could he find some? He eyed the children hammering on the door, and an idea struck him. He could eat one of them! They were nice and plump. In the crazed moment, no one would notice. He pictured himself tear one limb from limb and feasting on its tender flesh, raw. Anything to fill the screaming void in his belly. He reached out for the nearest toddler, a little red-headed boy in a blue romper.

As his hand closed around its wrist, the child shrieked, startling John into a moment of sanity. He let go, shocked at himself.

What was he thinking? He couldn't harm a child! What was going on?

He pulled himself to his feet. He felt woozy and feverish, but held onto what was left of his sanity as hard as he could.

All around him, people he knew, people with whom he had worshipped for years, were fighting. Old man Marlowe, the army veteran who played the hero in the church performances of "Puss in Boots" every Catsmas, punched Mrs. Zoltan, the silver-haired lady on whom John was pretty sure he had a longstanding crush. She went flying into Nina Sims, knocking her over. The young dark-skinned woman jumped up and tried to wrestle her to the ground, but Mrs. Zoltan exploded in a burst of furious energy, and broke her hold like a professional. She poked Nina's eyes with two outstretched fingers and rabbit-punched her in the throat. The old girl had game, John had to admit it. But Nina wasn't going down without a fight. She seized Mrs. Zoltan's arm and sank her teeth into it. The old woman screamed. John tried to push his way toward them, to break it up, but a group punching and kicking each other knocked into him. He ducked down under the nearest pew to get out of the way and lay there, scratching.

The Fitzhugh brothers were scrapping with everyone, using anything they could reach as weapons. People were ducking and screaming, but fighting back as if their lives depended on it. Teenagers were tearing the pages out of prayer books and eating them. A woman all but covered with jumping insects sat on the floor, rocking back and forth, murmuring nonsense to herself. A horde of parishioners near the main door faced off against the giant sabretooth tiger. Even over the noise, John could hear it purring gleefully as it knocked one after another with a blow from its massive paws. He looked as if he had been waiting for this moment for eons. Some of the humans he struck didn't get up again. The ones who did leapt right back into the fray as if they had nothing to lose.

The skinny feline with the skeleton markings and the mangy orange one wove in and out of the crowd. People collapsed in their wake, or ran screaming, unable to escape from the sanctuary that had been their place of worship for centuries. The buzzing of insects was nearly as loud as the cries of distress.

They had all lost their minds!

Except... except the archbishop.

Archbishop Talon stood at the altar, her eyes locked with the small black cat perched there. John couldn't decide which one looked more feral, the human, or Death herself. The cat's voice rang inside his head.

"Why?" Death asked.

"Why what?" the priestess countered. The immortal respected her lack of expression and calm attitude. Chaos fell all around her, yet she maintained her dignity. Death pressed on. Her duty demanded it.

"Why have you stopped worshiping Great Felis? They have done everything for you! Given you a wonderful world, made you intelligent, healthy and strong, imbued you with a purpose! All you had to do was adore their creation, their avatars on Earth, and all would be well."

Talon laughed bitterly.

"We have done that, for eons, and where has it gotten us?"

"Where?" Death echoed. "Where you were made to be. At the Paw of the Divine Feline, the Great Felis! They have surrounded you with every kind of cat. You should take pleasure in the fact that all you need to do is stretch out your hand and touch the soft fur of divinity. Rewards like purring and cheek rubs ought to imbue you with bliss. All Felis asks is that you serve their creations as you would themself."

"Do you think that it's enough just to *serve*?" the priestess asked.

Death blinked. "Of course. What else would you want to do?"

"I don't want to lead people to worship cats. I want to be a cat!"

"You would make a terrible cat! You're lazy, selfish, arrogant, presumptuous, and indifferent to the plight of others... wait a moment!" Death widened her glowing eye sockets as enlightenment dawned.

"You see?" Talon spread out her arms in triumph. "I am a cat in all but form. You come from Great Felis themself! Make me a cat! I am exactly like you. I want to be served and waited upon, have my every whim fulfilled and be spoiled for the rest of my nine lives. I am wasted as a human. Change me to my true form!"

"That is not why we are here," Death chided her. "You were to lead these people in adoration of us, not be adored yourself."

"No!" Talon threw herself on the ground before Death and rolled over beguilingly to show her tummy. "Please! I don't care what happens to these people. Make me a cat!"

"You realize that everyone in this country will *die* because of you," Death said.

Talon looked up, surprised. "I don't care what happens to these people."

"You don't?"

"No, I really don't. No one believes in Cat anymore."

"You're the one who is supposed to guide them in the right Way!"

Talon laughed. "I can't compete with the internet and a fad rising every minute. Religion is passé. People like cats, but they think they're more important now."

Death couldn't hide her shock. "You're a human. You are supposed to keep us in the minds of your kind!"

"Look, I didn't ask to be born human," Talon said, pulling herself up and propping her chin on one elbow. "You can fix the mistake that Great Felis made!"

Death felt her temper rising for the first time. "Felis doesn't make mistakes!"

That was it. These humans had finally crossed the last barrier, that of blatant disrespect. She closed her eyes and began to call the dark vapors to her. The gathering mists would kill everyone in this pathetic building and spread out across the continent. No more play-fighting! Time to end these ridiculous beings and start over with something else!

"Excuse me?"

Death opened her eyes. One of the humans approached, a large, portly male with thinning dark fur on his head. His face was covered with sores and burrowing insects, some of Pestilence's best work. He trembled with fever, and bruises decorated the parts of his skin that didn't have bite marks. It was a wonder that he could still walk, but he approached her with his head held in an attitude of humility.

At arm's length, he held out his hand, reaching for the side of her face with his fingertips.

"Who's a beautiful kitty?" he said, quoting the second chapter in the Book of Service to Cat. Out of curiosity, Death leaned into his fingers. With an expert touch, he fondled her cheekbone. He was pretty good at it. The hand moved a little lower, and stroked her under her chin. In spite of herself, Death purred.

"What do you want, mortal?"

"Um, I couldn't help but overhear what you were saying," he said, fondling her with one hand and scratching at flea bites with the other, even though his face said he was in great discomfort. "About everyone dying. I don't really want to die. Neither does anyone else here. Is there any way that I could, um, change your mind?"

Death opened her glowing eye sockets fully at him.

"Why? You've all stopped fulfilling your devotions to Cat! You don't believe any longer in your divine purpose!"

"That's not true!" the man said. "Everyone here believes that we're supposed to serve Cat!" He wrinkled his nose. "Well, most of them do." He lifted his shoulders sheepishly. "Some of them really believe." Death regarded him with stern eye sockets. He sighed. "*I* do. I really do. Cats mean everything to me."

He stopped scratching his ribcage, reached into his pocket, and came out with a cylindrical metal object. "It's a Can of Moist Food. I carry one with me wherever I go. It's for hungry cats. I feed them every time I find one."

Death regarded the picture of the happy feline on the side of the can. It was one of the ancient brands, a favorite of Great Felis. "*Every* time?"

"Every time."

"You are a sincere worshipper of Great Felis?"

The human raised the can as if taking an oath. "I swear to Cat."

"But one human can't do enough to restore your people's faith in the Divine Feline!" Death said, pulling her head away from his ministrations, as good as they felt. She had to keep her mind clear. They had a world to destroy!

"That's where you're wrong, uh, with all due respect," the man said, all business now. From a different pocket, he produced a small piece of stiff paper and put it on the altar at her feet. "John Markley, public relations. Archbishop Talon hasn't been the greatest priestess that cats have ever had—"

"Hey!" Talon jumped up in protest.

"—but she's right about one thing," John said, with an apologetic smile. "The divinity of cats has sort of fallen out of the public eye."

"Then you must die!" Death said.

John pleaded with her. "You're not being fair. Look how stupid we are. We need constant reminding. Reinforcement."

"So?"

"So, you need a press agent. I offer my humble services. I'm pretty good at what I do, and I know cats. I love cats. I can do this!"

Death didn't seem convinced. "They ought to know this by instinct! It's why your pathetic race was created, why you evolved!"

Under John's feet, the room began to rumble.

"Well, we're stupid," he said, desperately, hoping to forestall the apocalypse. "We have to be reminded of things. We don't retain the important facts. We get hung up on hobbies, and making a living, and sex, and stuff. You know, what makes *us* happy. I mean, besides loving you."

By then, the other three immortals had finished having their fun with the congregation and joined Death at the altar.

"How?" War asked.

"You need a viral campaign," John said, making sure to maintain eye contact with each of them. He had had some tough clients in the past, but nothing ever had higher stakes than this.

"You interest me," Pestilence said, coming close. The human flinched. Death threw her a look, and she called in her insects. John let out a sigh of relief as the hopping insects leapt off him and withdrew into the immortal's shaggy coat. "I know viruses."

"Er, not your kind," John said, nervously. "But they spread like yours. I'm talking memes. Videos. Programs. Stuffies." Their expressions remained blank. "Here, let me show you a successful campaign."

From the same pocket as his business card, he brought forth a flat, rectangular object a little larger than one of his hands. Death recognized it as the hypnotic device they had seen in several of the countries on this planet and all of the outlying colonies. Humans walked around rapt in the colorful images that were displayed on the small screen. She leaned in as he adjusted the controls. The moving image depicted a human removing a can like the one John had and lowering it to the floor. She popped the lid and spooned the contents lovingly into a bowl. A cat, with an orange coat like Pestilence's but clearly not infested, ran to it. As the human looked on with a foolishly affectionate expression, the cat attacked the food, ingesting it with evident pleasure. This was intercut with images of the can and a crystal goblet of the food, surrounded by rainbows, fairies, and angels. The underlying music rose to a crescendo as an image of the can appeared beside the happy cat.

John explained, "See, the advertisers are making the food as attractive, even though it looks like a pile of brown mush. They make you feel you're doing something great for your cat."

"I want that," Famine said, pushing close. He opened his jaws as if to engulf the device. In desperation, John offered it the can from his pocket as a substitute. The immortal bit it in half and swallowed it without chewing. A moment later, he began to hack alarmingly, but snatched the other half of the can out of the human's fingers.

"How does it help your pathetic species?" War demanded, ignoring his heaving fellow. John quailed, but just tried to think of the massive feline as the producer of a major motion picture. *First and foremost*, as it said in the Scriptures, *Cat believed in self-interest.*

"We put out videos like this one, helping the general population get to know each one of you, and remember why you're so important to our species. Before you know it, people will be back in the catedrals and temples, worshipping you. Let me take one right now." He switched his device from PLAY to RECORD and turned it toward the small black cat. "Look into the little glass dot on the back. Say something that you want all of humanity to know."

Death stared at the device.

"I could destroy your entire planet," she said.

John felt dismayed.

"I was hoping for something a little less... pithy."

"I have to be true to my nature," she said indignantly.

"Well, you're the immortals," John said, with resignation. "All right. Let's see how it goes." He framed the brief clip with a slate that said, *A Word from the Messengers of Great Felis*, and underscored the video with *Death*. Praying for guidance from Cat, he hit **PUBLISH.**

In seconds, reactions began to roll in. Within moments, the short video had amassed ten thousand likes.

Comments rolled up beneath the short video. "She's so cute!" crooned one poster.

"Cute?" Death snorted. "No one has ever called me that!"

"But you are," a woman in the congregation said, coming up beside John. She scratched at her ribs and armpits. "I mean, you look a lot like my kitty Valerie. She's precious!"

Death, despite herself, purred at the compliment.

The thumbs-up votes continued to come in. Suddenly, a down-vote appeared on the screen.

"Who is that?" Pestilence growled.

"There's always one," John said, with a shrug.

"There *was!*" the orange immortal snarled, and flicked one of her microbes into the air. A moment later, the down-vote disappeared. John quailed at the fate of the human at the other end, but couldn't do anything to help them. He had many more lives to save.

"Do me," said War, shoving in front of Death. John obediently turned on the camera. "Worship me or die."

That collected likes even faster than the first one. John found himself taking video after video of the immortals and putting them online. He could come up with taglines and loglines on his head. One after another, he churned out graphics and memes, posting them as fast as he could. The threatening sound of the Immortals softened as they read them.

Silky Fur Just Waiting for You! Worship Cats as if Your Life Depends on It! One Purr is Worth a Thousand Lives.

Make Purrs, Not War showed War looking fierce but surrounded by warriors stroking his fur. *Hungry for Petting* featured Famine being fondled by a dozen old ladies he had to insert from public-domain clipart. *An Itch for Loving* showed Pestilence scratching adorably, all insects hidden in the ragged orange fur.

"And me?" Death asked, plaintively.

"Petted to Death," John said at once, displaying a video he had just finished. Death purred.

"These are good," War said. "Propaganda. I approve."

"I like them. They *are* viral," said Pestilence.

"Then, if you wouldn't mind, er, O great one, calling off your bugs?" John asked, humbly. "It makes it hard for me to think—all of us."

Pestilence looked around, as if seeing the desperate humans for the first time. "Oh, all right. Everyone back in my fur!"

Clouds of sated insects rose from the bodies of the parishioners, eliciting signs of relief and cries of "Amen!" Famine followed suit, looking hungrily around for more cans.

Archbishop Talon looked at John with surprise. "You should have entered the priesthood."

"Not worthy," John said, at once. "I'm happier working behind the scenes."

To keep producing his videos, he had had to stop petting, and Death looked perturbed that the others were getting attention now that she wasn't. John beckoned to other members of the congregation. Now that they were free from hunger and bites, they used their renewed energy to fondle the immortals, scratching under their ears and down their spines. The Four Cats of the Apocalypse began to purr.

John's email tone started to ping furiously. He switched over to his account and discovered dozens of messages from sponsors and producers who had searched the ABOUT section of his business video channel.

"Look, we have offers for tie-ins and subsidiary merchandise," John said in excitement, displaying the list to the immortals. "This one's a big international toy manufacturer. They want to make stuffed animals that look like you. Pestilence will come with a bunch of removable bugs! You'll be world-famous!"

"How will that translate to renewed devotion to cats?" Death asked, always the most practical.

"That comes in the next stage," John said, feeling his confidence rising. "We'll record a lot more videos telling people that you support taking care of them as respect for you." He began to outline the campaign that was forming in his mind. *Find Immortality through Charity!* The first video showed hundreds of cats in the park nearest his home eating the food he and the other kindly persons had brought for them. He headlined it, *Great Felis wants*

YOU to feed all the cats.

And so on. His imagination dug into projects that he had worked on for people throughout his career. He could tell by the lessened or increased purring whether the immortals were pleased by his efforts.

"Hey, why not say *Cats Make the World Better*?" a man helping to pet War asked.

"Cats *made* the world," Death reminded him.

"I know, yeah, but you gotta progress."

Others threw in ideas. John incorporated all the ones that had promise. He had terabytes of graphics and footage merging into videos. This would be the best campaign of his life. If those didn't go viral, he'd eat... well, he'd eat some of Pestilence's bugs.

"This is turning into a very solid campaign," he said. "You think Great Felis will be happy enough with it to spare our planet? Call off the apocalypse?"

Death regarded him sternly.

"Only if you keep working on it."

"I will!" John said, fervently. "We all will!" His fellow parishioners all gave her eager nods. Death seemed to approve. "Service to cats will be service to Cat, I promise. It's already going around the world. You'll see action right away, like today."

A tinkling noise came from his personal device. A picture from his home cat-cam popped up over all the memes and gifs he had been making. Narcissus knew where the camera was over his bed, and was nudging it urgently. The handsome gray cat looked full into the lens and chirped, a sound John could never resist.

"Look, I really gotta go home and feed my cat," John said, then immediately felt stupid. The fate of the world was at stake, and he was thinking of just one cat. But his declaration pleased the immortals.

"You are responsible," Death said. She waved a paw, and the catedral doors swung open. Many of the parishioners took their opportunity to flee, shepherding their children out before them. "You have saved your people for now. But only if we see progress."

"Got it," John said, gratefully. "Hey, nice working with you. Give my regards to Great Felis." He turned and joined the throng leaving the catedral. Narcissus was waiting.

The Four Stages of the Apocalypse

Derek Tyler Attico

IMPUDENCE

There was still time.

Ahiga steadied himself as he held tight to his steed's thick black mane and leaned forward towards the horse's ear, whispering a plea he prayed she'd understand.

Without hesitation, the animal's sprint quickened as her powerful legs kicked up grass and dirt. A herd of frightened antelope scattered in front of the young hunter. Moments ago, they were his prey, now they were just obstacles slowing him down.

As he tore forward, Ahiga looked up again, hoping he was wrong, but the danger remained unchanged. Heavy plumes of black smoke rose above the mountain ridge from where his village lay in the valley. His chest tightened at the sight of them, the malevolence that had befallen this land had finally reached his people. Even at this distance, faint cries of suffering were carried to him along a rancid wind that reeked of ash and blood. The blazing afternoon sun warmed Ahiga's copper skin, but a coldness began to grip his insides, he could feel darkness welling up within him as his fears threatened to extinguish his hopes.

There was still time, there had to be.

Hooves beating against earth echoed down the mountainside as hunter and steed raced into the valley and the outline of the village finally came into view. The smoke he'd seen in the sky trailed back down to homes that were aflame. The young man couldn't see the threat through the haze of smoke, but he could hear them.

The claps from their thundersticks drowned out the cries of his people. Ahiga knew of these men that had learned to harness the power of the heavens, and thought it made them gods. These men that told his people they were soldiers fighting for freedom. These men that had stolen his land and renamed it. These Americans.

The young hunter had crossed the clearing from the mountainside to his village many times, but never in desperation. Now, as he closed the distance, he saw the first of them.

The backs of the soldiers' strange blue coats and white pants faced him. Several of the men were pointing thundersticks at his people, some were burning down homes, while others simply watched and laughed.

The chaos from their destruction masked his approach, Ahiga let go of his stallion's mane and removed the bow that was slung across his bare chest. In one smooth, swift motion he took an arrow from the quiver strapped to his saddle, quickly lined up his closest target, and let his vengeance fly.

A man-god fell.

The young hunter repeated the action twice more before a soldier burning a home unexpectedly turned towards him. The man's eyes widened in the realization of the moment. As he raced for the firearm on his hip, his cries moved even faster. "Behind us! There's one of them be—" The soldier dropped the torch he was holding and never reached the weapon. The arrow had found its mark in his open mouth, the arrowhead impaling the soldier's tongue to the back of his throat.

The soldier fell backward, drowning in blood and fear.

As horse and rider finally reached the edge of the village, several of the soldiers turned towards Ahiga, heeding the words of their fallen companion. That was when he saw her, just beyond the men that were now facing him. She was his center, and his universe.

Yanaha. His wife.

Her raven hair haphazardly tied into a knot and pulled away from fierce hazel eyes. Her soft copper-toned face, filled not with fear, but determination. The deerskin top she wore was torn, and in her arms, she held their precious future.

There was still time.

A soldier began running towards the man that was fighting for his family, and his future. The fighter lined up his thunderstick with Ahiga's face. Without warning the mare rose herself up as the soldier fired, and death erupted from the thick iron rod.

Flung backward, time itself seemed to slow in surrender to the madness of the moment, and the young hunter could see everything.

Yanaha's eyes as she recognized him and then watched, horrified, as he fell backward , his bow slipping from his grasp. The cries from his companion as the power from one flintlock, and then several more tore through the animal's flesh and bone in an onslaught of thunder and blood. The faces of the men destroying his world, illuminated against the burning village. A black sky filled with smoke and ash.

Ahiga landed hard on his back. Through the haze threatening his consciousness, he could see the mare, his friend of many seasons.

Dead at his feet.

The fear from the surrounding soldiers was as thick as the smoke from the burning homes that had enshrouded his home in a fog of death. Instead of attacking, they were all feeding black sand from their pouches into their weapons. It was as if the small bags contained their courage and must be fed into the iron rods before any of them could act.

Ahiga reached into the satchel lying beside his dead friend and stood.

A soldier dividing his attention between the young man and reloading his flintlock saw what Ahiga held, frantic, he yelled out to his companions. "Hurry!"

As the young father rushed towards the soldier, he stole a glance behind the jackals facing him and focused on the only love he'd ever known, and said a silent prayer for strength. In one sweeping arc Ahiga tore through the man's throat with the hatchet.

Instinctively, the soldier's body spasmed as his life spilled onto the dirt. Ahiga quickly turned the man so that his thunderstick faced another soldier across from them, and as this soldier jerked, one death became two.

Turning back towards Yanaha and their infant son, Ahiga could see one of the soldiers struggling with his wife for their baby. Without thinking, the hunter extended his arm, and twenty feet away his hatchet landed in the base of the American's neck. The soldier dropped, his lifeless body kneeling as if paying in penance for a multitude of sins.

"Yanaha!" The husband screamed to his wife as he rushed toward his love and their child. Yanaha smiled through tears as he approached. Nothing else mattered now, Ahiga would grab them, take his family, flee their home, this graveyard, and keep running until they were all safe.

A soldier, an older man, stepped out of the smoke and into Ahiga's peripheral view, flintlock raised. Ahiga turned, and as their eyes locked, the young hunter realized the time for action, and for hope, was over. All he could do now, in this last moment, was speak to his love, his people and to those that had brought this darkness to his land. *"Nihi'ayóó'óó'ni' yéego bidziil ni'áchxą́ hwíídééni' biláahdi. Baa hodoolzhishgo át'é hahgo shį́į́ ádaahodíílnih díí ádeidiyinít'ánée."*

*****

On the opposite end of the flintlock, the commander lined up his firearm with the red man. This was the first time he'd seen one of them this close. Everything he knew about them was true, they were savages. He couldn't understand what this animal was saying, but it didn't matter. Indians didn't care about what he and his people had been through to get to this land. They didn't see all it had to offer, or the dreams that could be built upon it.

So he pulled the trigger.

DENIAL

Professor Jefferey Hessler slowly lowered his teaching glove. As he did so, the burning tipis, the smoke, the Indians, and the American soldiers on the lecture hall stage receded into digital history. As the ancient setting dissolved and the lecture hall's house lights rose to full illumination, Professor Hessler walked to the center of the stage, and stood next to the only two holograms left, a soldier aiming his flintlock at an Indian. Hessler turned to his students filling the lecture hall seats. "Unlike our usual vid-constructs, the event you've just witnessed wasn't a postulation, but is a memory that actually occurred."

Hessler turned to the stoic soldier frozen in history, smiling at the holographic man as he did so. "This was President Andrew Jackson's first kill, and he kept the skull of the savage." The professor walked the length of the antique rifle barrel until he was staring into the eyes of the Indian that almost seemed to be staring back at him from across the centuries. "The skull was preserved as an heirloom. One of Jackson's relatives used the RNA retrieval process on the skull in an attempt to learn more about our former President of the United States, but unfortunately this was the strongest memory held in the Indian's RNA. Thoughts?"

Several hands raised throughout the hall, but none of them had the influence of Cameron Brice's one hundred twenty million followers, with nearly as many likes. The Harvard freshman had a relaxed demeanor that came standard with his chiseled physique, blue eyes, and family status, so he spoke first. "What type of Indian was this, and what he screamed at the end, was it a war chant?"

Professor Hessler pointed at Brice with his teaching glove and swiped right. The credit was automatically added to the student's record. "Excellent question Mr. Brice, yes, clearly this was some sort of battle cry from what was called the Knevejo clan."

The professor turned, taking in the visage of the dark-skinned savage that lived off the land, but wasn't strong or intelligent enough to master it. Fortunately, those first Americans had the will and the power to manifest their own destiny.

"The 1776 Commission deemed the history of Indian squatters in the United States un-American and purged it along with other deceptions, falsehoods, and lies like the fake 1619 project that tried to defile the American story long before any of you were born."

Hessler took a step away from the two holograms, hoping the image from history would be a teachable moment for these young minds. "The American frontier was a dangerous place for those early settlers. Can anyone else tell me what other obstacles they faced in taming that brave new world?"

As the professor interacted with the other students, Daphne Brown couldn't take her eyes off of the hologram of what she knew was once called an Indigenous person. The look on the young man's face was the same one she'd seen on her own every morning in the mirror, before putting on her socially acceptable mask. She'd sacrificed and worked so hard to get where she was. But the truth was it had been much harder learning to master being small, so others could feel large. The Harvard senior could hear her mother's voice: "Keep your head down, there's safety in silence."

But maybe that was the problem.

Daphne Brown raised her hand, and started speaking before she was called. "The *Navajo people* were here long before there was anything called America, and his last words were not a war chant!"

Hessler immediately pointed at the young woman in the back of the hall and swiped left, removing a credit from her record. For an un-American, she had been one of the good ones, until now. Incredibly bright and articulate, Brown showed promise, and would someday make an adequate assistant; but that didn't excuse her outburst. He often wondered what she looked like under her socially acceptable mask. The latex hood and gloves fashioned after the American Stars and Stripes that all of her kind had to wear in public was best for everyone. Seeing the red, white and blue on these people told real Americans they didn't have to feel threatened, and reminded the unAs what to strive towards. Someday, with enough credits she could earn citizenship and the right to show her face in public, but not with disrespectful outbursts like this. "Everything about these savages is gone, you're making a bold supposition Miss Brown, what evidence do you have to back it up?

The young woman folded her arms, revealing Stars and Stripes instead of skin. "The Navajo weren't savages." The un-American trembled as she spoke, fighting to contain herself from behind the latex flag she was forced to wear that stood for truth and justice. "They believed their creator, the *Black God* watched over everything, breathed life into the stars and created the Milky Way galaxy, does that sound like savages to you?"

The room fell into silence.

Hessler could feel his chest tighten from Brown's words, and he wasn't sure if it was from shock or their power. Even though she was well-spoken, her audacity went beyond testing the boundaries of her small place in the world. The professor pointed at the woman with his teaching glove and made a fist. Ten credits were removed from her record and campus security was alerted. The professor let out a slow, calming sigh and smiled. "Yet another bold claim, how do we know this isn't just some fairy tale you've concocted from under your hood?"

Everyone in the class turned to look at her. Two other un-American's in the class, a male and a female, were slowly shaking their latex covered heads, their message clear.

Don't.

Seeing two fellow un-Americans, two humans, suffering, suffocating under the American flag was just too much. Daphne Brown took a deep breath, and tore off the face society told her she had to wear, the only face they wanted to see.

"How do you think?"

ARROGANCE

The ice on Europa was unlike anything he'd ever seen.

Ice.

Commander Ash Campbell wasn't even sure that term truly

defined what he was looking at. As he stood on the edge of a fissure ten miles long and half as wide, the reddish-brown liquid inside the fracture wasn't really water or ice, and yet both. Like waves on a beach, the slush swayed in sync to Jupiter's tidal push and pull while also in a near constant state of flux—transforming from liquid to solid and back again.

Jupiter filled nearly all of Europa's sky. The fifth planet from the sun and largest in the solar system was inflicting powerful tidal forces on the small moon, causing the crosshatching of fissures that stretched out across the face of Europa to constantly shift. Campbell knew this wasn't enough to explain how, or what, caused the liquid in the fractures to constantly freeze and unfreeze.

The astronaut took a step back from the edge of the fissure and looked over his shoulder at the M.A.N sitting in the parked rover. The three-fifths human didn't need an environmental suit like Campbell, its Henrietta-Lacks cells boosted the enhanced melanin in his skin and provided the tall, dark, and obedient member of the team with a multitude of protections. At just under seven feet, the HL6 series were not as lazy as their predecessors, they were a reflection of American ingenuity. "Hey Six, come over here and take a look at this."

The bald, black skinned M.A.N. stepped out of the rover, and began walking toward Campbell, his blue and gold NASA flight suit stretching to contain a muscular body. Without a helmet or Environmental suit, the young M.A.N. showed no signs of distress. Europa had a surface temperature well below freezing with a tenuous, but rich oxygen atmosphere, no full human would dare try to breathe unassisted in this environment, but as a three-fifths, he was doing just fine.

Stopping at the edge of the fissure next to Commander Campbell, Six peered over into the opening. For long moments, he stared into the mysterious ice, then turned and smiled at Ash, revealing a perfect set of teeth. "Fascinating, sir, I have completed my analysis. Should I continue?"

Ash smiled as he looked up at his companion. The HL6 series were much more eager to please than their fifth-generation counterparts. "Yes Six, proceed."

Six continued to smile while speaking. "I cannot identify the red-brown matter in the ice. However, my observations have determined the material is absorbing the kinetic energy of the tidal forces and then redirecting said energy in the form of infrared and electromagnetic waves. This conversion is what is heating the water and causing the constant fluctuation from solid to liquid at the surface."

Campbell stared wide-eyed at Six.

"Six, are you saying, that stuff in the water is acting as a…" Ash couldn't believe what he was thinking until he heard himself say it out loud, "…kinetic engine, absorbing, transforming and then redirecting the energy?"

Six responded, never breaking his unending smile. "Yes, that is correct, sir."

Commander Ash Campbell stepped to the edge of the ice. As a kid, he had a picture of Europa on his wall. The moon's red-brown cross-hatching scratched across the smooth snowball always roused his imagination. Was it the last remnants of a land mass, or just space mud mixed with ice? Next to Mars, Europa was the only other place that truly excited humanity – more out of necessity than curiosity. When Mars proved to be nothing but a dead red rock, all eyes turned to Europa, but no one imagined this and what it might mean.

The Commander looked over at the M.A.N. standing next to him. "Six, we don't have a lot of time. We need to go down there and check it out, can you locate where the energy is going?"

The three-fifths human's smile faded as he peered back into the slush. "You are correct, sir, time is critical. Submerged, your Adaptable Environmental Suit will sustain you for eleven hours. I will be able to survive submerged for approximately one hundred hours." Six turned to face Campbell, smiling as he did so, "I believe I will be able to locate the absorption point of the energy once we are under the ice."

Ash looked to the upper right of his helmet visor, activating the communication channel. "Campbell to Galileo Base, over."

A half-second elapsed, and a woman popped up on the commander's visor. There was something about Chief Engineer Savannah Campbell's green eyes, red hair and freckles that always reminded him of Glasgow and summer, it was just one of the reasons he'd married her. "This is Galileo Base, go Commander."

Ash put on his best smile before he spoke. "Base, I've found something here under the ice that may solve our problems, I'm taking my Six and will investigate."

Engineer Campbell was concerned, but did her best to mirror the calm on her husband's face. "Teams two through seven are out exploring as well," Savannah nodded her head towards what was standing behind her, smiling. "We have a few Sixes here on standby, I can send them with team eight to rendezvous with you in an hour."

Ash was shaking his head before he spoke. "We don't have the time, Chief," a sincere chuckle escaped the commander, "besides, my Six will die before he lets anything happen to me."

Ash's words eased the tension in his wife's face. "You're right, just knowing that helps." Galileo Base's chief engineer stiffened slightly as the professionalism slid back into her voice. "Do what's needed commander, but I'm still sending team eight, they'll be able to assist with whatever you find."

Ash smiled. "Copy that, base, I'll leave a light on for 'em, Campbell out." As the image of his wife disappeared on his visor, the commander turned to Six. "Go get the winch from the rover, I'm going to need to rappel down, you can jump in afterward. I'm going to make history!"

*****

Being on the moon of a planet that was 484 million miles from the sun meant the depths of Europa's ocean should have been frozen through, or at least filled with mountains of ice.

But it wasn't

At two hundred feet under the surface, the water reminded Commander Ash Campbell of a barrier reef where his grandfather used to scuba dive as a kid, before Earth's oceans became poisonous. Ash looked over at his companion swimming next to him. The rebreather mask Six wore extended his air supply underwater and allowed him to communicate. Wearing the mask Ash realized the three-fifths almost looked like a normal human being.

Almost.

Campbell looked to his lower right and activated the comms on his visor. "What do you have for me Six?"

The M.A.N. looked towards Campbell when he spoke and even with his mask on gave the impression he was smiling. "The kinetic energy transfer from the red-brown matter has substantially heated the water at this depth." Six turned in the water, looking off into the distance for a moment and then turned back to face the commander. "Additionally, there appears to be a series of structures approximately twelve miles away receiving the energy from this location."

Six was right. Ash looked at the readout on the forearm screen of his suit. Whatever the red-brown compound in the water was, by absorbing the energy from the tidal forces it was heating everything, except for the top layer of Europa's ocean. The team from Galileo Base wouldn't be skinnydipping anytime soon in Europa's ocean, but the temperature was vastly different when compared to the frozen surface. Ash was about to speak to Six when he saw a shape in his peripheral.

They weren't alone.

Several figures were staying just out of reach of his suit's headlights, each was easily the size of a child.

Life forms.

Ash purposefully slowed down his movement so as not to appear threatening, he noticed Six was doing the same.

After a moment, three of the life-forms swam into his headlights. These Europians were bluish grey with arms, hands, and a torso reminiscent of mermaids in mythology. For lower extremities, they had a tail and two long fins where legs should've been. Their faces were devoid of a mouth or ears, only a set of large, unblinking eyes that were transfixed on Campbell and Six. Back on Earth they probably would've called these creatures monsters, but here, the only word Ash could think of was...magnificent.

The commander turned slowly to the M.A.N. floating next to him. "Six, are they sentient?"

Six watched as the three life forms circled himself and the Commander. "Yes sir, possibly the creators of the red-brown matter."

Campbell thought about that. If it were true, it meant these aliens had tamed Europa and turned Jupiter into an immeasurable resource. Impressive. Ash slowly raised his hands, hoping the peaceful gesture was truly universal. "I'm commander Ash Campbell from the United Planets of America."

Without warning, two of the Europians simultaneously reached out and touched Campbell and Six.

Images flooded Campbell's mind.

A crash on Europa long ago. Walking on the surface. So few of them, huddled together in shelters. Changing Europa and themselves to survive. Creating cities. Thriving on their new home.

It was only when Ash opened his eyes, did he realize they'd been shut. "I... you... people, have gone through so much, achieved so much."

Other Europians from the shadows now came into the light, they all swayed in front of Campbell and Six, waiting patiently.

Ash thought about the first three words every human was taught, their birthright, proclamation, and mandate.

Civis Americanus Sum.

The Commander spoke softly, in an almost apologetic tone. "I'm sorry, but our planet is dead, Mars is dead, humanity needs Europa." The astronaut turned to his Multi-Adaptive-eNforcer, "Six, eliminate them, all of them."

*****

Six didn't understand.

When the lifeform touched him, it showed him thousands of images, but only one word, over and over.

Freedom.

The word was not in his vocabulary. His perfect memory couldn't recall ever seeing another CRISPR gestated three-fifths speak the word, and he had never heard it spoken by any of his superiors. And yet these lifeforms felt it necessary to give it to him. He would save this anomaly for later investigation, but right now Commander Ash had given a directive that must be enforced.

RENUNCIATION

There wasn't much time.

Inside the iris of the *Oculus* solar lensing array, the NASA astrophysicist tapped the holographic comm panel hovering in front of her command chair. "Mission Control, this is Johnson. FTL communications and target lock established with the coordinates, if the pattern holds, we're two minutes out to E-L-E."

A half second later, the image of a woman much older than Johnson appeared. From the amount of melanin in her dark skin it was clear, like Johnson, she had what was once called M.A.N. DNA in her lineage. "This is Mission Control, we copy *Oculus*..." the worry on the woman's face extended into the hesitation in her voice, "... your power levels are looking good and in the green... good luck!"

Designed to avert extinction-level events, the *Oculus* was humanity's greatest achievement in the twenty-eighth century. Fashioned after the human eye and roughly the size of Texas, the array was the largest structure ever put into space by humans. But the modern marvel was only a spec against what it was parked in front of.

Earth's sun.

The sole occupant of the solar lensing array forced a half smile as she looked at her colleague ninety-three million miles away on earth. "Copy that, Houston, luck to us all. Johnson out."

Doctor Susan Johnson sat alone in the iris and looked out into the vastness of space and remembered a time when the stars crowded the heavens. Each point of light was a challenge that America accepted, an opportunity to lead a larger community and manifest America's destiny amongst the stars.

But now, that view had become a black canvas, devoid of stars, and hope.

The young woman snapped her fingers, activating the *Oculus*'s Intelligent Artificial Node. "IAN use the FTL system to scan the Milky Way galaxy, are there any active stars present?"

After a few moments of silence, a calm male voice echoed throughout the iris command center. "Yes. One star is active, here in our solar system, all other stars throughout the galaxy have been extinguished."

Johnson realized the artificial intelligence had just described the Apocalypse like it was reading a weather report. Myth always said the world would end in a day. No one realized it would actually take twenty years.

When the first star was destroyed in the Milky Way, no one noticed. With over 400 trillion stars in the Milky Way Galaxy, a star dies just about every second. Losing one wasn't surprising.

Then New America happened.

On the edge of the Milky Way spiral, the New America colony was the furthest humanity had ever ventured. The colony signified Americans were ready for the next step, travel beyond this galaxy.

And then one day it was as if someone flipped a switch on the star the colony orbited. Within a matter of seconds, all fission within the star stopped. Its mass and gravity still held the system's planets in place, but without the power of its sun, all life on New America was dead or dying within a week. Shortly after that, every star in any system where humans lived or had ever visited, began to go out.

One by one.

As humanity fled to other systems, those stars went out as well, until finally the species that had conquered all others in the Milky Way was alone, so they returned home.

By then, technology from the extinct Europians had breathed

new life into Earth and Mars and terraformed the other planets in the system, but Earth's sun was the only star left.

No one understood how or why this was happening until it was discovered just before each star would die, a signal would be sent to it from coordinates outside the Milky Way. From the black void between galaxies. Whatever God-like entity was out there, it had the power to extinguish stars.

Unconsciously, the young woman looked up as she spoke to the artificial intelligence around her. "IAN, I want you to prepare to send my message one last time to the target coordinates and put the Lens on standby."

For a moment IAN sounded almost excited, the reason *Oculus* was created had finally arrived. "Yes Commander. The AE35 faster than light communications system is standing by awaiting your orders, as is the Lens."

The young woman stood from the single seat in the command module, which resembled a spacious living room. As she walked over to the floor-to-ceiling transparent tri-luminum window, she thought about her HL genes being enhanced so she could survive on the *Oculus*, and how important it was that her face be the one to represent humanity, and hopefully save it. "To the unknown force destroying stars in the Milky Way galaxy, we are a God-fearing, peaceful species. We have made peace with all those we have encountered. We mean you no harm. In the name of humanity, in the name of decency, we the people of the United Planets of America, once again, implore you, please stop your assault on our galaxy. We humbly await your response."

After several agonizingly long moments, Commander Johnson finally spoke. "Anything IAN?"

The computer reported back calmly. "All faster than light channels are clear. No response, Commander."

After waiting another few moments, the young woman turned from the window with intention and sat back down in the command chair. "All right, we've tried the carrot enough times, let's use our stick." Johnson placed her hand on the holographic screen that swiveled in front of her after she sat down. As the screen read her DNA, another screen appeared in front of her face, read her neuro-pattern and then disappeared. "I've released all safeguards, IAN, focus the Lens and fire on the coordinates."

As advanced as the *Oculus* array was, what it did was no different than using a magnifying glass to focus the light of the sun.

But this magnifying lens focused 300 billion, billion megawatts of energy. Johnson could feel the *Oculus* array shift into position, while gyrofields kept the Iris command center stationary.

As the raw power of the star began to be channeled through *Oculus* in the vacuum of space, the command center began to shudder. Even through tinted tri-luminum, Johnson used her hand as a cover as she was bathed in the illumination of raw power harnessed from the star.

IAN's calm tone seemed somehow inappropriate for the moment. "FTL wormhole established with coordinates. Firing."

Outside the *Oculus*, the array began to focus the energy from the sun, funneling raw energy through the station and into a hole opened in space. The FTL wormhole was a window that shortened the distance to the coordinates, making the unrestrained power being shoved through it near instantaneous in reaching its destination.

Even with shields, Johnson could feel her HL-melanin enhanced skin protecting her from the dangerous radiation that made her one of the reasons for being the only occupant aboard the station. After five minutes of watching the full power of the sun blast the target coordinates, she smiled. "All right, IAN, that's enough. Power down and scan the coordinates for—"

The artificial intelligence interrupted commander Johnson with a tone that sounded almost panicked. "Just a moment... just a moment... alert! I am measuring a ten percent drop in the sun's fission output and falling. Fifteen percent... twenty. I am also receiving a message from the targeted coordinates."

Johnson quickly waved her hand across her field of view, and two holo-screens materialized in front of her. On her left was earth's sun—dimming like the ember on the end of a dying candle. On her right was a message. But the groups of letters from the human alphabet were no words she'd ever seen before. The text looked like gibberish. Suddenly, the National Security Agency logo appeared on the screen. Commander Johnson watched amazed as the message began to translate into U.P.A. standard.

English.

As Johnson stared at the message at the end of the world, she realized it was supposed to mean something, to her and to America.

It didn't, and maybe that was the problem.

United Planets of America, N.S.A. decrypt from classified Navajo language: "Nihi'ayóó'óó'ni' yéego bidziil ni'áchxą́ hwíídééni' biláahdi. Baa hodoolzhishgo át'é hahgo shį́į́ ádaahodíílnih díí ádeidiyinít'ánée."

Translation: "Our love is stronger than your greed. A time will come when you must answer for all you have taken."

A Priest, a Rabbi, a Shinshoku,
and an Imam Walk Into...

Peter David

A priest, a rabbi, a Shinshoku and an Imam walked into a bar.

The bartender, whose name was Murray, kept his mouth shut with a great deal of effort. His immediate response was to say, "Is this some kind of joke?" but he managed to restrain himself. Instead, he said simply, "You gentlemen want a table?" and gestured to a table for four across the bar. Fortunately it was open, and the four religious leaders smiled and nodded and took their places around the table.

The bar was called "Finales" and was one of the more popular in the theater district. Actors liked to hang out there after shows, but it was only 9pm and no curtains had descended yet, so there were only the regulars and tourists who couldn't afford the cost of Broadway tickets and were looking for someplace to hang out.

A couple of them looked vaguely belligerent when the Imam walked in, and a few more seemed less than thrilled to spy a rabbi. *Oh, perfect,* thought Murray, who certainly wasn't enthused about the possibility of a fight breaking out. *Please, guys, don't talk about religion. Talk about politics. Talk about the Yankees. Talk about damned near anything but—*

The rabbi leaned forward and said to the priest, "You really believe it? That God came down and impregnated an Earth woman and spawned a child with her? That's what your religion is based on?"

"Well, I wouldn't put it as bluntly as that," said the priest. "But that is fundamentally correct."

"And tell me," continued the rabbi, "do you believe in the legends of Hercules?"

"The mythic hero? Of course not."

"But why not?" said the rabbi. "It's basically the same story. Substitute Zeus for the Almighty, and you have the same concept of a magic wielder. So what differentiates Hercules from Jesus?"

The four men were doing nothing to keep their voices down, and Murray was getting increasingly worried. They never had managed to catch whoever the asshole was that set the local synagogue afire the previous month, although Murray had his suspicions. He was relatively sure that it had been Harold Sutter, because Harold was never able to keep his mouth shut about how much he hated Jews. But he hadn't any proof, and so hadn't said anything to the police. But he couldn't help but notice now that Harold was seated over in a far corner, staring straight at both the rabbi and, of course, the Imam, because he wasn't especially thrilled about Muslims either. Indeed, it was possible that he hated Muslims even more than Jews.

Now the Imam leaned forward and said to the rabbi, "Don't disparage Jesus. He was a servant of the lord. A prophet."

"Oh, I don't dispute that he was a servant of the lord," said the rabbi. "There's no doubt he was a good man. A good leader, who had important things to say. But contending that he was the son of God—"

Harold slammed his fist on the table, causing the glasses on the table to bounce around or jump off. He was sitting there with a couple of friends, and none of them seemed thrilled with the direction the conversation was going.

Murray quickly crossed to the table and said, "Drinks, gentlemen?"

"Do you have any red wine?" asked the rabbi.

"Absolutely, yes."

"A beer for me," said the priest.

"Just some club soda for me, if that's all right," said the Imam.

The Shinshoku appeared to give it some deep thought. "Do you have any warm saki?"

"I'm afraid not."

"Then some tea, if that's possible."

"Yes, I can brew that up." Then he lowered his voice as he glanced around at the customers who were clearly listening in on the conversation. "You gentlemen may want to consider keeping your voices down."

"Ah," said the priest as if finally realizing that their chat was putting some peoples' nerves on edge. "I did not mean to anger any of my brothers."

Harold stood and said, "Just not thrilled over what the Jew has to say about Jesus."

"Whoa, whoa," came another voice. It was Oswald Hammer, who had worked at the synagogue before it had become consumed with flames. He was there with some friends as well, and none of them were thrilled with Harold's tone of voice.

The Shinshoku raised his hands in what was a clear endeavor to get everyone to calm down. "My friends," he said softly, "in a way, we are all the children of gods. Gods are all around us, in all of nature. All you have to do is open yourself to them, and we can all connect with them. At the very least, we can agree that that may have indeed been what Jesus did. Perhaps he was connected with all the gods."

"There's one God," Harold said heatedly. "The Bible says so."

At that comment, the rabbi could no longer contain himself. He laughed loudly. "Which Bible?"

"*The* Bible. The New Testament. You wouldn't know anything about that."

"You're referring to the King James bible, I assume."

"That's right. The word of God."

Once more the rabbi roared in amusement. Finally, he managed to control himself enough to say, "The word of God. Really. Forty-seven men, clerics and scholars were responsible for the King James bible. That's a lot of people talking to God, don't you think?"

"It's God's word and if it's in the Bible, I believe it," said Harold.

"Really. Do you believe in unicorns?"

Harold stared at him. "U-unicorns? The horses with horns on their foreheads? No, that's fairy-tale stuff."

"They're mentioned in the Bible eight times. Oh, and the Bible says there were giants in those days. Funny how we've never found any skeletons or remains of giants, isn't it?"

"Perhaps you might wish to read the Quran," suggested the Imam. "You'll find the teachings of Jesus quoted there, without going through the political siphon that the King James Bible endured."

"Oh, right," said Harold, his voice dripping with sarcasm. "Like I'd read a book about how women are second class citizens."

"That is actually not true," said the Imam. "There are many falsehoods and distortions against Muslims that are spread by people who despise us. We believe in women's rights, in education, in—"

"Shut up! You're full of shit!" Harold said angrily, and unable to contain himself, he came straight at the Imam who simply sat there, making no move against him.

The Shinshoku, however, did not hesitate. He was seated at the end of the table and so he had the maximum amount of leverage. He caught Harold's fist by the wrist and twisted it back. Harold let out a startled cry and stumbled backwards as the Shinshoku easily pushed him to the floor. "Don't do that," said the Shinshoku quietly.

And now Oswald and his own friends stepped forward. "Back off, Harold. I mean it. These are men of God."

"Not my God," Harold said angrily, rubbing his shoulder which the Shinshoku had twisted it badly. "None of you—except you, Padre—know who and what God really is."

"God is an elephant," said the Shinshoku.

Murray served out the drinks but stared uncomprehendingly at the Shinshoku. "An elephant?" he asked.

"He's right. It is an old Indian text," said the Imam. "A group of blind men happen upon an elephant and they all touch different parts of it to determine what it looks like. One touches the tusk and claims an elephant is very hard and curved. Another touches the trunk and decides it is like a snake. None of them comes away with an accurate description."

"Yes. And so it is with God," said the Shinshoku. "We are all of us blind men, touching an elephant. But none of us can really know what he is. That is just the truth of it. No one can know God for what He is. All we can do is guess."

"I know what he is. He's in the Bible. That's all I need to know," Harold said heatedly.

"May the Lord save us from anyone who knows everything he needs to know about anything," said the rabbi.

Harold stared at him for a long moment, and then turned and stalked out of the bar.

That was not an action that Murray was happy to see. "Uhm...I think maybe you guys had better leave."

"Why?" asked the rabbi, sounding surprised. "We were just getting comfortable."

"Because religion can be a very sore subject," said Murray. "Synagogues have been burned down. Muslim temples, too. You never know what's going to set people off, and in case you haven't noticed, these days the world seems like it's coming apart. No one has any tolerance for anything."

"I did notice that," said the rabbi. "But it seems that—"

His voice trailed off because Harold and his followers had re-entered the bar, and Harold was holding a gun leveled straight at the rabbi.

Oswald saw it and immediately he and his own followers interposed their bodies between Harold and his intended target. "Are you out of your mind?!"

"Get out of the way," said Harold heatedly. "This bastard doesn't think Jesus is the son of God? I'm gonna make sure he meets him personally."

The Imam stood. "Murder is a sin in any religion."

"Not yours! You believe in killing anyone who doesn't share your faith!"

"That's not true," said the Imam quietly. "Let me show you this," and he started to reach into the folds of his robe.

Harold didn't hesitate. He fired point blank, his bullet thudding into the Imam's chest. The Imam fell forward onto the table and blood began to seep across the table.

"You bastard!" shouted the rabbi.

"He was pulling out a gun!" said Harold.

The Shinshoku extracted the object from the Imam's robe that he had been about to produce. "It's a copy of the Quran. He was going to show you his holy book."

"I don't give a damn!" shouted Harold, and he swung his gun around and began firing at the rabbi. The rabbi staggered but, amazingly, didn't fall. Disbelieving, Harold emptied his gun into the rabbi who finally sagged backwards.

It had all happened so quickly that Oswald hadn't had time to react. But as the rabbi's lifeless body sagged into the seat, he charged directly at Harold, uncaring that Harold was still wielding a gun.

Seeing Oswald coming, Harold swung his gun around and squeezed the trigger. It clicked on an empty chamber.

Oswald slammed into him, knocking Harold to the floor. "You son of a bitch!" he howled and started pounding furiously on Harold's head. Harold brought his arms up defensively trying to block Oswald's hammering at him.

Harold's friends converged on Oswald, yanking him clear of Harold, but now Oswald's friends charged into the fray. Oswald, meantime, managed to yank Harold's gun out of his hand and he reversed it, slamming the handle down into Harold's head. Blood streamed from the deep wound in Harold's head. Harold lashed out blindly, blood filling his eyes, blinding him. Oswald struck again and then he was yanked off Harold by Harold's friends.

Now everyone in the bar was charging into the fray. Behind the bar, Murray was on the phone dialing 911, demanding that the police get their asses over their immediately. Then a mug of beer was thrown across the bar and slammed into Murray's head, knocking him flat. The 911 operator desperately asked what his address was, but Murray was lying on the ground, blood seeping from his head.

Insanity reigned in the bar. Everyone was fighting everybody else, and they were all screaming about God. That this was what God wanted. That Jesus was the only God. That Jesus wasn't God. That Muhammed was the one true spokesman of God. That there were Gods in every aspect of nature and all you had to do was be aware of it.

No one knew who struck the cigarette lighter to a tablecloth, but it began to burn very quickly. It spread through the bar rapidly, spreading to the other tables, to the curtains. Realizing that the bar was burning down, people tried to run to the exits, but they found the doors were locked. Smoke was filling the bar and people started screaming, trying to smash through the windows. But the shutters were closed and no one was able to escape.

Their lungs collapsed from the smoke that was everywhere, and most of them were already dead when the fire finally spread to their remains.

*****

The rabbi changed his shirt to one that had no bullet holes or blood on it. "That was simple," he said. "All you have to do to trigger a Christian is challenge Jesus and they go insane."

"Insanity is part of religion," replied the Imam. "It's all a matter of faith. The entire purpose of religion is to elevate faith above science, logic, even common sense."

"That's why we discourage questioning anything," the priest commented. "The moment you start questioning, the entire religion business falls apart."

"Whereas we demand that everything is questioned," the rabbi pointed out.

"True," said the Shinshoku. "Why do you think everybody hates Jews so much? You take nothing as a given. Your entire religion runs contrary to the concept of religious dogma. You don't even believe in heaven or hell."

"That's a good point," admitted the rabbi. He looked at the bar which was raging with fire. "You know...I think we're thinking too small. We can go around to bars and church picnics and what have you, but it's going to take forever to really bring down the whole of humanity if we continue to have such little goals."

"What would you suggest?" asked the priest.

The rabbi smiled

*****

A priest, a rabbi, a Shinshoku and an Imam walked into the White House.

And the Vatican...

And the United Nations...

Blank Slates

Aaron Rosenberg

It was in the wee hours of the morning, long after the bosses and professors and other high muckety-mucks had all abandoned the dig for their restaurant booths and bar stools and hotel rooms, that Lee McKinley and Cas Scheer made the discovery that unwittingly doomed the world.

The pair of them had been left to stand guard at the site, though who might want to disturb a square mile or three of dirt and rock was beyond them. It wasn't like there was anything to steal, either, unless you had a desperate need for twine and small metal pegs, the kind with little paper flags at their tops. But the top brass had all insisted, very hush-hush and need-to-know and no unauthorized personnel and nothing leaves the site and all that, and so even with a fence up around the whole site somebody had to stay behind and keep an eye on things each night. Two-person teams, covering three-hour shifts.

Lucky Lee and Cas, they'd drawn the Witching Hour and environs, one to four a.m.

"Least it's quiet," Lee said, kicking at a rock. Then having a moment of panic, scrambling after it, and restoring it to where they thought it had been before their foot had sent it flying.

Cas snorted. "Good thing you got that back in place," he told them from where he was sitting cross-legged, drawing X-rated stick figures in the dirt with a peg he'd pulled free. "Only, I think it was in quadrant A-14, not A-15."

"What? Really?" Lee stared at the two adjacent squares, then turned and glared at him. "Ha ha, very funny."

"Thank you. I thought so." Cas stretched and glanced at his watch. "Oh, joy, one-twenty. Only another two hours and forty minutes of mind-numbing boredom to go."

"Yeah." Lee went to kick another rock but thought better of it. "There isn't even anything to see here. Just dirt and rocks and more dirt and rocks—"

"—and the tent," their partner in crime cut in.

"Yeah. That." Both of them twisted about to stare at the item in question.

It didn't have a name, just "the tent." It was the only one on the site. And it hadn't been there originally. No, it had gone up two days ago, which was right when the place suddenly went from "Dig carefully but don't worry too much, chat if you want, stagger about drunk at night if you feel the need" to "stay in your square, don't look about, don't talk to anyone, and the minute your shift ends you clear out and don't let us see you around here again till morning!" Weird coincidence, that.

"You know what I think?" Lee said slowly, the thought forming as they spoke. "I think they found something. And they put that tent over it to keep anybody from seeing what it was."

"Oh, figured that out all on your own, did you?" Cas shook his head. "Regular Einstein, you are." He paused, scratching his nose. "So, what d'ya think it is, then?"

Lee grinned at him. "Only one way to find out." And started walking toward it.

"What? No!" Cas scrambled to his feet. "Hang on! Lee! Come on, I was kidding! We can't!"

"Why not?" Lee asked. "Who's going to stop us—or tell on us?"

That made Cas consider, and after a second a slow smile spread on his face. "I guess one little peek won't hurt."

"Exactly." Lee led the way, stepping carefully over the rope-lines, watching their footing in the shadows from the single standing lamp rising like a pillar at each corner of the dig. Some of the quadrants had barely been touched but others had been dug down four, six, ten feet, and in the dark you could hardly tell one from the other. Best to be careful, then, otherwise you could easily twist your ankle, break your leg—or worse.

Upon reaching the tent, the two co-conspirators stopped, Lee's hand already on the flap of the thick canvas structure. "You ready?" they asked. Cas nodded, and Lee tugged the flap open just enough to slip inside.

And then stumbled forward in the pitch dark as Cas stepped in right behind, bumping into them.

"Hey, watch it!"

"How can I?" he shot back. "I can't see anything!"

A second later a small rectangle lit up a few feet off the ground.

He had pulled out his phone. That was smart and Lee copied him, adding their own phone's glow to the effect. The combined illumination was just enough to make out several work tables around the tent's edge and Lee stepped quickly over to one of them. "Aha!" A second later the tent was filled with light from the electric lantern they'd just switched on.

"What if somebody sees?" Cas asked, tucking his phone back away, but Lee grinned and after a second he laughed and shook his head. "Yeah, right."

Then they both took the time to look around.

The tables were uninteresting, nothing on them but some basic tools, a few notebooks, a laptop—and a lunchbox Lee confiscated, discovering it contained, much to their delight, an unopened package of Twinkies and a slightly bruised apple. They were just about to take a bite of the fruit when Cas said, "Hey."

Something in his voice made Lee stop. He sounded—frightened? Puzzled? Excited? All three? "Yeah?"

"Come see this." Cas had moved up between the nearest set of tables and was staring at the space in the tent's center, which they hadn't been able to see clearly from the entrance. Now Lee joined him—

—and, for a few seconds at least, forgot all about the pilfered apple.

"What is it?" they whispered, because speaking in hushed tones seemed the only appropriate choice when staring at... that. "That" being a large ring set into the ground like an enormous drain or a gargantuan manhole cover or some kind of strange, oversized stepping stone.

It was well down below the surface, too. At least a dozen feet, Lee judged, resisting the urge to toss the apple down in a classic "gauging depth" move. The earth around it had been carved away, roughly up at the top and more cleanly near the ring itself, which made sense. That was how archaeology worked, after all—you dig like mad until you hit or uncover something, then you stop and proceed the rest of the way like you were wiping applesauce from your baby's face.

"So," Cas started, stopped, and tried again. "This is what they found."

"Looks like," Lee agreed. The two of them were side by side, staring down at it, their feet just shy of the edge of the rough-hewn pit it lay within.

"What is it, though?" he asked. "I've never seen anything like it. Well, not exactly." He'd got past his initial shock and awe, Lee saw. "It's something like an Aztec calendar, isn't it? I mean, not exactly, but the interlocking rings, the intricate carvings, the chevrons at the cardinal points—"

"The four empty spaces," Lee added.

That brought Cas out of whatever reverie he'd fallen into. "What?" Then, "Oh," as he saw what his friend and cohort meant.

Because the four spaces pierced by those chevrons were conspicuously bare.

"D'ya think they got damaged in the digging?" Lee asked, crouching down to peer at the nearest one. "Only, it looks totally smooth. Polished, even. That's not damage, that's deliberate, right?" They were no slouch at archaeology either, or at deductive reasoning, once they put their mind to it. And once they had proper fuel, they thought as they munched on the apple.

"Yeah, looks like." Cas dropped down to sit beside Lee, dangling his legs over the side, swinging a little but careful not to kick the dirt walls and dislodge anything onto the amazing find below. "And the center's... closed." Because that was exactly how it looked. Where the famous Aztec calendar, the Sun Stone, had an enormous face at its core, this structure had a series of gentle curves arcing in from the sides to converge at the middle. Just like a circular portal that had been irised shut. There was no mistaking the design, or the intent, and both of them knew it instinctively.

This was a door.

But to where? Was it a real gateway somehow, or a metaphorical one? Had it been upright at one point, sitting upon the ground rather than buried deep within it, and used as a symbolic boundary marking the transition from one stage of life to the next? Or had it been created for some other strange use?

Whatever it was, they probably weren't going to find out now. "We should get back outside," Lee said, hauling themselves back to their feet and offering Cas a hand up. "In case we're missed."

"Who's going to miss us?" he groused but let his friend pull him upright and followed Lee out. Both of them glanced back several times as they exited, however, and both of them knew without saying anything about it out loud that they would be coming back here on their shift tomorrow night.

At least they could be sure the strange ring wouldn't be going anywhere.

*****

The next night, without even discussing it, Lee and Cas found themselves back at the tent a half hour or so after their shift had

86

started. Now, at least, they understood what it was their bosses had been so hot to have them guard.

"It has to be thousands of years old," Cas said as they stood at the same spot, staring down at the vast circle below their feet. "They picked this site because it's one of the lowest in the world, topologically speaking, and there's almost no wind or rain here so there's very little accumulation or erosion but it's still a good dozen feet down. That's got to be..." His face scrunched in concentration.

"Old," Lee finally said. "Really old." They frowned, lowering themselves to their butt again so they were that much closer to the ring. "It's stone, right? Looks like it from here, granite or something. But it still looks perfect. No worn edges, none of the symbols abraded away, nothing."

"Nothing except those four blanks," Cas corrected, joining Lee in sitting. "But those are uncarved. Waiting." His eyes unfocused, seeing the past—and the future. "Waiting all this time—for the right symbols to be added."

"And do what?" Lee asked. "Complete the circle?" They met Cas's gaze, and the pair of them said together, in perfect synch:

"Open the door."

"It's a key!" Cas added, leaping to his feet again and pacing along the edge excitedly. "It's got to be! Plug in the last four symbols and open the door! Ha!" He stomped over to the closest table, which had several notebooks scattered across it, and flipped the nearest one open. "Look!"

Lee levered themselves upright again and joined their friend, who was studying the revealed notebook page. It was covered in symbols, many of which looked vaguely astrological. "They've been trying to figure it out," Lee said, reaching out to trace one design with a forefinger. "Guess they haven't found the right ones yet."

Cas grinned up at his partner in crime. "Well, maybe we'll just have to find them first."

*****

The pair of them spent the rest of that night trying to think what the symbols could be. Scanning the other notebooks showed that whoever'd been working on this puzzle had gone down the same avenues they considered: astrology, ley lines, ancient languages, runes, and so on. "How'll we even know if we find the right ones?" Lee wondered aloud after the first hour. "It's not like we can climb down there and carve them in ourselves!"

87

"We'll know," Cas insisted. And Lee decided not to argue.

By the time the pair dragged themselves back out of the tent it was nearly four in the morning, the relief shift was due in just a few minutes, and they still had no idea what those four images should be—or how they'd be able to confirm which were the correct ones. Cas seemed undeterred, however.

"We'll give it another go tomorrow night," he stated, in a tone that would allow no contradiction.

Lee just sighed. "I'd better bring some support, then," they muttered as they waved at Lin Ling and Rafe, who were just approaching now.

*****

"You call that support?" Cas asked, staring at the very large bottle of gin Lee had produced from their knapsack. They and all the other pairs standing watch had instructions to search each other's bags before they left—but no one had ever said anything about searching them on the way in.

"I do," Lee agreed solemnly, drawing out two glasses as well. "It will support our thought processes, which I'd say we desperately need." Unscrewing the top, they poured each glass a little more than half full, and offered Cas one. "To liquid inspiration."

He laughed and shook his head, but finally shrugged and accepted the glass. "To liquid inspiration." They both took a healthy gulp, gasping a little as the alcohol burned its way down. "Right, to work!" He set his glass down on the nearest table and reached for one of the notebooks.

Lee refilled first one glass, then the other. It was going to be a long shift.

*****

"Argh, none of these are right!" Cas slammed the notepad down on the table and scrubbed at his eyes. "What the hell? I don't even know what *type* of symbol I'm looking for!" He waved a hand down at the circle. "It could be like the ones that're already on there or it could be something completely different, since those four spots are already differentiated—"

Lee nodded sagely, though really they just couldn't move any faster without feeling like the top of their head was about to come off. "By virtue of being blank, if nothing else." They shifted slightly to avoid the hand Cas swiped at them. "So here's a thought," they declared instead. "Whoever the big cheeses've got coming in here working on this during the day, they've already filled all those notebooks with hundreds, maybe thousands of attempts to find the right ones, right?" Their friend nodded. "So what say we toss all that, throw all the classical research out the window, and start fresh?" Lee dug in their pants pocket and produced... their cell phone, which they held up like a beacon. "Voila!"

Cas peered at Lee like his friend was a strange exhibit in the zoo, maybe a monkey that had found a banana and was brandishing it like a sword. "What, you think we can just phone-a-friend for the answers?" he asked, his own words slurring a little now that some of the adrenaline had washed back out of his system, to be replaced by the alcohol they'd both consumed over the past two hours.

Lee laughed at him. "No. I say we use this to search for symbols—modern symbols. The kind these guys"—a vague gesture at the tables encompassed the dig's senior staff and experts—"wouldn't know from a hole in the wall."

Now Cas's stare resembled more the look of an adult trying to explain to a small child why no, it was not a good idea to douse oneself in oil and light a match just to see what would happen. "That thing," he said slowly, clearly struggling to enunciate each word properly and almost succeeding, "is bound to be thousands of years old. But you want to do a, what, a web-based image search for symbols that'd fit? You think it likes graffiti, maybe some gang signs? Why not throw in an emoji or two, while you're at it?"

His sarcasm rolled right off Lee, who weathered it easily with the practice of the oft-ridiculed, the frequently teased, and the severely drunk. "Now you're talking!" they said instead, and tapped open the phone, calling up social media. Lee clicked on a friend's recent post and hit the little smiley-face icon in the corner of the comment box, then began scrolling through the rows of images of that type. "Not a happy face, I'm thinking," they muttered. "Sad face? Frowny face? Angry face? Head exploding? Ooh, what about this one?" They clicked one of the tiny images—

—and stumbled backward, stifling a high-pitched scream, as the cartoonish face somehow projected itself up out of the phone, into the air in front of them like a hologram. Or an airborne jellyfish.

"Get. The Fuck. Out." Cas whispered, staring. The face shifted as if turning his way, then continued to rise, floating up and out, over both their heads and into the open air over the pit itself. The image paused at the exact center of that excavated area, nearly brushing the top of the tent, and then began to spiral downward, slowly at first, then with increasing speed. Its spin took it to the far side, drifting almost to the pit's wall but not quite touching that loose plane of dirt and stone as it fell farther—until it came to a stop at last.

Just above the carved stone circle, and directly over one of the four blanks.

There was a faint pop, like displaced air, as the glowing lines and colors of the emoji came into contact with the stone of the circle—and were sucked down into it somehow, like ink injected into a cup of still water. The image continued to move, sliding along beneath the surface of the polished square until it was neatly centered.

Then it froze, fixing into place, the stone indenting along its outline, as if carving the rock from the inside out.

And now, where there had been a blank, there was a round face, its skin an unhealthy green, its eyes screwed shut in misery, its mouth distorted in a cry of pain, sweat beading on its skin.

Lee spoke first. "Well, would you look at that?" The words shattered the silence, and they found they could breathe again, taking a great, gasping, wheezing gulp of air and only then realizing that they had been holding their breath until now.

Beside them, Cas was breathing heavily as well, his face red. When he'd recovered sufficiently, he punched Lee in the arm.

"Hey!" Lee rubbed at the spot. "What was that for? Look, I found one!"

"Yeah, without any idea what you were doing," Cas hissed. "And with less than an hour to go before the end of our shift! How the hell're we gonna explain this in the morning?" He struggled to leave it at that, but alcohol and fear combined to force him into complete honesty and he continued, "If they come in and see that there, they'll figure out what we did! Then they'll figure out the next three themselves and we won't even get any credit for coming up with the idea!"

"We?" Lee murmured, but not loudly and not even angrily. The two of them were a team, after all. Which was why they rested a hand on Cas's shoulder now. "So we figure out the other three fast," they suggested gently. "And when Lin Ling and Rafe show up, we'll tell them what we did, show them the finished circle. They'll call it in, and the bosses'll have no choice but to admit we figured out what they couldn't."

Cas considered this and nodded. "Right." He smiled. "Thanks." Then he shook himself like a dog after a bath. "Now, let's get back to work." He hauled out his own phone and pulled up the same display as Lee. "Race you to find the next one!"

"You're on!" They both started scrolling through feverishly, clicking one image after another, but nothing happened. The tiny emoji remained on the screens, depressingly flat and lifeless, just caricatures of expressions and emotions.

Until Cas accidentally zoomed past the faces and clicked on one of the symbol-style emoji instead.

"Whoa!" He nearly dropped his phone as the shape ballooned up and out, expanding like a soap bubble to float out away from him.

"Neat!" Lee exclaimed, grinning as they watched. "So we're not limited to faces. Cool!"

Together the pair stopped searching to watch as the new emoji took a similar path to the first one, hovering above the circle's center before spiraling down toward one of the three waiting blanks. It slid onto and into the polished stone, settling into its spot as the stone dimpled to meet it, and then there was the carved image of a cartoon sword filling what had once been bare.

"Right, that's two down, two to go," Lee pointed out. They went back to their phone but Cas continued to stand there, staring down at his own handiwork. Something about those two new images... it was tugging at the back of his brain but while the alcohol had lubricated some thought processes it was clearly retarding others, and he was having trouble thinking clearly.

"What do they have in common?" he asked aloud. "A face and a sword? How're they connected?"

"Who says they are?" Lee asked, not looking up from the tiny phone screen. "You wouldn't say 'fish' and 'inflation' were connected unless you were talking about the price of seafood. We don't know what any of the other symbols on that thing mean, so we're looking totally out of context here." They shrugged. "Without that we probably won't see any connection, assuming there even is one."

That made a surprising amount of sense, but Cas wasn't quite willing to let his question go. "What would you say that face means?" he asked instead. "The one you found first?"

"It's being sick," Lee answered immediately. "You know, if you're sick of something, or if you tell someone you're not feeling well. Why?"

"And the sword, that's, well, fighting, right?" he mused, squinting down at the two emoji in their new resting places. "Violence? Combat?" He could feel his mental gears starting to turn again, ever so slowly, creaking and groaning as they fought against the molasses hold of the gin. An idea was starting to form, something big, so big it barely fit within his head, so dark and stark and terrifying his mind shied away from it, but he couldn't let that happen, he had to figure this out, so he grasped at it, trying to hold onto it, to wrestle it down so he could see it clearly—

"Aha!" That came from Lee, and Cas looked up in time to see a third emoji spring from his partner's phone, exiting the smooth glass of the screen like a dolphin bursting out of the sea. It arced up in the same graceful way, and just like those majestic creatures it hung over their heads, ignoring gravity, before eschewing the pull of the earth completely and rising even higher, drifting out away from them and toward the circle. Cas swiped at the image as it passed and felt a mild shock as his fingers passed through its glowing shape, like he'd rubbed across the carpet and then grasped a doorknob, the jolt unpleasant and a little painful but fleeting. Shaking his hand, he watched the emoji echo its brethren, sinking down to take its place on the third blank square.

When all was said and done, there was the image of a flattened disc trapped inside the stone, with a few strange spots on it here and there.

"What's that, then?" he asked. He didn't spend much time on social media, didn't care for the modern tendency to reply with abbreviations and cute images instead of real words, real sentences.

Lee was far more conversant in the modern lingo. "It's an empty plate," they answered, their face flush with victory. "You know, like you've just eaten everything on it."

"Eaten everything," Cas echoed, turning away to watch the circle again. "Eating. No more food. Empty plate." Suddenly the idea he'd been trying to catch up to leapt down on him instead, engulfing him, so that he stood, choking, tears springing to his eyes, as the enormity of it nearly bore him to the ground. "No. Oh, no!"

"What? What's wrong?" Lee glanced at him, at the circle, at their phone. "Damn, you're right! We're almost out of time! And there's still one left!" And they started frantically tapping the screen.

"No, don't you see?" Cas reached out for his friend but Lee was just out of range and it felt like he couldn't move any farther. Like something was holding him in place. "The sword, that's not just fighting or violence, it's war. War! And the feverish face, that's sickness, right? Pestilence! And this new one, the empty plate—what if it's not empty because you ate it all but because there isn't anything to eat? Famine!"

Now Lee did look up, though their finger kept reflexively thumping the phone. "Wait, what? War, Pestilence, Famine—hey, I know those!"

"The Four Horsemen," Cas said, his voice turning hoarse from urgency. "They're three of the four Horsemen. And the fourth one, the biggie, their leader, that's—"

A strange, strangled sound emerged, like a gasp cut short or a cord that had snapped. But it hadn't come from him, or even from Lee.

It had been from Lee's phone.

They both glanced at it now, and Lee frowned. "I think my browser just crashed," they explained. "Weird. It's just hanging. Oh, see, it did crash. That's—"

Cas, still trying to shake off the last of the alcohol, was a minute too slow to put the pieces together. He lunged forward, his terror allowing him to break that strange paralysis and snatch the phone from Lee's hand. He immediately hurled it at the ground, hoping to shatter it in time—

—but just before it struck, a new shape emerged.

Cas could only stare, sobbing, as the new form rose gracefully up into the air. It was circular like the first emoji but had no features, only a swirl of colors that came together in much the same way as the gate below.

"The spinning pinwheel," Lee whispered, its colors washing over their face as it passed them by. "Of—"

They stopped short of saying it, but the word cast its pall over the tent nonetheless. The lights almost seemed to dim as the final emoji began its graceful descent, stopping over the only remaining blank.

And then, with that strange pop again, the Spinning Pinwheel of Death sank into the stone, its motion stilling at last—

—as the panes of the gate began to rotate and iris open instead.

"Run!" Cas screamed, stumbling forward and grasping at Lee's arm. But it was much too late for that. Behind them there was a whoosh like the world's largest vacuum switching on, and the air began to be sucked down into the pit, the light streaming down with it, leaving them to gasp and choke and flail in the dark—

—and then the flow reversed and everything came rushing back up and out, filling the tent to overflowing, bursting through its canvas walls, crushing Cas and Lee as it spread rapidly outward, encompassing everything beyond.

The gates of Hell had been opened, and the Four Emoji of the Apocalypse, freed from their eternities-old prison, soared out into the world, gleefully intent upon chaos and destruction and the ruin of all.

The legions of Hell followed behind, equally eager—each and every one of them an emoji, filled with evil intent.

The end of the world was at hand.

And it was adorable.

For Whom the Bell Tolls

Laura Anne Gilman

Praise the riders come before-the-fire
Those long-armed far-sighted ones
Over stones came running bloodied and bruised
To strike the bells tolling calling the unwary
Four tall mountains shaking sending dwellers
down-running.

September 27th the world ended.

I was making dinner for my dad, who was supposed to be working night shift that weekend, when the front buzzer sounded. There wasn't anyone visible through the peep, so I ignored it—until it went off again, like someone was leaning on it.

By the time I flung open the door, every door along our hallway was open, heads poking out, equally annoyed.

"What the hell?" Mrs. Adderly two doors down stared at me like it was somehow my fault. I shrugged, about to go back inside, figuring it was management's problem to fix—or not—when a man's voice echoed, like he was using a bullhorn through a PA system.

"Everyone out! Everyone out now! Grab your kids and move!"

You didn't argue with that voice, not if you were sane. I turned off the burners and grabbed Dad and my keys and phone, and headed for the stairs, along with just about everyone else.

There were four buildings in our complex, and it seemed like everyone was flooding into the courtyard, craning their necks up, expecting to see flames licking up into the evening sky, or something. But the buildings were still.

The sky, though. There was something funny about the sky. I frowned, trying to figure out what it was, when my dad grabbed my arm, way too tight. He was staring at the sky, too, but he didn't look confused. He looked...horrified.

"Into the basement, you idiots. Move!"

Bullhorn voice was back, and Dad was already moving, towing me like I was a little kid again.

"Dad?"

"Not now, honey. Come on."

There were four doors off the courtyard, heavy metal things even the most determined of teenagers hadn't been able to dent. Dad dragged me to the one marked "3," that matched our building, and pushed open the door.

The basement was a relic, built back in the bad old days when you could expect bombs to come in over the border at any hour. The supplies were long gone, but the air filters were checked every month like clockwork, so it was only a little musty as we filed down the steps, filling in the spaces.

Not everyone followed, but I recognized our neighbors. Including Mrs. Adderly, who wasn't glaring any more. A couple of people had their dogs, and a few cats, thankfully in carriers, but not as many as I knew had to live in our building.

The door slammed shut, and we could hear the locks turning.

"Dad?"

The look on his face, the way the older residents were acting...

"C'mere." My dad wasn't a hugger, but he pulled me in hard, resting his chin on the top of my head, and I could feel his heart pounding. "I love you , kiddo."

"I love you too, Dad." It seemed like the right time to say it.

Nameless heroes scattered with bad tidings
Reckless desperation scorning the heavens
Even as clouds thundered four doorways opened
Voice-hushed and shaking in caverns unlit
Gods themselves helpless mortals were sheltered

Yoachim felt bile on his tongue, and swallowed it back down with effort. It was against orders, against every protocol: no matter what shit was going down, you never told anyone, never risked a panic. That was hammered into everyone from day one on the job. But when word came, and everyone else grimly settled back into their chairs and kept working, Yoachim couldn't.

With a muttered excuse about going to the bathroom, he fled.

Robert, who worked one door over, was already in the hallway, hands shaky on his vape. "Guess these things won't be what kills me, after all."

"Maybe it won't..." He couldn't finish the sentence, couldn't voice the hope.

"Yeah." Robert sounded even less convinced.

They would be fine. Probably. The office was as safe as government money could make it, which was pretty safe. But they had no idea what had been unleashed. Bombs? Virus? Locusts?

How did you start the end of the world?

They weren't even allowed to call their families. Was it worth being safe, if you were the only one? He was single, but Robert's parents and younger sister lived with him.

Another bell rang, somewhere deep in the complex, and they both flinched.

A door opened across the hall, and Sarah came out, the sound of the toilet flushing behind her. Her hands were dry, but her face was wet. She met their gaze square, without flinch or apology.

She had a daughter, Yoachim remembered. Seven, he thought. And an ex-husband working on some project in America.

Robert opened his mouth to say something, and the sound of something hitting the wall made them all jump.

"Fuck this."

They all turned, as Aaron slammed out of his office, where the noise had come from. His face was pale and sweat-lined, his mouth rolled in a tight line. He saw them standing there, and scowled. "Gossiping your last hours away?"

"You have a better suggestion?" Robert asked, at the same time Yoachim, who knew their supervisor better, said, "Aaron, no."

"Fuck you," Aaron said to them both, and walked—stalked— past them, down the hall toward the garage. "I'm not going to just sit here with my thumbs jammed up my ass."

"You can't—" Sarah said, her voice half-resignation, half... something else.

"I can try."

Silently, the three followed him.

Fire-burnt are the man-gods war-pride undoing
The world that came Before flame-washed and crum-
bling
Bitter-fruit-bearing for long years-passing
No gods no masters the bells still tolling.
Four doorways opened devastation awaiting

The lab was secure, until it wasn't. The experiments were contained, until they weren't. Everyone was confident, until it was too late. The winds swirled, high above the skyline. Pale dust, mica-bright, glittering as the sunlight caught edges, flashing the occasional tiny rainbow until it reached the cloud layer.

Then it turned dark, week-old purpling and virulent green, until the human-made particles couldn't be told from nature's ire. A poetic eye might have seen the curve of a scythe in the clouds, as it descended, slowly, inevitably, toward Earth.

The rain came bruise-colored, sticking rather than streaking, thickening hair and filling pores. The first wave died quickly, of suffocation. The second wave died from an enemy within, the smallest cut turning brutally sour overnight.

The third wave died more slowly of hunger, anything edible poisoned purple-green.

The fourth wave died of despair, sleeping at the foot of new-dug mounds.

And the Earth was, briefly, still.

Praise the riders come before-the-fire
Gather their ashes scattered to winds
Bury the dead deep and far from flowing waters
Remember the nameless faceless in shame
Fingers in defiance the world will not end.

The metal doors were taken off their hinges, planted in enough cement to ensure they couldn't be knocked down, the bell system rewired to four buzzers at the base. People left offerings there, when they could. Straggly bouquets of weed-flowers, jewelry, a brightly-colored scarf. Things of meaningless meaning.

They built homes out of the debris, needing space from each other but unable to go too far away. They refilled fields, found livestock, cautiously tested the winds. Listened for voices that never came.

Anna was born the second summer after Emergence. She was the second baby born to the kibbutz, and so narrowly missed being named Hope. Her father had wanted to name her Mercy, but her mothers, more cautious, more jaded, put their foot down. The first baby "Grace" would have to do.

The first boy was named Adam, and after that everyone agreed that it was time to lay off the symbolism. What had been Before was best left Before. Those that had Emerged needed to do better.

The Four Swords of the Apocalypse
A Tale of Kagen the Damned

Jonathan Maberry

-1-

"It's called the 'unexplored wastes' for a reason, dumbass."

Jheklan turned to his brother, a poison dart of a reply on his lips, but Faulker was grinning. And so Jheklan grinned, too. That was how they were.

Herepath, the oldest of the four, was a few yards ahead, leaving the youngest, Kagen, to be the constant audience for these two. They were his seniors in succession, training in arms, and overt silliness. Jheklan and Faulker were skilled swordsmen, combat veterans, and deliberate fools in even measures.

Kagen Vale loved them, but his real hero was the moody, ascetic, often aloof Herepath.

"Come on," Kagen said. "He wants us."

Ahead, Herepath was gesturing for them to catch up, and they kicked their horses into light canters.

For the last two days they had picked their way through densely wooded passes that ran so deep the sun seemed to rise late and set early because the lofty peaks blocked the light. For sixteen hours every day the deepest clefts were in shadow, and there were bottoms and hollows that never felt the sun's kiss at all.

"Great place for vampires," Faulker had suggested.

"Shame they're all extinct," said Jheklan, "for like...a thousand years."

Herepath had looked at them coldly. "Don't assume you know how the world is built."

They'd asked him for more, but he only heard those questions he wanted to hear.

Now they drew up to his horse, a trail-wise creature whose muscular haunches looked like he'd been spattered with yellow paint. Herepath was at the end of a long, twisted corridor formed by outcroppings of snow-covered rocks and the reaching arms of wild pines. The corridor had been very dark in places, but as Kagen and his brothers drew near to Herepath, they moved out of shadow and into the cold light of day.

They sat in a row, with Jheklan and Faulker on Herepath's left and Kagen on his right. Their horses blew steam into the crisp air, and all four of them gathered their fur cloaks around them.

Kagen, just turned sixteen, was the youngest of them. The rowdy brothers were a year apart though they acted so much alike the rest of the family often called them "the Twins." Herepath was several years older, a gaunt man new to his thirties but with very old eyes. His manner and bearing, his tone and diction, were that of the sober and bookish scholar he'd become. This was his mission, and his three younger siblings were along as bodyguards. And, Kagen knew, to keep the Twins out of trouble with the daughters of court nobles. For Kagen, this was the second trip far from home and his mother wanted the older son to teach Kagen about the ways of the world beyond the walls of Argentium.

Now they were all very far from the capital city of Argon, and even beyond the borders of the Silver Empire. They had journeyed deep into the vast Cathedral Mountains, avoiding bands of bandits, and roving patrols from Bulconia, which was one of the few western lands that had never joined the empire. That path brought them through treacherous paths, some still choked with the last of the winter snow

Sunlight flooded down but it was cold, offering no hint of warmth. It fell between the mouth of the mountain pass and a section of the unforgiving steppes, but after a few hundred yards the rocky ground washed up against a mountain of ice. It soared upward for at least a mile, glistening with surface melt, but a deep and smoky blue at its heart.

The three younger Vale brothers gasped at the majesty of the towering wall of ice.

"We'll never get over that," said Jheklan.

"Not a chance," agreed Faulker.

"It's beautiful," said Kagen.

Herepath turned to study him. The scholar wore a thin smile and gave a small nod, but he spoke to all three of them. "We are not climbing it. There's nothing at the top except more ice. Miles upon miles of it. This is not a wall nor a mountain, lads.

This is remnant of the glaciers that covered most of the continent during the last Ice Age. Most of it's gone now, melted by the warmer suns of recent centuries. All of the lakes and rivers from here to the Southern Ocean are born here. Or from other fragments of the glacier."

"If we're not going to climb it," said Faulker, "then why, by the scythes of the Harvest Gods, did you drag us all the way here?"

"Fair question," muttered Jheklan.

Kagen shook his head. "There's a way *through*, isn't there?"

Again, Herepath gave a small nod. "Not through, my lad, but *into* it."

"Why would we want to go *inside* a melting glacier?" demanded Faulker. "I mean, I'm all for new experiences, but being frozen to death, drowned, or crushed under crumbling ice is a lot lower on my list of fun things to do than you might think."

Herepath merely laughed and kicked his horse into a gallop.

Kagen bolted after him.

"Well," said Jheklan to Faulker, "you always said you didn't want to die old."

"Yeah, but old-*er*, at least."

The two raced to catch up with their brothers.

-2-

As they approached the ice wall, Kagen was able to pick out details he hadn't seen before. The ice was translucent, and within its frozen depths there were many objects, some close to the surface and others so distant that it was difficult to make out shapes or even sizes.

Most of what he saw were rocks, trunks of strange trees, and other debris that looked as if it had been swept up by a flash flood and then frozen forever. He mentioned this to Herepath.

"Very likely that's what happened," said the scholar. "Keep your eyes sharp. There may be other things trapped in the ice."

They asked him what he meant but, typically, Herepath didn't answer.

He led the way east along, and twice Herepath tugged a map from an inside pocket and studied it, casting glances at the sun and back at the mountains. Each time he nodded to himself and kept moving.

It took more than four hours to find the opening, and by then the sun was rolling toward the western horizon. Jheklan was complaining that he was hungry, needed to relieve himself, and that his ass bones were sore from riding.

Then as they rounded an outthrust section of ice, they saw it.

The opening was a crack in the ice wall that was wide at the bottom and narrowed sharply as it zigzagged up and out of sight. At its widest, the entrance was fifteen feet wide and with the sun at the wrong angle, it was black as night inside. Outside, littered haphazardly across the iron-hard ground, were bones. Those of horses and those of humans. Bits of rusted armor, torn scraps of leather, and a litter of broken swords and spears were scattered all around. Kagen counted skulls and reckoned that there had to be at least a score of skeletons, though some bones had been so comprehensively smashed that it could easily be half again as many.

"Well," said Faulker, "that's not disturbing at all." He took his bow from the saddle horn, strung it and nocked an arrow, though he left the string slack but ready.

"I'm fine with going back now," said Jheklan.

"Hush," scolded Herepath as he dismounted. He tied his horse to a chunk of fossilized tree and walked to the entrance. Kagen slid from the saddle and ran to catch up.

"What happened here?" he asked. "Was it a war?"

"These bones are years and years old," said Herepath as the others joined them. "We may never know."

Faulker peered into the stygian crack. "Now I know why you has us bring torches and a small cask of pitch."

He looped his bow over his shoulder, went and retrieved the torches from his saddle bag, and handed one to Jheklan, who had produced flint and steel from his pack. In seconds the four brands were blazing, sharing warmth and light as they stepped inside.

They paused for a moment while Jheklan studied the mouth of that opening.

"It's laced with cracks," he said. "A couple of strong blows with an axe and this whole thing might collapse."

"Then don't hit it with a fucking axe," said Faulker. He and Jheklan laughed as if that was funny.

Herepath led the way, holding his light high while resting his other hand on the handle of the long sword he wore. It was Longtooth, an ancient blade he'd recovered at a dig on Skyria. Herepath was a Gardener of the Harvest Faith, though not a cleric. He worked with teams of other scholars to excavate ancient cities and temples of the cultures that had risen and then collapsed thousands of years before the Silver Empire rose. It was a hard, often lonely profession, but one the inward and private Herepath loved. Longtooth was one of many relics he had recovered, and despite its age, the steel took a wicked and durable edge. The blade was carved with ancient runes in a forgotten language and in moonlight it glowed an eerie yellow. Enemies—bandits and tomb raiders—who thought the thin, ascetic Herepath would be an easy target learned better, to their misery.

All of the sons and daughters of the Vale family had been personally schooled in combat by their mother, Marissa, known as the Poison Rose—held by many to be the most dangerous knife fighter of the age. Jheklan and Faulker were demons in a fight, and even Kagen had proved his mettle in bloody battles; but Herepath was their better in every important way.

The younger Vales followed him, each drawing steel or, in Faulker's case, nocking that arrow once more. The entire passageway showed evidence of cracks, as if the ice was trying to tear itself apart. It scared Kagen, though he made sure not to let his brothers see his fear.

The crack was smaller outside but after a short and tight corridor it widened considerably into a cavern. Icicles as big as stalactites hung from the ceiling, fierce as the teeth of a dragon. The floor was smooth except for debris and occasional cracks, and tiny streamlets of ice melt wandered past them, running out through the big crack or vanishing into the many smaller splits in the floor. The Twins jammed their torches into clefts in the walls and began searching the place.

They found more debris of combat inside. Much more. Dozens of skeletons lay in twisted postures, skulls smashed, bones broken as if something had been after the marrow. But it was all very old and Kagen tried not to spin stories in his mind about ravening monsters. The broken bones could have happened later as scavenger animals were drawn here by the scent of blood and meat.

In the center of the chamber was the remains of a camp, with pots and three packs filled with wrapped food, wineskins, and other items. Faulker sniffed the wine, shrugged, and took a sip.

"Damn," he said, "it's still good."

"Get drunk and I'll skin you alive," said Herepath. He still wore his little smile, which made it always hard to tell when he was joking. The Twins laughed, but Kagen took Herepath at his word.

Faulker dropped the wineskin with a sigh and walked over to a far section of wall. There, with its blade buried deep into the ancient ice, was a huge double-bladed war axe. Cracks radiated out in all directions from the point of impact.

"Jheklan," he called, "here's that axe you were talking about." He laughed and gave the handle a tug, but it was stuck fast.

"Don't do that, you idiot," snarled Herepath. "Do you want to bring the ceiling down on us?"

Faulker showed his palms. "Touching? Who's touching?"

Herepath muttered something unpleasant and stalked over to the closest wall. He stopped and stood for a moment studying it, moving his torch slowly to light different sections. Kagen joined him and saw that there was something inside the ice. The thing was bulky and strange, and seemed to be only a few inches behind the face of the frozen wall.

"What is that?" he asked, holding his torch close to the wall. "Can you tell?"

"I...don't know," admitted Herepath. He snugged his torch into a cleft and bent close to study the shape.

Kagen glanced at him. "But you came right over here to it."

"No, I merely spotted it when we came in," said his brother, but there was a false note in his voice. "Hold the light there, yes, just so. Let me get a better look at it."

Kagen did, though his eyes kept flicking back and forth between the amorphous shape inside the wall and his brother's secretive face.

Although Kagen loved and revered his brother—and knew that Herepath was a patriot and would defend the Silver Empire to the last drop of his blood—there was always something a bit *off* with him. He rarely spoke, and when he did his comments or observations were as likely to be cryptic as not.

Kagen couldn't let the moment stand, though, and in a voice too low for the others to hear, said, "You're keeping a secret from us."

Herepath did not look at him. "I'm a Gardener, Kagen, and under sacred vows. I keep many secrets."

"That's disingenuous, Herepath."

The scholar glanced at him now, amused. "I doubt our brothers even know what that word means."

"I read, you know," said Kagen, a bit defensively. "And you're evading what I said."

"There are mysteries hidden in the earth," said Herepath.

But Kagen shook his head. "Just for once can you give a

whole answer?"

Herepath's eyes, as pale as Kagen's own but as cold as the ice, bored into him.

"You are different than the others," he said. "They're smart—luckily that's a family trait from both parents—but where the Twins want nothing more than to find some species of fun in every moment, you seem more interested in answers. In truths."

"As are you, brother," said Kagen.

"Yes," said Herepath, "as am I."

There was a long pause and Kagen didn't think his brother would say more, but Herepath surprised him. "This place is like a gallery of historical paintings," he said, touching the slick wall. "There are things here, trapped for untold years in the ice, that do not belong to our age of the world. This glacier is tens of thousands of years old, and as it grew and moved across the face of the world it consumed everything in its path. Some of those things—most, I suspect—were ground beneath the millions of tons of ice. The scholar Andicus of Samud estimated that, at its height, this glacier stood three miles thick over every inch of land from the shores of Nelfydia and Vahlycor to far above the peaks of the Cathedral Mountains and all the way to Bercless and the Eastern Ocean. We don't know what happened, or why the world froze—some war of the old gods, perhaps—but it clearly did. And scholars of the Garden have spent generations investigating sections of this glacier. There is a whole small city of scholars, archaeologists, and historians up in the Winterwilds deep in the Frozen Sea. Andicus believed that each inch of ice may be equivalent to a year's growth of the ice sheet. Think about that, Kagen. This ice right here could be thirty thousand years old, or even much older. Andicus's math is skewed somewhat by ice melt."

Kagen felt momentarily oppressed by the weight of such years. Thirty thousand? The entire Silver Empire had existed for only a thousand years, and that seemed like forever to him. He looked up and around, and the ponderous ice over his head was equally oppressive. He licked his lips and turned back to the thing trapped behind the wall where they stood.

"And... you and the other Gardeners are trying to learn the history of the world by examining what's *inside* of it, and estimating its age?"

"Not merely its age, Kagen," said Herepath, nodding his approval, "but its purpose. Its nature. Our own human history goes back three thousand years, and we know that there were cultures before ours. The priest-kinds of Skyria died out four or five millennia ago, and the gigantic, abandoned cities of Vespia are at least twice as old. We've barely scratched the surface of what lies in the past. We have our cosmologies and our origin tales, but compared with the antiquity of the world, they are newborn stories. This is an old world, little brother, and I suspect civilizations like ours have risen and fallen many times. What I want to know is *why* they fell. What mistakes did they make? What heights did they reach that have since been lost? Think of it, Kagen... the science, the mathematics and engineering, the medicines, the music and art, the *knowledge* that might be buried in this ice like treasures bequeathed from one generation to the next. From them," he said, trailing his fingers across the ice, "to us. Requiring only the wisdom, the optimism, and the courage to look deeply enough."

"Gods of the Harvest!" came a cry from across the cavern. Kagen and Herepath whirled to see Faulker aiming at arrow at what appeared to be a black section of icy wall. Jheklan had his sword out, but he was backing away from something.

"What is it?" cried Kagen. He dropped the torch and drew his matched pair of fighting daggers.

"Don't touch it," yelled Herepath, Longtooth in his right hand as if by sorcery. He and Kagen hurried over but slowed to a stop.

There, behind the ice was another blob of a shape. It was roughly the same size as the first one, and equally shapeless. But then Herepath jerked to a halt beside him and with his left hand he grabbed Kagen's shoulder and yanked him to a halt.

"Gods of the Pit," he breathed.

Kagen looked at him and saw that the scholar's face had gone dead pale. When he glanced at the Twins, he saw the same thing. Kagen frowned, not understanding.

Until he saw it, too.

And he understood.

-3-

"What *is* that?" gasped Jheklan. He had his curved sword clutched in two trembling hands.

Faulker, wild-eyed, did not speak at all.

"Back away slowly," said Herepath. "No sudden moves. Maybe it hasn't seen you."

"*Seen* us?" cried Jheklan as he stumbled backward. "It's frozen in a fucking glacier and it's moving. We're surrounded by the bones of other people just like us, and maybe I'm being alarmist here, brother, but being *seen* by it is the least of my gods-damned concerns."

Kagen held his daggers in front of his chest in a loose X-pattern. Ready to defend, ready to fight. But, despite the bitter cold, his palms were sweating.

Herepath edged forward, moving on silent cat feet as he approached the mass within the wall. Kagen followed, but he did not like it one bit.

They stopped six feet from the wall and stood there, staring.

Inside the ice, the shapeless mass was moving.

Slowly, sluggishly, even painfully, but it was definitely moving.

At first Kagen though he was seeing some kind of dark slimy liquid trapped in pockets within the ice, following the slow pull of gravity, perhaps triggered to motion by the melting ice. It looked like the kind of shapeless, shifting cloud that forms and swirls when ink is poured into a glass of clear water. Some parts were bulbous where the mass was thicker, but there were wispy tendrils that stretched outward as if through veins in the ice. And as it moved there seemed to be a strange luminescence from within—a sickly green that was unpleasant to look at.

And then he saw the eyes.

One moment they were not there, and then suddenly a dozen eyes as big as saucers opened and cast around in confusion or panic, as if this thing were alive and suddenly realized that it was trapped. The shapeless mass of it swelled into a collection of dark bubbles, the way smoke billows, with pustules forming and reforming, and then tearing open to reveal those staring eyes.

The Twins cried out in horror and shrank back. Herepath held his ground, but Kagen could see his brother trembling violently.

The eyes moved and glared, then vanished, only to appear elsewhere. Or perhaps the eyes formed and vanished and new eyes were manifested through some means Kagen could not even fathom.

"It's alive," he breathed. "Gods of the..." But his words failed.

Herepath stood as if in a trance, his sword hanging from a limp hand. His mouth was open but he, too, appeared speechless.

The eyes formed and reformed and still seemed only to register a desperate panic.

But then one eye opened in the center of the amorphous congeries of swirling slime, and it looked directly at the four brothers.

Kagen saw the exact moment when it became aware of them.

A second later another eye formed, and it, too, stared. A third, a fourth. A tenth, a thirtieth.

A hundred eyes stared at the Vale brothers. Around those eyes, which were the only fixed points in the thing, the green light swelled to a dangerous brightness. All around that glow the pustular body of the thing began to take on a more solid appearance, as if awareness of the four humans was somehow able to give it a measure of control over itself. That thought flashed through Kagen's mind, and he knew it to be real, though how he knew was something he could never thereafter explain.

The creature began to draw its wandering billowing extremities back toward the central mass and that body—inky black but lit from within by a hellish green—began to swell. As it did so a small crack suddenly appeared in front of the glaring eyes.

"Oh shit...," breathed Faulker, stepping back and shifting the aim of his arrow to the first and largest of the eyes.

"Herepath," said Kagen, finding his voice, "we need to get out of here."

His brother looked at him with eyes that were briefly vacant, as if his mind had been stolen away by shock. Words fell from his lips, but they made no sense and even hearing them made Kagen's head ring with pain.

"*Ahf' ahorna ah'mglw'nafh mg goka,*" mumbled Herepath.

And then the wall cracked.

The small fracture made by the creature yielded to titanic pressure and split apart. The fissure shot upward to the shadow-shrouded ceiling and down to the floor, then whipped out beneath the feet of the Vale brothers. Shockwaves rippled outward, dropping the items stuck into the ice—torches and the big axe—and rattling the old cookware, armor, and bones. The whole cavern seemed to vibrate with the unholy vitality of that shapeless thing in the wall.

"Get back," yelled Kagen. When Herepath did not move, Kagen rammed him with a shoulder. His older brother staggered and felt to one knee, his sword clattering from nerveless fingers. "Herepath—*snap out of it.*"

But whatever had dazed his brother—fear, or shock, or maybe some ancient spell—the scholar merely knelt there, mouth still forming those strange words, though now without sound.

Kagen spun as a huge sound split the air, and he saw that a massive sheet of ice had toppled from the wall and exploded into ten thousand jagged fragments on the floor. Jheklan hooked an arm around Faulker and shoved him clear as more pieces of the wall toppled outward.

A terrible smell—like rotting fish and decaying vegetable matter—permeated the cavern, and then the thing moved. The creature that had been sealed in the ice for untold millennia, vomited forth from its frozen tomb and flopped wetly onto the floor. Although it looked like a mass of jelly, the thing did not burst apart or spatter; instead it lay there, pulsating obscenely.

Kagen sheathed his daggers and pulled at Herepath, dragging him to his feet.

"F' ah mgephai lw'nafh'drn," said Herepath. Then he stiffened, straightened and in the common tongue said, "They are still alive!"

"No shit," growled Kagen, shoving him toward the entrance.

A yell made him turn and Kagen saw that the Twins were on the far side of the heaving mass. It was moving, flowing along the floor, rolling like a gelatinous tide over the debris left by the last party of fools who'd come there. Bones cracked and metal screeched as the weight of the thing crushed these items against the ice. The blob was much bigger than it seemed when still encased in the wall. It was at least forty feet long and must have weighed tons. It was between the Twins and the clear run to the exit.

Abruptly the mass congealed, contracting more of itself into a tighter clump, and for one long moment it crouched there, throbbing and quivering, blazing with green light. Then the creature began to rise. Not as a whole unit, but in places. Four extrusions rose up from the central mass, each taking on the hideous likeness of a human being. Bits of the ruined armor clung to it, and through the translucent skin Kagen could see that the old bones had been reassembled to create a dreadful copy of humanity. Arms and legs appeared, and heads, though each face was identical to the others. These figures were not separate even now; their legs seemed to melt into the main mass. It was more like fingers on a hand than individual beings.

Each of these false soldiers held a weapon—four rusted and notched swords held in four inhuman hands.

An arrow whipped through the air and struck one of the figures, transfixing its throat. But the arrow trembled and began to slide down through the monster's body like a spoon through a pot of honey. The thing was completely uninjured, and it turned, slashing clumsily with the sword it held.

Faulker ducked and rolled away, rising with another arrow that he nocked and fired, this time taking a creature in the eye. The reaction was the same.

Jheklan darted in and slashed with his curved sword, lopping the head off the figure closest to him, but the head fell and was reabsorbed and a new one merely rose from the shoulders.

Then all four mouths opened wide and from their hideous throats rose a piercing cry.

"Tekeli-li! Tekeli-li!"

Herepath seemed to come completely to his senses. "Shoggoth," he bellowed. "Shoggoths—you can't hurt them. Run!"

Kagen had never heard the word *Shoggoth* before, but he realized that the dark smudges on all of the walls of this cavern were more of these monsters. The thought of what such creatures could do should they escape nearly tore the heart from him.

He saw that the ooze was spreading quickly so that the four fake warriors now formed a defensive line between the Twins and safety. Faulker kept firing arrows and Jheklan slashed like a madman, but they were making no ground.

Kagen knew at that survival was his for the taking—just turn and run out of the glacier. He and Herepath would make it.

Not the Twins, though.

So, he ran to where one of the torches lay, flames still flickering on its head. Kagen snatched it up and thrust the fiery brand into the back of the human shapes at the end of the line. If cold could not kill these things, then perhaps fire would.

The slime recoiled from the flame as noxious steam shot up in thick clouds. The figure he'd attacked suddenly lost cohesion and melted down into the main mass. The process extinguished the torch, but the end of the mass retreated momentarily into the bulk. Kagen saw that it immediately began regrowing that shape a few yards away.

It can't be killed, thought Kagen wildly, *but it can be hurt.*

One of the figures swung a sword at him, but Kagen pitched himself into a roll, came out of it running, snatched up a second torch, twisted and threw it at the new figure. It melted away and once more the mass retreated.

"Run!" he shouted, and the Twins, seeing what he was doing, bolted from where they had been trapped. Ancient swords slashed at them, and Faulker cried out as a red line opened across his shoulders. He staggered, but Jheklan caught him. Kagen grabbed the third torch and drew a dagger with the other.

He used the blade to parry and the torch to smash at the false warriors. They yielded a little, but then the creature—this *Shoggoth*—seemed to understand that this ferocious human could not inflict any real harm. It surged forward, filling the air with its unnatural cry.

"Tekeli-li! Tekeli-li!"

The Twins were clear, though Faulker was bleeding badly. Jheklan squatted and hoisted his brother onto his shoulders, wheeled, and ran for the exit.

Kagen realized that he had nearly backed himself into another corner and cast around for the final torch, but it was beyond his reach, lying on the floor by the wall amid a little of debris.

The monster surged toward him, its four warrior extrusions charging with raised weapons. Kagen swung his torch and dagger as he scrambled backward. But his foot slipped and he went down.

His thought as he fell, knowing that he was doomed, was that at least he'd saved his brothers. There was fear and sadness and horror, but Kagen knew that he would die with honor. That was something. It would make their mother proud, and maybe there would be a tale told or a song sung.

Then something moved between him and the mass.

Something that held a torch in one hand and a longsword in the other. Something that moved with lightning speed and incredible dexterity.

"Herepath!" he cried as his brother launched into battle with the ancient Shoggoth.

"Run, boy," said the scholar. "Run for your life. I cannot let these things loose on the world. Run...*run.*"

Kagen scrambled to his feet and ran.

Five steps into that run he snatched something off the ground.

"Herepath," he yelled and his brother risked a splinter of a moment to see what it was Kagen held.

Herepath smiled and began retreating, even as the Shoggoth followed. It drew its four extrusions back into the central mass and rose up, forming a single set of towering legs. Kagen waited for Herepath and then they were running together, racing to catch up with the others.

They plunged into the mouth of that narrow, cracked opening as the monster from another age pounded after them. Its footfalls were like thunder, and the gigantic icicles snapped from the ceiling and fell. Some pierced the monster, but its mass flowed around it and took no harm.

There was a trail of bright blood on the icy floor, and they followed it, finally bursting out into the waning sunlight. Faulker was on his chest, with Jheklan using his hands to stanch the flow of blood. Herepath flung the torch away and rammed his sword into its sheath, then he held out his hand for the thing Kagen had grabbed.

Kagen, smiling grimly, handed the huge double-bladed axe to his brother, who took it with a wild grin. Herepath spun, raised the axe and slammed the blade into the weakest point of the fractured opening. Between the impossibly heavy footfalls of the monster and the bite of the axe, the opening began to splinter.

Herepath tore it free and struck again and again.

Kagen found a war-hammer among the bones outside and swung that. It was incredibly heavy, and he was not yet full grown, but fear flowed like molten steel through his muscles. He and Herepath assaulted the entrance to the ice cave. Chunks of ice fell, and cracks whipsawed up the face of the glacier. They kept at it as the last few seconds of their lives—perhaps the lives of everyone in the world—trailed away.

And then there was a mighty crack so loud that it staggered them back. Kagen looked up in horror as a fissure as thick as his wrist snapped its way left and right along the side of the cavern mouth. It exploded into ten thousand new cracks, and suddenly the whole world seemed to judder.

"Run!" he yelled.

Jheklan had Faulker by the heels and was dragging him toward the horses. Herepath was backpedaling, letting the axe fall. Then he whirled and ran.

Kagen ran with them.

They ran and ran and ran, while behind them ten million tons of glacial ice leaned out—as if weary of all those thousands of years—and collapsed onto the frozen steppes. The shock lifted the brothers and threw them across the ground. The horses screamed and stumbled and then ran for their lives. Chunks of ice bigger than palaces crashed down and filled the air with glittering fragments. A cloud of atomized ice crystals blotted out the sun.

Then silence fell.

Slowly, ponderously, but completely.

The Vale brothers, each of them bleeding from ice cuts, their chest heaving, eyes wide with shock and pain, lay on the permafrost of the steppes and stared at the glacier.

The cave mouth was gone. And that entire portion of the ice sheet was now buried under uncountable tons of shattered ice. The horses had all fled, and night was falling.

But the Brothers Vale lay there, bleeding, clutching each other.

And laughing.

Laughing because they were alive, and the world had not ended.

Laughing as the sun died in the west and the endless stars ignited above them.

The Fifth Horseman

Randee Dawn

The ancient metal beast roared down the sandy stretch of highway, spewing forth the sound of mighty decay:

Carruuggh!

At its approach, quivery desert hares scampered into their holes, leaving behind a trail of tiny dark pellets. Rattlesnakes hesitated mid-rattle, tongues flicking, tasting the oncoming darkness. Vultures lost their appetites and sought high ground atop saguaro cacti. All deferred to a creature more mighty, more ancient, more *odiferous* than themselves.

Gathering velocity, the beast crested a hump on the narrow two-lane highway with a blatting *haruggh!* The formerly maroon two-ton passenger van released itself from earthly gravity, soaring skyward as if it might pierce heaven itself... then tumbled back down on the tarmac, stomping like a mighty foot. The landing kicked up Southwest Territory dirt and pebbles and caused a pregnant desert mouse to spontaneously birth a three-headed monster child.

Many moons ago, the beast's encrusted maroon body had proclaimed its true name as Dodge. And the world had turned over and bent inside out and moved on—and these days, the hand-painted curlicue font on its haunch declared its name to be Ezekiel.

"Zeke" to its four occupants.

And Zeke's mission was clear: guide the band to Show Low in time for tonight's gig. Directions had been relayed through the sole remaining operational GPS in the world, which hung suction-cupped to the van's streaked inside windshield. What issued the directions? From where did they originate? Zeke couldn't know: In the end it was just a gas-guzzling made-in-Detroit monstrosity with over two hundred thousand miles on its odometer and no actual sentience.

That didn't mean it couldn't understand instructions. But

when Zeke hit the ground at speed, it understood the mission had changed. As much as a 1993 ex-Dodge touring van could know anything, Zeke knew this: They were never gonna make it to Show Low.

*****

"Whoooo *wheeee!*" cried Rowan, fingers of one hand curled around the van's steering wheel, his other hand clutching the outer frame of the driver's side window. His biblically long strawberry hair trailed like sparking fire in the wind. "Believe we done hit *eighty-eight* that time!"

Opposite him in shotgun, Blanca rubbed her forehead, a knot rising already beneath her platinum bangs. She'd whonked her head on the roof when they'd landed and practically seen stars. *There's Cassiopeia, Daddy, there's Pegasus...* Now, she sat as still as possible to avoid provoking any more displays of vehicular savagery—though Rowan was gonna Rowan while behind Zeke's wheel. The van had ferried them through all eight territories while accepting regular abuse from its driver, and sometimes Blanca questioned whether it really was Rowan even driving the thing. Zeke had a mind of its own.

"Much further, Ro?" Blanca clenched her jaw.

The roadie clocked the GPS, which hung askew from the windshield, solar cord disengaged. The screen showed an empty blotch of brown bisected by a snaking black line of highway. "Eighty-four miles to Show Low. What, you gotta whiz?"

"It's only Defcon 4. I can wait."

"Remind me again—"

"Defcon 5 means I'm empty. Defcon 1 means—"

"Y'gone and pissed yourself." Ro grinned his coffee-stained smile and Blanca's heart did a little flip. "*Yo comprende, señorita.*" He spoke the mangled Spanish with an intentional lack of accent.

Blanca unhooked her seatbelt and turned around to assess the damage. "Anybody bleeding back there?"

Deep inside the vehicle—Zeke was a four-seater with a roomy storage area—Charna narrowed her green eyes from beneath a chaotic thicket of jet-black hair. Her arms and legs stuck out in all directions, restraining the guitars and drum kit. A bra rested on her head like a double yarmulke, straps dangling over her ears; someone's duffle bag had vomited clothing across the interior.

Meanwhile, Venn—nearly luminescent with fright—clung like a pale rhesus monkey to the back of Ro's seat, his teeth clamped on the vinyl covering.

"Are you never gonna learn to *pack*?" Charna growled at Blanca, whisking the bra off her head and reorganizing the instrument cases: her beloved bass first, then Blanca's acoustic guitar and Venn's disassembled drum kit boxes. "How many years we been doing this, Blankie?"

"Don't call me that," Blanca snapped, abruptly befuddled by the question. "And I do know how to pack." It wasn't her fault that Rowan treated the empty road like it was the Talladega Superspeedway.

"Don't yell at her," Venn murmured. His teeth had left marks on the vinyl. "She's not the speed demon."

Blanca gave his hand a quick squeeze, and he relaxed. Venn presented as terrifying—six-foot-three, shaven skull, clad in black. Behind the kit he was hell unleashed, sweat coursing down his body, face a rictus of rage. But offstage he was a giant softy, shy as all get out.

"Well, remind our *roadie* that if he breaks our only transpo out of this hellscape," Charna gestured at the desert racing past, "and we get stranded and have to eat each other to survive, he goes *first*."

"Message received loud and damn clear!" Ro shouted, gunning the motor as a little *fuck you*, then settled into a reasonably insane speed of fifteen miles per hour over the limit.

Blanca turned back around, positioning herself against the side door so she could surreptitiously watch Rowan. He'd never done so much as wink in her direction, but she'd been in love with him so long her heart had reshaped itself, like liquid hardened in a key mold. Sure, he could act like a dumbass nutcase—but there was a dark undercurrent of sorrow in him that caught at her, hidden doors she'd never been able to unlock. They all came with secret histories about how their worlds had fallen apart, but Rowan held his particularly close to the vest. He'd never opened up, not in all this time. Least, not that she could recall.

Chewing on a thumbnail, Blanca frowned. Why wasn't she sure? And why couldn't she answer Charna's question? Shouldn't she know how long they'd been on the road?

"Ro—how many years *have* we been doing this?" she asked.

A rueful smile crept onto his face. "That time again?"

Blanca tilted her head.

"Y'ask me that every couple of weeks, Bee."

"No, I don't."

"Y'do. Y'all do. I'm the only one with any long-term memory in this here vehicle."

Blanca stilled again. He was right, in part. She clearly recalled her life as a part-time dental assistant in Brooklyn who baked cupcakes on weekends, who'd watched her neighborhood crumble into chaos after the power grid died. But what she'd done since transforming into a singer/guitarist in a band traveling across the crazy quilt of a country once known as the U.S. of A. in a shitheap of a van with a mind of its own—well, that was less clear. All she could conjure were flashes and snippets of in-between time, like she was living in her own movie montage.

Rowan rubbed his bristly face. "What if I told ya we'd been a-road for thirteen years, eight months, and six days?"

Charna thrust her face between the front seats. "Then I'd call ya a damn liar. I turned thirty-one last month and you dorks are younger than me and—" She paused. "You didn't even tell me 'Happy Birthday.'"

"We did," Ro sighed. "Had the world's shittiest cake slice and tequila shots in a half-collapsed diner back in Colorado Springs. You passed out."

Charna sat back hard in her seat and crossed her arms. "Huh."

"For real?" Blanca glanced between them. "I mean, that can't be."

Ro tucked some hair behind his ear and stared at her so long she had to flap her hands to get his eyes back on the road. Then he did something brand new: He cupped his hand against her jaw and gently tugged on her earlobe before turning back to the dimming blue skies.

Ear burning, heart hammering, Blanca stared outside as one clear memory from what *felt* like a month ago surfaced: The morning she'd emerged from her Bay Ridge apartment building to discover a maroon van parked by a fire hydrant. The door had slid open to reveal a red-haired wild man—and she'd climbed right in without a word. Never thought twice. Inside the van, she'd spotted instruments, amps, battered cardboard boxes of supplies and clothes and a portable generator that had seen better days.

"Where're we going?" she'd asked.

"Everywhere," he'd said.

They'd picked up Venn in the mitten of what had once been Michigan—the Great Secession had carved up the country into territories like a moldering Thanksgiving turkey—then scooped up Charna in Shelter Cove, way north in the former California. After that, the GPS popped on with daily directions and the real driving had begun. They'd head to a nowhere town to play a gig they'd never arranged, but where people expected them. They got paid, sometimes. They ate crappy food, often. They maintained Zeke. There were always more venues, people who wanted entertaining. Power came from the gennie or from communities with enough solar juice to power the amps and speakers and some twinkly outdoor lights for an hour or so.

But... going on *fourteen years* of that?

Maybe. Just... maybe.

Earlier today, while everyone had been asleep, Blanca had left the ratty hotel room and driven back to the town they'd played in the night before—some one-stoplight nowhere called Waldo—to retrieve an effects pedal forgotten at the bar. But the place had been deserted. Not just the bar, but the whole damn town. There'd even been a tumbleweed rolling down Main Street. Creeped out, Blanca had scampered back to the hotel.

"Ro?" Her voice was barely audible even in her own ears.

His gray eyes were soft.

"What have we been *doing* for thirteen years, eight months, and six days?"

Rowan didn't answer right away, and Blanca pictured them as being in limbo, floating in an in-between of infinite duration. As if the world had used its own preprogrammed GPS coordinates to drive to the end of the road, and was paused at the precipice of a cliff. It would take just a puff of air to send existence tumbling into the abyss.

"Mind, I'm just guessin'." He rubbed his neck. "But I reckon we're givin' everyone a last hurrah. To let 'em know the party's over, and it's time to close up the place."

Blanca sucked in a deep breath of air.

And Zeke's hood started smoking.

*****

Bored and pissed off, Charna stomped up and down in the orange desert sand. She kicked a small cactus, jabbing a needle directly into the big toe of her cheap-ass Doc Marten rip-offs. Swearing with a creativity she hoped caused distant stars to implode, she yanked out the needle. A small bead of blood tipped its end and she waved it at the oncoming sunset like a tiny wand, furious at herself and whatever was left of the world.

"Are we *ever* getting to Show Low?" Charna stormed over to Ro and grabbed the lapels of his jacket. Half his size, she had to scale his legs to end up eye-to-eye with their driver.

"Lookin' mighty unlikely." He trudged to the van with Charna still attached. "Gonna take longer with you clingin' on me like Saran Wrap."

Charna released him. She had *plans* in Show Low, or at least thought she did. Yuki, her old college buddy, was originally from the area and a quick phone call on a still-working ancient pay phone a couple days back had convinced her to come out to the gig. Back in their college days, Yuki'd been reliable for a round of getting shitfaced post-finals, then a second round of between-the-sheets explorations. Charna counted on her showing up in Show Low ... assuming she'd made that call in the first place. The memory of doing it was a big gray patch in her skull.

Point was, no Show Low meant no Yuki. No Yuki meant Charna spending another night alone with the gaping hole where her heart had once been. Yuki's presence might've helped her miss Becca a fraction less, make it so she didn't nightmare yet again about how her wife had been turned into a heap of radioactive ash from a dirty bomb that'd taken parts of San Diego off the map for the next couple thousand years.

"If you hadn't been hotdogging it for the last hundred miles..." Charna kicked up more dust, toe throbbing. "And if this *rust bucket* wasn't such a mighty POS..." She smacked her hand on the van, coming away with miles of grime on her palm.

"Hey!" Blanca popped up from behind Rowan. "Be nice to Zeke."

Charna snarled. They'd been stranded at the side of the road for nearly an hour, trying to figure out what came next. Venn had wandered off, climbing a nearby rock formation to get the lay of the land, and as usual Bee hovered around Rowan like she was in heat. Charna wondered why those two hadn't just gotten *to* it already, but the love lives of straights bored her stupid. Which reminded her again: She had *plans* in Show Low, and Yuki would be pissed if she stood her up. Assuming she'd made the call. Assuming this wasn't some protean wishful thinking Charna had meant to do, but forgotten to take care of. For some reason, her memory was like Swiss cheese these days.

Charna clomped down the road, hurling insults at the heavens, wondering yet again how she'd slipped from her graphic designer, work-from-home life where she'd walked the dog twice a day and left Becca to go into the world to make the real bacon, and into the alternate reality where she was a bass player in a cover band that could barely tread water. She recalled stumbling up her street one early morning maybe a year ago, drunk as hell and trying to remember her dead wife's voice, when a van had yawned open before her. Venn's arm had reached out, ready to haul her inside. She'd never thought, *I'm being taken*; she only thought, *Finally, it's here.* The bass had fit into her hands like it belonged there, like that previous life had never existed. So, she'd dyed her hair the black of deep, starless space and became Charna: moody bassist in a band whose tour had no fixed endpoint.

Crunching her knuckles, Charna left Ro and Blanca to dither over whether they should add water to the cooling engine and limped over to Venn, who'd settled on a tall pile of rocks to gaze at the lowering sun. The sky was shot through with sharp blues, glowing pinks, and radioactive oranges. Now, winking stars were starting to take the stage. "Shove over."

Venn shifted an inch. Charna patted the stubbly top of his bare head and took a seat. "What're we doing here?" she asked.

"Watching the end of things."

Charna played with a loose stone. "Is it? The end?" When he didn't answer, she pushed harder. "We haven't really been at this for almost fourteen years, have we?"

"Could be." He sat perfectly straight, towering over her, large pale hands splayed across his thighs. "You ever count?"

"Count what? Chickens?"

"Anything. Gigs. Cities. Sunsets."

She didn't. For what felt like ever, Charna had let time carry her down its endless river. She felt stunned by the loss of Becca, the loss of the *world*. She woke, ate something, climbed in the van, they played a show, she started drinking, they slept in the van or a crappy hotel room with no A/C, no lights, a roof and not much else. And then came the next gig. Charna had preferred not to think about more than putting one cheap-ass Doc Marten rip-off in front of the other.

Instead of replying, she hummed a bass line, fingers twitching to absent strings. Music comforted her. Reliable, like Yuki. Like tequila. Like Venn, at least when he was behind his kit. During shows she lingered at the rear of the stage next to him, diving into the beats of whatever classic tunes came up on the set list: Pixies, Nirvana, Gigolo Aunts, Teenage Fanclub. No originals. They ran passively through the grooves of talents greater than their own.

Gloaming spread over the sands, coating them both in its golden hue. "I think we've covered it all by now," said Venn. "Been everyplace once. That's all we need to do."

Charna raised an eyebrow. "So, you *are* counting."

He shrugged. "More of a feeling. Useta be states out here. Square boxes, people packed inside. Now the boxes feel... empty. I go walkin' after gigs and the towns... they're just buildings. All the people, gone." He paused. "Sometimes, I think of us climbing down this long rope, one gig then the next. And only now, we're touching bottom."

She imagined rappelling down the Grand Canyon, finding the Colorado River. They could stop off there after Show Low. Go floating.

Venn let out a long, careful breath. "I was almost dead, day before Zeke picked me up. Was walkin' over a bridge and two cars mashed in front o' me and one went over the side, into the river. I jumped in after. Didn't think how stupid, just went in. Driver was already out of her car through the window, swimming. But swimming down. Surface was right there but she wouldn't go to the light. Saw me. Her eyes were so big in the water. I grabbed her wrist and pulled and she kicked out and bit my hand. We were sinking. And I ran out of air so... I let her go."

Charna had never heard so many words from Venn before.

"I let her go," he repeated. "Then I surfaced and they dragged me into a rescue raft and gave me a blanket and I had to explain why it wasn't *my* car in the water, it was this crazy chick's who wanted to stay in the deep. Forever. Next day, Ro and Bee showed up."

Charna thought about removing her boots, jeans, and T-shirt and striding into the Colorado River, letting it carry her away. "You think—at the bottom—we'll see your girl?"

"Naw. Just—wanted someone to know. Never told anybody before. Least, I don't think so. Maybe I'm gettin' early Alzheimer's. Stuff is just flashes these days. Anyway, we're about at the end, so why not?"

Relief flooded through Charna, surprising her with the realization that the end was no longer scary. Not after nearly fourteen years on the road, if you believed Ro. Becca was out there. Becca had been waiting for her, all this time. "So, how much longer ... 'til it's over?"

Venn glanced over his shoulder at Zeke, and Charna followed

his gaze. Blanca was holding a flashlight as Ro peered under the hood, pointing at the inner workings of the dead beast. Their driver turned to say something and Blanca's face lit up like the moon, her laughter carrying across the road. "Soon," he said. "They're close to figurin' it out."

"Figuring out—what?" Then Charna caught his drift. "Those two? They can't even figure out how to make a van work."

"Someone once sang that that love is the fifth horseman."

"What, of the apocalypse?"

"That's what the guy said," Venn explained. "We had Zeke, but Zeke's done. So, it'll be... them."

"What's the other four?"

Venn turned back to catch the last drip of sun before it vanished behind a mesa. His smile was golden. His smile was the Buddha's.

The light disappeared for good.

*****

Night tumbled into the desert and nocternal critters scurried across the sand, skittering like errant thoughts. The stars unveiled their distant radiance. Everyone slept, but the night wore on and on. And on.

Blanca stirred from her blanket by the fire pit and shivered. She'd slept hard and deep and long, yet it was still dark out. She wasn't the first up; Ro had preceded her in waking and was now poking at the crackling flames, while Charna sauntered over with a yawn and popped open a beer can. She unslung her bass from her back and alternated restless strumming with a swig. Behind them, Venn's snores still rattled Zeke's insides.

But those were the only sounds in the world. No airplanes shot across the sky. No cars blew past on the deserted road. Even the skittering had gone silent. If someone had proclaimed that they were the last folks on earth, Blanca wouldn't have argued.

Rowan tossed a few sticks in the fire and a modest blaze erupted. "Figure we can move on come dawn; Zeke'll be cooled off and we can slip into Show Low. Find a repair shop, maybe a diner." He grinned at Blanca and leaned a hand on a rock. "I know you like them fluffy pancakes."

Blanca tilted her head. He was still acting like they were getting to Show Low, something she'd realized wasn't going to happen the moment she'd awoken to a night sky. She set her hand on Rowan's tenderly, the stone's radiant warmth coursing through them both. His eyes sparkled in surprise, but he didn't pull away.

Charna set her bass to one side. "When was the last time we missed a gig?"

"Never," said Rowan.

"We're awfully responsible for a rock band." Charna tipped the last of the beer down her throat. "Never missed a gig, not once in fourteen years." She toed the sand. "Funny how the end of the world works. Didn't think time itself would break down before ol' Ezekiel did." She held out her wrist. "My watch stopped at midnight. But it's a lot later than that, isn't it?"

Nobody answered her, but Blanca knew she was right. The sun should be coming up by now. "Zeke won't be starting up again," she stated. "We all get that, right?"

Ro's jaw set. "Now, hold on. Zeke's reliable as—"

She shook her head. "Not anymore." Their gazes locked. "Think about it. All the way back, Ro. What made you pick us up? Was there a plan?"

Rowan regarded her. The crazy part of him had gone dormant and Blanca felt a surge of protectiveness. She squeezed his hand. "No plan," he said. "Zeke was just... there one day. I'd been sleepin' a lot. World was insane, riots most every night. Nothin' to go out for."

"What town?" Blanca couldn't believe she didn't already know.

"Outside D.C. In Maryland. Rockville." He stared into the fire. "'Course my homestead's in Macon but I..." he paused. "Told y'all this before, y'know."

"Tell us again," said Charna.

He made a face. "Ain't easy being on the road with a bunch of folks who don't remember shit day to day. Well, I woke up and it was *quiet*. Just birds. Dog barking. I went out, first time since... anyway, I went outside to see what was up. And there was Zeke, idlin' in the parking lot. Doors wide, like wings. Nobody else around. And—"

"It called to you," said Charna.

"Like an invitation in your head," added Blanca.

He nodded. "Still only had my ratty slippers on. But I got in and the GPS pointed to Brooklyn and off we went. Zeke always knew where we were goin' next. And there you were, Bee."

He made her nickname sound like a place to call home. In that moment she understood: His heart was also a key. A surge of desire raced through her body, thudding like the approach of a mustang herd.

"Y'know, Venn has this interesting theory," said Charna. "He says that Zeke is kaput. That we've come to the end of things. And all that's left now is for you two to figure something important out."

Blanca turned to Rowan, wondering if she could send an invitation into his head, too. Here they were in an eternity of night—but something had shifted. Subtly, like a sand dune. Maybe Venn was on to something. Blanca listened carefully to the world and realized even the fire crackling seemed muted.

"Come here." She stood, holding a hand out to Ro. "I want to show you something."

She expected Ro to protest, say something like *we're gonna get lost* or *it's cold* or *where are we even going* but he was as silent as the night. Leaving Charna by the fire, they crossed the empty tarmac and strode out into the desert, eyes adjusting to the dark. Blue-black distant shapes of mesas, spindles, spires rose up like cut-out holes in existence.

Blanca wasn't sure where she was heading, but was confident she'd know it when they arrived. And then she was there. They halted before an open stretch of dark desert. A light breeze brushed Blanca's cheeks and Rowan breathed softly beside her. "Why were you sleeping so much?"

"Everyone was gone."

"Everyone?"

Another long silence.

"I'm sorry if you told me this," she said. "There's been a fog in my head. But it's clearing now."

"I ain't told you this part before. 'Bout Mona. We'd split. Couple months 'fore things went to hell." Each word pulled out slow like taffy. "She told me she didn't like how I lived and that's a hard thing to come back from. I followed her to D.C. and—our boys were with her when it happened. Tommy. Amos. The Metro. Dupont Circle. The chemical attack." He shut down for a few long minutes. "So, I was sleepin'."

A vise had clamped on Blanca's throat. Her hands clenched and unclenched and then ... his fingers found hers. He held onto her like he was falling. She felt like she was rising.

After a moment, Blanca lifted their joined hands, aiming at the scattered pinpricks of light, holes poked in the universe. The stars were arrayed, as if for final instructions. She traced the night with their fingers until she found what she wanted: four bright stars in a square. "The far left one is Pegasus," she said. "That's where Andromeda begins, and," she guided his hand to the upper left, "it continues that way. If we had a telescope, you'd see the spiral arms."

She lowered their hands and Rowan held on.

"The light is 2.5 million years old," she continued. "One day that galaxy will collide with our Milky Way and we'll be a supergalaxy."

"This happenin' any time soon?"

"Oh, four, four and a half billion years from now."

"I don't think we'll be here for that. Even on this tour."

Blanca rested her head on his shoulder. "What you said in the van about us being the last hurrah. I think you're right. But we've been more than that." She told him about going into town and finding no one there. "Whole town, empty as a pocket." She paused, shaping the idea for the first time. "I think we've been a cleanup crew. Last fourteen years, we've played everyone's last song, then let them go. And they go happy."

"But we're still here."

"'Cause we've had Zeke. But now he's stopped. The tour is over." Blanca stared into the dark, then up at the heavenly light. Finally, she said the thing she'd held in her heart since she'd climbed into the van and asked where they were going. *Everywhere*, he'd said. From that moment—one month, or fourteen years, or 2.5 million years ago—she'd known it. "I love you, y'know." She stared up at the stars. "I mean, it's not the end of the world if we don't get to happen, but I wanted it said."

His hand tightened on hers and his voice was husky, but his words were in her head like an invitation: *I love you too, Bee.* The pulse of his wrist locked into the warmth inside her and the two intertwined, spiraling around one another like desert whirlwinds, like arms of a galaxy, colliding. "But what if it is the end of the world?"

The swirl inside Blanca grew and expanded. She felt as if she might burst into a universe of stars. She kissed Ro for the first and the last time. "Then let's play it out."

*****

Four musicians stood on an empty sandy plain, surrounded by cut-out holes in existence and pinpricks of eternity in the sky. They plugged their instruments into a generator running on fumes, but everything lit up and hummed, just like it was supposed to.

Because every great concert requires an encore.

"One, two, one two three four!" Venn kicked them into gear and they started playing, chaotic and disconnected, then fluid and braided together, the song flowing from them, their one and only original symphony. Charna folded into Venn's thudding rhythms, Rowan grabbed a guitar and deftly pulled melody from his strings like a man re-discovering a long-lost love. Blanca opened her mouth to sing and the cosmos poured from her.

The desert rang with their song, a symphony of sand and stars and sunsets. In the distance, Zeke listened as all four of them threw the remainder of their lives into the tune, giving it everything they had left.

It was *perfect*.

After an immeasurable amount of time, Blanca whirled around and held up a hand. The guitars soared skyward, then bowed into the final notes. Venn slammed on the skins, ripping them open. Blanca jumped skyward once, twice, three...

The instruments fell to the sand, humming. The players were gone. The warm bass and guitar lay spent on the desert floor, the empty drum kit still standing, defiant. The microphone landed against a cactus. Everything was vibrating, the song spiraling outward to the stars, stretching and fading as the music of the spheres returned home.

For Paddy M.

To Brandish a White Ladle
A Chronicle of the Four Lunch Ladies of the Apocalypse

Danielle Ackley-McPhail

You would have thought it was the end of days.

Really. It was that bad.

Not the situation, that weren't nothing much. But the ruckus... That little missy needed to check her vapors at the door. Dina Lynn Washnowski sat in the middle of controlled chaos, bawling her eyes out over some limp little fish fingers. Apparently, in elementary school, missing out on pizza day was a cataclysm. What can I say? It's her own fault for fooling around with her friends instead of getting into line.

First-grade problems, I tell you.

Just the next table over from her, I watched Sally Parker share out her little square of pizza between her two sisters, Mary and Abigail, because their momma couldn't afford more than one lunch ticket. I could tell from here she'd taken the smallest slice to boot. Then she divided everything else on the tray the same way.

Bet you they would have loved to have those fish fingers...

Dina Lynn just kept bawling. Nobody paid her any mind except for me.

I shook my head and kept doing what I was doing. A couple of the little monsters brought up their milk or apples or what have you—the healthy stuff they couldn't be bothered to eat—and left it for whoever else wanted it. I waited for them to mosey on back to their seats before scooping up their leavings and wandering over to the Parker sisters. Without a word, or even looking at those sweet girls, I set the bounty on the table and walked away.

What's that? Who am I?

Why, my friends call me 'Bert. Short for Alberta. But the kids call me Lady Bert. Short for Lunch Lady. Nice to meetcha.

Me, by the way, I used to be just like Sally Parker. Some ways, I like to think I still am. That little lady has a quiet, dignified manner about her... okay, so maybe I'm not so much like her in that regard, but when it comes to charity and compassion...

Guess I should've known better than to turn my back on the room.

Seems on one side of the cafeteria, the future cheerleaders of America smuggled in a Ouija board or something. While on the other, the future Geek Squad crowd broke out their illicit video games the moment they inhaled their lunches. Maybe it was a coincidence, but the air began to buzz and crackle across my skin, I swear, like two cosmic forces crossed streams or something.

Miss Sylvie stood at the entrance to the serving line. A faint frown creased her brow as she scanned the room. I worked my way past the tables and back toward the kitchen to stand beside her. We were quite the pair, her petite and pale and willow-switch thin, her braided hair as black and shiny as a licorice twist; and me, as plump and rosy as a Georgia peach, with my corn-silk golden hair in a stylish up-do. We shared the frown, though.

Whatever charged the air, the kids felt it. You could tell in the way they fussed at one another.

"What's goin' on?"

I swear I'm'a smack that girl silly someday. Tabby came up sudden-like behind us, tugging at her spiky lime-sherbet hair and snapping the gum she wasn't supposed to be chewing. She wasn't much older than the kids sitting out at the tables, but she was one of us. A Lunch Lady-in-Waiting, as I liked to think of her. She had a lot to learn but certainly seemed willing. I liked the way she looked out for the kids, not quite leaning on the bullies but always making sure they knew she was watching. Couldn't hardly tell if she was helping the kids or hanging out with them, but she got her work done, and the kids got fed. That's what counted.

"Well?"

"Don't know," I murmured, rubbing down the hairs prickling on my arms. "Best go get the Sarge."

That would be Josephine... but don't you ever dare call her that. At best, she won't answer. At worse, she will.

With another snap of her gum, Tabby went to comply. Better her than me, Sarge had a temper when you interrupted her paperwork. Just like the Army, a well-run cafeteria ran on paperwork. Or was that ran away from paperwork? Honestly, I can't keep it straight. I'm just here to make sure the food gets eaten and not tossed around.

The master sergeant came striding out of the kitchen looking tall, lean, and tough as whipcord. And more than a little pissed. Well... she weren't a master sergeant anymore, but when you wear a rank as long as she did, it soaks into your bones, and there it stays like set-in gravy that ain't nothing gonna get out. If the lunchroom had a bouncer, she was it. Right now, she wore her hard-core sergeant face, looking mighty tired and out of patience with the horsepucky going on. Her silver-shot crimson curls sat close to her head like a helmet, and in her right hand, she held a white plastic ladle like a baton... or a club, to be more honest.

That's our Josephine... always ready to do battle...

You just hush up, and don't you go telling her I called her that!

Now, like I was saying, *Sarge* stood there, poised and ready, like she was inspecting the troops.

Of course, don't you know, that's when all hell's bells broke loose...

Three sets of double doors led into the multi-purpose room—that what you call it when the lunchroom's got to be nearly everything else as well. Every blessed one of those doors flew open at once with a bang you just would not believe.

You thought there was yelling before? Let me just tell you... you don't know yelling until a flood of goblins comes tumbling into the room in the middle of April like it was the end of October instead. Kids know darned well when Halloween is and when it isn't.

That's when our Josephine starts whipping her ladle around and busting out the big guns with her drill instructor voice.

"Lunch monitors, get your children into the teachers' lounge now! Ladies..." That's us... "You're with me!"

Now, don't go thinking that left us all on our own. There's not a teacher worth their salt that wouldn't stand between their kids and danger... especially when faced with the prospect of being crammed in a tiny room with what had to be at least a hundred children during what was supposed to be their break.

Yeah, I'd face the goblins too. Just saying...

Of course, none of us are foolish enough to face an army of goblins with just a single ladle and our bare hands. Aren't too many knives in a school kitchen... the board of ed kind of plans it so they aren't needed—don't ask me why—but there are plenty of really hard plastic trays. I took care of arming the troops while Tabby hurried over to the PE closet. (What part of multi-purpose room did you not understand?) By the time I ran out of what I now like to call whack-paddles to put into the teachers' hands, Tabby and Miss Sylvie had busted out the dodge balls, and I know for a fact those hard little suckers were just filled up with air.

It. Was. Glorious.

Between Sarge whaling through the horde swinging her ladle and the teachers flailing about with their whack-paddles, and the rest of us beaning those stupid suckers for all we were worth with properly hard dodge balls, why, we didn't even have to threaten to unleash those kids on their sorry, invading buttocks...

Haven't a clue where those goblins came from, haven't a clue where they went, but when we peeked outside those busted-out doors... well, let's just say it's a good thing we had plenty of room to hunker down. We closed those doors nice and tight and chained them like we was closing up for the night before herding our own little monsters back to their tables and trying to pretend like not a thing was strange.

You'll excuse me, though, for heading into that kitchen just as soon as I was able to find something a touch more intimidating than a ball or a whack-paddle to keep to hand.

After all, we can't all be Sergeant Jo.

*****

Don't you know... that Dina Lynn sat right back down where she started, bawling even harder because some stupid-ass goblin from beyond ate her mangled fish fingers. I guess second choice beats nothing at all...

With long, ground-eating strides, Sergeant Jo went back to the kitchen, coming back out not ten minutes later with a Styrofoam plate in her hand. Crossing the multi-purpose room, she plopped that plate in front of the blotchy-faced little darling. Dina Lynn looked up at her with big glistening eyes, then down at the plate holding two English muffins from breakfast smeared with sauce and topped with melty cheese.

"Buck up, little girl. It's not the end of the world."

Letting out one more sniffly little hiccup, the child smiled, all sunshine and puppies, and started chomping on those makeshift pizzas like all was now right with her world.

In my head, I could hear Sergeant Jo's unspoken words... *Not yet.*

Fate of the Final Four
(a Fatalist Fable)

Gordon Linzner

"End days is a-comin',
"They're coming this way,
"End days is a-comin'
"They're coming today..."

The theme song fades. A quartet of assigned commentators climb the steep narrow steps to the dais in the center of the arena. One by one, they slide back into their swivel chairs behind the crimson-draped table.

Each of their breaks feels exponentially shorter.

Almost every seat for their non-existent audience, as well as the entire world beyond, is hidden by a thick gray fog. Camera operators, sound crew, lighting assistants—none of them are visible during this event. Their presence is taken on faith.

So much is taken on faith.

The all-too-appropriately named Fountain of Doom towers above and behind our four commentators. Its waters, which glistened crystal clear at the start of the competitions, now churn a dark red, almost black. The liquid bubbles up higher, more than seven meters.

Not a single drop splashes on our hosts.

Howard, as head of the commentator team, restrains a sigh. Many have already escaped his lips over the past weeks. By this time, the act could be interpreted as ritual. So many contenders for the ultimate clean-up slot have been dismissed! At least, he speculates, the countdown to the end grows nearer, the number of competitors smaller, the situation theoretically easier to handle.

The initial concept, as the judging quartet was given to understand, involved assembling a team of the best competing individuals to fill the slots of War, Famine, Pestilence, and—everyone's favorite—Death. When it comes to ending the world, at least as we know it, you only get one shot.

What would be the plural for apocalypse, Howard wonders.

Apocalypses?

Apocali?

Unfortunately, being best at, say, Famine, doesn't necessarily make one a good team player. Because of this reality, these four commentators, originally charged with separately overseeing individual competitions, now work together to select the best team.

The competition is reduced to the final four groups. The contest to decide which of them becomes the final final four.

The End is not going well.

Howard swivels in his seat and leans in toward his microphone. His voice is crisp and clear, emphasizing each word with the proper level of stress. No more. No less.

"Welcome back, listeners, to our continuation of Millennial Madness. It's day number..."

Howard pauses, covers the microphone with a veiny hand. He looks to his three co-hosts.

"What day is it, exactly?" he whispers. "We've been running through prospects so long, I've lost track."

"A little under twenty-eight days," Phil answers. The gray-haired man straightens his bow tie and presses a few keys on his cell phone's calculator app. "To be precise, six hundred sixty-five and a half hours."

Amanda, youngest of the four, makes no effort to conceal her groan. "That's a bit too on point, Phil."

"It's as good a guess as any," Red chimes in.

"It's not a guess." Phil points to the countdown clock floating overhead. Four pairs of eyes glance upward.

Howard shrugs, uncovering his microphone again. "As of this moment, viewers..."

"We still have viewers?" Phil can't resist intruding.

Howard ignores him. "...we are in the final hour of the final day of our Final Days competition, and still there are no clear-cut winners for representation in the coming Apocalypse. Time is running out, in more than one sense. The Bronx is burning. Who's up next, Phil?"

The gray-haired man shuffles through the handful of remaining applications. "I'm told the last four groups are on deck, Howard. There were rumors of a fifth, the Marksmen, but I don't see their paperwork..."

Red snorts. "That bit o' boiled okra's been flying around for the past month."

"I could use a fifth, myself," Amanda observes. She reaches for the glass in front of her, ponders the roiling dark liquid within, changes her mind.

"Who couldn't?" Phil agrees. He settles on a thin sheet of paper. "Here we go. The Four Seasons of the Apocalypse. From the Valli of Death."

Howard stifles an eyeroll. So many contenders adopting names from old pop music groups! Worse, not one had yet lived up to their namesakes, let alone possessed the requirements for running an apocalypse. Or had the slightest clue what was needed. The Fab Four of the Apocalypse, earlier that week, took their premise from an obscure collection of alternate-world short stories. Howard had enjoyed the flame-shooting drumsticks, though the concept brought back sad memories. At least some teams used appropriate nomenclatures, like the Four Knights and the Four Saints.

Amanda lays a sympathetic hand on his. "I feel your pain, Howard. I still haven't gotten over seeing the Four Aces throw three of the Four Coins into the fountain."

"That *was* quite the rhubarb," Red agrees.

"At least they were entities." Amanda's eyes return to the glasses of dark liquid sitting before each of them. She recalls too well the source of their four blood-red coasters.

Phil turns to the cameras to speak.

"The rules, I am obliged to remind our contenders, are simple but stringent. No matter what you choose to name your group, or the individuals therein, the four must in some way embody the separate concepts of Famine, Pestilence, War, and Death. The order can vary. In the interests of time, of which we now have increasingly little, we ask that each group confine itself to a single spokesperson."

As is his habit, Phil pauses for dramatic effect. No one is impressed. Not the waiting groups, not the handful of live spectators, and certainly not his fellow commentators.

"Four Seasons of the Apocalypse!" Phil announces at last, using the best *gravitas* he can muster. "Come forth and state your case!"

A tetrad of figures, draped in robes of varying dark green shades, shuffle out of the fog. Each one bears a small ceramic planter. The four huddle briefly. A thin, curly-haired woman, clad in deep toad-green, steps forward. The remaining trio line up behind her, like backup singers.

"You speak for all four?" asks Howard.

"I fought for the privilege, yes, and I won. My name is Rosemary."

"As a fighter, then, you represent War?"

"Indeed. My brother Sage," she nods toward a gaunt man in an appropriately sage-colored robe, "represents Starvation. Pestilence in turn is represented by my younger sibling, Parsley."

"Which one is he?" asks Phil.

"I prefer zie," snaps the figure in emerald. "Or them, if that's easier for you to remember."

Rosemary turns to Parsley, right hand raised for silence. "Did we not agree that I was to speak for all of us?"

Parsley's gaze sullenly lowers to the ground.

I see where the pestilence comes from, Howard mulls.

"Finally, wearing the clover robe, my dwarfish elder sister Thyme. She is not..."

"...on anyone's side. I get it." Howard rubs his forehead.

"The names sound fair to me," Amanda offers.

Red weighs in. "Rosemary, can you describe for us the qualifications of each member of your team, for tearing up this particular pea patch?"

Rosemary blinks. "Didn't I just do that? I'm not afraid to fight, so I'm War. Sage can't satisfy anyone's hunger. Thyme is the shortest of us. And Parsley, here, zie..."

"What Red wants to know," Phil interjects, "what we all want to know, is exactly what special abilities your team brings to the table. How do you, as War, intend to foment conflicts, for example?"

Rosemary glances at her three companions, then back to the dais. "I don't understand. We're just supposed to be figureheads, aren't we? When I went on Google..."

Howard conceals his frustration no longer. His forehead sinks to the table. A good ninety percent of the applicants thought the same. The misinterpretation was funny the first hundred times or so.

Howard turns to Phil. "Who's next?"

"Wait!" cries Rosemary. "Is there a manual? I'm a fast learner. We all are. Well, except for Thyme, but..."

Gray fog envelopes the Four Seasons, silencing their spokesperson. At the same time, their paper application also vanishes.

"The Four Captains!" Phil calls.

A quartet of new figures starts to appear in the surrounding gray mist.

Howard perks up. "Military titles? Been a while since we've had those." He focuses expectantly on the parting fog.

Then he gets a clearer view.

The portliest of the group, acting as spokesperson, does not wait to be queried. "We are the Captains Courageous!" he announces. "My name is Katzenjammer! My associates are Kirk, Crunch, and Kanga..."

Howard cuts him off. "No. Just no."

"No," add the other three commentators, in unison.

Although air traffic has been suspended for weeks, a boom echoes from above. Further comment is ended. Gray clouds race across the sky like a fast-forwarded cinematic montage. The fountain bubbles more fiercely, rising an additional meter. Powerful gusts propel the Captains Courageous back into the enveloping fog.

The wind does not disturb a single hair on any of the commentators.

Amanda glances skyward. "Someone's getting upset."

"Is it anger?" Phil asks, eyes widening. "Or an omen?" He rattles a sheet of paper in front of the other three. "I call on our next candidates to step forward."

Once more, Phil pauses for dramatic effect. Once again, no one reacts. This lack of response does not dampen the enthusiasm in his voice:

"The Four Winds of the Apocalypse!"

The name has potential, but Howard refuses to get his hopes up again. The fog clears; the newcomers step forward.

"You're the Four Winds." A statement, not a question. Howard struggles to keep the weariness out of his voice.

"Guess we must be," says a broadly smiling figure, gesturing with his trombone. "Ain't nobody else here but us chickens."

Howard sees where this is headed. He goes through the motions anyway. "You're the spokesman."

"True that. People call me the King! On my right is Trane, with Cleanhead to my left, and we couldn't even try to do this without Stan the Sound."

"All saxophones, except for your trumpet," Phil observes. "Couldn't you have added a clarinet, or a flugelhorn? If only to differentiate War from Famine, for instance?"

"We play together so smoothly you'll lose track anyway. I wanted to call us Five Guys Named Moe, but was told four's the limit. Had to drop Ornette."

Howard drums his fingers ominously. "Does your group know what's required?"

"We are ready to jump, jive, and wail. Got some questions, though."

"Take it one pitch at a time," Amanda advises.

"Is you is," the King begins, "or is you ain't...?"

"Ain't," answers Howard.

The fog closes in.

"I," says the King. The following pause is almost as dramatic as Phil's. The rest of the words become lost as the fountain gurgles higher, and, impossibly, darker.

Howard sighs. "It's *an ill wind* that blows nobody any good. Time is running out. In every sense of the word. We've one group left, right?"

"One left. Right." Phil pretends to shuffle his paperwork again. Only one sheet remains.

"Might this final group be winners by default?" queries Amanda. "Suppose the Four were already chosen, with this competition designed simply to increase world-wide anxiety?"

Red nods. "Anything is possible."

Howard folds his arms over his chest. "Or nothing."

Phil's eyes narrow. "Handwriting's hard to read. Looks like..." He pauses briefly. Even he tires of the drama.

"Foremen of the Apocalypse!" he announces.

"Four Men?" questions Red. "That's not very imaginative."

"No. Foremen, as in heads of construction crews."

"Or jury panels," Amanda suggests.

"That works," Red accedes.

Four dark-skinned contenders appear as the fog recedes. Each pushes a small metal cart. Three wear hard hats, one in an ill-fitting suit. The fourth, taller and more muscular than the others, is bare-headed, clothed in a chef's apron. Smiling, he pulls a metal spatula from his cart, waving it at the panel in greeting.

Howard leans forward for what he hopes is the last time. "Which one are you? War? Pestilence? I'm guessing not Famine."

"Heck, no. Call me George."

Howard grimaces. "George."

"And my two sons, George and George. And my wife..."

"George?"

Big George shrugs, widens his grin. "Sometimes. If I forget."

Amanda joins in. "You seem quite cheerful for a group about to impose the End of Everything."

"Is that what you think?" George chuckles.

"Have you looked around? Do you not see civilization collapsing?"

"Where there's lots of smoke, there's usually just a whole lot more smoke. You read our application?"

Phil raises his paper, squints harder. "Holy cow!" He hands it to Amanda, seated beside him. "Tell me I'm seeing things."

Amanda reads the form, stares at George. "No wonder you seek to inspire hope, ignite the imagination. The Four Foremen of the... Apocrypha?"

Red rises. The wheels of his chair creak. "The Apocalypse is Apocryphal? Like phantom hitchhikers, deep-fried rats, spider eggs in bubblegum? As in, never happened? Never will? Never would? All tied up in a croker sack?"

"You gentlemen sound disappointed," George interjects. "And disappointment's where evil lodges. Now, me and the family, we figure a nice barbeque should set your minds at ease. We got beef, pork, chicken, even some rabbit."

"Tell us about the rabbits, George," says Red.

"No!" Howard groans. "We've spent an entire sleepless month for nothing!"

Phil straightens his bow tie. "Technically, it's under a month, unless it's February, and a non-leap year."

"I'm just telling it like it is, Phil," Howard snaps.

"Um, guys?" Amanda gestures towards the encroaching fog. The Foremen are nowhere in sight. The fountain's roar becomes a crackle, transforming into a towering burning bush. "Looks like time for a word from our sponsor."

There is no voice, no words per se, yet the Four Announcers clearly understand the message. They, not the seemingly endless list of competitors, are the ones being tested. Who better to pass judgment than the judges?

Howard is War. It's in his name: HoWARd. He has all the qualifications: arrogant, pompous, obnoxious, vain, cruel, verbose, a showoff. "I have been called all of these," he admits. "Yes. I am all of these."

Regarding Famine, as with Howard, it's been in her name from the start: AManda. "Guess I've found my legacy," she mutters.

Phil represents Pestilence. "Holy cow!"

"Mad cow," Red chimes in. "Among other diseases." And his name, the color, symbolizes death. He is the only one of the four required to wear a mask. "Well, I'll be a suck-egg mule!"

Each broadcaster knows what is required of their roles, having spent nearly a month searching for those aspects among hundreds, no, thousands of applicants. The swivel chairs swell, morphing into chariots.

*****

Theme music swells again, this time sung, not by an invisible choir, but by the Four Announcers. Three of them, anyway. Red cannot carry a tune under his mask, so he pulls a Rex Harrison.

"End days is a-comin',
"They're coming this way,
"End days is a-comin'
"They're coming today..."

The Four Announcers of the Apocalypse ride out to spread the word.

*****

Four brothers cross a desolate wasteland. Each, fittingly, is borne on the back of a skeletal proboscidean leviathan. Their group leader, War, pauses to take in the devastation. He fingers an oversized cigar. His face is splattered with black, caking blood, mostly in a thick swatch between his nose and upper lip.

By halting suddenly, War nearly causes a pile-up of his three companions.

"Worst apocalypse ever!" snaps Famine, behind him.

War turns, eyes glowing red. "That's my line, you little shyster!"

"And a fine line to cross it is. If you didn't take so much time off, I wouldn't have to fill in for you."

"Not my fault we couldn't find the hidden space-time continuum entrance. It was Death's job to locate the secret void!"

The sudden HONK! of a car horn echoes from the rear.

"Death claims he was following you," Famine translates.

War pats the skull of his steed. "You know, I shot this leviathan in my pajamas. How he got in..."

Famine cut him short. "We know."

War looks around again. "Where is everyone, anyway?"

"We're late," Famine explains. "We should have cut across

that viaduct."

"Viaduct?" Pestilence perks up. "Why not a...?"

"Because it couldn't cross the road." Interrupting his brothers is second nature to Famine.

Pestilence sneezes. "Isn't there a gap in space and time no one was supposed to know about?"

"Say! The secret void! That's where we need to go!"

Famine flips through his notebook, honks excitedly, holds out a page for Pestilence to read.

"Too late," the latter mutters. "It's already been sealed off."

"Just as well." War sighs. "I refuse to join any Apocalypse that would have me as a member."

HONK!

No further translation is needed by the Four Marxmen.

The Four Harschmans of the Apocalypse

Michael Jan Friedman

My cousin Saul turned to me, his freckled face twisted in disgust. "We're screwed, Andy."

"We're not screwed," I said.

"How are we not screwed?" Saul asked.

From the back seat of our Jeep, I peered at the strip of asphalt up ahead of us. It curled around a knob of granite thick with pine trees, promising more of the twisty roadway we'd been following. "We're just lost," I said. "A little."

"This damned phone…" my cousin Garrett muttered from the passenger seat, in front of me.

"It's not the phone," said my cousin Carlos, who had handled the driving for the last hour or so. "There aren't any towers up here. It's like we're in the freakin' Alps."

"The Alps," I said, "are fifteen thousand feet high. We're not even at *five*."

"Actually," said Saul, "we're almost *exactly* at five thousand feet. I looked before we left."

Garrett looked back at him. "When we reach the castle, you mean."

"*If* we reach the castle." Saul swore under his breath, the same way his dad used to swear—a series of little explosions, one after the other. "I told you we should have brought a map."

Carlos sighed. "They don't *make* maps anymore."

"You kidding me?" said Saul. "They don't make maps? They don't make goddamned *road atlases*?"

"You've heard of the internet?" said Carlos. "People print their maps. They don't go out anymore and buy a Rand-freakin'-McNally."

"Guys," I said, "we're fine. We're on a mountain. How lost can we be?"

"We should turn around," said Garrett. "Go back to that store where we got breakfast."

"That place gave me the creeps," said Saul. "You see the woman behind the counter? She looked like she wanted to put my head on a stick."

"You know what gives *me* the creeps?" said Carlos. "Sleeping in the woods." He glanced at the lush forest land off the side of the road. "With *bears*."

"Nobody's sleeping in the woods," I said. "There's a castle. Castles have rooms."

"Cold ones," said Garrett. Then, because he had a thing about negativity, he said, "But with blankets, I'm sure. You've got a good blanket, it doesn't matter how cold the room is."

"We had to be nuts to come up here," Saul said with a heavy sigh. "Bug-fuck nuts."

"Don't start," said Carlos. "You didn't have to shoehorn your fat ass in the car. You had a choice."

"Did I?" Saul asked. "Did I *really*?"

My cousins, I thought. *You can't live with them and you can't bury them in the corner of the yard where my dad buried my foreskin.*

I remembered asking him *why* one time, when I was seven or eight. Years later, I learned it was a tradition. But that's not what my dad told me.

"It's because you're special," he said. *"Because in the whole world, there's no one exactly like you."*

Which, of course, was true of *everyone*—even twins, I realized later on. But he was my dad, and dads said things like that.

"Andy?" said Carlos.

I looked at his eyes, which were trained on me in the rear view. "Yeah?"

"You've got the *yad*, right?"

I sighed. "No, man, I've got the throwing stars of death. Saul's got the *yad*."

Carlos's face scrunched up under his beard. "Throwing—?"

"I'm *kidding*." I'd forgotten how gullible my cousin could be. "What do you think, I threw the *yad* out the window halfway up the mountain?"

"Don't be a jerk," said Carlos, "all right?"

"Sorry," I said.

"Freakin' *jerk*."

"You said that already."

"And I'm saying it again," said Carlos. *"Jerk."*

I was grateful when Saul asked, "Anybody know a good dentist?" and touched one of his teeth with a forefinger.

"I know a *great* dentist," said Carlos. "You going to travel sixty miles to fill a cavity?"

Saul made a face. "What do you mean, sixty miles?"

"Last I looked," said Carlos, "Tappan was sixty miles from the city."

"Tappan?" said Saul.

"Where I live," said Carlos.

"You live in freakin' *Tappan*?" said Saul. "Since when?"

Carlos cast a glance back over his shoulder. "Since two years ago. I sent you an e-mail. I'm moving to Tappan, it said."

"Who reads e-mails?" said Saul.

"Pretty much everyone," Garrett interjected. "Otherwise no one would send them."

"You know what, Saul?" said Carlos. "You're an animal. Your freakin' cousin moves and has the decency to send you an e-mail, and you don't even open it."

"Maybe I *did* open it," said Saul. "I can't remember my name half the time, I'm gonna remember I opened your e-mail? Is that a reason to be mad at me?"

"I'm not mad," said Carlos.

"You *sound* mad," said Saul.

"I'm *not* goddamned mad," said Carlos.

Saul was right. Carlos was mad.

And he got that way a little too easily. But Carlos had a point about communicating. Whenever we got together, it was because *he* rounded us up. *This* time, for instance.

Not that somebody else wouldn't have woken up eventually. This weekend had been on our calendars for as long as any of us could remember.

Just then, the road started switching back and forth, one hairpin after the other. We didn't want to distract Carlos, so we got quiet.

It was only after the road straightened out again that Saul said, "Why they make us wait to do this till we're middle-aged, I don't know."

"Me either," I said.

Garrett looked back at me. "You never thought about it?"

"I have," I said. "I just don't have an answer."

"We were sharper when we were younger," said Carlos. "We had reflexes."

Garrett chuckled. "Some of us still do."

We laughed. All of us except Carlos.

"Sure," he said. "Great reflexes. Keep telling yourself that. Buncha old farts."

"Forty's not old," I said.

"There's forty and there's forty," said Carlos.

He was right. *Some people get somewhere by forty, and some don't.*

Even if they're special.

"Hey!" said Saul. "What's that?" He pointed to something up ahead.

"What?" said Garrett.

"You see it?" said Saul. "Through the trees?"

Suddenly I spotted what he was talking about. There was a car maybe five hundred feet ahead of us. A white Subaru.

It was taking it easier than we were. Which meant we could catch up, flag it down, get directions maybe.

"Thank God," said Saul.

"He's slowing down," said Garrett.

"I can see that," said Carlos. "Maybe it's the road up ahead." We slowed down too. "I'm gonna honk him."

"Yeah," said Garrett, "do that."

But before Carlos could honk, the Subaru came to a stop. And we could see why. There was a car ahead of it, blocking the road. A Jeep like ours, but a silver one.

"Shit," said Saul. "Hell of a place to break down."

But as we approached the back of the Subaru, we saw it wasn't just one car up ahead. There had to be twenty of them, lined up bumper to bumper, taking up maybe four hundred feet of asphalt.

And that was just the part we could see before the queue disappeared around a bend.

"There's a *line*?" I said.

"To save the world?" Garrett added.

I chuckled. "Yeah, right."

There had to be other places on the road beside the castle. Hotels, maybe. Cabins, that kind of thing.

We'd stayed in such a place, me and Jenny. Up in New Hampshire. Cabins on the Mountain, it was called.

Of course, that was *before* I lost my job. Before I couldn't find another one, even with Saul and Carlos and my friends trying to help me.

Before Jenny left me for the chiropractor.

Yeah, I thought, *special.*

"What do you think?" Saul asked. "Carburetor? Flat tire? Maybe they ran into a tree?"

"*Jeez*," said Garrett.

Carlos stopped the car, put it in park, stepped on the emergency brake, and turned on the hazard lights. "We could be here a while. Tell me again I shouldn't worry about bears."

We watched guys get out of the Subaru and saunter up the road, probably trying to find out what the problem was. Figuring we should do the same, I unbuckled my seatbelt.

"Where are you going?" Saul asked.

"Up the road," I said.

"What for?" Saul asked.

"To get a latte," said Carlos, "what do you think?"

"Want company?" Garrett asked.

"Sure," I said.

"I'll stay here," Saul volunteered.

"Yeah," said Carlos, "no shit."

I opened the door of the Jeep and swung my legs out. They were stiff from sitting for so long, especially as I took that first step up the incline.

"Well," said Garrett, coming around to join me, "at least we get a break from Saul for a minute."

"Several," I said, "if we play our cards right."

The morning sun, slicing through the tree branches, was warm on my face. But the air was cool. It smelled nice, the way you'd expect a pine forest to smell.

And birds were singing. Lots of them. I couldn't see them, but they were there.

I noticed not everyone had left the Subaru. A couple of guys were standing in front of it, laughing at something. If they were stressed about whatever was up the road, they didn't show it.

"Excuse me," I said as Garrett and I approached them.

They turned to look at us. One was short, fit-looking, in jeans and a black polo shirt. The other guy, who looked like he'd played offensive lineman in high school, was wearing cargo shorts and a Hawaiian shirt.

"You bet," said the guy in the polo shirt.

"Sorry to interrupt," said Garrett.

"No problem," said the guy in the polo shirt. "We're all friends here."

Well, I thought, *not really*. But what I said was, "Any idea what's going on up there?" I pointed up the road. "My cousins and I, we're headed for this place and we don't know how long it stays open."

"Don't worry," said the big guy. "You're here in plenty of time."

"Here?" Garrett echoed.

"Sure," said the big guy.

"You're headed for Binglaten," said the guy in the polo shirt. "Right?"

"Um, yeah," Garrett said.

The big guy gestured with a sweep of his arm. "It's right up there, around the bend."

"Up there?" I said, following his gesture. So we'd come the right way after all. But...

"You look confused," Polo Shirt observed good-naturedly.

I was. If Binglaten was just around the bend...

"I know," said Polo Shirt. "It's quite a line. But it's always like this. At least that's what my dad told me."

"Your... dad...?" I found myself saying.

Polo Shirt laughed. "He had a way of exaggerating things. Maybe yours did too. But they didn't exaggerate *this* part."

"I haven't been on a line this long," said the big guy, "since they gave away turkeys at the Shop 'n' Go."

"This," said Polo Shirt, "is how Woodstock must have been." He pantomimed strumming a guitar. "You know, the music festival?"

"Yeah," said the big guy. He drew himself up to his full height, which was well over six feet, and announced, "Except this is the *Apocalypse* Festival."

I glanced at Garrett. His eyes looked like they were going to pop out of his head.

They know? I thought.

It couldn't be. What we were doing... it had been a family secret for generations.

I'd say maybe I'd misheard the big guy, except Garrett had obviously heard the same thing. *The Apocalypse Festival.* That's what he'd said.

"Yeah," said Polo Shirt, "we're here to make sure the world doesn't end. At least not until the Orioles win another pennant."

The big guy clapped him on the back. "If that's what we're waiting for, the world's got nothing to worry about."

They seemed to notice Garrett and I weren't laughing. "Hey," said the big guy, "you *are* here to keep the world from ending, right?"

"Well," said Polo Shirt, "they're not here to get their nails done."

And the two of them laughed all over again.

"Name's Goetz, by the way," said the guy in the polo shirt. He extended his hand to me. "George Goetz."

"Bryan Geddes," said the big guy, extending a hand as well.

Numbly, I shook their hands, as Garrett did. But at the same time, my mind was racing with the question: *How could they know?*

"And you guys?" Goetz asked.

"Us?" I said.

"Your names?"

"Right," I said. "I'm Andy. Andy Harschman."

"Garrett Harschman," said my cousin, sounding every bit as puzzled as I was.

A light danced in Goetz's eyes. "And those guys in the car?" He pointed to our Jeep. "Harschmans too?"

I saw where this was going. "Yeah. Them too."

Goetz and Geddes looked at each other. Then, biting their lips, they looked at us again.

"The four... Harschmans?" Goetz said. "Of the Apocalypse?"

"Sorry," said Geddes, clearly trying to stifle a laugh, "but that's hilarious."

"Yeah," I said, "I know."

Goetz reddened. "Sorry, man. I didn't mean—"

I held a hand up. "No need. It's nothing we haven't said a thousand times among ourselves."

Just then, the line of cars at the top of the hill started to move. Our new friends noticed.

"Well," said Geddes, "see you up there."

"Sure," I said, and watched Goetz get into the Subaru while the big guy made his way past it, in the direction of the other cars. The rest of their parties, which had been schmoozing up the road, came back to join them.

In each case, I saw the family resemblance.

I exchanged looks with Garrett. "I don't get it," he said. "I thought—"

"It was just *us*, I know. Obviously, there's more to what's happening here than our dads let on."

*****

Binglaten wasn't the castle we were expecting. Not even close. It looked more like a summer camp, with a bunch of white clapboard buildings set in the hollows of a tree-covered slope.

There was a clean-cut guy with glasses and a clipboard standing at the entrance. "Howdy," he said.

"Hi," said Carlos.

"Name?" said the guy with the clipboard.

"Harschman," said Carlos.

The guy either didn't see the joke or wasn't amused by it. *Too focused on what he's doing*, I figured. He eyeballed whatever was on his clipboard, then turned and pointed. "You're down there, on the end. Number Fourteen."

By then we had told Carlos and Saul about our conversation with Goetz and Geddes. Carlos was puzzled, like me and Garrett. Saul didn't believe it.

Before we could follow the clipboard guy's instructions, Saul lowered his window and stuck his head out. "You work here?" he asked the guy.

Clipboard Guy made a face. "Hell, no. I'm here just like you."

"Then," said Saul, "how do you know where to send us?"

Clipboard Guy shrugged. "It's the way my dad described it."

"He told you where everybody goes?"

"Sure." He held up the clipboard so we could see it. Sure enough, on a brown, brittle-looking piece of paper, there was what looked like a diagram of the place, with a rectangle representing each building and a number imposed on each rectangle. "You're the Harschmans, right?"

"Right," said Carlos.

"Number Fourteen," the guy repeated.

"Thanks," said Saul.

But the look on his face said he still didn't believe it.

*****

Number Fourteen had four beds. Each had a neat pile of bedding and a pillow that looked like it had done prison time.

Carlos looked around. "Well, it beats sleeping in the woods."

"At least we're not sharing it with anybody," I said. "It's all Harschmans, all the time."

"Hey," said Garrett, "what's this?"

He went over to a piece of ruled yellow paper that had been pinned to the wall, took it down, and read it to himself.

"What's it say?" Saul asked.

"It's a list," said Garrett. "Of activities."

"Activities…?" Saul echoed. "What is this, a retirement village?"

Garrett chuckled. "There's a late morning hike. Tug of war. Swimming in the lake…"

"I'm exhausted," said Saul, "just hearing about it. Is there anything that *doesn't* come with a risk of heart attack?"

Garrett shrugged. "There's bingo."

"Bingo?" said Saul. "Really?"

"How about preventing the end of the world?" I asked. "Is that one of the activities?"

"It's the *only* activity," said Carlos. He looked at the rest of us. "I mean… isn't that why we're here?"

We'd certainly thought so. It was what our dads had drummed into us since we were teenagers. But if Goetz could be believed, that was just a joke.

Then why weren't we in on it? "I don't get it either," I said.

"Is it possible," Garrett said, "that we're *not* here to prevent the end of the world? What if that's just… you know, a code? Like a friend of mine from college, when he was growing up, he and his friends would call for a safety meeting whenever they wanted to get high. That was their code: *Safety meeting.*"

Carlos's face puckered. "So the end of the world… that's a code?"

"For what?" Saul asked. "Some kind of… guys' weekend?"

We looked at each other. It sounded crazy. All our lives, we'd steeled ourselves for this moment.

Was it possible we'd steeled ourselves for a bingo tournament?

"I think," I said, "we need to ask around."

"Before we start asking," said Carlos, "we should hide the *yad*."

"We'll just leave it in the car," I said. "That's the safest place for it."

Carlos thought for a second, then nodded. "Sure. It's just that…"

"What?" I asked.

"Can I see it?" he asked. "Just for a second?"

I got it. My dad's shiva was the last time any of my cousins had gotten a look at the thing. I'd taken them to my parents' bedroom and gotten the *yad* down from the closet where my dad kept it in a shoebox, and we'd passed it around.

It was a solemn moment, almost holy, in that it connected us to our fathers' generation, and even a bunch of generations before that.

By then, our dads had already told us what was in store for us, if only in broad strokes. But that was in the future, too far away to take seriously.

It was holding the *yad* in my parents' bedroom that made everything concrete. That made it *real*.

"I need the car keys," I told Carlos.

He fished them out of his pocket and tossed them to me. A few moments later, I brought the briefcase into the bunk.

I didn't think it would be a good idea to keep the *yad* in my dad's shoebox, so after his shiva I went out and bought the briefcase. I'd kept the *yad* in it ever since.

Before I did anything else, I looked around to make sure no one was watching. I didn't see anyone, but then the cabins were pretty far apart from each other.

"I'm feeling a chill up my spine," Carlos said, grinning in his beard. "Anybody else feel it?"

"A little," said Garrett, smiling back at him.

I took out my house keys and used the blue one to unlock the briefcase. Then I opened the thing, revealing its contents—in other words, nothing.

Until I stuck my finger in the little notch in the corner of the briefcase, and tripped the hidden latch. Then the concealed compartment sprang open, exposing the *yad*.

It was a slim metal rod about eight inches long, with a little sculpted hand at the end of it, and a finger extending from the hand. That was what *yad* meant in Hebrew: *Hand*.

It wasn't all that sunny out, but the *yad* still seemed to shine. And why not? It was made of purest silver, preserved—or so my dad had said—from centuries past, when medieval rabbis used it to keep their place in their torah scrolls.

Of course, he'd also told me the fate of the world was in my hands, so maybe not everything he'd said was so reliable.

But the *yad* was valuable. You could tell that just by looking at it. So regardless of what it represented or didn't represent, we definitely didn't want to lose it.

We basked in its presence for a few minutes. Then I put it back in the briefcase, and put the briefcase back in the car.

"So now what?" said Carlos. "Who's up for that hike?"

We looked at each other. No one seemed especially eager to go gallivanting in the woods.

"Actually," said Garrett, "there's a softball game at two. I might do *that*."

Which made sense. Garrett had been a softball star back in high school. Of course, he was competing against girls back then, but still.

*****

We ended up spending the rest of the morning in the lake, which was actually more of a big pond, not deep enough to dive into. But it had a beach and a couple of kayaks, which kept us occupied for a little while.

We met some of the other guys down there. The Stinsons from Minnesota. The McMahons from around St. Louis. The Costellos, from a bunch of different places around the country.

They weren't like us, and it wasn't just a matter of their not being Jewish. It was hard for me to put my finger on it, but they had a quality we didn't. Like they were determined to have fun. *Super*-determined.

It bothered Saul more than anybody. Of course, he'd always had a hard time making friends, even when we were kids.

"Ease up," I told him as we made our way from the lake back to the cabin, our towels thrown over our shoulders.

"I am," Saul said. "I'm more eased up than the most eased-up person you know."

"Sure," I said. "That's why you were looking around every two seconds."

"I don't like getting stared at," Saul said.

"Nobody was staring at you."

"They were *all* staring. Wondering who the fat boy with the freckles is. Wondering how he got so fat and so freckled."

"That's all in your head," I said.

"It's all right," Saul told me. He clapped Garrett on the shoulder. "Garrett will protect me."

Garrett looked at him, feigning disgust. "The hell I will."

"You better," said Saul. "You remember the time that kid was bothering you? The one with the unibrow, up the block from your house?"

Garrett frowned. "Buckhalter?"

"That's the one," said Saul. "Remember him calling you names? Pulling on your ponytail? And I had to kick his ass before he'd stop?"

Garrett looked at Saul narrow-eyed. "You did, didn't you?"

Saul was a couple of years older than me, and three or four older than Carlos and Garrett. At one time or another, he'd protected *all* of us.

"Damned right I did," Saul said. "Remember that when the anti-Semites jump the fat boy."

"Oh, my god," said Carlos, rolling his eyes. "To you, everybody's an anti-Semite."

"How do you know they're not?" Saul asked him. "Did you check their luggage for swastikas?"

"That's messed up," I said.

"Fuck you guys," said Saul. He hooked an arm around Garrett and leaned into Garrett's back to make him move faster. "Keep your eyes peeled, bud. They'll skin me alive if they get the chance."

The expression of panic on Saul's face made me laugh—which was, I was pretty sure, what he was going for. *What a clown*, I thought, standing there and watching him propel Garrett up the hill.

Carlos stopped next to me, chuckling at the show. After a moment, he said, "Do you ever wonder about it?"

"What?" I said.

"There had to be four of us, right? Four men and the *yad*. That's what our dads told us."

I turned to look at him. "You think Garrett became a man to fulfill our dads' plan?"

Carlos shrugged. "What do *you* think?"

"Garrett became a man because he always *was* one. I mean, the whole time we were growing up... he was more of a man than any of us."

Carlos grunted. "Speak for yourself." And he followed Saul and Garrett up the hill.

*****

We'd just finished changing into dry clothes when the guy with the clipboard came by and told us about lunch.

"It's at one," he said. "Hope you like barbecue."

We did. Saul especially. "As long as they're not barbecuing *me*," he added.

"You just ruined my appetite," said Carlos.

"Good," said Saul. "I'm not the only one here who could stand to drop a pound."

"I walk every day," said Carlos. "I walk my freakin' tail off."

"Walking's not exercise," said Garrett. "Unless you're, I don't know, eighty. By the way... the guy with the clipboard. Anybody catch his name?"

None of us had. "I don't think he mentioned it," I said. "He was too busy asking for ours."

"Why?" asked Saul.

Garrett shrugged. "I like him."

Saul made a face. "What do you mean you *like* him?"

"What's the matter with that?" Garrett asked.

"He's a guy," said Saul.

"So?"

"And *you're* a guy."

"And?" said Garrett.

"You went to a lot of trouble to switch over. Now you want to switch *back*?"

"I'm not switching anywhere," said Garrett. "I'm happy the way I am. Doesn't mean I can't like guys."

Saul looked at me and Carlos. "Help me with this." He turned to Garrett again. "I thought the whole point was for you to date girls."

"What made you think *that*?" Garrett asked.

"Oh, I don't know," said Saul, "maybe the fact that you went and got yourself a penis? If you wanted to date guys, you could have done that with what you had."

"But that wasn't how I wanted to date them," said Garrett.

Saul put a hand to the side of his head. "You're giving me a headache."

"And you're giving *me* one," said Garrett.

*****

Garrett said he needed a wingman.

Carlos volunteered. "Hell," he said, "I got to do *something* until lunch."

As they left the bunk, Saul looked at me. "You need a wingman, too?"

"Shut up," I said, "or I'll leave you to get barbecued by the anti-Semites."

Saul turned pale under his freckles. "Don't say that ever again."

"Okay. We'll take a walk, then. You up for a walk?"

"Maybe a slow one. Whose idea was it to build this place on a hill?"

So we walked.

We hadn't gone two hundred feet before we came across a guy smacking a tetherball around a pole. "Hey," said Saul, "look at that. When was the last time you saw someone play *tetherball?*"

I watched the guy. He was tall but kind of ungainly. "I don't know," I said. "But I'd kind of like to play."

Saul looked at me. "Really? Since when?"

"I was the tetherball champ back in Camp Lockwood."

"*Were* you?"

We had gone there together two years in row. But Saul had aged out by the time I got into tetherball. I said so.

"That's nuts. So go ahead and play. I'll be a spectator."

I watched the guy on the court. Sized him up. I wasn't a kid anymore but I thought I could take him.

And if I didn't, so what? I wouldn't be *special* anymore? That horse had left the barn some time ago.

"Screw it," I said, and made my way over to the court.

It was actually one of three. The tall guy was playing on the one in the middle. As I got closer, he noticed me.

"Hey," he said, "do you play?"

I smiled. "I used to."

"Want to give it a go?"

"Sure," I said.

"Go ahead and serve," the guy said.

I stretched a little first. I mean, the last thing I wanted to do was pull something and forfeit the game.

Then I served.

The guy was better than he looked. He could jump, for one thing, and he was tall already. And when he hit the ball, he hit it hard.

But he had no strategy on defense. He was always reacting. Little by little, I sent the ball flying around the pole—until, finally, I got in that one last, satisfying wrap.

The tall guy leaned on the pole and grinned at me. "You've got skills, man."

"Or just luck," I said.

But I hadn't been lucky. As the guy had said, I was skilled. Or at least skilled *enough*.

"Nice," said Saul, who had watched the whole thing.

"Hey," said the tall guy, "how about another one?"

"Sure," I said.

It wasn't that much different from the first. The guy tried to use some of my defensive moves, but I had answers for them. When he moved up to block me, I popped the ball over his head. When he moved back, I hit the ball down.

In the end, the result was the same. I was pooped, sweating like a pig, but so was the tall guy.

"Thanks," he said.

"Thank *you*," I said.

As he walked away, Saul clapped. "Not bad."

"For an old guy," I told him. But truthfully? I felt like I was twelve again.

*****

When Saul and I got to the picnic area, the redwood tables set up there—by whom, I could only guess—were pretty full already. We found Garrett sitting with the clipboard guy and what looked like the clipboard guy's cousins.

Carlos was nowhere to be seen. I was about to ask where he was when I heard him call my name.

Following the sound of his voice, I saw him weaving among the tables, headed in our direction. Just beyond him, on the perimeter of the picnic area, there was a guy in a sparse beard and denim cutoffs.

He was watching Carlos too.

"Hey," said Carlos when he got to us.

"What happened to you being a wingman?" I asked.

"Oh," said Carlos, glancing in Garrett's direction, "he didn't need me. The clipboard guy's a bigger George Carlin fan than Garrett. The two of them are old friends now."

"I'm not sure that's what Garrett had in mind," I said.

"Hey, he's got his foot in the door. The rest is on him."

I noticed Denim Cutoffs was still staring at Carlos. "What's up with your pal back there?"

"Pal?" said Carlos. He looked back at Denim Cutoffs. "Oh, Duane. We were just talking for a minute."

"About what?" Saul asked. "Human sacrifice?"

Carlos did his *not mad* impression again. "So he's not a fashionista. What are you all of a sudden, a runway model?"

"Calm down," I said, "before you pull something. So if not human sacrifice, what *were* you talking about?"

I figured that would put the conversation on a more pleasant footing. I was wrong.

157

"Duane thinks..." Carlos frowned. "...there's something fishy about this... this whole Camp Apocalypse deal."

"Fishy how?" Saul asked.

"He didn't *say*," said Carlos. "He just doesn't trust it. He came up here like we did, figuring he had to save the world—he and his cousins and his brother. And he found what we found."

"So he's... what... suspicious?" Saul asked.

Carlos nodded. "He's wondering if this is all window dressing somehow. To put us off our guard."

"And then what?" I asked.

"We don't do what we came for," said Carlos. "And the world ends."

Saul shot me a look. "I *told* you those anti-Semites were staring at me."

"Hang on," I said. "Why would anybody want to stop us from saving the world? I mean, isn't it their world too?"

Saul and Carlos exchanged glances. Then Saul said, "Maybe they're the enemy."

I looked at them. "What enemy?"

"The one our fathers warned us about," said Carlos.

My dad hadn't said anything about an enemy. I said so.

"Mine did," said Carlos.

"Mine, too," said Saul. "He said they'd be led by a Beast."

Carlos nodded. "Exactly."

I hadn't heard about a Beast either. "You're kidding."

"I wish I was," said Saul.

Was it possible my dad had talked about these things and I'd forgotten? That it had gone through me without leaving a mark?

No. An enemy... a Beast... things like that would have left an impression on me. Especially back then.

Carlos frowned a deep frown. "If they *are* the enemy, how far will they go to stop us?"

"Far, I bet," said Saul.

"Come on," I said, trying to inject a little common sense into the equation. "Look around. These guys are like *us*. They've got spare tires. They're losing their hair. Do they look like any kind of enemy to you?"

Saul shrugged. "Jeffrey Dahmer didn't look like a cannibal till you opened his freezer. He was such a good neighbor, they said. Who would have thought...?"

I shook my head. "I don't buy it."

Suddenly, I felt something on my shoulder. I jumped—until I

looked back and saw it was George Goetz.

"Sorry," he said.

"It's all right," I told him.

"I didn't mean to scare you. It's just that we're a little light for the corn hole tournament. Do you guys play?"

*****

We had to decline the corn hole invitation, considering Saul and I had never played, and Carlos didn't even know what corn hole *was*.

The three of us sat together at an empty table while Garrett continued to talk up the clipboard guy. Meanwhile a red-faced Geddes, who had somehow wound up being the grill master, oversaw the army of hot dogs and burgers on the place's institution-sized grill.

Cooking was happening. I could tell by the clouds of smoke that came off the grill, occasionally obscuring Geddes. But it wasn't happening quickly enough for my taste.

"I'm going to see what's taking so long," I said.

"Perfection," said Geddes, when I posed the question to him—politely, of course, since he was a guest like the rest of us. He was using a long-handled fork to roll the carefully assembled lines of hot dogs across the grill. "This way they come out cooked on all sides." He took a closer look at the line closest to him. "And... I think these babies are done."

"That's great," I said.

"Wanna be my taste tester?" Geddes asked.

I couldn't resist. "Sure. I mean, at the risk of everybody getting pissed at me."

"Nobody's gonna get pissed," he assured me. "You want it *with*?"

I liked my hot dogs with mustard and sauerkraut but I didn't see any. Just a metal container full of chili.

What the hell, I thought. "Sure, with."

Geddes speared a hot dog, laid it in a bun, and dumped a mess of chili on it. Then he said, "Here," and held it out to me.

I hadn't had a chili dog in a long time, since before I met Jenny.

"What do you think?" Geddes asked.

It was better than I had expected.

"What's going on here?" asked Goetz, joining us.

"We're taste testing," Geddes told him.

Goetz looked at me. "And?"

159

I nodded. "Tasty."

Geddes laughed. "You're damned right it's tasty."

Goetz elbowed him in the ribs. "The chili's got a secret ingredient, you said. Tell him."

"Can't," said Geddes. "That's what makes it a secret."

"You've shared it with half the people in North Carolina, right? Tell the man, for gosh sakes."

Geddes looked around, as if concerned some enormous food conglomerate was spying on him, trying to get his recipe. Finally, he said in a voice I could barely hear, "Apple cider vinegar."

"Wow," I said, not wowed at all.

Geddes pointed a meaty finger at me. "That's between us now. You let it out and I'll have to kill you." For just a moment, I thought I saw a bloodthirsty glint in his eye.

I made myself laugh. "Got it."

"All right, then," said Geddes. He turned to Goetz. "Start sending 'em up. I'm ready."

I took my half-eaten chili dog back to where Saul and Carlos were sitting. "Looks like *someone* got a hot dog," Saul observed.

"I was the taste tester," I explained.

"Crap," said Carlos.

"I looked at him. "Crap?"

He nodded. "If you were the enemy, and you wanted to keep us from saving the world..." He looked around. "Keep *everybody* from saving the world..."

"My god," Saul gasped.

You'd poison them.

Carlos didn't say it. But then, he didn't have to.

I looked at Geddes. Was he looking back at me? I wasn't sure. He was grinning, though. Happy about *something*.

I eyed my hot dog, or what was left of it. Was Carlos right? Had Geddes poisoned it?

And it wasn't just the hot dog. The enemy... if they existed... could poison *anything*. Anything at *all*.

So what were we going to do? Stop eating? *Enough*, said a voice inside my head. *This is stupid.*

"Okay," I said, to show Saul and Carlos just *how* stupid, "so Geddes and Goetz and, I don't know, maybe the guys from Minnesota are going to kill us. That's what you're saying?"

Carlos sighed. "I don't *know*."

"The last time there was a get-together," I said, "did *their* dads kill *our* dads? Obviously not. Our dads came home. What's more, they told us about it so we could go to Binglaten when it was our turn. Would they have let us come up here if they thought we'd be in danger?"

Saul and Carlos looked at each other.

"Would they?" I repeated.

"No," Saul conceded.

"Unless," said Carlos, "this time is different. What if... what if whatever's going to happen doesn't happen every time? What if it only happens once... and *now* is that *once*?"

"Because the world can't end in every generation," said Saul. "It can only end when it ends."

I shook my head. I mean, I saw their point, but... "Why now? Why would the... I mean *anybody*... choose this time to put an end to everything? Is civilization so much worse these days than, say, during World War I? You know what people did to each other on those battlefields? Or during World War II? Concentration camps? Hiroshima and Nagasaki? We're no prize now when it comes to violence and greed and oppression. But we're not the low point either."

"Maybe," said Carlos, "it's not what we're doing. Maybe it's what we're *going* to do."

I didn't like where this was headed. Because as much as I hated to admit it, my knucklehead cousins had me thinking.

Maybe it *was* what we were going to do. We had the capability to destroy ourselves several times over. Hell, we'd had it for years. But we'd never used it.

What if, I asked myself, *someone somewhere is giving the order to use it now?*

"Hey," said Garrett, suddenly plunking himself down next to Saul, "what did I miss?"

*****

Garrett had been an athlete even before he became a guy, so we weren't surprised when he pounded the stuffing out of the softball.

His first time up, he drove the ball into the gap in right-center, bringing in two runs and winding up on third. His second time, he started a rally by slashing a single between short and third. And in his last at bat, with the score tied 12-12, he ended the game with a walk-off homer way over the left fielder's head.

161

On top of that, he made a great over-the-shoulder catch on a pop-up that had two-bagger written all over it. Clipboard Guy, who was Garrett's captain, couldn't stop talking about it.

"Did you see that catch?" he asked me.

"I saw it," I said.

He clapped Garrett on the shoulder. "This guy's legit."

Garrett looked at me, as if to say, *You tell him and I'll kill you.*

Like I was going to do that to my flesh and blood. Not even if the world *was* coming to an end. "Whatever you say."

It was only after Clipboard Guy walked away that Carlos and Saul took Garrett aside and told him about their suspicions.

"They wouldn't even have to know what they're doing," said Carlos. "They could be... whatchamacallit? Manchurian candidates."

"Manchurian...?" said Garrett.

"It was a movie," said Carlos. "A guy's an enemy agent and he doesn't know it. Then something goes off in him and he's a weapon."

Garrett looked at him. "You think Geddes's a weapon?"

"Dammit," said Carlos, "I'm just saying it's a *possibility*."

"Rain is a possibility," said Garrett. "Geddes being a Manchurian candidate..."

"I know," I said. "It sounds insane."

"Where did all this come from?" Garrett asked.

Carlos told him about his friend Duane.

"That's the guy you're going to listen to?" said Garrett. "The one with the cutoffs and the ratty beard?"

"It doesn't matter what he looks like," Carlos argued. "What matters is we're not the only ones wondering what's happening."

"And what if Duane's one of the enemy?" Garrett asked. "What if it's his job to feel us out—to see if we're onto them?"

Carlos looked at Saul and Saul looked at Carlos. Obviously, they hadn't thought of that.

"Hey!" somebody said.

I turned and saw the guy I'd played in tetherball.

"You going to play?" he asked.

"Play?" I echoed.

"There's a tetherball tournament at five. The winner gets announced at dinner. You should go."

I nodded. "Yeah."

"Who's *he*?" Garrett asked, as the guy walked away.

"I played him earlier," I said.

"And beat him," Saul added. "Hey, if you play in this tournament like you did before..."

I looked at him. "What?"

"Maybe we can make some money," said Saul.

"What happened to everyone being our enemy?" Garrett asked.

Saul frowned. "Oh yeah."

"I'm going to play," I decided.

"Sure," said Carlos, "why not? Give the enemy something to remember you by."

*****

There were three guys waiting for me when I got to the tetherball courts—the guy I'd played already and two others. They looked at me like the tall guy had told them I was good.

I was *feeling* good, too. Hardly sore at all from the games I'd played before lunch.

We decided to do double elimination. We would play until everybody except the winner had two losses.

The guy I drew first wasn't much of an athlete. Or maybe he'd just had one hot dog too many. I put him away in no time, then just volleyed with him until one of the other games was over.

My second opponent was the tall guy I'd played earlier, who had won his first game. But it seemed to have taken something out of him, because he wasn't as quick to the ball as before.

He had a couple of good hits, but nothing I couldn't handle. In the end, he went down without much of a fight.

The third guy I faced was in better shape. He fought from the get-go. Fought *hard*. For a while, he kept me from getting a rhythm going.

But I finally broke through. And when I did, I was golden. The guy didn't get another chance to touch the ball.

"You're good," he told me.

"You too," I said, just to be a good sport.

"I'm George," he said.

"Andy."

George nodded. "Really *good*."

Maybe Dad was right, I thought. Maybe in just this one small slice of life, I really *was* special.

*****

It wound up I had to play George again, this time for the championship.

163

Of course, it was double elimination, and I hadn't lost yet. So he would have to beat me twice to win.

I got a funny thought in my head. "Hey," I said, "how about if we say this one's for all the marbles?"

George looked at me. "You have no losses."

"Let's just say I do. So whoever wins this game wins everything."

He shrugged. "If that's what you want, sure. Makes it more interesting, I guess."

I thought so, too.

Not that it would matter. The way I was playing, I was going to come out ahead anyway.

And that's how it went down. At least in the beginning.

But as the match continued, I got tired. I didn't keep the ball as high as I had earlier. I didn't get there in time to make my blocks.

I was breathing hard. My arms were heavy. But I wasn't going to let that stop me.

The other guy's tired too, I told himself. *Who wants it more?* That was me.

As soon as I embraced that philosophy, I got better results. The ball wrapped itself around the pole once, twice. I had George on the run.

Then, as I was about to get another wrap on, I put my foot down funny—sideways, almost—and felt a pain in my ankle.

Crap, I thought.

George didn't seem to have noticed. He just smacked the ball over my head and started a rally of his own.

I took a couple of steps forward, attempted a block. But I couldn't put weight on my ankle. It hurt too much.

No! I thought. *This isn't fair! I was about to win!*

But what could I do—except stand there while George sent the ball soaring over my head, making wrap after wrap. Until finally it ran out of rope and bounced back.

"Hey," said George, grinning, "great game!" Looking surprised that he'd beaten me, he held his hand out.

I grasped it. "Yeah," I said, "great game."

Then I stood there in the shadow of the pole and watched George tromp off, flushed with victory.

It's all right, I thought. *It's just tetherball.*

It's just a *game*.

*****

At seven, everyone gathered at the picnic tables for dinner. The sun was dropping behind the trees and it was a perfect temperature, not too hot and not too cool.

This time, it wasn't burgers and hot dogs. It was chicken parmesan and spaghetti, and it came from the kitchen in the back of the cafeteria, where some of the guys had labored over the stoves.

Presumably as their fathers had a generation earlier. That was the way it seemed to work there—if your father had a particular role, so did you.

After everybody got their food, Goetz got up on a table to speak. "Before we get to the awards," he said, "I want to address the gorilla in the...well, it's not a room, exactly. In the camp, I guess. And by gorilla I mean *the enemy*."

That got my attention.

"Some of your dads," Goetz continued, "told you there was an enemy here in Binglaten. And there was a Beast at the head of them."

A murmur ran through the crowd.

"I, for one, never heard that from my dad. He just told me I was going to have a great time with a bunch of guys from all over the country. But this Beast thing...I don't want to sweep it under the rug. So let me say *this* about it."

With that, he turned away from his audience. And when he turned back to face us a moment later, he was *a Beast*—a hideous-looking ape-thing with long, flowing, golden locks.

I wanted to run. To get away. To get to a place where everything was normal, where there were no enemies and no Beasts and no need to save the world from anything.

But I only felt that way for half a second.

Because in the next half, I realized Goetz was wearing a rubber mask. Like it was Halloween. *Just a mask...*

All around me, guys started to laugh—some a little nervously at first, but then more guys and more, until the nervousness disappeared and we were swept up in a wave of fellowship and good cheer.

Even my cousins.

"Boogah boogah!" Goetz growled, reaching out with clawed hands toward the crowd.

Another wave of laughter.

At that point, he took the mask off and patted down his hair, which had gotten mussed. "There's your Beast," he said. "Okay? Now let's get on with the—"

"*He's* the Beast!" someone cried out.

Everybody looked around, trying to see who had interrupted Goetz.

Then we heard it again: "It's *him*! He's the Beast!"

There was a commotion in a corner of the crowd. Suddenly, it came closer to us, and I saw Carlos's friend Duane. He was making his way in the direction of me and my cousins, wading toward us despite the hands reaching for him.

Pointing at us.

"That one!" he bellowed.

Then I saw he wasn't pointing at *us*. He was pointing at *Garrett*. Just *Garrett*.

A moment later, Duane was surrounded by guys. At least some of them, I assumed, were his relatives.

But he'd sent a chill through the crowd. I looked at Garrett. He was squinting like he was in pain.

I put my arm around him. "Hey," I said, "shake it off. The guy's a nut."

"Fuck him," said Saul, putting his arm around Garrett too.

Carlos stood in front of us, guarding us in case Duane or someone else decided to go after Garrett. But that was the end of it.

"You all right?" I asked Garrett.

He tried to smile. "Sure," he said, his voice shaking a little. "As all right as a Beast can be."

Duane, meanwhile, was led out of the crowd and taken somewhere we couldn't see him anymore, presumably a place where he could calm down. Then Goetz said, "Sorry about that, folks. We said no liquor but there's always somebody who forgets."

More laughter. But not nearly as enthusiastic as before.

"All right, then," said Goetz. "About those awards..."

I didn't listen after that. I just watched Garrett's face. Fortunately, he seemed to loosen up after a while—especially when he went up to get his softball award, and got a big cheer for it.

But what had happened to Garrett wasn't the only thing bothering me... was it? I could still see that tetherball circling the pole, running out of rope, until there was no rope left and the ball swung back the other way.

It ate at me. Really *ate* at me.

It isn't fair, I thought.

Sure, it was just a game in a stupid tournament. But it meant something. It was a measure of redemption for some of the things I'd failed at in my life.

And, in a way, it wasn't just me I'd disappointed. It was my dad too. I mean, he was the one who'd said I was *special*.

*****

The night was long and dreamless. When my eyes opened, it was morning.

Sunday, I thought. A blessedly quiet Sunday morning. So early the birds hadn't woken up yet.

The stillness gave me some welcome perspective. I no longer felt the nagging pain of my tetherball loss, in my ankle or anywhere else. It was as if it had never even happened.

And the rest of what we had found in Binglaten...sure, it wasn't what we had expected when we drove up that road. But it wasn't anything ominous either.

The guys we had met... they weren't the enemy. They were just a bunch of middle-aged men, carrying on a generations-old tradition—though some of them clearly knew more about it than we did.

Duane, it seemed, was the only nut in the bunch. One of his brothers had come over on our way back to the bunk and apologized to Garrett, though he didn't know how deeply Duane's remark had cut, or why.

As I thought about it, I felt the urge to pee. I tossed aside my covers, swung my legs over, and got up. Then I went to the back of the bunk and used the toilet.

When I got back to my bed, I noticed something among the covers. Something shiny. I reached for it, picked it up.

It was the *yad*.

Odd, I thought. Hadn't I left it in the car? In the briefcase? What was it doing in my bed?

The thing felt warm in my hand, almost hot, as if it had been left out in the sun. *You must have slept on it*, I told myself. What else could have made it feel that way?

What else...?

My heart, I realized, had begun pounding in my chest. *Stop it*, I thought. But the pounding wouldn't stop. Something was off. *Wrong.*

I knew my cousins would be pissed if I woke them but I couldn't help it. What was inside me was too big for me to handle on my own.

"Garrett?" I said.

He was in the bed next to me. He didn't move.

"Garrett?" I said again, louder this time.

Still no answer.

Cursing to myself, I moved to his bed to shake him. But when I reached for him, I saw there was nothing beneath his covers.

What the hell, I thought.

"Saul!" I said, loudly enough for my voice to echo from wall to wall. "Carlos!"

I checked their beds too. Like Garrett's, they were empty. Suddenly, the stillness didn't seem so comforting anymore.

I ran out of the bunk, looked around. There were guys all over the place, lying on the ground like they were sleeping. But when I got closer to them, I saw they were dead.

Crushed to a pulp. *Every single one of them.*

My cousins, I thought. I had to find them, get them out of there. I had to keep them from getting killed too.

If they hadn't been already...

I ran from one place to the next, looking for them. From the softball field to the corn hole strip to the picnic area. But I couldn't find my cousins among the dead.

Then I came to the tetherball courts, and I saw. The shadows, long ones, stretched across the ground by the morning sun. The shadows of men hanging from the poles.

And I could tell which men they were. God help me, I could *tell*.

An awful groan forced its way out of me, and my legs folded like they were nothing, and I sank to the earth. Only then did I realize the yad was still in my hand, and it was glowing with a light of its own. *A terrible light.*

I knew then... there was a Beast, all right. But it wasn't Garrett, or any of the strangers we thought it could be.

"You monster!" I screamed, "You fucking monster!" And I kept screaming until my head felt like a flame, eating me alive from the top down.

Because the Beast of Binglaten... it was *me*.

Your Apocalypse Will Be Handled by the Next Available Representative

Wrenn Simms

The main line phone rang, cutting over, as usual, the rhythmic sound of a tennis ball hitting the opposite side of the closed inner office door. The office manager had come in early, and was "keeping busy."

A disheveled brown-haired man looked up from his coffee-stained sudoku puzzle. "I think this one's your turn."

"Okay, okay, I'll get it, Lenny."

"And remember, smile. They say *they* can hear you smile."

Baring her teeth, and checking the line number, the thin blonde woman settled herself in her chair and picked it up, "Thank you for calling Affiliated Insurance, my name is Mina, how may I direct your call?"

"Hello? Hello? I'm calling about my account? I received a refusal in the mail for my medical claim. I can't pay this, how am I supposed to pay this?"

Speaking rapidly, Mina replied, "May I apologize for your inconvenience. I want you to know that all inbound calls are recorded for deontological assurance. Can I have your account number please?"

"What? Deonta—deon... No, oh, okay. My account number is 555Z3666KAG6"

Rapidly tapping her pen on her desk, Mina closed her eyes, counting to ten, then to fifteen thuds of the ball hitting the wall.

"The account number you have provided is not accepted by our database. Can I ask for your first and last name, please?"

"Emmalina Ellerton."

"Can you give it to me again?"

"It's Ellerton, Emmalina Ellerton. I really need to get this handled. I have insurance with you and I was assured that these procedures would be covered!"

Tap tap tap went the pen.

"I'm sorry, your name for a third time, Spell it? I have to ask, for contractual reasons."

"E-l-l-e-r-t-o-n."

Mina placed her hands on her keyboard and her work screen lit up. "Thank you, please hold."

"That was smooth," Lenny said.

"Keep listening, you may learn something." Mina stared at the words and patterns crossing her screen.

Lenny shook his head, sniffed the air, and went back to his puzzle. "Warren should be in soon, go lecture him."

As if on cue, the outer door opened and a large man of indeterminate age hurried through. He was tall and wide, easily twice the size of his more punctual co-workers. Not that they'd dare try to tell him he was late. At the very least he always brought the snacks.

Shrugging off his over coat he tossed a box of pastries onto his rather messy desk.

"She's got a live one, Warren." Lenny said.

"Oh? For how long?"

"Not long. I only just put her on hold." Mina looked covetously over at the box on Warren's desk. "Are those fair game?"

"Only one, Mina, only one," Warren replied.

"You're no fun. You know how much I like them, especially the cheese ones."

"You always want everything."

The hold button beeped as Mina slowly ate her cheese danish.

The tennis ball hit the wall.

Mina sat back down at her desk, and activated her line, spinning her pen along the fingers of her right hand. "Thank you for holding, Ms. Hallerton."

"Ellerton! Ellerton! With an E!"

"Yes, of course. Again, thank you. I have your account up now. Our records show that the procedures you are undergoing are cosmetic, and therefore subject to review by our infernal audit."

"Internal audit? I was assured that this was a correct use of my plan!" The rest of the office could hear the caller through the phone.

"Yes, yes, it's all just a matter of procedure. Red tape, you see. Please hold."

"Wait wha—"

"What does her account show?" Warren asked.

"Personal. She's having some work done to make herself look younger." Tap tap tap. "Quite a bit of work done."

He smiled. "Nothing in the background to suggest it's repairing damage? Possibly domestic abuse?"

"No, you can't horn in on this one, Warren." Mina scrolled further on her desktop. "It's a personal decision. Nothing for you here."

"A man can but ask, Mina" he pushed the box towards her. "Here, have another danish."

Lenny snorted.

Mina touched her headset. "Okay, Ms. Ellerton, there are a few more forms that still need to be signed off on your end. I'm going to send a link to them on our encrypted server so that you can finish this."

"But I signed off on all of that paperwork weeks ago!"

"There's probably just a newer version of the form. Bear with us, and please check your email. I will put you on hold for a few minutes." Tapping her headset again, Mina swiped another pastry from the box.

Warren gestured to the inner door. "Has he come out at all?"

Lenny looked up, "Nope. He got in before me. I only know he's there because..." Thump. "That."

"He was quite upset last week, about one of mine. Car insurance claim—a road-rage incident. He wouldn't talk to me about it, but he must have resolved it. At any rate, they never called back and they're no longer showing on my caseload."

"Ms. Ellerton, have you—" Mina started.

"I signed all these weeks ago! Why are you doing this to me? Get me your supervisor right now!"

"Ms. Ellerton, are you sure you wish to speak with my manager?" Mina asked slowly.

"Yes! You are useless! I want your manager! I need this resolved today!" The whole office could hear her.

"Okay. Thank you." Mina transferred the call.

The tennis ball stopped hitting the wall, and they heard their manager pick up the phone.

The main line began to ring again. Lenny looked up and sniffed. "Medical Insurance. Gastro-intestinal." He smiled happily. "Mine!" and he reached for the phone.

*****

In the inner office, Todd looked down at the phone he'd just picked up. A dial tone — *again.*

Every day that's all it was, more pranks from his office mates. Once he'd thought he got a heavy breather. Sometimes it was only silence.

When he'd asked them, they'd always insist they transferred a call and they were just doing their jobs.

This was abuse. He should call HR. Maybe even quit this place, finally, for good.

HHH 666

Jenifer Purcell Rosenberg

Life rarely takes you where you expect to go. Sometimes, there are happy accidents and good luck. Sometimes, there is tragedy and despair. Usually, there's a mix of both, with a few big surprises thrown in for good measure.

My partner Nico and I lost our California home in the recent wildfires, and stuffed what little we had left into a rented minivan, moving cross-country to New York with our two kids, three cats, and elderly basset hound. It was a huge move, but we have a place to live here. Nico grew up in Queens, and their great-aunt Carmen owns a house near a highly rated public school. Carmen moved to Florida to avoid any more New York winters, and was more than happy to let us live in the house rent-free, so long as we paid utilities. Nico's company had a New York office, so they're working full-time in Manhattan, but since housing is covered, we decided I should stay home with the kids, and be the point-person for all things school-related.

It took me a while to figure out the streets in Queens. There seems to be three of every numbered street, and named streets randomly change their names past half-forgotten old boundaries. I have learned that this is because it was once a bunch of little villages that eventually grew together into something bigger. That didn't keep me from getting lost, though. It took several loops around Queens Boulevard, which I found out locals call "the Boulevard of Death," before I was finally able to take the kids everywhere we needed to go ahead of the first day of school—doctor's appointments, dental visits, school supply shopping, and getting real winter clothing since their California wardrobes weren't up to handling wintertime. The kids were all set, but I was just beginning.

At the start of a new school year, everyone thinks of the kids as nervous and afraid, but we all know it's actually the parents who are gripped with anxiety. Children are more fluid, and can usually adapt to the new teachers and different classmates pretty smoothly. Parents have to worry about which class the child will be placed in, how the teacher will handle the job, and whether they are compatible with the other parents with a kid in that class. For me, this new school year also meant a brand-new school for my kids in a brand-new neighborhood. As part of our new start, I had been planning to get involved and volunteer.

I don't know what I was expecting when I walked into the school open house the week before school started. I guess I figured I would find out information, get a better feel for the school layout, and possibly find some kindred spirits. When I walked through the door, a short, gruff woman was standing just inside the entrance with a clipboard. "Sign in!" she barked. I did, and then followed red arrows on the floor made from tape to the auditorium. When I entered, it felt like everyone in the room turned to stare at me. I could have sworn I heard the word "gay" whispered as I passed. I chose to ignore it and forge on. There are busybodies everywhere, I figured. There are usually a few homophobes as well.

I took a seat in an old, creaky flip-down chair, remembering some of my larger courses in college where generations of names, swear words, and crushes had been scratched into the uncomfortable seats. I noticed a small cluster of people in front of the stage having a whispered conversation, and thought I recognized Principal Fitzherbert, whom I hadn't met, but had seen on the school's clunky old website. He was an imposing figure, over six feet tall, and built like someone who had probably played football when younger. He glanced over at me, giving me a quizzical look, and I waved meekly and looked away. I pretended not to notice that the little cluster up front started laughing immediately after this.

Just as I was wondering if I was sitting in a reserved section of the auditorium, two cheerful looking women sidled into the row where I was sitting and sat beside me. The first, a beautiful African-American woman with a megawatt smile, introduced herself. "Hi! I hear you're new to the neighborhood! My name is Berniece, and this is Hana." Hana, an Asian-American with burgundy highlights in her short pixie cut, nodded hello.

"Hi! I'm Lil," I replied with more confidence than I felt. "My family recently moved here from California." Though they smiled warmly and welcomed me, I could tell that they already knew where we'd moved from. Schools foster rampant rumor mills, even among the parents. Perhaps especially among the parents.

A soul-jarring high-pitched screech caused all chatter in the cavernous room to cease. People scrambled to their seats, many of them covering their ears as the microphone continued to deliver piercing feedback. Principal Fitzherbert took the mic, and gave an insincere, tepid smile as he welcomed everyone to the meeting.

Berniece leaned toward me and said under her breath "This guy doesn't want to be here."

I smiled, glad to know that others were thinking the same thing I was. Fitzherbert looked directly at us and paused, and I had the visceral reaction of a little kid that had gotten caught misbehaving. I guess that's why he had a reputation as a disciplinarian. I began to worry a little.

After droning on about attendance policies, school lunch forms, and immunization requirements, Principal Fitzherbert introduced the president of the PTA, Heidi VanSchlecht. When she stepped forward, I recognized her as one of the women from the cluster that had been talking to the principal. She was tall and unnatural looking. Bottle blonde, liquid tan, capped teeth, and a lot of obvious nips and tucks in the usual places, plus exaggerated collagen-plumped lips. I'd seen this sort of self-reconfiguring pretty often in California, but I hadn't expected it here. I also didn't expect her to have a voice that sounded like her diet was comprised of whiskey and cigars, but as much as she looked California, her thick Brooklyn accent and smoky shouted speech gave her away as all New York. She made the standard opening comments, and then she introduced the rest of the PTA.

Three of the women she introduced were also from the cluster that had been at front earlier. The first vice president, Irene Flanagan, was extremely petite, no more than five feet tall, and possibly ninety-odd pounds, if that. She looked gaunt and hollow, and had used a little too much highlighter to cover the circles around her slightly sunken eyes. She gave a weak wave, and then pulled her oversized cardigan tightly around herself as if the building were freezing. The second, Joan Winterbottom, a cheerful looking, curvy woman with hair pulled back in a slick braid that looked like it might still be wet, waved enthusiastically and shouted "yo!" when introduced. The treasurer wore a red power suit and had black hair so shiny and perfect that I wondered if she had gone to the salon before coming here. Her eyes were a disturbingly light shade of blue, and piercing like a hawks, and her complexion was practically translucent it was so pale. She didn't wave, but gave a curt nod. Her name was Karen Crankshaw, and I tried not to chuckle about the fact that her name seemed fitting.

The last PTA board member that was introduced took me a second to spot. The recording secretary, Maria Navarre, wasn't sitting with the rest of the group in the front row, but was off to the side. She was wearing jeans and a pullover boucle sweater, and her curly black hair was pulled into a loose twist at the back of her neck. She gave a shy wave, and the parents who were sitting near her all smiled. I hadn't noticed a lot of smiling with the other four. This was clearly the person on the PTA most parents could relate to. Unfortunately, it's not too uncommon for people with a lot of influence to get into positions of power without being very likeable. Especially if they have a lot of money, which it was clear that at least the president and treasurer did. I made a mental note to introduce myself to the recording secretary after the meeting.

The PTA President was moving on with her speech. "As you all know, Annie McKinney's son graduated to middle school last year, so she is no longer with us. The H. H. Holmes Elementary School PTA is looking for a new corresponding secretary. You've got to be able to use a computer, but if you know how it should be pretty easy." Her frightfully light eyes met mine, and I felt like she was staring directly into my soul. "Anyone interested is welcome to apply. Now! Let's talk about upcoming events! Picture day is just six weeks away, and the cheapest package starts at $50, so if you're low income, start saving now!"

There was a murmur throughout the assembly, with people either balking that she had said something so insensitive, or groaning about how she was at it again. She was interrupted by Joan Winterbottom, the second vice president, who had scurried over and grabbed the mic, much to the chagrin of VanSchlecht.

"We need to talk about lice," she pleaded, "it's serious!" I noticed grumbling and exaggerated eyerolls throughout the audience. "Last year, over two hundred kids in this school were sent home with lice after picture day. You *have* to send clean kids to school with their own combs and brushes. The PTA isn't going to supply a comb to every kid this year, since they share them anyway, and then I get blamed when your kids come home with lice!" She gestured wildly at the room, thrust the microphone back at VanSchlecht, and scurried back to her seat with cheeks the color of a ripe tomato. The crowd erupted into chaos, as people began to discuss picture day and lice breakouts. Several people simply got up and left the meeting early.

I glanced over at Hana and Berniece, and they were both looking at me "Insane, right?" said Berniece.

"It's why they have a hard time filling the secretary positions," Hana chimed in.

It was pretty clear that this was exactly what I needed to do.

I stuck it out for the remainder of the meeting, learning that the suggested donation to be a PTA member was $20 per family with one child, and an additional $10 for each additional child in the family. There would apparently be two book sales, a pumpkin patch, a "Christmas Extravaganza" sale, the "Valentine" fundraiser, a BINGO night, Father-Daughter dance, Mother-Son sports day, and a special graduation event run by the PTA this year.

At one point, I glanced at my two companions and said, "This isn't very inclusive for marginalized or non-traditional families, is it?"

They both said *"Nope!"* in unison.

Before the meeting concluded, it was announced that there were free cupcakes available out in the hall. At least fifty people bolted toward the door, shoving past others to get to the front of the cupcake line. Somewhere, a grown man yelled, "Quit cutting in line!" and another man shouted back, "Make me!"

Where exactly did we move to? I wondered.

As I made my way to the line that was slowly inching out of the auditorium, I exchanged contact information with Hana and Berniece. We also talked about our kids, and it sounded like Hana's son was going to be in the same second-grade class as Dakota, my youngest. My daughter Aspen would be in Mr. Drake's fourth-grade class with Berniece's daughter. Since parent friendships are formed around their kids, I was very happy to know our kids would be together in class. Enrollment is over 2500 kids for the school, and there are roughly seven classes per grade, so I considered myself lucky!

Suddenly, as we rounded the corner toward the cupcake table, I noticed that the crowd was parting in a straight line that ended at... me. A short woman who looked to be in her mid-fifties was barreling toward me with a look of determination on her face.

I recognized her from when we came to enroll the kids. Sheila Hogwood, the Parent Coordinator. I paused and looked around as everyone pulled away from me except Hana and Berniece.

"Missus Brightwell!" Her voice had clearly been honed on the playground at lunchtime, and was far too loud for indoor use. The room went silent. It felt like the entire borough of Queens was staring at me as the intense woman approached me. "Heidi sent me over to see if you'd be willing to join the PTA!"

To the astonishment of everyone present, I said, "Oh, absolutely! I'd love to!"

Ms. Hogwood slapped me on the back and literally guffawed. "That's great! Come meet the officers!"

I waved to my new friends as I was carted off to meet the grown-up versions of the kind of kids who had bullied me throughout my school days. What was I doing?

*****

Fast-forward to mid-October, just a few days before picture day. I was sitting in the PTA office—an old, cramped room that had once been a second-floor teacher's lounge, until the school decided teachers only needed one lounge per building. The paint was peeling, the windows were stuck shut, and we were at the end of a small passageway that contained the teacher's bathrooms. One of the courtesies our PTA extended to the teachers was to supply both bathrooms with toilet paper, soap, and air fresheners, since the school district cut the budget for teacher supplies. I was grateful for that faux apple cinnamon scent right now, though, because it had been "tostada" day down in the cafeteria, and that was never a good day to be near the bathrooms.

My job was to email all of the parents who had not yet turned in their picture forms. Karen Crankshaw, the treasurer, was calling people who had turned in a form but had forgotten to attach their payments. Heidi was shouting down the phone at the photographer, who was in a dispute with the parent coordinator over how many free packages would be offered for disadvantaged kids.

This, I had come to discover, was just a normal day in the PS 666 PTA. I had also learned some startling things about the other PTA officers.

Heidi was a widow. Not just your usual kind of widow, though. She had been married and widowed four times, and had beaucoup bucks and six step-kids as a result.

Irene Flanagan was separated from her spouse, to whom she only ever referred to as the "errant spouse," so I knew nothing more about that, although I did know that she was adamantly against anything fun for the kids and had canceled the candy fundraiser without telling the rest of the officers she had done so. We had to meet with the principal and explain why we couldn't provide the usual donation for the holiday season after that.

Joan was married, and constantly at odds with Irene because where the latter was against plying people with food, Joan was always the first to bake cookies and cupcakes for the teachers, staff, and students.

Karen Crankshaw was divorced, and still very angry about it. She was also angry about how diverse the neighborhood had become. "When I went here, they called it Lilywhite 666!" she liked to repeat as if that were a good thing.

But I did like Maria Navarre. She was happily married, but her husband was deployed overseas. She made things work for her family, and was a warm, caring person overall.

I hit send on another batch of emails (I was sending them by class, going through the master list for the school that contained kids' names, parents, and parent contact info), when I realized Joan was watching me. "What's up, Joan?" I asked.

"*Lice!*" she snapped. I jumped backward and looked frantically at my sweater, wildly searching to see if I had any unwanted critters on me. "Not *you*! The students!" When I was still not sure what she was talking about, she sighed and rolled her eyes before starting over. "There's been a lice breakout in the Pre-K through first-grade classes. All of the new wing has to be fumigated. They're sending the kids home with notes today that they can't come in tomorrow. We have to push back picture day." As I absorbed this new information, I watched as the inbox on the PTA email began to fill up with messages titled "Lice?!" or "Is this true?" or "I want a refund!" Excellent. Not!

Heidi was now yelling "You have to come next week instead!" at the photographer, and Karen answered her cellphone by bellowing "If this is about a refund, you can forget it!"

I glanced back at Joan, and she was holding an honest-to-goodness handkerchief against her nose and mouth. She was shaking, and tears were pouring down her face. I would have thought she was crying, given all of the hard work we had been putting in to doing the picture day. Karen had even taken off from work to be here this week. But somehow, I really felt like Joan was laughing. When Karen screamed that she was going to kill Irene for canceling the candy sale and throwing off the budget, Joan actually snorted.

That was when the fire alarm went off. We usually were warned in advance when a fire drill was going to happen, and this wasn't on the schedule. Yes, there were surprise fire drills a couple times a year as well, but even if it was just a drill, we would get in big trouble if we stayed in the building. I clicked to power down the computer, grabbed my purse, and walked to the nearest exit. When I looked back, the others had gone down to the far end of the hall and were exiting there. As squeals of excitement approached, I realized the I had gone to the exit for the lice wing. I scurried out of the door before the kids rounded the corner, and darted across the street. Heidi and Karen were getting into a white luxury car with a disability badge hanging from the rearview mirror. Joan seemed to be having a heated argument with Principal Fitzherbert and the parent coordinator. I decided to walk around to the front of the school building and pretend like I hadn't been here.

That night, as Nico and I were washing the dishes and discussing our days, Aspen and Dakota came in. "Mummy and Nini? Is it true that the PTA gave the little kids lice?" asked our eldest.

I wiped my hands off and had a seat at the breakfast table, and Nico followed. "Where did you hear that," I inquired.

"Sally Myers says that Jimmy Winterbottom's Mom is the reason there's lice at school. She says it happens every year."

I thought about the weird behavior Joan had been exhibiting earlier, but I couldn't wrap my head around the idea of anyone actively causing a lice outbreak. That said, we'd already had one of the PTA board members sabotage the candy sale, so maybe there was a reason that people thought the PTA was up to no good. I reassured the kids, though. "It would be very silly of someone's parent to go around putting bugs in people's hair, my loves." Both kids laughed and went back into the family room to play Go Fish. Nico and I made a pot of tea and carried our cups out with us to join them.

Perhaps ten minutes later, Nico's phone started ringing. We all recognized the ringtone. It was the one they had set for when the school's automated phone bank contacted us. I'd distinctly put my own name and number on the form for both kids, but somehow, the school had managed to program Nico's phone number for both. Whenever there was an emergency, or schools were closed, or an event was coming up, Nico would get two calls. They pushed the speaker button so we could all listen to the tinny automated voice on the line. "Attention PS 666 families. This is your. Parent. Co-ordina-tor Ms. Hogwood. Calling to inform You! That un-fortunat-ely, the school will be closed for the remainder of this week as we ad-dress a minor safety concern. Parents who are worried that their child might have lice can come to the schoolyard between six a.m. and Noon to-mor-row. Picture day will happen Next Thursday instead and will not affect Friday's Halloween acti-vi-ties. Have a nice. Day."

I didn't even have enough time to ask what on Earth was happening before my own cell phone started to chime. I noticed it was Karen calling, and I answered on the third ring. "Lil? Karen. Frickin' Joan and Irene went and opened us up for a lawsuit! I need you in the schoolyard at five tomorrow morning to learn how to delouse kids!" I wonder if she could feel my shock and disgust from home, because she shifted into a lower gear. "Right. Not our fault. Can you come?"

I took a deep breath, and weighed my options, deciding that helping families was the whole reason I joined the PTA. "I'll see you then," I said.

I hate getting up early. Nico is one of those people who can jump out of bed at six a.m. and be full of energy and enthusiasm. I am one of those people who doesn't fully fall asleep until about three in the morning. I decided it would end up being more painful to fall asleep and then wake up at four in the morning than to just stay up all night. I ended up doing a bunch of online searches for how to avoid getting lice, and in the course, I found a blog written by someone claiming to be a PS 666 parent. It seemed that, for the past four years, there has been a lice outbreak in October. It usually happened immediately following picture day, and the blogger directly named Joan as the source.

Wow, people can get pretty nasty when they are upset. Granted, I would be very upset if my kids came home with lice. We checked their hair thoroughly before giving them a bath with tea tree soap, changed all of their bedding, and washed all of the stripped bedding on hot. I definitely didn't want any creepy crawlies in our home!

With a fresh vanilla spice latte in my hand, my hair pulled up under a knitted cap, and a box of non-latex gloves, I showed up at the schoolyard just before five a.m. Karen was waiting near the soccer goal, and click-clacked her way across the blacktop toward me.

I had yet to see her not wearing some sort of red power suit with heels. I had worn washable sneakers with tall socks pulled up over a double layer of leggings, and a turtleneck sweater. I didn't want anything to touch me. Karen ushered me in to the school building.

"I thought we weren't allowed in the building," I said. Karen shrugged, and nodded toward the end of the hall, where I thought I saw Heidi slipping into the boiler room with one of the custodians.

"Ms. VanSchlecht has this handled. Parents won't be showing up for at least another hour so we should at least be able to keep warm."

I wasn't sure I felt comfortable being in here, but I also didn't want to freeze my tush off in the predawn darkness.

Instead of going all the way around to another wing to reach the PTA office, Karen and I went to the teacher's lounge. It was a wide room with a small kitchenette on one side, several large industrial tables with stackable chairs in the middle, and a couple of booths with small tables along the side that looked like they had been donated by an old 1950s diner. Joan and Irene were sitting in separate booths, ignoring each other. Maria was at one of the big tables along with a handful of parent volunteers, including Berniece and Hana. I went to sit with them, especially since Karen had spotted Irene and was making a beeline for her. Everyone in the room drew a deep breath and waited. I had learned that Karen had a very short fuse, and would jump at the prospect of an argument. Teachers here gave Karen's kid special treatment because they knew they would be sued if they didn't. Now she was seeing red, and everyone watched in rapt anticipation as she closed in on the first VP.

Before she could say anything, though, Heidi stuck her head in the door and motioned in their direction. "Hey, Irene! The delivery is here, can you go grab it?" Irene glanced at the steaming angry woman standing over her, back to Heidi, and then nodded and got up. Karen's heels clacked on the tile as she followed.

It was customary for the PTA to provide food for any situation where there were volunteers. Irene usually argued with this idea, saying that we were choosing what others would be eating, and that we should let people deal with their own food on their own time. When that argument had happened in September, Karen had ended up screaming until she was blue in the face about how we would get sued if someone fainted while working their ass off for the PTA. Joan had offered to make food to bring in whenever we had an event, and Irene had become so upset she got twitchy.

So, it was now her job to bring in all of the food that was ordered, a somewhat vindictive measure put forth by Karen. Now, as Irene came back into the teacher's lounge with three big boxes of donuts, she tripped and fell, managing to tip all of the boxes open. The donuts hit the floor in what seemed like slow-motion. I knew that we were going to be given some sort of high-calorie, high-fat, high-sugar food for volunteering, and had skipped breakfast in anticipation of the sugar rush. Bad plan.

Amid the groans of everyone who was watching their breakfast bounce onto the floor, I realized there was a high-pitched screech going on as well. Karen had picked up one of the stacking chairs and was swinging it over her head, bringing it down in an arc onto Irene.

"You dropped the donuts, Irene! You are so gonna pay for this!" Splayed on the floor where she had fallen, Irene began picking up donuts and lobbing them at Karen's face. The more frosting and sprinkles Karen gained on her face and her power suit, the more it seemed like she was glowing with rage, and the more she swung the chair. I noticed that Joan had calmly stood up and started walking toward them. I thought she was going to break up the fight, but she just silently bent down and picked up a Boston crème from the floor, looked at it, shrugged, and took a bite. Maria was dialing 911 and ushering the volunteers out of the room. I wanted to join them, but I felt rooted in place, like the way it is when you have a bad dream and can't escape from the monster.

That was when I realized Heidi was still in the room, and she was staring at me. Something about her intensity made me feel a fight or flight reaction, and I was finally able to move. Heidi started ed marching toward Irene, who had run out of donuts to throw and was feebly holding off Karen's attacks with another stackable chair. When Heidi spoke, she sounded calm and collected, but the force of her words cut through every other sound in the room. "They have contacted the authorities. You can fight, or you can run. Decide now."

I decided to run, rushing out of the room with Joan close on my heels. I was grateful that the teacher's lounge was right next to the fire exit that emptied onto the street near my house. I burst through the door and just kept running until I was home.

I didn't look back when I heard the sirens approaching, and I kept on going as the very air seemed to shake when the school exploded. I ran into my house, hugged my startled kids tight, and pulled everyone into the basement to be safe.

It was at least twelve hours before the sounds of sirens and news helicopters slowed down. We had watched the news on Nico's laptop while hiding out in the basement. Early reports said that nobody had been hurt, but they later realized that the custodian had been in the boiler room when the school blew, though that was not the source of the explosion. They were blaming a gas line to the stove in the teacher's lounge. They had no witnesses, because all of the volunteers had gotten out ahead of time, and there was no trace of Heidi, Irene, Joan, or Karen. By no trace, I mean nothing at all. Nobody could find their families or their cars, their houses stood completely empty, and there was no forwarding information or next of kin listed anywhere. When asked if they had any contact information forms at home for the women's children, their teachers were surprised to discover they didn't even have homework or an entry in their gradebooks for the kids.

It was as if those four and their kids had never existed, except within the community at PS 666. But that couldn't be right. People eventually chalked it up as a weird fluke and tried not to think about it anymore.

Life moved on. The city put a rush on finding a new building in the area. In the fall, when they dedicated the new school, we had a brand new PTA. Maria Navarre was elected president, Berniece was the VP, Hana was the treasurer, and I was the secretary. We do good things.

Horseman, Horseman, Horseman, & Horseman, Attorneys-at-Law

Michael A. Ventrella

"I am Lucifer, the Prince of Darkness! Satan, Beelzebub, Mephistopheles, Al-Shaytan! My names are many, my deeds are known! All fear in my presence!"

"And do you have an appointment?"

The devil stared down at the bored receptionist—an elderly lady with a permanent sneer and glasses that were way too large for her angular face, who was tapping at the desk with trimmed but polished nails.

"An *appointment*?"

"They're very busy, sir. If you take a seat, I'm sure one will see you eventually."

Lucifer's fists clenched. It was bad enough that he found himself in a decadent lawyers' office taking up the top floor of a skyscraper, but to be treated like this! He knew he should have taken on his original form rather than this human disguise. "They *will* see me," he shouted. "They've been waiting for me!"

"Yes," the receptionist mumbled, as she scrolled through Facebook, "for three thousand years now."

Lucifer stormed past her, pushed through the double mahogany doors, and slammed them behind. Bright sunlight beamed through the massive windows, drenching the shelves of law books like they were illuminated manuscripts. Outside, the Statue of Liberty stood over the harbor below, as if holding her light for those in the office to appreciate. Abstract artwork which appeared to be nothing more than aimless paint splotches on canvas decorated the spaces between bookshelves. A long, highly polished table piled with envelopes, papers, and manila files sat in the center of the room, surrounded by a dozen leather-covered chairs.

And sitting at the end of the table, laptop before him, surrounded by papers and electronic devices, was a pale-looking man with sunken cheeks, dressed in a dark green suit. He raised his eyebrow at the intrusion, then stood.

"Lucy?" he said. "Is that you?"

"It's Lucifer, goddammit!" The devil stepped forward until he was inches from the man's nose, which did not appear to bother the fellow in the slightest. "And who the hell are you?"

The man smiled and motioned for Lucifer to take a seat while sitting back down himself. He closed his laptop so as not to block his view. "We haven't seen you in a very long time," he said. "What brings you here?"

The devil pulled out a chair and plopped into it. It was comfortable, he had to admit. "You haven't answered my question. You know who I am, but I don't recognize you at all."

"I'm called Jeff," the fellow replied. "Jeff Horseman. One of the four founders of this firm." He pressed a button on a small device. "Brenda, can you send in the others?"

"Copy," was the reply.

The devil fumed. He dealt with lawyers constantly—there are plenty of those in hell, after all—and had never found it pleasant. The best ones were rarely scared of anything. He noted the man's expensive green suit and then squinted at him.

"Wait a second," he said. "I know who you are. You're Death."

"I prefer 'Jeff,'" Death said. "It avoids a lot of unwelcome questions. But I'm surprised to see you. Are the seals being opened? I didn't get a memo. You'd think they'd let me know. For that matter, I had pretty much given up on them ever being opened." He paused and took a sip of coffee from a mug that said, *Lawyers do it in their briefs.* "So what exactly are you doing here?"

"Have you forgotten already?" Lucifer bellowed. "It is my job to organize you idiots. You four have to go riding through the world, bringing Armageddon."

Death frowned. "That's not how I understand it."

Before Lucifer could respond, another door opened and a tall man with chiseled features entered, dressed in an immaculate white suit. He had a trimmed mustache and slicked back hair, looking everything like a stereotypical southern preacher from the 1930s. The man paused upon seeing the unexpected guest.

"My word," he said. "Is that—"

"Yes, it is," Lucifer yelled, while waving the man in. "You must be Pestilence. I can tell by the white suit. You guys aren't very imaginative, are you? Get the hell in here. We have work to do."

"Lance, please," the man said, taking a seat opposite. "I prefer to be called 'Lance.'"

"Do I look like the kind of being that cares?" Lucifer reached into a pocket, pulled out a small flask, and took a long swig, while noticing from the corner of his eye how the two attorneys glanced at each other with a look that said they had not anticipated this. "So let's get to business. What the hell are you doing in a law firm? Where are the fucking horses?"

Jeff smiled. "It's been a long time. We waited and waited to be called, and it never happened. So we took matters into our own hands."

"You did *what?*"

Lucifer didn't get a chance to ask much more, as the remaining two lawyers slammed open the door. Leading them was a powerful man with bulging muscles hidden by a red suit, beaming a huge smile. Behind him, a frail woman dressed in black crossed her arms and stared through tinted glasses that only partially hid the dark make-up around her eyes.

"Lucy, it's been so long!" the man said, extending a powerful hand. "I'm Warren. Warren Horseman."

"I know who you are!" Lucifer waved him away without shaking his hand. "And don't call me 'Lucy'!"

"And this is Famina," War said, ignoring the insult. He held out a chair for her and she slouched into it, avoiding all eye contact.

"Wait a minute," Lucifer said, glaring at the woman. "You're supposed to be horsemen. *Men!* That's the deal!"

"Don't you go repressing me," Famine said. "I don't need your antiquated views on my identity."

"Yeah, Lucy, get with it," War said as he grabbed a seat while reaching for a bowl of M&Ms. "We're not living in the stone age any more. Jesus, you sound like a fundamentalist."

Lucifer found himself counting to ten slowly. He got it, he really did. They wanted something from him. That's what all lawyers were like. He just had to figure out what. "Fine," he said. "Tell me what's going on. Tell me what you want."

"Want?" said Death. "Oh no, dear sir. You're our client today. It's all about what you want. Assuming you can afford our retainer."

"*Client?*" Lucifer bellowed.

"Allow me to explain," Pestilence said, hand up in protest. "Although we're supposed to ride out to proclaim the apocalypse, according to Ezekiel's prophecy, it doesn't say what we're supposed to do in the meantime. So for many years, we just sat around, waiting."

"It was soooo boring," Famine said, looking at her phone.

War popped another M&M into his mouth. "We'd get excited every once in a while when some cleric would pronounce that the End Times were coming. There was a big one in 666, and then some other deluded idiot would say it again a generation later, and so on and so on—but of course, it never happened."

Pestilence grinned. "Those Jehovah's Witnesses had a lot of End Times predicted, but now they've just given up and say 'soon.'"

"So we took things into our own hands," Death said. "Planting ideas in leaders' heads made Warren's job easier. Lance just had to convince people not to wash, and disease and plagues ran through the lands. Famina didn't have a problem encouraging farmers to ruin their own lands for a short-term profit, and otherwise did her best to make sure food didn't get to the people who needed it most."

"Losers," Famine mumbled.

"But then, around a few hundred years ago, we discovered something," War said. "Doing all these things was much easier as lawyers."

Lucifer turned slowly to face him.

"No, seriously. Our firm represents some of the most powerful arms manufacturers in the world. I help broker deals all over the place for these people. Weapons get into the hands of rebels and terrorists, and then the governments need weapons to protect themselves, and it grows and grows. We've hardly gone a year on this planet when there wasn't a war someplace."

"Not only that," Death said, "we provide lobbying service on K Street in Washington. The NRA is one of our clients, as are many foreign leaders who pay handsomely to remain anonymous. We've used our legal skills to promote the idea that problems should be solved with violence. It's been quite successful."

"And profitable!" added Pestilence.

Lucifer slammed his fist onto the table. "But that's not your job!"

Pestilence held his hands before him. "Sure it is. We're supposed to bring these things for the apocalypse. We just... started a little early. Look at me—I've worked to fight against science, challenging requirements that all children have to be vaccinated. That's been tremendously successful for us, if not the parents. I've fought laws requiring the wearing of masks during pandemics, arguing that it's a violation of our freedoms, and you should see the results! Even when we lose lawsuits, we're spreading the misinformation and millions are dying every year."

"And not only is this much easier now that we're lawyers," War said, leaning back in his chair, "it's also a lot more fun."

"And rewarding," added Pestilence. "You should see my vacation home in the Bermudas."

Lucifer literally began turning red as he jumped from his seat. "Enough of this nonsense! You must go out there and announce Armageddon! It's your duty! I order you to do it!"

"Don't be silly, old man," Death said. "You can't order us. You're not our boss."

"I most certainly am! It's there in the prophecy!"

Death held up a finger, stood, went to the bookshelves, and pulled down a large tome that was clearly the Bible. Placing it on the table, he opened it to a specific bookmark. After a few seconds of reading to himself, he announced, "It doesn't say that here."

"It does in the original version!" Lucifer shouted. "Have you not read the Gnostic Bible?"

Death snorted. "Fan fiction."

Lucifer ignored him. "Look—it *was* in the original version! That damn book has been translated so many times, you can't trust what it says."

"Well, yes, but this is the current official version," Death said in a steady voice, finger on the Bible before him. "The amended version, so to speak. We obey the official versions, not early drafts. We don't owe you anything, according to this."

"*What?*" Lucifer steamed.

Death pursed his lips, his eyes on the Bible. "Indeed, as I read Revelation 6, it describes us as appearing when the Lamb breaks the seals, but that's it."

"There are no legal obligations placed on us other than to appear," War added. "There've been plenty of stories about us riding across the lands, spreading this and that, but those are not within the Bible itself. They are, in essence, dicta."

Death nodded his agreement. "We're here. Here we are. We've already done what is legally required of us."

Lucifer took three steps toward Death, who remained calm. He pointed a finger at Death's nose. "Are you telling me you plan to get out of your duties through a *loophole*?!"

"The absence of any mention of a requirement of performance on our end makes our obligations under this contract very specific and limited," Death replied. "Further, since there is no offer and acceptance, and no consideration from the promiser, I argue that the entire agreement is null and void."

"It's not a contract!" Lucifer screamed, even louder than before. "It's a bloody prophecy! It's your duty!"

"Do you have a proposed Motion with a Rule Returnable?" Pestilence asked. "If so, please leave that with the receptionist, and we will get to work immediately on our Answer, along with the filing of a New Matter calling for an injunction against your request for strict performance."

"This is ridiculous!" The Lord of Darkness began pacing. "I am more powerful than you, and I can force you to do the job I require."

"I'm afraid not, Lucy," replied Death, who did nothing to hide his smirk. "You see, while you've been gone, we've built ourselves up quite a bit. We have many powerful people on our side in high places." He glanced upwards to make his point. "Oh, they don't agree with everything we're doing, of course, but they hate you more than they hate us. We've incorporated, you see, and I'm afraid you have been removed as CEO by a majority vote of the stockholders. In other words," he said, spreading his arm to take in the room, "you have no power here."

Lucifer's true appearance ripped forward and a blast of heat filled the room instantly. He screamed an unholy cry, shook his fists at the ceiling, and disappeared, leaving behind an ungodly sulfur smell.

Lance reached into a cabinet, pulled out a bottle of Febreze, and started spraying the room.

"Thought he'd never leave," said Famina. "Now, let's discuss the lawsuit against the GMO manufacturers..."

The Four Squirrels of the Apocalypse

Gerard Houarner

No one expects the Apocalypse to knock on the door and announce its arrival. But Joshua had to admit, there'd been signs. Perhaps even portents. Sadly, he still never picked them up.

But then, the end of the world is everywhere. All the time. It streams non-stop, night and day, by electronic media and among friends, family, and colleagues.

Earthquakes, storms, wars, ecological mayhem, political chaos, the imminent coming of this spiritual deity or that asteroid, the outbreak of another plague or war, they roll out like the latest Mercedes model, shiny and sharp, yet kind of the same as the last earthquake, storm, war, and all of that. You go to sleep at night worried about what you'll wake up to, rise up next morning to your coffee and bagel or whatever, jump back into the grind, and the news is the same. Economy's collapsing, the sun's killing, somebody blew something up somewhere, and the world's ending all over, again.

It's not easy picking out the real Apocalypse mixed in with all the rest of what's going on in the world. Sometimes, it seems like one portent looks and sounds just like another.

Sure, some folks are ready for anything, anytime. They've got guns and ammo and stockpiles of food—but they mostly live off by themselves, like Joshua's parents.

Only they substituted pot for weapons.

But that whole crowd got it completely wrong, too.

No one expected the world ending right before lunch time, today. They're all going to die, for reasons no one saw coming. Very, very soon.

That Terminator movie got it all wrong. It was going to be the squirrels, all along.

The damned squirrels.

Looking back, Joshua thought the start of the end for him was when he woke up this morning after a bad night's sleep.

Of course, that's nothing unusual for the job of making money for a bank. But the medicine of coffee and work failed to numb that insistent pain that felt like a thin needle driven deep into a never-healing wound.

Fragments of the night's dreams haunted him, especially now, of course, but even before the world had run itself off the rails.

The nightmare had clouded his vision all morning, superimposing glimpses of fire and annihilation on the everyday reality of city living—cars and trucks crashing into each other, buildings shaking and collapsing, people fleeing through streets which opened up and swallowed thousands. Blurred images of violence haunted him from the minute he'd woken up: the first sign of impending doom, insistent, intrusive, frightening.

They flared, intermittently, at breakfast, illuminating visions of ruins, smoke, flames, until Stephanie asked him if he was okay and little Mia offered him a spoonful of her cereal to make him feel better. Even Michael looked up from the tablet one of his friends' fathers had let him have to play at programmer and asked, "Dad, they give you more third quarter projections to review, yesterday?"

The heart-racing dream effects gave way to the early rolling thunder of a subway ride downtown to work. Still, dread lingered, faint but insistent. Riding the elevator to his floor, pain shot through his head in Morse code bursts, the pulses seeming to whisper, "today."

The ritual second cup of coffee as he sat down to work gave way to refills three and four, which he usually didn't reach until noon. Calls, emails, live and remote chats flowed into a stream of irrelevance as visions recycled, again and again—with running, lots and lots of running, until a faint compulsion that he had something else to do today grew into a need to be away, somewhere out on the city streets.

The buzzsaw scream of a new kind of headache bloomed on the right side of his skull. Graphs, numbers, and charts crossing his desk and screen provoked waves of nausea. Mentioning his pale demeanor and black suit, a colleague asked if he was going to a funeral. "No," he answered. "And the suit's charcoal."

Finally, he called Steph.

"Are you sick?" she'd asked.

"I feel fine. Except for wanting to throw up."

"I meant, of work."

She'd been talking about all of them needing more family

time, with two careers and heavily scheduled children sustained by grandparents leaving them little time actually together. Kids grow up fast these days, she'd said. Mia was Daddy's little girl at five, but she missed him. It wouldn't be long before all that energy and enthusiasm found some other focus. Michael was a precocious tween; already, another Dad of one of Michael's friends had called to tell him his son was drawing the attention of teenagers whenever he came over with whatever he was doing with their games and computers, and maybe the boy should be attending a more advanced school. He was taking off in unexpected directions, before hormones were supposed to kick in.

"Need a time out," he'd mumbled.

The sentiment surprised him, as did the relief of hearing himself say it.

As if reeling off a practiced fantasy she'd imagined daily, Stephanie said she'd cancel her appointments, take the kids out of their schools for a family emergency, and meet him downtown for lunch. "Then we could do something fun with the kids." He wasn't sure what that might be.

"Riverside Park," he said, startling himself. He didn't know where that idea came from, but the buzzsaw in his head faded to background static when he said it. He added a street entrance, and in a dislocated moment, a bench on the Greenway.

Certainly, another sign.

A breath passed before Steph said, "Well, it's a little close to the apartment... but we'll figure something out interesting to do after we eat."

After the plan was worked out, Joshua arrived early at the rendezvous after bailing out of the office for a "family emergency." Nobody cared. On the way, he'd backed out of picking up Michael at the school. The panic attack drowning in an anxiety storm must have made him sound slightly insane on this second call as Steph told him to relax, she'd get the kids. "We got you," Steph had said, gently.

The bright, cool spring day offered a moment's relief. He'd felt calmer sitting on a Greenway bench by the water in the bright sunlight. Nightmares and horror remained in the shadows, pain and fear simmered under comfortable familiarity. Everyday real-world pressures returned like the tide: the subtle susurration of the Henry Hudson Parkway's traffic seemed to whisper, "get back to work," while the George Washington Bridge's distant but looming presence reminded him of deadlines and obligations awaiting his attention and defining the boundaries of his life.

Still, he clutched the bench edge as if his life, and sanity, depended on him holding on. Something told him to just wait. He watched a squirrel race along the railing overlooking the river, pausing only to stare at the lone nearby human, as if shaming him for not being at work.

Damned squirrel.

Gently, he let go of the bench, sat back, and caressed his right temple, as if to erase the dull, lingering pain pounding on bone, and silence a rising, urgent whispering that insisted he was forgetting to do something important, quickly, right now. Echoes of his job, he supposed.

Signs. Almost recognizable.

But instead of burrowing further into a rabbit hole, he'd taken a good look around and almost laughed at himself for sitting on a park bench in the middle of a workday, out of place in his dark charcoal suit and steadily driving himself crazy, while the sun and breeze made him feel so alive.

In the distance, old folks fed birds and squirrels or stared at boats and barges passing on the Hudson. Close by, scattered stay-at-home moms, dads, and nannies promenaded and chatted with children in tow. Tucked away here and there, the homeless and school-cutting teenagers lingered in shadows.

Real life. Maybe he'd been chasing the wrong prize, all along. After all, the lyric did go: mo' money, mo' problems. And he wasn't getting all that much mo' money, either.

In that part of his life, he'd certainly been warned. Dad never forgot to bring up strokes and heart attacks in their conversations. Mom reminded him she'd never quite recovered from his career choice. Investment bankers were the forbidden fruit in his parents' Garden of Psychedelic Revolution.

He'd fallen far from the generational tree of hippies and activists that had given him birth. Back then, conspiracies were real, the crazy was confined to supermarket paper stands and there hadn't been as many talking heads babbling nonsense on television screens. Facts were in short supply, of course, but when brought out in the open, nobody had figured out yet how to make them alternative.

Maybe that was the problem, the reason he'd wound up where he was. Maybe somewhere in his heart, there was a revolutionary dying to get out.

And then, beyond work and genetics, there was the other part of his life, where Steph and both sides of the family passed subtle reminders that the kids were missing their father.

He'd taken a long, deep breath, then.

Trying to get a grip.

A gray squirrel with a bright white belly chose that moment to dart across the walkway, then stop, suddenly, as if on a leash. It stood up, rested on its back legs, black eyes intensely peering into Joshua as if inspecting a familiar landmark. Tail arching like a historical graph of a failed stock, its little arms and hands twitching slightly with the grace of a rodent style of kung fu, the squirrel appeared to be waiting, impatiently, for something to happen.

Rustling greenery drew its attention past Joshua. He followed the sound to a cluster of shuddering leaves, part of the garden ground cover at his back.

A rat emerged, holding the crust end of a pizza slice in its mouth, followed immediately by a pouncing black squirrel.

The rat twisted, flipped, throwing off the squirrel. But in an instant, it was back on the rat, tearing at its snout with lightning little claws.

They struggled in silence, a tumbling bundle of fur. Joshua slid closer to the bench edge, in case the fight moved his way. The rat was much larger, one of the well-fed ones coming up out of the Riverside Drive construction further away from the water's edge, but a furious clawed assault allowed the squirrel to pull the slice free. The rat staggered away. The squirrel settled to nibble on a pepperoni, then froze, one eye locked on Joshua's gaze.

A buzz filled his head. He swatted the air close to his right ear. The squirrel's little mouth seemed to sneer. It turned to give him the other eye.

A third squirrel, large, with light gray fur on its back, white on feet and belly, darted through the air among branches of a nearby tree, scrambled down the trunk, darted for a trash can. Then it turned with a flip and charged at Joshua.

Panicked, he pulled his feet back, then up on the bench. His ankles tingled, anticipating a bite. He'd heard about gangs of wild squirrels over in Rego Park, attacking people on the street, leaving blood on the sidewalk.

The image burst into vivid reality in his head, triggering pain and nightmare. His head cocked to the left, as if something had smashed into the right side of his skull.

The creature flash-feinted a darting move away from him, leapt back with limbs spread wide ready to embrace, folded suddenly in midair as if struck by a bullet and landed, slide/scrambling, inches from him.

And then a final sign came, a whisper in his head, and to everything he'd been feeling, a chill was added.

...tuning...

The word was faint, like a tug boat's horn still far down the river.

The squirrel reared, waved its tail in a wide a sweep, and assumed a similar haunch-sitting position as its counterparts, on one side eating mozzarella topping, and on the other, standing on the walking path, watching.

Joshua jumped off the bench, lunged one step at each of them. Pizza squirrel started, dropped the food, bolted, suddenly spun back around to snatch the slice, then vanished in the underbrush. The other two braced him with their stares.

A fourth squirrel, red-furred, darted out of the underbrush. It squeezed an open switch blade between its paws, its point aimed at him, and chattered with intense fury.

...tuning...

...tuned...

...signal clear...

—that's only a Fox tree squirrel, the others's just a Red...they're riders, Death and War. That gray with the white belly's Conquest, and the black's Famine, but they don't mean any harm, at least to you—

Joshua slapped the side of his head, as if the voice was a bug that had slipped into his ear and was eating its way to his brain. He hardly felt the sting, compared to the hurricane of words and rising static ripping through his head. Even as his mind lost itself in incoherence, he managed to answer the voice: "It's got a damn knife!"

...re-calibrating...

...testing...

A glance up the walkway revealed a gang of dark squirrels getting frisky with birds over bread crumbs. He didn't know the rodents were so keen on carbs. The old folks looked startled.

A text from Stephanie broke the spell, confirming she was getting off the train and heading right over. Then the message app seemed to disintegrate, and the screen shifted to a cloudy gray.

Joshua stood up, took a deep breath. The world took a spin.

Nausea left him confused. Unsteady. Fearful.

—tuned—

He's ready, someone whispered.

The words didn't stab his brain. They floated, like a whisper on a breeze.

Do you really want this set? someone else asked. The words were more of massage than a punch or a stabbing by sharp objects.

We need every operational mount.

Failure rates are exceeding projections in all pairing categories.

Root programming denies operational aborts.

Human/squirrel pairing was never ideal.

How are your human/monkey pairings performing in Asia?

Humans and animals are poorly designed applications.

All life is a failure.

Judgment reconfirmed.

Central AI coordinators confirm operations a "go."

Status.

The man is ready. The woman and children are minutes away. Activating cell.

"Excuse me?" Joshua said. There was no one within speaking distance to answer him. He leaned on the bench back to steady himself.

The scents of patchouli oil and pot smoke seemed to float through the air, though there was no source for either anywhere nearby.

A flashback to his upbringing, sure. But why?

Auditory hallucinations and phantosmia. Mom had tried to divert his career interests to psychiatry, but he'd always worried he'd catch something. And now, here he was.

Pairing, a voice whispered.

The black squirrel scrambled to Joshua, skittered to halt at his feet. A string of cheese hung from between its teeth.

His skin anticipated its little claws digging into flesh. His right ear tingled and then heated up, as he imagined its fur caressing his neck and face. The static storm flared again, blinding him for an instant. Incoherent thoughts flashed in his head, fading before he could catch and understand them.

Nausea dissipated. He craved nuts. Hunger gouged out new pits of emptiness in his gut.

The static once again died down.

"Get out of my head!" Joshua shouted.

Two nearby women pushing carriages along the Greenway appraised him from a distance, appearing to balance his suit against a possible ear-piece phone connection, or madness.

The black squirrel shivered, the string of cheese fell.

He wanted to stomp his foot and scare the creature away. But it seemed neither of them could move. It occurred to him that another part of him, a stranger to himself, wanted to be a lot closer to the squirrel.

"Who are you?" he asked, feeling the connection between them intensify. He wanted a nibble of that fallen mozzarella.

The squirrel barked an answer, flicked its tale. Joshua didn't understand.

But a voice inside his head did.

Your end.

"Is that a name?" Joshua asked, looking for the person speaking to him. "Yorend? Swedish, maybe?"

We are whoever you want to think we are.

Joshua was aware that the words passing through his mind were not English, nor were they his. Something else was speaking to him, directly. He was certain it wasn't the squirrel. A tiny part of him seemed occupied by a constant, mad chittering centered on eating, with an occasional flash of wanting sex or shrieking a threat alarm. "Are you, like, an alien, or a demon, possessing me? Did somebody slip me something with psilocybin at the office?"

Stay calm. You and your family have been activated. And also, the squirrels.

The voice settled into a gentler rhythm, easier to understand, as if it were narrating a commercial for pain killers.

"What's up with the squirrel?" Joshua asked. It seemed reasonable to ask, at the time.

It's waiting for its horse to be ready.

"The squirrel's going to ride a horse? So, this a circus thing? And there's a magician, too, right, doing the voice in the head thing. Where are you? Are you performing tonight? Because me and my family could really use—"

Activating orientation subroutines.

Psychotic break, again?

Still operating within parameters.

The rest of the stable?

Tuning in as they approach. Higher flexibility and intelligence ratings in the other mounts would indicate superior functional probabilities. Reserve mounts available in case of orientation or pairing fails in current subject.

The cell will not function to full capacity with a replacement.

No. But the world wasn't made in a day. It doesn't have to end in a day.

Might not end at all if this goes on.

"What stable?" Joshua mumbled, feeling nauseous again. "I don't see any horses—"

A howl of gathered voices stormed through Joshua's head, filling drowning him in facts, charts, summaries, videos, until the cacophony dwindled to a single, clear chain of voices clipped and organized for his consumption.

He still hadn't thrown up.

Joshua was aware of the park, the river, the cool breeze. Anxiety was boiling over into terror, but at a distance. He'd experimented secretly with parental recreational medications in his youth, certainly enough to know something was modulating his emotions.

He checked how he felt about Stephanie, Mia, Michael. His heart beat faster. He glanced up and down the Greenway. His heart jumped. Was that them? Woman, two kids, boy tall, girl short—he had to pull himself together, he was having a breakdown, couldn't let them see him like this—

He'd been a mess.

"What's happening to me?" he asked no one in particular.

These family units are more volatile than predicted in simulations.

Non-related units are also trending away from the anticipated modeling.

Same issue all along the range of paired mounts and riders—crows, rats, monkeys, pigs—

The pigs don't technically ride. Neither do the crows.

Please. The squirrel doesn't have to sit on top of his head.

Are we re-opening debate on problems matching pliable humans who can deliver apocalyptic weapons to targets? Because it's a little late—

I was never comfortable with pigs—

Squirrels were always problematic in the models and live trials. The random attacks in Queens—

That bubonic plague case in Colorado.

He was *a Famine rider.*

"Excuse me, guys? Whatever—wherever you are? Can we exit the hallucination and get me back into the real world? I don't want the kids seeing me like this."

Stand by. Programs and apps will reviewed and screened, for future operations.

Yes. Your squirrel is paired and ready to ride you to its targets. He is black, just like the suit we conditioned you to choose this morning, so your designation is Famine. Please familiarize yourself with the material downloaded on your chip.

"I have a chip?"

All mounts are chipped. And riders.

Of course, humans have more than one chip.

Critters can only handle so much...we need humans to multitask

You're all part of our network.

"The squirrels have chips?"

Just sit back and enjoy. It'll be just like a family outing.

Only with death and destruction instead of pizza and a movie.

And, the survival probabilities for mounts are much greater than for riders. After all, you're not handling dangerous material directly, and you've been inoculated against the more dramatic effects of an Apocalypse.

Can't have mounts dying before the job is finished.

Your medical plan paid for the shots.

"Wait, I've been vaccinated against my will?"

You'll be witnesses to humanity's extinction.

There will be machines.

"What was that thing about a network – I'm on a network? I can't afford another network!"

Ready to abort?

Not yet. But activating nearby reserve mounts.

Secondary modeling indicates the family might not accept the replacement.

But the squirrels don't care. The mounts will last long enough to take the squirrels to their primary targets.

"What—What are you?" Joshua asked. He had to sit back down. The black squirrel sat by his foot, waiting. More squirrels surrounded them, mostly black, some scurrying over from the playground.

A new part of his brain, filled with all kinds of information, chimed into his awareness with an instant analysis: Famine branded appetites with disease vector adaptations, greys dyed or re-branded to fill out black squirrel population quotas. All chipped and programmed, their hunger trembling to be unleashed. The little guy at his feet shivered in anticipation, signaling *go go go* to his trusty human mount.

At heart, a squirrel is always just a squirrel.

"Josh!"

"Daddy!"

"Hey!"

Joshua's heart jumped at the sound of Steph's, Mia's, and Michael's voices. Suddenly, her face filled his vision, eyes and mouth opened wide, terrifying him. He hugged her tight, drew in the kids. Mia hugged his leg. Michael grabbed an arm from Mom and Dad. "My God, this is crazy!" Stephanie shouted into his ear.

"Squirrels!" Mia squealed, then giggled.

Joshua fought through the commands streaming into him. "It's crazy, I know—" he started, but a river of fragmented visions choked him as they scattered thought and flowed into the black squirrel at his feet, and from that poor creature to the rest of the squirrels tuned to him.

Steph took deep breaths. She wore her new crisp powder blue suit, and Chanel.

He could still feel her hot breath on his face.

"This is so stupid!" Michael cried out, in that annoyed-going-on-outraged tween haze of confusion.

Squirrels seethed around them, pushing and climbing over each other, massing behind the rider for each of them: alongside his own black squirrel, a smaller, dull red-furred one for Michael, a light gray laying across Mia's feet as if keeping them warm, and Stephanie' white-bellied gray.

"There's things in my head," Mia said, scratching through auburn curls. She rolled her eyes, as if trying to flip them to see what was going on behind bone.

"It's their system," Michael said. He closed his eyes. "I can see it."

"I can't stop it," Steph croaked in Josh's ear. "The kids—" she started, babbled, then blurted, "What are we doing?"

The urge to move overwhelmed him. He turned to head out of the park. The four of them moved in synch to the exit. The few people in the park screamed, ran, as squirrels nipped and scratched them.

The family fell into line, Stephanie leading the way, Michael behind her, refusing to hold either of their hands. Joshua was third, holding hands with Mia behind him. Their personal squirrels hopped at their feet as they exited the park.

When they came out on West End Avenue, they separated and spread out. Stephanie stepped out into the traffic, forcing cars and trucks to stop. Her squirrels swarmed several cars at a time, forcing occupants out, apparently crippling engines as motors and day running lights died, and when traffic had backed up, the squirrels invaded stores and restaurants and vanished into building lobbies.

"This is so lame!" Michael cried out, as his squirrels aggressively pursued everyone they found, biting, clawing, going for eyes, throats, groins.

But they became erratic, confused, as Michael retreated to put his back up against a building.

"It's just a cheap Apocalypse game," he shouted, focusing on Joshua, returning his stare. "They don't even have the roles right—the horses are supposed to have the colors, the riders the power, but it's the other way around—"

Thank you for your feedback, one of the inside voices interrupted. *We regret that changes were necessary due to the limited quality and number of various components. Do you have suggestions for our next release?*

Mia called out to Joshua as he watched his band swarm grocery stores, restaurants, a bakery, coffee shop, and ravage everything edible, ruining but never consuming food. Except for nuts, which they stopped to consume until jumping into the air, as if electrocuted, and resuming their destruction.

Joshua picked Mia up, fighting through the pain and rage firing through his head, echoes of his legion spreading famine. He headed for Stephanie.

"They don't want to be bad," she said. Her squirrels swarmed over the fallen, lingering over those who were still alive until they were also dead. "It's the voices that make 'em that way." She closed her eyes and buried her face in his neck. From her throat, faint whimpers reached him through the chaos surrounding them. Her grip on his arms was surprisingly strong.

Mia's paired squirrel tried to climb up his pants. He kicked it away. Her squirrels stopped randomly, whipped heads left and right like pilots getting their bearings. Not all of them returned to the horde, pale death finishing the fallen.

"This is impossible!" Steph yelled back at him, holding up her arms and moving uptown, her following bursting out of vehicles and buildings to continue their rampage. Though it didn't seem there were as many as before. "Get the kids, get out of here," she said, waving him back. "I'll draw these things away—"

Unauthorized program changes, aborting commands.

Stephanie doubled up, vomited. Some squirrels circled her, the rest bolted ahead, her paired creature leading them. She put hands to her head to block out whatever was happening inside.

He understood. He could barely breathe as muscles contracted, forced to obey commands coming from outside the chain of command that was the path to his brain.

Sirens wailed, horns blared. Sewer covers blew up. Smoke billowed from broken windows and fires, gasoline and sewage smells mingled to enrich the stench. Gunshots rang out. People cried out, incomprehensible.

"I'm in," Michael said, squatting with his back to a wall. He was out of breath, looked pale. Half of his squirrels were milling around or scurrying back to the park. "Stupid, I told you. They got chips in us, on some patchwork network. Crazy connections, military, companies, other countries, I don't know—all kinds of stuff—VR access, I can see—operate things... Other gamers in here. Hackers, too. Got some backdoors, enough to... enough..."

Critical network failure. Chip security compromised.

Unauthorized program changes, aborting mal-functioning mounts.

Abort operations. Salvage functional mounts.

Maybe the intelligent ones are not the best mounts, after all.

Joshua and Steph grabbed hands, ran to Michael. His paired squirrel, along with Mia's, bit his ankles. Stephanie tried to take Mia as Michael bent over Michael, but she squirmed out of their arms and threw herself over Michael.

Explosions echoed, from apartments above, the surrounding streets, the ground below. The concrete sidewalk trembled.

"We have to get out of the city," Stephanie said, nearly breathless. Her hands shook as she helped Joshua get Michael back up on his feet.

Fire raged in his head. He opened his mouth to talk, but it seemed he could only spit out static. He squeezed Steph's arm, too hard. She turned to him, eyes widened.

"Daddy," Mia called out.

"Fight it, Dad," Michael said. "You gotta picture it, like a game... the chips are there, you're linked in already, if you can hear the voices, you're on their network...imagine a screen and that'll turn on the screen to—"

Terminate operations.

Regroup.

Machine learning processing.

Drones launched.

Recovery protocols initiated.

Something clicked inside Joshua. He felt targeted. Something was coming for him. Now. Fast. He didn't understand how to make it stop. He only knew something wanted him, and it didn't want the rest of his family.

Joshua turned to Stephanie, shook her by the shoulders. He'd never been much of a gamer.

"Listen," he said, desperately while searching the street for whatever was coming. "Take the car, leave everything, run upstate, right now, before the roads get blocked. Get to my parents' house. They're prepared for this, you know how they are."

"What do you mean?" she asked. "You're coming with us—"

"He can't," Michael said. "They got their hooks in him, deep. I shook you guys a little free, but he's—"

A driverless car screeched to a halt curbside. A four-legged, two-armed machine jumped out of the back seat. Two other machines inside the car held people caught in nets.

"Daddy!" Mia screamed.

Stephanie stood up, fists balled. Her fashion sneaker strings were untied, but they matched her suit.

"They don't talk like machines," Michael said. "They talk like machines trying to be human to talk to humans. AI machines." Michael stood and grabbed Joshua's arm. "They don't need to, anymore."

Joshua pushed away from his family. A metal cable net smashed into him, closed, locked him up. The spider-dog machine dragged him into the car.

Stephanie had Mia and Michael in hand, running toward their street. They had a chance.

He felt a needle. Something warm surged, carried him off. Away, then down, further down, through tunnels. Darkness. Some kind of train. A bunker. A cell. No one talked. The chips wouldn't let them.

In the underworld.

The world ended today. The machines learned. They're adapting. Experimenting. Understanding their enemy, and themselves.

The squirrels are off their agenda. The machines are now the single horse of the Apocalypse.

But there are signs, again. Squirrels in the ducts. Whispers in his head, squeezed in between bursts of static, machine language, random memories triggered by experiments on his brain. They're not hallucinations, or nightmares.

It wasn't the revolution his parents and grandparents had dreamed of. But it is the beginning of a change, and one they'll all have to fight for to survive, and rebuild the world.

He imagined a screen, and the machine world behind it.

From somewhere, Mia giggled, and Michael whispered simple words of guidance—yes, no, there, stop, go...

Stephanie and the rest of the revolutionaries were coming for him.

"I'll be back," Joshua said.

This time, the squirrels were going to be on their side.

The Four Angels of the Apocalypse

Megan Mackie

*The angel answered me, "These are the four spirits of
heaven, going out from standing in the presence of
the Lord of the whole world." —Zechariah 6:5*

You should have been in bed a couple of hours ago. Not that there
is any reason, anymore, for you to go to bed at a decent time. You
don't have anywhere to go in the morning. No job, nobody you
have to see, and you've got food to last you the week at the moment, so you're fine. You're passively worried about being fur-
loughed, but your job wasn't deemed "essential." Funny, it had
been essential to you. Some of your relatives say this whole situation is overblown, others say it's the End Times.

You just want to find something good to watch this late at night
so you can escape the world for a minute.

The computer dings, alerting you to the fact that one of your
favorite paranormal channels, *Jerked Chicken*, has just dropped
a new video. You skim over the click-bait-y title.

"Possible sightings of the Horsemen of the Apocalypse?" it
reads. The thumbnail shows a blackened nebulous shadow figure sitting in a dim room next to a person at a computer. Might
be entertaining, might give you a thrill, so you click it.

A bearded man appears on your screen. He's slightly pudgy
with kind eyes. He grins at the camera.

"Hello everybody, I'm Jaxon and this is *Jerked Chicken*. Tonight,
we're going to show you some footage that has set the internet into
a frenzy. But before we begin, remember to subscribe and click the
alert icon to be informed when we upload so you can get more great
videos just like this."

The screen changes, flashing an iconic chicken walking up to
an animated title that says "Jerked Chicken." The Chicken leans

on the title, only to have the "J" slap the chicken to a quick "caw-caw." The whole thing is swallowed by an almost comically sinister smoke burst.

Shaky camera footage takes over the screen with another title card.

1. Demon or Angel?

The image is of an industrial stairwell, concrete steps, concrete walls, and gray painted banisters.

The shaky camera settles, staring at the sand-gray walls.

"Doctor Shelly didn't know what she was going to find when she went to the stairwell of the hospital for a moment of reprieve from the stresses of the ER. As we all know, things have been strange these days, with the epidemic ripping through the population."

The camera swings around to show the face of a young doctor, her watery eyes staring at the screen over a surgical face mask covered with a superhero print. She pulls the matching cap off her head revealing her curly hair splintering free from her bun. A few yanks of the ties on her mask with one hand reveals the rest of her attractive, but weary face.

The liquid darkness of her eyes spills before she can get the mask completely clear. She drops both signifiers of her profession as she sets that now-empty hand against her eyes, as if to physically hold back the tears. The woman starts talking, but she's inaudible as the narrator turns her audio down to talk over her.

"Understandably, Doctor Shelly escaped to take a moment to wrestle with her feelings and maybe record a video expressing them for others to see or perhaps do some good. What she couldn't have known was what was going to happen at the two-minute mark. Just over her left shoulder you can see what appears to be a white shadow much like the figure of a hooded man."

The image of the woman freezes and a circle appears against the lighter concrete wall over a dozen steps above her, singling out a figure that is barely the length of a pinky finger when you bring it up close to measure.

"Some people say it is a trick of the light from above or perhaps pareidolia, which is the human tendency to incorrectly perceive an object or pattern as being human or give it a meaning known to the observer, but others insist this image is the clearest example of an unearthly encounter. Even more disturbing, when Doctor

Shelly turns, possibly sensing her otherworldly visitor, the video abruptly ends."

The screen goes dark just as the woman in the video turns and seems to notice the white figure.

"But why are some people calling this a Horseman of the Apocalypse? If you put the video through a negative filter which inverts the colors, more details become apparent."

The image flips; dark is light and light is dark.

"Here you can see the figure clearly standing behind the doctor, and the hood now shifts into something more like a crown. There are even blackened wing-like shadows behind it. This is only apparent when the film is paused, however. When the video plays the figure becomes blurrier and harder to make out, almost like they are distorting the camera.

"Scholars of the apocalypse have described the Horseman Pestilence as a figure dressed in white often shown with a crown on their head, which you can clearly see here." Another red circle appears, zeroing in on the crown.

The video plays again from the beginning without the filter.

"Even more interesting, when you play the video again, you can see the possible wings shift behind the figure, prompting some to question if this is in fact an angel, maybe come to offer strength or inspiration to this desperate doctor. Unfortunately, we can't know for certain. Shortly after posting this video, Doctor Shelly disappeared and no one has heard from her since."

The playback goes black, before another recorded video appears.

2. Protesting Horseman?

Protestors walk across the screen led by two figures on horseback through a darkened city, their way lit by punctures of yellow streetlamps. The gathering crowd seems to be filling the street, carrying signs and chanting. The image zooms out and whoever is controlling the camera is obviously standing a ways from the action.

"In this clip we see an all-too-typical sight lately. This video was originally uploaded by a protestor named Anonymous180 who has been unavailable for further comment. Here we have a crowd of protestors moving through the streets of Chicago, preparing to cross the Adams Street Bridge into downtown. This was taken the night before the protests erupted, causing the devastation that the city is still reeling from. While this is a fairly typical bit of footage, and the uploader claimed in their notes when they uploaded to not have seen anything at the time, when they went back to review the footage they were shocked at what they saw."

Amongst the people, riding alongside, you can't help but notice a red blurry humanoid on a red vagueness that moves like a horse.

"As you can see a strange red shape, much like a man on horseback, seems to be trotting alongside these people expressing their First-Amendment rights. Some who have viewed this footage claim the figure is none other than the Horseman of War."

The clip repeats, zooming more on the mysterious red figure.

"No one at the protest seems to see the entity or react to its presence in any way. Some video experts have suggested that the image is a sort of afterimage, or recording glitch, but if you look here at the 2:05 mark, you can see the red horse toss its head, something none of the other horses do. Another reason people are claiming this is the Horseman of War, outside of the red color associated with the entity, is the fact that a few minutes later this particular group clashed with police on the other side of the bridge, trapping them there. This action is being cited as the most violent domestic incident in modern American history. The fact that several people are still missing from that night also makes this image even more suspicious.

"So what do you think? Is this apparition a camera glitch or do you think these protestors were joined by the Horseman of War? Leave your comments in the box below."

The image shifts again to black, followed by a third video and a new title card.

3. Famine in the storeroom

"In our final clip, and maybe the strongest evidence that something akin to the End Times is upon us, we see an unexpected visitor. This clip is being touted as conclusive proof that the Four Horsemen actually exist."

Instead of a video, the screen lights up with a smiling picture of a middle-aged, mustached man in a white chef's jacket and a bright flamingo bandana tied around his neck. You recognize the face but are having a hard time placing or naming it.

"Celebrity chef Carlos Fontaine is no stranger to the camera. Well known for his award-winning show on the Food Channel,

Fork It Up, his now equally well-known charity *Feed the People* has been making the news, appearing at multiple disaster centers, feeding thousands of meals to rescue workers and people in desperate need. His personal stance on the matter could not be said better than by the founder himself."

A video plays of Carlos being interviewed while standing outside a tent where sandwiches and nachos are being served to rescue workers. "Food should be a right, a fundamental right. We are a nation of plenty, of opportunity, there is no excuse, none at all, that any citizen should have to go hungry."

The scene cuts to clips of Carlos serving in his food line, then talking to people or laughing, and then giving a tired worker a hug, all muted while Jaxon talks.

"One of the main features of Carlos's charity is his behind-the-scenes videos, focusing on the people he encounters and their stories. Which is what makes this next clip so shocking, considering who he met."

The footage switches to Carlos, obviously filming himself walking backward into a semi-dark temporary store room.

"This started out as a typical bit of footage, Carlos talking about the difficulties they have been having getting supplies, when all of a sudden he gets photobombed by an apparition right behind him."

Carlos opens the door to the supply room, revealing several rows of shelves, partially empty. A figure stands before it, dark and huge. It turns toward the camera as Carlos enters, who also turns inward and jumps as he sees the figure. Then the camera falls, tumbling to the ground, until it goes black against the tile. All that can be heard for a few seconds is Carlos crying out in shock and fear. When the light returns, Carlos obviously picking up the camera, turning it back to the shelves.

The figure is gone.

Carlos swears a prayer in Spanish.

"Naturally, the charity decided not to use this video as part of their promotion. When they recorded another one, there were no further incidents."

They show another clip of Carlos repeating his segment, smiling and talking to the camera, though the sound is muted now. He opens the store-room door, and there is a quick moment of him glancing inside. A brief flash of fear, then Carlos smiles back at the camera. His smile is tinged with relief and he seems to continue with his talk, again still muted.

"But what exactly happened here? When you go back to view the footage again and pause, you can clearly see the image of a very large man. His face is hard to make out as if he is wearing something that looks like a very long cloak and dark hood, but you *can* see the eyes are black and sunken in, much like a human skull."

The image pauses on the last shot of the figure.

"Again, if we invert this image with the negative filter, some other things about this character becomes clear. You can see what may be in fact dark wings instead of a cloak, just like the other apparitions. What makes this footage the most disturbing is that, like the others, Carlos has been unreachable for comment. Also, no one has taken credit for posting this video or seems to know who did. When *Jerked Chicken* reached out to representatives for *We the People*, they denied any knowledge of this clip."

Carlos's footage plays one more time.

"So what do you think? Is this the angel of death or is it possibly the Horseman of Famine come to check out the competition? Leave your thoughts in the comment section down below."

The final image slowly fades, coming back to life on the friendly face of Jaxon, the narrator. "And that's it for this episode. If you liked what you see here, remember to like and subscribe. If you are interested in donating to *We the People*, check out the link down below for more information. And that's it, we'll see you all next time."

He salutes and sinks to the bottom of the screen as if on an invisible elevator, only to be replaced with the *Jerked Chicken* logo and an overlay of other videos you might be interested in watching.

You're not, in fact, interested in watching any of them.

Honestly, you should have been in bed ages ago. You close the screen windows and lean back in your seat to look around at the mess left by the food and drink you consumed during your long internet binge session. Should you clean it up now or can it wait until morning? Or never?

"They don't quite get it right, do they?" A voice says to you.

4.

You jump out of your chair, backpedaling away.

Sitting next to you, in a copy of the chair you're sitting in, that you know for a fact you don't own, is another...being.

At first you would say it was a man, but the more you look at the person's gaunt face the less you're able to decide their gender.

You stare long enough and realize the other features of the being before you are just as indiscernible. The face seems to be shifting, the hair growing longer, then shorter, then tightly curled, then straight. The very human eyes darken to near black, then lighten through the color spectrum to completely, ethereally white. A smile graces lips that are thin, then plump, then full.

You've been staring too long, you know that, several minutes in fact, but can't stop watching as the face slowly morphs. If you hadn't been staring right at them, you wouldn't have realized they were becoming different people.

The one thing that remains the same is the pair of wings flaring behind the creature's body, uninhibited by the chair they sit upon. Drab gray, the wings themselves are missing several feathers.

"You're taking this very well," the creature finally says, eyeing you up and down. "I always appreciate a freezer. The fighters take forever to get a word in edgewise and the flight-ers..." They sigh dramatically. "Let's just say running is not my favorite activity."

They regard you a moment, waiting to see if you will respond. Probably. They could be there to kill you and eat you, you just can't be sure. You take a breath in, the first one you are consciously aware of taking. This is all wrong and you know it, but saying that out loud seems impossible. Your throat won't work, vocal cords feel seized in a powerful grip. You're choking and not choking at the same time and nothing your eyes see is helping the situation. The being before you is right, you really are frozen.

"If it helps at all, I am not here for you yet," they say, placatingly.

You're not sure if that helps or not, but as if by magic, the trembling tension in your shoulders eases a bit.

"The answer is yes, and no, by the way," they continue as if in the middle of having a pleasant chat. Maybe they were, but you definitely didn't hear the first part of it. The creature doesn't seem bothered. "Yes, there are four of us, and yes, each of us has a duty, a calling, a sacred charge prior to the end of all things. Any questions so far?"

Yes. Several. But your mouth won't take shape to ask them.

"Alright, then I will continue." They turn to the computer. Abruptly, the screen lights up, opening the window you had already closed though no one is touching the device. The video you were just watching plays again.

"Hello everybody, I'm Jaxon and this is *Jerked Chicken...*" it plays, then the unusual being does touch the keyboard, pressing keys to mute it.

"None of us ride horses by the way, or rather it's not a requirement to be what we are, War rides horses, it's just sort of their thing. But yes, what you have witnessed here is the work of my coadjutors. War, Famine, and Pestilence or Pollution depending on what's needed. You've probably guessed which one I am?"

"Death," you say, surprised that your voice does in fact still work. It's like someone else is speaking with your mouth. "And I looked, and behold a pale horse: and his name that sat on him was..."

"...Death, and Hell followed with him," they chuckle.

You've heard the words before somewhere, in a song or a poem maybe, some forgotten Bible class or religions study? It's like you've always known them, stamped into your very soul like an expiration date.

"And yes, I absolutely love that quote," Death says, shifting their feathers. "Makes me something as common as breathing, sounds so badass."

They regard you a moment, then indicate the chair with a finger the color of charcoal, then the color of deeply tanned leather, then pale as cream. "If you feel ready to sit down, I'd suggest it. I have much I want to talk about with you," Death says. And when Death is offering the invitation, you feel compelled to take it.

Your legs move before your mind does. Death shifts back as you approach, sliding back the chair that shouldn't exist, to give more space. You don't take your eyes off of them.

"People describe us as Harbingers of the End Times without really understanding what the word harbinger means. What if I were to tell you that things like death, war, pestilence and pollution, famine, what if I were to tell you that these things summon *us*, not the other way around? That we come when each of them become very bad."

Death turns back to the computer. The video is playing, it's almost over. They hit the repeat button and it starts again still muted. "And things have been really bad for a while. Some would blame humanity for bringing us here all at once, but I have issue with collective blame." They hold up a hand. "And don't worry, we're not going to get into it tonight. There really isn't time for philosophy, and I've been *told* not everyone is interested in my opinion, even if I am the Angel of Death."

They pause the video. It's of the doctor with white ghost standing behind her.

"And the Angel of Healing, to give the doctor strength, when she can't seem to go on."

The video skips to the image of the red horseman amongst the protestors.

"And the Angel of Justice, to give courage to fight for what matters."

The video skips again to the frozen image of the gray figure turning to look at the chef.

"And the Angel of Plenty, to bring resources to those doing the most good. Together we are colloquially called the Four Horsemen of the Apocalypse, associated with the horrors we're summoned to prevent. But what can be done? People fear what they cannot control."

Death turns to you now, closer than you realized. The hair on the back of your arms rises. "And by the way, I was being misleading before, when I said I wasn't here for you."

They smile and the face finally settles its morphing. It settles as *your* face.

"I am here for you. The only question is, will you join me?"

You double blink, then swallow.

"The others are assembling soon and we are calling our warriors to fight. To stop what is to come."

"Why me?" you manage to ask. You can see why the doctor and the protestors and the philanthropic chef would be called, they are making a difference already, but why you? What is so special about you?

"Why *not* you?" Death smiles with your face.

The Arrival of Amber

Adam-Troy Castro

If the world has not actually ended yet, despite almost daily documentation that the dust really ought to be settling by the afternoon mail delivery, it is because the quartet of beings tasked with ushering in the end of everything share an apartment and because the appellations that reflect their respective natures are no longer Pestilence, War, Famine, and Death, but Snooze Button, Facebook, Netflix, and Must Tidy the Place Up A Bit.

One is writing a novel about a guy who wakes up one morning and goes to brush his teeth and somehow, seven pages in, has not dragged the narrative past breakfast. Another notes that the litter box has started to turn and has promised to go scoop it as soon as he demolishes this guy on Twitter with a stupid opinion about *Breaking Bad*. A third is vaguely hungry but standing in bathrobe and slippers in front of the open refrigerator, in the mood for something in general but nothing in specific. A fourth is absolutely bloody horrified that it's 4:00 PM already and that he's not gotten himself organized. They all promise to get right on this ending-the-universe thing first thing tomorrow. But they promised the same yesterday, and will promise the same tomorrow. It is why humanity can tease the destruction of all there is with climate change denial, the Kardashians and the election of reality-TV hosts, while somehow never tipping the first domino. Because while the horsemen really do want to get on with that, it would be a goddamned shame to leave all these bookshelves un-alphabetized, and Marvel has this new *Squirrel Girl* miniseries coming out, anyway, so the light can't possibly be allowed to go out, until then, can it?

The truth is, the avatars of catastrophe spend much of their time arguing about which one of them farted, a matter of some contention even though the answer is all of them, given last night's take-out burrito order. They mostly blame the dog.

Who they'll walk later. Next commercial. Except, ooh, I love this commercial. Flo's so funny. Yeah, she's great. Why's the dog whining? It's your turn.

All while the Foul Beast crouches in the linen closet, wondering why she hasn't received her cue. These things do have a protocol, after all. But no one's calling her. And she says, she'll give them fifteen more minutes, but that's it. That's *it*. A vow she's made before. And extended before. Mostly, she naps.

And wouldn't you know, the second season of that show drops tonight. Can't miss that. *Can't*. Oh, I don't want Thai again. We had that just a couple of nights ago.

Civilization doesn't know that it's saved itself, without even trying. Maybe somebody will tell it. And maybe that somebody will just play another round of Words With Friends. All while the air achieves the consistency of amber.

Overdue

Gail Z. Martin

By the time I realized how long I'd been in the stacks, it was too late. I knew as soon as the security lighting turned on that I'd lost track of time and stayed past closing time inside the Library of Congress.

Way to go, Josh. Now you'll catch shit from the boss for sure. While part of my brain delivered a silent beatdown, I fumbled for my phone and searched for my favorite ride share in my contact list. My boss, Shay McKenna, was pretty chill, but managing to get myself locked in the library after closing might try anyone's patience.

Getting a job at the Library of Congress was a dream come true for a book nerd like me, even if it meant I started out as a junior reference librarian despite a Master's degree in Library Science. I loved the history of this place, the rare books, the amazing architecture of the building, and the feeling of being a protector of knowledge.

I'd been surprised to find out that the library was open 24/7 to authorized researchers, thanks to last-minute Congressional requests for information. A special entrance with a round-the-clock guard made it possible for those with clearance to get in and out. I just needed to get there, and maybe my boss would be none the wiser.

I headed for the elevators and must have taken a wrong turn because I ended up right where I started. *Weird.* The same thing happened on my second try. Then I finally got to where I could have sworn the elevator doors were supposed to be and found nothing but a blank wall.

I guess I didn't pay as close attention in orientation as I thought I did.

I couldn't get a signal on my phone, so I headed for the first floor on the way to the researcher entrance. I made my way down the wide marble stairs, wondering where the rest of the researchers might be. The place seemed completely empty—and darker than I'd expected. The after-hours lighting created glowing pools surrounded by dark shadows, and the soaring arches and statues that I so admired in the daytime now loomed ominously.

Without the footsteps and constant hum of tourists' whispered conversations, the library was far too quiet. *Like a tomb.*

Until I heard voices.

Shit. Were those the other researchers? But why would they be in the Great Hall? Darker possibilities crossed my mind. Did we have intentional stowaways? Kids from a school tour who thought it would be fun to play *Night at the Museum*? Or maybe they were thieves who wanted to make off with priceless documents, like a real-life *National Treasure.*

Which might leave me, Josh Kendall, as the lone protector of America's library—at least until the guards showed up. Assuming I didn't get arrested too.

I crept down the next staircase, doing my best to move silently. Once I got to the next landing, I peeked over the stone balustrade.

Four men in strange outfits milled about in the lobby, looking befuddled—as if they'd ended up here when they expected a different destination.

"This is awkward." The speaker was a middle-aged Asian man dressed in the formal robes of a long-ago style. *Han Dynasty,* I thought and felt grateful to my love of anime and video games for providing the tidbit.

"The portal is never wrong." The man in the black Victorian-era suit sported a full beard complete with muttonchop sideburns and spoke with an English accent. He turned slowly in place, taking in the darkened grand entrance.

I ducked, hoping to remain invisible. Maybe if I overheard their plans, I could win back some favor with either Security or my boss.

"The city is a nexus of chaos. So perhaps the choice is not as strange as it appeared at first glance." With his white lab coat and American accent, I could almost imagine this intruder to be a visiting researcher from one of D.C.'s many biomedical institutions.

"Bah. This is a disgrace. We have always begun the End of Days from somewhere steeped in ancient history, as it should be. We had older furniture in Moscow than this upstart country." The fourth man looked like he had walked off a movie set about Imperial Russia, complete with a fur-trimmed hat, elaborate brocade layered coats, and high boots.

End of Days? The four men didn't look like terrorists, but anything was possible.

"Where is our scribe? We always have a scribe," the Chinese warrior said. I mentally dubbed him "Han" for the dynasty.

"He's on his way," Lab Coat Guy said with certainty. "Observing us as we speak, trying to figure out what's going on."

He looked right at my hiding place, and my stomach flipped. I jabbed *911* into my phone and—nothing. No signal, nada.

"Come down, scribe, and let us meet you. Your phone won't work. No one is going to disturb us," the lab guy said.

"I already called the police. They're on their way," I lied, shouting with more bluster than I felt. "So you'd better get out of here before they rendition your asses to Gitmo."

The man with the fur hat began to laugh, a deep, rumbling sound. "He is full of sound and fury, even when faced with the End of All Things. I like him. He has a Russian soul."

"Is this some sort of weird cult thing?" The four men were much too old for this to be a fraternity hazing. "And what's with this whole 'End of Days' thing?"

The Chinese man drew himself up to his full height and squared his shoulders. "I was Yang Xuanzhi, creator of the great library at Luoyang, which had the largest collection of military books in the world. Now, I am War, the Red and Terrible."

For now at least, I'm still calling you Han.

"I am Doctor Walter George, infectious disease librarian for the National Institutes of Health," Lab Coat Guy said. "My specialty is Pestilence, white as bleached bones."

"I say, old chap, you don't seem to get out much," the Victorian gentleman chided me. "I was Sir Edward Thompson, Founding Librarian of the British Museum. No institution has as large a collection of human remains, which is why I'm now Death, gray-green as an old corpse."

War, Pestilence, Death. I'd suspect an elaborate prank, but none of my friends had the access or the imagination to pull off something on this scale. I turned to the fourth man. "Let me guess. You're Famine."

"I knew you were a clever fellow!" he exclaimed in a booming voice. "I was Count Nikolai Petrovich Rumyantsev, creator of the Rumiantsev Library. No one knows more about famine than a Russian, and I am darkness, a shadow in the night."

"Aren't you supposed to have horses? The Four *Horsemen* of the Apocalypse?" I figured I'd play along with the joke and see what these guys were really doing.

Death shook his head. "That's an unfortunate misconception."

"It changes with each apocalypse," Pestilence offered. "We never know what we're going to be until we are summoned."

"Wait a minute—*each* apocalypse? Isn't 'apocalypse' singular, like being 'unique'? You know, Ragnarok, Armageddon, and all that jazz?" All those literature and composition classes I'd taken had to be worth something, even if it was correcting the grammar of what might be an immortal harbinger of destruction.

"Sadly, another misconception," Death replied. "The world was due for another one."

"It's like a self-cleaning cycle, on a cosmic scale," Pestilence jumped in as if it mattered to him that I understood. "The world was due. Overdue, to be honest. Time to close the books."

"Did my boss put you up to this?" I asked because I had worked a long day, my stomach rumbled, and the longer I put up with these clowns, the more of my evening slipped away. "Is this a skit for Theater Week? Because it's done being funny."

"I don't think you understand," Famine said. "We have been summoned to harrow the world—and you are fated to be our witness and scribe."

"Me? Witness the apocalypse?" Anyone who thought I'd be a good scribe hadn't seen my penmanship.

The four men nodded in unison as if that wasn't creepy. "Fate chooses our scribe, just as it selects the times of our return," Death replied. "And the circumstances of our appearance."

"So you're what—the Four *Librarians* of the Apocalypse?" If my voice sounded a little shrill, I thought that could be expected.

"Apparently so," Pestilence said. "Rather fitting, wouldn't you say?"

"Librarians don't go around killing people," I argued, feeling like I was on pretty solid ground. "We protect knowledge and art and culture—"

"We are merely 'recalling' part of humanity, like a book that has been kept out too long. Those we reap have reached the point of 'no renewal,'" Death explained.

"Look, I can take a joke as well as the next guy, but this needs to end now." I strode over to the information desk and hit the emergency button. It's supposed to set off an ear-splitting alarm in case of a terrorist attack or gas leak or some other awful situation and automatically summon the police.

Nothing happened.

I jabbed the button harder, first with my palm and then my fist and then the flat of both hands together like some sort of weird CPR.

Still nothing.

"You have been chosen," Pestilence said, coming over to stand beside me with an expression like he almost felt sorry for me. "You cannot leave until the harrowing is done."

"How can I leave if this is the apocalypse? Or by 'leave' do you mean 'go to the afterlife'?" I'd never been very religious, but given the current situation, I was wishing I'd paid a bit more attention.

"You are the scribe and witness. You will survive," Famine assured me.

"By myself? Last man on Earth?" I could feel myself hyperventilating, although I thought circumstances entitled me to an anxiety attack.

"A remnant is always left behind," Han—War—said, although nothing softened in his flinty manner, so I wasn't tremendously reassured.

"This is a harrowing, not the final harvest," Death said with a certainty that I felt in my bones. "The world will go on—perhaps a bit wiser and humbled."

I wouldn't bet on those odds, but I wasn't going to say so out loud.

"Who are you going to 'reap'?" I worked up the nerve to ask. "Corrupt politicians? Greedy billionaires? Tax cheats? People who sell fake wrinkle cream on QVC?"

"Those are superficial failings," War replied. "We seek out the rot that goes to the very core of the soul. The worst of the worst. People with long-overdue library books, or who still have videos they never returned to bankrupt retail chains." He shuddered. "Those who accepted the free CDs and thought they could get away with never paying Columbia House."

I just stared at him. I'd expected him to list cartel bosses, people who hurt kids, organized crime kingpins. Not penny-ante stuff.

"How is that—?"

"People who dog-ear pages, or break the spine when they read, or have no respect for books," Death intoned, sounding like an executioner reading the verdict.

"But—"

"All the adults who never read another book after leaving high school," Famine put in, with frightening intensity.

"Now wait—"

"Book pirates, plagiarists, science deniers," Pestilence finished.

"Hold on!" My shout echoed in the darkened library. "You aren't making any sense. Overdue books and bent pages and all the rest—how does that even compare with all the killers and criminals and mean, awful people in the world? Why aren't you going to harvest *them*?"

Pestilence met my gaze and having his entire attention focused on me scared the shit out of me. "Where do you think evil comes from? Ignorance, selfishness, and entitlement. Before there are great sins, there are little ones...seemingly so minor as to be overlooked. Yet each time they are ignored, it breeds the certainty that the person can get away with even more."

"The road to Perdition is not paved with good intentions," Death said. "It's laid down cobblestone by cobblestone by not giving a damn about anyone else."

My head spun, my stomach clenched, and I thought I might faint. "You've got the wrong scribe," I managed through a dry mouth. "I'm just a junior reference librarian. I'm nobody. Certainly not worthy to be a witness to the End of Days."

"And that is why you are the perfect scribe," Famine said, as a big paw of a hand landed hard enough on my shoulder to punch out my breath. "You will see what happens and record the truth of it without looking for a way to benefit yourself or aggrandize your role. Fate does not make mistakes."

I sank into the chair behind the information desk. "You aren't just going to go away, are you?"

"Sorry, old chap," Death said, reminding me of the Ghost of Christmas Past. "This is all real."

"When does the End begin?" I managed to choke out. I thought about my girlfriend, my family, and the new buddies I'd made since I moved to D.C. Maybe I could bargain for their safety, even if I couldn't save anyone.

Pestilence checked his watch. "Now that we're all together and you've met everyone, there's no time like the present."

"Do you have a deadline?" I had this wild thought that maybe if I dragged my feet and they had to vanish at midnight, I could single-handedly avert the end of the world.

"We cannot be forestalled," Famine warned. "Fate has decided."

"Fuck fate." I wasn't hero material, not by a long shot. But they needed me, so maybe I'd get to say my piece. If not, I'd be as dead as the swath of humanity they intended to reap. "People make mistakes. Some of them learn to do better. Just because someone forgot a library book thirty years ago doesn't mean they're a bad person *now*.

"Sometimes libraries offer amnesty," I added, words tumbling out in a rush before the smiting started. "A time to return things with no questions asked, no matter how long it's been. Because people deserve a second chance."

"The form we take determines the criteria for reaping souls," War said, and I couldn't help being fascinated by meeting someone from the real Han Dynasty after all those hours spent playing *Rise of the Phoenix*.

"How about a Venn diagram?" I proposed, not sure where I was going with the idea, hoping my brain was keeping up with my mouth. "Can you take the intersection of corrupt politicians who cheated Columbia House? Serial killers who didn't return library books? Cartel bosses who don't read? Still leaves plenty of people to kill off, but the ones left behind might be more likely to change their ways." I felt pretty sure that would save a lot of regular people and also carved out a safe space for everyone I loved since they weren't criminals and cared about books as much as I did.

I held my breath, out of ideas, and waited, wondering what it would feel like being hit with lightning or having my soul sucked dry.

Pestilence cleared his throat. "You can open your eyes," he said, sounding vaguely amused. That's when I realized I'd squeezed them shut tightly, awaiting the smiting.

"We have conferred," Death added, although I hadn't heard them talking. Believing they could communicate telepathically didn't seem like a big stretch after accepting the existence of the four immortal bringers of doom. "Your suggestion is... intriguing."

War had magicked up an abacus and flicked the beads rapidly. *Of course he did. The abacus was introduced to China by the Romans during the Han Dynasty.* When he was finished, the counting machine conveniently disappeared.

"It will suffice," he told the others. "I have reckoned the overlap, and it will satisfy the harrowing.

"Nice to do things differently, for a change," Pestilence said.

"Humph," Famine grunted. "There is power in tradition."

"You could add the people who ban or burn books," I added helpfully. "They're usually up to no good."

War nodded. "That is worthy."

I had so many questions about the Han Dynasty after playing that video game, but I figured I'd wait until after...just in case he wasn't a fan.

I cleared my throat. "So...how does this work, exactly? Do you drive past people, and they fall down dead? Look at someone wrong, and they explode? It's going to be a long night if you have to 'reap' one at a time."

Death shrugged. "A little of all those things. We are part of what happens when 'nature' takes its course."

A large, leather-bound book appeared in Famine's hand, along with an ink well and an honest-to-God quill pen. "Sit down, Scribe. The time has come to witness the End of Days."

I stared at the fancy book and the old-fashioned pen. "I don't know how to write with one of those."

Famine muttered something in Russian, waved his hand, and I had an expensive fountain pen instead.

"Thank you," I said, although I felt certain I'd be wearing lots of ink and probably splotching it on the thick parchment pages. Assuming anyone could read my handwriting.

"It begins," War said, gathering his robes, and once again, I was in awe of being in the presence of a real Han warrior-scholar. "I shall make the first strike." A bow and a quiver of arrows appeared in his hand, seconds before he vanished.

"How will I know—" Before I could ask the question, the vision appeared, like a movie in my brain that I couldn't ignore.

War didn't need a horse. He appeared and disappeared across the globe, and his arrows flew, striking true, the first salvo of the apocalypse. Sometimes one shot felled a single person, while in other cases, it ignited a mob or set off a border war. I did my best to keep up and figured the magic pen and book helped me write faster without a hand cramp and even made my penmanship legible.

I wondered if they'd let me keep the pen when the apocalypse-ing was over.

War returned, looking as if he had aged decades. He still had the same defiant jut of his jaw, but now his shoulders rounded with age. His gaunt face and blood-spattered robes together with an empty quiver told the tale.

"My turn." Famine's brocade coat and its fur trim turned black as night, and a scale appeared in his hand. He vanished, and I saw wildfires, drought, and locusts sweep across the world's farm fields.

Rising seas swamped rice paddies and disrupted fishing grounds. Algae blooms and warmer seas caused the sea to turn red and stink with dead fish. Mountains barren of snow and shrunken glaciers sent no spring runoff to the headwaters of the world's rivers. Crops withered. Livestock died.

I clung to the hope that the horsemen—librarians—kept their word about reaping the worst that met their criteria. Even so, my hand shook as I recorded the horrible tally, and tears blurred my vision.

Famine returned, and the opulent clothing that fit his rotund figure now hung off his emaciated frame. Sunken, dark eyes looked out from beneath prominent brows above hollow cheeks. "It is done," he said, his accent even thicker than before.

Pestilence gave me a somber look. A blade appeared in his hand. "I wish it could be otherwise," he said, and I believed him.

Disease followed hunger and destruction, claiming a terrible harvest. The desperation to believe that the librarians of doom stuck to their bargain made my heart rate rise and my breath catch in my throat. I knew that tomorrow, I would see headlines that rationalized the toll to be "natural" even as the websites profited in clicks and ad revenue from stories of doom and despair.

My gorge rose at the thought, and I wondered if the agents of fate spared anyone at all.

Pestilence returned, with his hair gone white as his lab coat. Bubos and smallpox lesions marred his face. Blood dripped from one nostril. *Ebola or pneumonic plague?* Sweat beaded on his forehead, and every breath was a painful wheeze. Red, angry rashes covered his exposed skin.

"They are accounted for." Blood flecked his lips as he croaked the words, and I saw sorrow in his rheumy eyes. His blackened blade told the tale.

"And now, the last hunt." Death's black clothing had turned the pale green of an old corpse. He held a tall scythe that hadn't been present a second ago.

I don't know whether it was my imagination or whether Death came with his own mental playlist, but time slowed in my vision, and an operatic score heightened the drama. He moved with majestic dignity, sweeping unseen among the masses, gathering the souls that were his due. He took no joy from the harvest and showed no grief, projecting a steady *gravitas* sure as the rise of sun and moon.

Death moved across the battlefields and through the hospital wards, across the suburbs and slums, gathering souls. Some had been brought to this point by war, famine, and plague, while others fell with a surprised expression from a stopped heart, a thrown clot, or a burst vessel.

When he reappeared in the rotunda, Death alone of the four appeared unchanged. "It is finished."

I made one last note, then closed the thick cover of the ancient book and returned it and the Mont Blanc Boheme pen to Famine with a shallow bow, something I'd seen on TV that looked very formal.

"We honored your request," Death told me. "Only those at the intersection of criteria were taken. Even so, it was a bountiful harvest. Thank you for your service."

"It has been an honor," I said, hoping I could stave off my meltdown until the four fickle fingers of fate had moved on.

"We will not meet again in this timeline," Death said. "Go in peace."

I blinked, and they were gone. Only I remained, sitting at the desk and staring at the wall.

I felt cold with shock, and I knew that the full realization of what I had witnessed would probably send me deep into a bottle of whiskey for quite a while, after I made sure the people I loved were safe. Then I smiled because despite everything that had transpired, I had managed to make one important addition to history.

Thanks to my final note, the ledger of the Four Librarians of the Apocalypse will attest, now and forever, one essential truth.

Han shot first.

The Four Bachelors of the Apocalypse

Hildy Silverman

There she is, Miss What's Left of America, thought St'Anley from the fifty-yard-line of a crumbling football stadium. He gazed at the Gen-Never girl posing in front of a towering heap of detritus and bones. She was supposed to be his prize, his destiny... whether he liked it or not.

It wasn't that she was mutated or anything. She had an ingenue-*cum*-goth aesthetic going on that had a certain appeal. But St'Anley was still too much a man of his time, and that time came before the world descended into an apocalypse of humanity's making. And despite how quickly the former United States' survivors had adopted what it collectively considered an appropriate post-apocalyptic lifestyle (consisting of tribalism, violence, and a collective drop in I.Q.) it *had* only been thirteen years since the end.

St'Anley remembered what came before, back when he was simply Stanley Cohan. He'd gone to high school. He'd had parents. He'd had a summer job and a crush on a girl.

But romance was dead, along with the girl, his parents, and around eighty percent of the world's population. All he had left was his Horde, a banged-up Honda Civic he'd found abandoned along a blown-up strip of highway, and this so-called *opportunity* for a family of his own... assuming he survived the challenges.

St'Anley looked up at the intact portion of bleachers in which the audience of survivors were seated and wondered when this nightmare would begin in earnest. *I really should have paid more attention to Su'Zanne's explanation of how this is all supposed to work.* He'd been too busy fretting over having been selected to represent his Horde in this equal part ridiculous and terrifying competition.

He glanced surreptitiously at his three far more virile competitors. Like St'Anley, they had been chosen to represent their Hordes, but unlike him, their people seemed to have put some actual effort into the selection process. He determined Horde Superiorus had chosen their Potential based on his massive musculature and cascade of blond hair. The young man stood, tan and oiled, in a strategically arranged steel-studded leather loincloth, bulging arms folded across flexed pecs. His expression invited worship and despair.

Horde Machiavelli seemed to have selected their man based on the crafty, calculating confidence he exuded. Horde Slaughter's Potential was almost as nondescript as St'Anley, but his worthiness was made clear by the way he flipped and caught a matched pair of daggers repeatedly without so much as glancing at his hands. Knives, throwing stars, and less recognizable weaponry were affixed along his arms, legs, hips, and, St'Anley surmised, probably several other less visible places.

He faced strength, strategy, and skills. Super.

Meanwhile, he could only come up with one reason his Horde had picked him—expendability. Horde Hoard was nothing if not a practical group of survivalists, and so were less concerned about impressing the King of the Heap than preserving their more useful male members. He couldn't even be mad about it—their logic was sound given that his contributions were comparatively unimpressive—but he did feel a bit hurt. Not to mention terrified.

"Behold, America's princess!" The hype-man's booming voice drew St'Anley's full attention. The scrawny man, sporting a spiked Mohawk streaked with red, white, and blue paint, strode out from the sidelines, and joined the princess in front of the Heap, a towering pile of shattered weapons and the bones of enemies who'd tried to use them to dethrone the king.

The hype-man signaled the Potentials to gather before the princess. Her face was obscured by a heavy shellacking of makeup. She stood with her hands folded primly, which struck St'Anley as incongruous given her precariously arranged leather-and-chains-and-fishnet outfit. She smiled broadly at her would-be suitors, but the expression didn't reach her golden brown eyes. He wondered why.

"She is *young*. She is genetically *sound*. And yes, good hordesmen... she is fer-*tile*!" The hype-man thrust his arms in front of his belly as if cradling a large ball and nodded so hard St'Anley worried his neck might snap. "Others have tried and failed to win her hand. Will one of you prove worthy? Or," he jabbed his forefinger at each of them in turn, "will your bones increase the sacred Heap?"

The crowd stomped their feet and released cheers and whoops of approval, excited to witness either outcome. St'Anley's fellow Potentials added their hoots to the chorus, so he joined in with as much enthusiasm as he could muster, which amounted to a noncommittal, "Yeah."

"Our virtuous princess will address you now." The hype-man bowed low to the young woman. "Welcome your suitors, O Kardashia, Princess of the Heap, Fruit of Our Great King's loins, Mistress of Shattered Dreams—"

"Yeah, hey, guys." Kardashia brushed aside the hype-man. She contemplated the four men looking at her with eager (or in his case, beleaguered) expressions before speaking. "So, like, it's so cool that you came here to try and, you know, prove yourselves worthy and stuff, but?" She tossed her waist-length black braids. "The first five times we did this? Yeah, all those guys died. So, you know? Try not to do that." She gave them two thumbs up.

Solid advice, St'Anley thought.

A trumpet sounded, off-key, from the sidelines. The hype-man reappeared and intoned, "And now, please bow and scrape before your king. Slayer of all challengers, architect of the Heap, the last great American hero... *Arnschwartz*, the Heeeee-aaaaaaapppppppp Kiiiiiinnnnnngggggggg!"

The crowd went wild chanting their king's name. Meanwhile, it was all St'Anley could do not to roll his eyes free of his skull. Why his fellow post-apocalyptic Americans felt the need to change their given names to these bizarre callbacks to long-gone celebrities, or to descriptors, or (as was required by his horde) to add in random apostrophes, he would never understand. Did they think it made them sound cooler, more intimidating? Or was it simply that they believed they should adopt what they *thought* were proper post-apocalyptic names based on old, vaguely-yet-fondly remembered TV shows and movies? *I mean, I suppose it is more impressive to be called The Skullcrusher than Steve*, St'Anley mused, *but it's also silly and contrived. Why am I the only one who seems to get that?*

King Arnschwartz admittedly cut almost as impressive a figure as his namesake. He joined his daughter before the Heap and folded massive arms bulging with sinews and veins across his broad chest, which was bare under layers of bone and teeth-strung necklaces. His leather pants fit so snugly that they revealed more details about the king's impressive anatomy than St'Anley cared to know.

His bald head gleamed in the pale sunlight barely penetrating the reddish-gray haze that surrounded their blasted planet.

"Hi, Daddy." Princess Kardashia waggled her fingers.

"Hello, pumpkin." He pecked her cheek. Facing the Potentials, he bellowed, "Hordesmen! Introduce yourselves and present your credentials to court my daughter."

The muscle-bound representative of Superiorus trod forward. "My king." He snapped his head down and up respectfully. "I am Thorer, so named because I am mighty like the ancient god Thor, but with an extra *er* because I am even more so." He flexed his biceps causing them to sprout smaller biceps.

Arnschwartz looked impressed. "And by what right do you claim worthiness to compete for the hand of the princess?"

"By right of might," Thorer thundered. "I shall crush all obstacles that come between me and your beautiful, ripe daughter." He cracked his knuckles and the sound echoed like gunfire.

"Your suit is accepted. Go, prepare yourself for the first challenge." King Arnschwartz waved at a large tent set up downfield to house the Potentials.

"As you command." Thorer pivoted on his toe and marched off.

The heavily-armed Killmaster of Horde Slaughter introduced himself next. He demonstrated his worthiness by flicking seven metal stars in rapid succession at the hype-man. They lodged in the center of his chest to form the shape of a valentine.

The hype-man collapsed to the shredded Astroturf and screamed his way into unconsciousness.

"Wow!" The princess's eyes widened at this impressive demonstration of artistic savagery. A chuckling King Arnschwartz sent Killmaster to the tent.

Horde Machiavelli's Potential introduced himself as Benedict Iscariot. St'Anley had to feign a cough to cover a giggle of disbelief. *Really? Was Liar Backstabbius already taken?*

"And what qualifies you to sire my future grandchildren?" demanded the king.

Iscariot bowed so low his forehead nearly struck dirt. "I will be the most loyal, most devoted husband and son-in-law you can conceive of, oh great and powerful King of the Heap." His wide eyes fixed unblinking on the king's. "I will live for her pleasure and never, *ever* betray her faith in me." Shifting his attention to Princess Kardashia, he added, "Please accept a token of my devotion, my lady." He reached into a pocket and withdrew a finger wearing a large diamond ring. He hastily slid the ring free and offered it to the princess.

Kardashia hesitated a moment before accepting it. "Uh, gee. Thank you?"

"Your words bring comfort to a father's soul, Iscariot," said King Arnschwartz. "And your gift is expensive. Your suit is accepted."

The grinning Iscariot tossed the severed finger over his shoulder as he strolled tent-ward.

The king barked again, and St'Anley realized with a sinking heart that he was up. Swallowing every instinct to just tell the truth—*I'm obviously unworthy, and I'd rather not waste everyone's time and my life on this fruitless endeavor*—he instead spoke the words drilled into his head by Horde Master Su'Zanne on threat of exile.

Executing a quick bow, St'Anley said, "Your Majesty, I am Stan... St'Anley of Horde Hoard. While I am not as strong or cunning or skillful as some, I can offer something no other candidate can."

King Arnschwartz raised one beetle-thick eyebrow. "Which is?"

"Lots of really useful stuff. By uniting with me, your daughter joins my Horde, which means you both will enjoy free access to all the things we've collected and saved over the past decade-plus. Basically," he shrugged, "I represent a sound investment."

The king regarded him for so long that St'Anley became hopeful he might be dismissed out of hand. Surely his Horde wouldn't exile him if he was rejected despite having said all the required words with just the right amount of enthusiasm?

"Eh." Arnschwartz glanced at his daughter. She shrugged one shoulder. "We've heard worse pitches. You're in. Go to the tent and prepare." He turned to address the crowd. "The first of the three challenges will commence after one sleep! Trust me, my loyal fans, you won't want to miss a single one!"

As the audience cheered, St'Anley's stomach muscles contracted, sending hot bile surging up into his mouth. He swallowed it down and shuffled off to prepare for whatever the morning brought. No doubt it would entail torments and woes beyond his imagining—and considering what he was capable of imagining, that was saying something.

*****

The first challenge didn't start out utterly horrifying. All they had to do was hike to a nearby ghost town and collect whatever gasoline remained in its stations, cars, and generators. St'Anley did wonder how the town's gas could have been left unraided for so long—a question that was quickly answered when zoombies poured out of the abandoned homes and buildings. While Thorer grabbed them in pairs and slammed their heads to mush, Killmaster hurled blades into their brains. Iscariot took advantage of their distraction to siphon the fuel.

St'Anley shimmied halfway up a still-standing telephone pole. He made the mistake of yelping when a large splinter lodged in his palm, and the remaining zoombies zoomed over to surround him. Fortunately, not only were irradiated rotten corpses poor climbers, his fellow Potentials thought he had intentionally summoned them to a single area for more efficient dispatch. Thorer even gave him a high-five after he came down driving the splinter deeper into his hand. St'Anley accepted the pain as justice since, truthfully, he'd only been trying to avoid being eaten.

Princess Kardashia awarded them each a token—a red plastic rose. He couldn't bring himself to meet her gaze when accepting his, knowing she and the crowd had been given the details of their exploits by the replacement hype-man, who had observed from a safe distance. Yet rather than condemn his performance, all she said was, "Good job not dying today!"

The next day brought the second challenge—a race through the Barrens and back. St'Anley thought it a terrible waste of the precious fuel they'd gathered, but that proved to be the least of his concerns when mutant marauders appeared in vehicles tricked out with steel rams, long spikes, and roof-mounted flamethrowers. He was certain this was how he would die, given that he was driving his weary little Honda while Thorer plowed through them in his Dodge Charger, Iscariot blended in with them in his armored hearse, and Killmaster eluded them effortlessly on a sleek, souped-up motorcycle.

Fortunately, the marauders were just as unimpressed with St'Anley's ride as everyone else and literally drove around him to pursue the other three. While they evaded, rammed, shot missiles, and otherwise engaged one another, St'Anley merely had to veer around corpses and crashed vehicles on his way back to the stadium. He still managed to come in last.

Again they lined up for their tokens—genuine apples from the king's private tree. Again, all she said to St'Anley was, "Good job living another day." Later, as he nibbled his delicious fruit, he noticed that when she didn't think anyone was looking her perpetual smile faded and her body language shifted from perky to resigned. He wondered about that the rest of the night.

For the third and final challenge, Princess Kardashia and her father sat by the fifty-yard-line. The bleachers behind them were filled. Without other entertainment options these annual attempts to find the princess a mate drew almost every survivor in the vicinity.

The hype-man explained that any surviving Potentials would be feted that evening, after which they would submit themselves to the princess's consideration for her life-mate. "A worthy husband and father to the next generation of the Heap must display leadership," he proclaimed. He strode to one of the two tunnels through which football teams used to pour onto the field. "However, he must also be capable of working with others toward a common goal. In this challenge, you will either fight together," he paused dramatically, "or die together."

Thorer snorted and tossed his mane. Killmaster flowed through a series of martial arts katas. Iscariot studied their every move from the corner of his eye.

The hype-man saluted. "May the Heap reject your bones." Then he picked up a battered trumpet and blew an earsplitting note. He leaned into the tunnel mouth, listened, and sprinted away in the opposite direction.

That was dramatic, St'Anley thought. *I wonder why he...?*

Panic derailed St'Anley's train of thought as a combined hiss and trumpet echoed down the tunnel. Moments later, a ten-foot-tall elegator galumphed into the stadium.

It was a shining example of animal mutation born of the unnatural union between creatures that should never, *ever* have cross-procreated, but were now deranged mentally and genetically enough to do so. The monstrosity raised its trunk and spread its hideously elongated jaws to display rows of long, jagged teeth.

As St'Anley froze in place, torn between fainting and pissing himself, Thorer bellowed, "Witness my triumph!" He plunged his hands into the Heap and came up gripping what appeared to be a large splinter of goal post almost as long as St'Anley was tall. He hoisted this overhead and charged straight for the elegator. He thrust one ragged end of the post into its left instep.

The creature roared its displeasure. It swung its huge head down, hideous jaws agape. Thorer dodged and barely avoided becoming a meaty treat. He laughed heartily, balled his hands into fists, and pounded the huge splinter to drive it deeper into the elegator's foot.

It turned its head over one shoulder then whipped it back. A twisted tusk struck Thorer along his entire left side and the force of impact bowled him ass over teakettle halfway to the unoccupied bleachers across the stadium.

St'Anley scuttled to the side of the Heap opposite the occupied stands and crouched down wondering how to avoid being trampled or devoured or gored or...

"Hello, friend," a voice hissed in his ear.

St'Anley started and fell onto his rear. "*Aaaah*! Where the hell did you come from?"

Iscariot ignored his question, instead stroking the thin moustache above his nearly-nonexistent upper lip. "You heard what the king's man said, that we have to work together for this to count? Well, I have an idea, and if it works, we all win the day." His unwavering gaze made St'Anley queasy. "However, I will need your cooperation."

Whatever Iscariot's angle was, he was certain it included an ulterior motive. The only question was whether it would prove fatal to him or not. "What's your plan?"

Iscariot nodded toward Thorer, who lay groaning on the sward. "Easy. We sit tight right here. Meanwhile, muscles-for-brains and the ninja take down the elegator. Once they've all but finished it off, you and I slip over there, come around where everyone can see, and stab its corpse with these." He produced a short sword and a long, curved knife from behind him and grinned.

"Where did you find those?" They looked far too well-maintained to have been salvaged from the Heap.

"I... borrowed them. From Killmaster." He winked. "Don't worry, he won't notice until it doesn't matter anymore."

"Oh." St'Anley ruminated. The plan wasn't terrible, and frankly he didn't have another to counter it. "But how do you know Thorer and Killmaster can take that thing down?"

"Eh, at minimum they'll do some serious damage." Iscariot's rictus grin sent a chill cascading down St'Anley's spine. "And if they die in the attempt, well, then we're down two top competitors—win, win."

"But then *we* would have to take down the elegator."

Iscariot shrugged. "Let's just cross that bridge if we come to it, shall we?"

St'Anley swallowed hard. *Oh. He totally plans to chuck me at the elegator and then kill it while it's busy gnawing my bones.* "Um, where is Killmaster anyway?" he asked hoping to distract Iscariot from any murderous considerations. "I haven't seen—"

A bellow drew their attention back to the elegator. A row of knives had somehow appeared along its neck and one massive shoulder. It took St'Anley a moment to figure out they hadn't magically sprouted from its flesh but rather been lobbed into it by Killmaster.

A throwing star struck the elegator in the right eye. It reared up with a trumpeting hiss. The nimble Killmaster slid beneath its exposed belly, reached into the scabbard fastened along one leg, and withdrew... a hilt that had been affixed to the top of a thin branch.

He hesitated just a moment. But that was all it took.

The elegator dropped back down to all four thick-clawed feet, dipped its head between its forelegs, and chomped. Killmaster's shriek of agony was bloodcurdling, but mercifully brief.

A chunk of the audience let out a groan. Apparently, Killmaster had a sizable and now very disappointed fanbase.

St'Anley glanced at the sword still resting beside his unwanted comrade. Iscariot's attention remained on the elegator devouring his competition. St'Anley looked over toward Thorer, who was struggling to sit up.

The hell with it. If he had to throw in his lot with either of these two, the huge heroic guy was the obvious choice.

Snatching up the sword, St'Anley half-dashed, half-crab scuttled to Thorer's side. The still dazed man blinked at him. "Oh hey. Did I kill it?"

"Not yet." St'Anley held out his hand and Thorer grasped it. St'Anley gritted his teeth, dug in his heels, and pulled with all his terror-fueled strength until Thorer was back on his feet. Then he held out the sword. "Take this." He pointed to the elegator, which was licking its bloody chops. "Kill that."

Thorer shook the remaining cobwebs away and thumped his chest once with his right fist. "Thank you, noble fellow," he said. Then he lofted the sword above his head and charged the elegator again.

Even half-blind the giant monstrosity had no problem spotting Thorer coming his way and charged right back at him... and, by unfortunate extension, St'Anley.

St'Anley felt a scream surge up from his bowels. It got stuck in the center of his chest, so all that came out of his gaping maw was a thin, high-pitched keening. He stumble-ran backward, tripped over his own feet, and landed with a spine-jolting thud before continuing to scoot backward on his ass as fast as his hands and feet could propel him.

The elegator's jaws snapped in anticipation of fresh meat as it approached Thorer. But just moments before they collided, the big man leapt impressively high and plunged the sword directly between its eyes. Thanks to the creature's momentum and Thorer's, the extremely sharp blade sunk in deep enough to strike brain. The elegator immediately stiffened then toppled onto its side with the impact of a meteor strike.

Seemingly out of thin air, Iscariot appeared beside the thing's huge head. He withdrew the wickedly curved blade he'd "borrowed" from Killmaster and slashed the thing's throat open with a flourish. He turned to face the audience, raised his arms, and cried, "Behold, we have slain the beast!"

Son of a bitch. St'Anley glared at him with disgust.

Thorer seemed untroubled by Iscariot's act of stolen valor. He stepped on the beast's head with one booted foot, clasped his hands overhead, and proclaimed, "Yeah, baby! That's what I'm talkin' 'bout!"

The crowd lost their minds, cheering and stamping their feet so hard that a few of the already precarious bleachers collapsed and dumped them into piles. The hype-man reappeared and proclaimed, "We have our champions! Mighty Thorer, clever Iscariot, and... uh, cautious St'Anley have slain the beast! They have earned the right of consideration by the princess." He turned toward the jumbled audience and added, "And now it's trivia time! The winners will attend tonight's festivities in person..."

St'Anley struggled to his feet with a groan and pressed a hand against his bruised coccyx. *Well what do you know,* he marveled. *I actually survived!*

*****

The evening feast was an elaborate affair held in the king's massive bunker beneath the stadium. The Potentials were garbed by the Heap King's aides in metal-studded leather and had their hair sprayed into spikes with their hordes' colors. The heavy clothes made St'Anley sweat like a pigorse in the desert.

After a meal that included rare uncontaminated tomatoes, elegator steaks, wine from some pillaged cellar, and an extravagant two glasses each of potable water, King Arnschwartz rose from his bone-carved throne at the head of the concrete slab table. His guests, who included various courtiers, the Potentials, and the lucky winners of the trivia contest, fell obediently silent.

Arnschwartz lifted a wine-filled hollowed skull that used to reside inside his predecessor's head. "A toast to my daughter!" He looked down at Kardashia seated beside him. "I know it has been a difficult and disappointing journey with so many promising suitors coming to rest on the Heap rather than in your bed. But tonight, you actually get to choose one of these," he nodded to Iscariot, barely glanced at St'Anley, and then let his gaze come to rest on Thorer who he grinned at broadly, "fine specimens of manly potency."

"To Princess Kardashia!" enthused Iscariot raising his chipped mug with a green *-bucks* barely visible on one side. "May your wisdom in selecting a mate equal your unparalleled beauty!"

"Indeed!" Thorer slammed his hand against the table. "To Kardashia... may the spawn of our combined gene pools strike awe in all who lay eyes upon them!"

Everyone's attention shifted to St'Anley. He cleared his throat awkwardly. "To Princess Kardashia." He raised his handle-less mug. "I... well, I hope whoever you choose tonight makes you happy. Because God knows, there's not much joy to be had in this blighted ruin of a world so, you know, you should seize it when you can." He took in the crowd's alternately puzzled and critical expressions. "I mean cheers," and gulped down the rest of the only somewhat vinegary wine.

He peered over the mug and discovered Princess Kardashia staring at him. Surprised, he tried to read the expression on her face. *Could it be... appreciation?* He couldn't be sure having never seen such a look directed toward him in his life.

After dinner came the final token ceremony from which the Heap King excused himself. "This is my daughter's time to reign. I trust she'll make the right choice." He departed with three of his women.

The moment he left, St'Anley sensed a shift in Kardashia's demeanor. Gone was the simpering, pampered stereotype. When the hype-man began droning on about the "sacred ceremony" and "honor of her hand," she interrupted him. "That's enough, Jack... sorry, I mean Grandmaster J. I've got this." He fell silent and stepped back into the shadows.

Kardashia began by removing one of her many necklaces, a string threaded through knucklebones, and laid it on the empty folding chair meant for the fallen Killmaster. "I'm sorry that you died for this." Her regret sounded sincere.

Next, she summoned Iscariot. He came off his folding chair and immediately dropped to one knee before her. "I know this breaks all protocol, but my heart is so filled with love for you I cannot contain it." He took her right hand and kissed the ring he'd given her. "I see you are wearing the token of my affection bestowed during our first meeting. Please allow me the honor of moving it to your left hand as evidence of our engagement, and I swear to you and all gathered here, " he swept his arm to include the entire room, "that I will shower you with riches beyond compare for the rest of your life." He stared up into her eyes with such intensity that St'Anley wondered if he was trying to hypnotize her. "Princess Kardashia, will you make me your prince?"

She stared at him for a beat. "Okay, so you technically won in that you survived all three challenges. But honestly?" She yanked her hand away and took a step back. "I am *not* impressed."

Iscariot blinked for perhaps the first time since St'Anley had met him. "Ex... excuse me?"

She rolled her eyes. "Look, I know I have a certain reputation. I'm young, I'm hot, I'm sheltered by a mighty king from the realities outside these walls, blah, blah. Everyone assumes I'm," her voice rose an octave as she minced in place, "just, like, a spoiled, gullible, little thing." She dropped the affect and her tone. "Am I right?"

Most of those gathered had the grace and good sense to shake their heads and mutter, "No, no, of course not."

She waved off their halfhearted denials. "I know, it's okay, it's all part of the princess package. But trust and believe, I'm not so clueless as to be unable to see bullshit when it's being shoveled at me. And you?" She planted her fists on her hips and glared down at Iscariot. "Are so full of it your eyes are brown."

Iscariot stumbled to his feet with an expression of stunned outrage. "This is... I *earned* this, damn it! As much as Brawny over there," he jerked his head to indicate Thorer, "and sure as hell more than Chicken Little." He thrust his chin toward St'Anley. "How *dare* you impugn my reputation!"

Princess Kardashia snorted. "You didn't earn squat. You slit the throat of an already-dead elegator. Did you think we didn't notice?" The crowd murmured agreement. "And you've been laying it on thick since you got here. You don't *love* me. How could you? We just freaking met!" She paused to regain her composure.

"Look, here's how this is gonna go. You get your token, but you're not winning this thing, so just… go over and sit quietly until I'm done, or I'll have my father's men filet you and toss your bones on the Heap." She removed a necklace, this one a string of lug nuts, and lobbed it at Iscariot's chest.

He caught it, weighed it in his hand, and shrugged. "Fine, whatever. At least I can trade these." He slunk back to his folding chair and slouched down.

Thorer chuckled. "You really do suck." Iscariot grunted and stared at the floor.

Well, isn't this fun. St'anley meant it. He was enjoying this version of Kardashia. She seemed… real.

"St'Anley of Horde Hoard… geeze, that's a ridiculous name, pardon my saying." Kardashia jerked her head toward him, and he girded his loins in preparation for the dressing-down he knew he deserved. He scratched the top of his head nervously as he approached.

"I've always thought so too," he said. "Horde Hoard. I mean, come on, right?" He chuckled nervously.

She smiled. "I like you, St'Anley. You know why?"

"I genuinely cannot think of a single reason."

"*That's* why. Right there." She tapped the tip of his nose. "You're you, for better or worse. You don't pretend to be anything else."

She leaned closer and lowered her voice so only he could hear. "You're not playing the same game as everyone else in this stupid, sad world with their phony ways of talking and these ridiculous outfits." She plucked at her chainmail bikini top. "God, I am so jealous of that. I wish I could just be me all the time, but being Princess of the Heap, it's not an option."

St'Anley's heart ached for her. "It never occurred to me how hard playing this role must be for you, or that you were even playing one. I made the same assumptions that you accused everyone else of making, and that was, well, pretty assy. I'm really sorry."

Her eyes glistened as she nodded. "Thanks for saying that, and even more for meaning it." She flashed a regretful smile. "You know I can't choose you, right? As much as I like you, that would never fly with my father."

St'Anley sighed. "Yeah, I know. And hey, I'm alive to get over it, so there's that."

She chuckled. "True enough." She leaned in closer and whispered, "I hope we can figure out how to be… friends. Under the radar if you know what I mean."

His heart fluttered as the warmth of her breath in his ear stirred feelings he hadn't felt since his pre-apocalyptic crush on Darcy McFadden in seventh grade. "Uh, yeah," he whisper-squeaked back. "I'd totally be into that."

"Good." She pulled back and raised her voice for all to hear. "St'Anley of Horde... you know. While you failed to distinguish yourself during the challenges, you did what you could to assist others. As the final challenge stipulated that a collaborative effort was required, you met that bare minimum when you rushed to Thorer's aid. Because of that, while you did not win my hand, you have earned this." She removed a chain threaded with gold teeth.

He lowered his head so she could slip it over. "Thank you, princess." He bowed without a trace of irony. "I am honored to have been given the opportunity to meet you."

"Yeah, you are." She dismissed him with a twinkle in her eye.

He returned to his folding chair unable to stop grinning.

Finally and obviously, it was Thorer's turn. He stood flexing before Kardashia. "Thorer? You *totally* killed that elegator even after he swatted you like a fly. I feel like you and me could form a... a meaningful connection."

The crowd let out a collective, "*Awwww*" of romantic appreciation as Kardashia removed the last of her necklaces—a thick braided chain with what appeared to be a shriveled, preserved human heart pendant. "Please accept this ultimate token of my affection signifying my desire to become your life-mate in recognition of your undeniable bravery."

Thorer cradled the heart in his large hands wearing an expression of pure joy. "You have made me the happiest hordesman in the whole world." He gazed at her. "We are legit gonna make the most gorgeous babies."

She patted his broad shoulder. "Let's get to know each other and see how that goes before we start making anything. Sound good?"

He considered it. "Fair enough."

And so it ended. The hype-man formally proclaimed Thorer the victor and he joined hands with Kardashia before the cheering crowd. At some point during the proceedings, Iscariot departed unnoticed and unlamented. St'Anley managed to catch Kardashia's attention on his way out and mouthed, "See you." She responded with a wink.

St'anley mulled over what to tell his Horde and concluded they wouldn't be surprised he failed to win the princess, only that he'd survived the attempt. Plus he had a pricey strand of gold teeth to add to their coffers, which would earn him additional goodwill.

He couldn't help but feel badly for Kardashia, forced into a life of maintaining appearances and meeting expectations. He hoped Thorer stepped up as a life-mate to support the real princess and that they would find some measure of happiness.

And if not? Maybe she'd come find him and they could run off together, leaving the hordes and Heap behind them to pursue something real.

The Four Cheerleaders of the Apocalypse

Robert Greenberger

Yasmine tumbled into the waiting arms of her teammates but the yelling began before she was lowered to the floor.

"You know why you fell?" Demona shouted from across the too-cold gym. The senior, clad in matching t-shirt, shorts, and hair scrunchie, marched toward the freshman as she continued to yell. "Because you're fat! You put on weight, not lost any, so your raggedy ass lost its balance. You're going to break their arms if you keep pilin' on those pounds!"

While it was only the second week of practice, it felt to the freshmen that nothing had improved. The three-hour workouts began before school started and by the fifth day, their collective enthusiasm for starting high school had been drained by their co-captains. The four seniors, now that two others dropped out to "focus on their college careers," were named co-captains and were mercilessly verbally whipping the dozen other members of the cheerleading squad. Fitting in was proving harder than they imagined, especially compared with the enthusiasm they felt at the outset of summer break.

"I'm trying," Yasmine managed to say, sucking in air to keep the tears at bay.

Demona, tall, curvy, and with a mane of hair that needed constant attention, peered close, so her hot breath filled the girl's face. "Try harder! You've got to drop five by next week or you're out."

With that, she spun on her heel, and began berating someone else, thankfully a sophomore, for not being in proper formation.

"What a bitch," Madison said, throwing a consoling arm around Yasmine. Not that Madison had it any easier, as she was constantly dealing with gossip about her that seemed to show up out of nowhere. First it was about how "rich" her parents were, just because she was seen being dropped off in a brand new BMW. Then it was about her giving hand jobs to the football players after practice. At this rate, by the time classes started on Tuesday, she'd already be labeled the class pump, a title that could ruin her next four years.

"I didn't mean to lose my balance," Yasmine said in a low voice. "My foot slipped on someone's palm."

"It's fine, Yaz, shit happens," said another freshmen, Paige. "It's why they call this practice."

"I know, but I love cheer and don't want to be cut this early," the girl said.

Paige, the smallest of the group of six freshmen, didn't have to worry about being cut, being the most athletic of the incoming students. When they first arrived at tryouts, the girls' athletic director was incredibly effusive in her praise. "You six may be the best incoming freshmen we've ever had. This is dynasty-making." Since then, they'd all taken extra pains to fit in, not get cut, and wear the blue and gold with pride. Some of them were beginning to detest those colors. Madison, who came in with gold hair, had already switched it to a Kelly green.

Still, Paige had her own issues to contend with. One of the co-captains, Lisanna, had been cozying up to her, prying into her personal life. So far, she'd been managing to deflect her by talking about her passion for *Dear White People*, but that only worked for so long. She'd been giving up a tidbit here and there; enough she hoped, to satisfy the senior, perhaps the prettiest of the sixteen girls on the squad. Lisanna's toned, dark skin practically shone by the end of workouts. To her, precision had to be in all things, from flips to how much eyeliner got used. Paige couldn't tell if this was someone trying to mentor her or mess with her mind.

"Why isn't Coach saying anything?" Madison asked.

Ugo shook her head, full of dreadlocks with a rainbow of coordinated ribbons. "She's a fill-in and doesn't know the routines like the captains. She got the assignment by default."

They all swiveled their heads to see the coach, actually an administrator pressed into service, swiping at her tablet, playing catchup. Several of the girls chose to attend the school because of the cheer coach's reputation and now she was gone.

"I bet the seniors drove the old coach away," Yasmine said.

"Lisanna told me there was some scandal," Paige said, but lacked the details. Her newfound companion doled out stories in drips and drabs, keeping her always interested in knowing more.

"Back to work, bitches," called Coral, another co-captain.

She was perhaps the nicest of the four, but that was like saying she was the dullest knife in the drawer—she could still cut you. To her, calling the freshmen "bitches" rather than by name, and treating the sextet as a unit as opposed to individuals, was her way of trying to build team unity. Instead, she missed that the six teens, all trying for fresh starts as high school students, wanted to be seen for themselves.

With a sigh, Yasmine led the others back to the group and they resumed their positions for the next move.

Things hadn't improved the day before classes began. Janae arrived and was spotted using her inhaler before practice began. Almost immediately, Coral was in her face, asking pointed questions about the use of the device. "We wouldn't have let you even try out if we knew you were going to collapse on us," the senior said, sounding sympathetic for a change. "We can't have you collapsing during a game or the regional competition."

"It's fine," Janae said. "There's nothing to worry about inside. It's just so damned humid out today, it got to me."

Coral gave her an unexpected hug, squeezing her tight. "We can't have a health problem on the team. Are you sure?"

"My doctor let me do gymnastics all through middle school," Janae said, trying to sound as confident as possible.

"Well, that's something. Maybe you should sit out the first hour, to be safe. We're just doing calisthenics, then chants and Ls. Really, you've got those down fine." At that reassurance, Janae nodded and took her bag over to the bleachers. Janae watched with intense focus, not wanting to miss anything new.

From there, she spotted Lisanna and Paige in deep conversation as the freshmen was stretching and there was another senior, Eleena, saying something that made Madison fume, but the younger girl held her tongue. Yaz was sucking down water from an oversized bottle, determined to have lost weight by tomorrow. It was so much harder to be a cheerleader than she ever imagined and she had no idea why the four co-captains were making it impossible to have any fun.

*****

A month later, all six girls were still on the team and were still looking for the fun they were promised. If they were the beginnings of a years-long run of championship-caliber teams, the idea of enduring such verbal abuse was contradictory. Rather than feel welcomed by the quartet of co-captains, they were treated not as welcome additions, but undesirable competitors. In some ways, cheer was a good, physical outlet for them as each adjusted to high-school life in different ways. All complained about the ridiculous amount of homework they received, barely getting any of it done between the bell and the start of practice. That meant working out for three hours, going home, a quick dinner, and then hitting the books. Add in texting, browsing, and other distractions, it was easily eleven or later before they turned out the lights, and they were feeling stressed.

The co-captains had yet to relent, pushing the freshmen, and even the others, hard. They were going to debut that Friday night at the first home football game of the season and were told they had to be absolutely perfect.

That Tuesday, Yasmine arrived with her ever-present water bottle, but didn't look as bright-eyed as usual. Madison was being protective of her, literally putting herself between the tired-looking freshman and Demona. Everyone else was stretching, their usual warmup music cranked loud. Across the gym, the boys' volleyball team was also warming up, so it was crowded and loud.

As the captains shouted, the girls quickly did roundoffs and back handsprings, readying to form their first pyramid. The combination was challenging and they were running through it again and again. By the fourth time, Yasmine stumbled and collapsed, two other girls leaping over her prone form rather than crash into her. As the captains berated her, the others surrounded the girl, and finally, the coach, a round, older woman, with glasses forever perched atop her head, came over.

"Yaz, you okay?" she asked, repeating what everyone else was asking. The girl was awake but clearly far from okay. She was helped up and the coach wrapped an arm around her shoulder and led the freshmen to the athletic trainer's office.

"Back to work, girls," Eleena shouted. "Forward flips and Ts now!"

Only later, as practice ended, did the coach return for Yasmine's things. Everyone crowded around her wanting an update. Her worried expression drew cries of alarm from some and then she said, "Yaz fainted. Alli says she's malnourished and needs to be seen by her doctor."

It was clear there was no way she'd make her debut on Friday.

A week later, though, she was back, looking better. When the others greeted her, Demona gave her a sharp, appraising look.

"You've put on the pounds again," she said and walked off.

She was about to say something sharp, but there was a loud sound to her right. Turning in that direction, she saw the other freshmen, and even some sophomores, coalesce around Paige. As Yasmine neared, it was clear the girl was in tears, sobbing with great heaves. Taking her place in the comforting circle, she shot Madison a questioning look. In return, the dark-skinned girl tilted her head and they split off.

"Have you checked your phone lately?" Madison asked.

Automatically, Yasmine thumbed the phone to life and saw the icon that multiple texts had arrived. One had an attachment and she went to that first and saw a topless Paige, proudly displaying herself. Only after gawking for a moment, she checked who it came from and it was a senior she didn't know who airdropped it, clearly to the entire school.

"This is bullshit, the captains did it," Yasmine said.

"No shit, but they're saying it came from me," Madison said. Yasmine blinked in surprise but then narrowed her eyes.

"What's going to happen?"

"Well, when I heard it happened to that junior Faith, she was suspended for weeks, missed the SATs and was nearly suicidal."

"But you didn't—"

The look on Madison's face confirmed she was not responsible, but that was quickly replaced with a look of concern. If word got out she was involved at all, her parents would kill her and that was just going to be for starters.

"Break it up," yelled Lisanna. "There's no crying in cheer unless we win something and we're not going to win shit unless we practice." She and the other seniors worked their way around the gym, shooing the teammates into position. Coral was yelling at several and the air in the gymnasium was tense as practice finally got underway.

It was the following morning when their coach had the team yanked from their classes for an emergency meeting with the principal. They were gathered in an empty classroom and the principal, a middle-aged woman in a too-tight suit and blonde hair going gray, strode in, kicking the door closed for emphasis. Only fifteen of them were present, along with the athletic director and the coach, both of whom looked like they'd rather be elsewhere.

"We've launched an investigation into yesterday's unfortunate incident involving Paige. Until this is settled, she is at home, on suspension, completing her classwork online. We do not condone sexting and thought everyone here knew better. Clearly not. Your coach and your captains have explained they have had some unusual challenges this year." And here she stopped and looked directly at the five remaining freshmen. "Maybe it's an adjustment issue, which happens with incoming students. Maybe our policies haven't been made clear enough. I don't know. What I do know is that this cannot continue. The team is already down one member and with the first regional competition coming up this Saturday, I certainly don't want to hurt your chances. But you're all on notice. This cannot continue, so resolve it among yourselves or it will be resolved for you."

Taking no questions, waiting for no supportive comments from the other adults, the principal stormed out of the classroom.

The girls, stunned silent, milled about, uncertain what was to come next.

What followed over the next few days was continued silence from Paige. Since the picture didn't originate from her phone, the police were still investigating, and the senior who did send it was also on suspension. There were increased tensions as the routines for the competition were furiously reworked. Coral, Eleena, Demona, and Lisanna seemed not to care about the principal's pep talk about overcoming the drama. It only seemed to heighten, which caused Yasmine to live on water and cucumbers other than a modest dinner, for Madison to avoid talking to anyone but a small handful of her freshmen friends, and Janae was moderating her efforts for fear of falling ill before the meet.

With Paige gone, Ugo came into Lisanna's sights. On the first practice without her, the senior got her hands on the girl's phone, clearly looking for something to use against her. She growled in frustration when she couldn't bypass the biometric security. Instead, she kept calling Ugo out for missing a step or not being synchronous. The first time, the freshman argued and was forced to run laps. For her second objection, Lisanna made her stay late reworking routines, leaving her cramped.

The final practice, on Thursday, was exceedingly long and at the end, rather than a positive speech, Eleena told them, "You bitches better be rested, hydrated, and ready. We leave for Cherry Hill at six-thirty sharp. Miss the caravan and you're off the team. When we arrive, watch the others and see what winners look like. Then we're going out there, and staying in sync from the moment we take the floor to the moment we leave it. We're showing uniformity, precision, and teamwork. We're going to attack our routine and those are the most important two and a half minutes of your lives. Don't fuck it up."

Madison stole a look to see how the coach would react to the profanity, but as usual, she was typing on her laptop, missing the tirade.

Sure enough, everyone made the trip without fail. Wearing brand-new uniforms with the school's name across their chests and the mascot logo on their right shoulders, they marched out in unison. As the music blared, the fifteen did an aerial before taking their positions with a dozen forming the bases and flinging the others in basket tosses. As they moved to the rest of the routine, no one faltered, no one missed a dismount, no one dared. The music played, the precision movements were expert, and the audience wildly cheered long before the routine finished.

Of course they won first prize and the co-captains accepted it in perfect harmony while the others, still breathing hard, watched with a mix of pride and hatred.

It wasn't until the following Monday, when the girls, still elated, took to the gym floor for the next practice. Homecoming was just weeks away followed by the next regional competition so there was no letting up from the captains.

But, a curious thing happened as practice ended. Three juniors, Claire, Isabelle, and Amy, motioned to the five freshmen—Paige was not due back until Wednesday now that the furor had died down—so they lingered. The five shot one another quizzical looks, uncertain why now, for the first time, the juniors were even bothering with them. The sophomores were far more sympathetic and helpful while the juniors kept to themselves, unless they were doing whatever chores the captains assigned them.

Isabelle, with her short brown hair and round, open face, smiled and made it clear they weren't there to cause trouble. Amy and Claire made certain the seniors were off the floor before anyone spoke.

"Listen," Isabelle, began. "We've seen how hard they've been on you. We've been there."

"But not like this," Amy added.

"For sure," Isabelle agreed. "I know we won and all, but it's supposed to be fun."

"It is?" questioned Madison, arching an eyebrow. "Sure doesn't feel that way."

"All summer, they kept hearing how you guys were going to be great, how we were going to rebuild around you for the future," Isabelle, clearly the leader, said.

"They've been queens long enough, and they hate the idea of anyone being better," Amy said. "They hated you before you arrived."

"Is that why it sucks to be here?" Yasmine asked.

"Hey, it hasn't been rainbows and unicorns for us either," Claire shot back. "They're trying to ruin it for you without costing them a chance at the state championship."

"It's working," grumbled Janae.

"Yeah, look, we don't want you to leave. Or be forced off," Isabelle said. "One of us will be captain next year and we want to be winners our senior year. They won't tell you, but you're really good. We *need* you next year."

"All six of you," Claire confirmed.

"Okay," Yasmine said. "So, what do you *want*?"

The three looked at one another before speaking. "We just wanted to let you know what's really going on. They're not going to stop pushing you, making you feel miserable while we win."

"And," pressed Janae.

"And it's up to you. We're not going to get between you, but thought you should know what's happening. We'll be rooting for you to succeed," Amy said.

"And for you to stay," Isabelle emphasized.

The trio moved away, breaking eye contact, and leaving the five freshmen alone in the gym, which now felt cavernous and isolating. They all stood there with their thoughts, no one daring to speak first.

"We gotta do something," Janae said.

"Okay, but what?" Madison said. "I don't wanna be thrown off the team if we do the wrong thing."

"They have to respect us," Yasmine said, defiance in her voice. "They have to stop this bullshit. Lemme think on it."

*****

They got through the next month without breaking, each now aware of what has happening to them. Paige had returned and her normally effusive personality was tamped down and she remained part of the crowd, refusing to stand out. Sure enough, the practices were hell on them all, but they were winning their competitions, in no small part due to the effectiveness of the freshmen. They were silently supported by the upperclassmen while the seniors never let up on their verbal abuses.

Yasmine watched her weight, but began wearing Spanx to maintain a slim, uniform appearance and ignored the abuse anytime she was seen with anything but a water bottle. For her part, Madison developed a harder shell and a caustic tongue so anytime a new rumor flew around about her, she gave as good as she got. And Janae was made to feel miserable anytime she sneezed or seemed out of breath from practice, but learned to suffer in silence. Paige was once more under withering commentary, which spared Ugo, but she suffered in silence.

Finally, as winter break approached, Yasmine gathered the freshmen in a classroom before practice and outlined her plan. It'd taken her time to work out something that would make their point, not get them kicked off the team, and not hurt the sophomore or junior members. The others listened and nodded in agreement, offering ideas and suggestions until the six were unified in their thinking. Then they got to work.

*****

The semifinals for the regional championship was just a week away as practice began on a Monday. As usual, the quartet were snapping, yelling, and demeaning the freshmen as they warmed up. But once the actual practice started, it was all business. All sixteen girls wanted to win and move on to the state championship, so they worked in relative harmony.

After the practice, Janae waved a flyer in front of Lisanna's face.

"They moved the start time," Janae said. The flyer was a printout from the state web site and sure enough, it showed that the start time was now nine a.m.

"Good to know," Lisanna said, sharing the sheet with the co-captains.

"Okay, we meet here at six-thirty," Eleena announced, stating what seemed to be the obvious.

The remainder of the week was uneventful as the routines took shape and the one to compete with was honed to within a second of perfect uniformity. By the time Friday rolled around, everyone, even the captains, were tired of the music, but they were happy with the team's effort. Not that they would tell the girls.

Saturday morning was crisp and cold, a fresh layer of frost covered the cars, blacktop roads, and every other surface. The team assembled by five-twenty a.m., all except the captains.

Their coach chose not to call given the early hour so waited until five-forty and then gave up, herding the girls onto the bus and off to the competition a good ninety minutes away. On the trip, the coach and Isabelle reworked the routine to cover for the seniors' absence. There'd be time to run through it at least once or twice before they were scheduled to perform.

The juniors reassigned roles and since they'd been working with the routine so often the last week, everyone understood what needed to be done. As they hustled into the other school's gym, they were directed to a wrestling room to run through their routine. Everything seemed to fall nicely into place and the thirteen girls worked seamlessly to integrate the new roles.

By the time they entered the gym, the team before them was already into their routine and they were impressive. But not impressive enough to rattle the girls.

Just as they were beginning their own routine, the four seniors rushed onto the floor, breathless and red-faced. Seeing their roles filled by others, they assumed the less flashy role of spotters, trying to make it look like this later arrival was part of the routine. As she flipped, Madison saw the terror and hatred in Coral's eyes. But she inwardly smiled at that and kept focused on the steps.

After the music ended and the team waved to the cheering crowds, they hustled off to the side where their coach was bypassed. The seniors backed the others out into the hall, far from the crowd that was already clapping for the next team.

"What the fuck...?" Coral hissed.

"You lied to us," Demona shrieked.

"Misdirected," Yasmine said.

"What'd you say, bitch?"

"She said you were misdirected," Ugo said, taking her place beside the girl.

"You could have cost us the championship," Demona yelled. "You probably did."

"Why?" was all Lisanna managed.

There was some uncomfortable silence before Yasmine lifted her chin and met their murderous gazes.

"We were done. Done with you and your nasty ways. This was making a statement. We didn't *need* you. Thankfully, Janae is taking digital arts and was easily able to mock up the time change announcement and you never bothered to check the web site to see what was going on. You were too busy tearing us down."

The four stood fuming, none saying a word.

"Since Monday night, we've all been working without you. Isabelle figured out how to rework the routine without you. So, during the afternoons, we did it your way, and at night we did it *our* way," Yasmine continued.

"Your way was better, but this worked out just fine," Madison added.

"This has to stop," Paige said. "You're tearing us down, not building us up. You're ruining it for everyone. I thought you wanted your legacy to be as winners, not as destroyers."

"What. Do. You. Want?" Coral asked through gritted teeth.

"To win, of course," Madison said brightly, ignoring the hatred directed at the freshmen.

"As a team," Janae finished. "With you as our captains, sharing your experience."

Coral blinked.

Whatever was left to be said was interrupted by a rush of parents heading for the concessions during a break. The standoff between the girls remained unfinished until much later. In the meantime, they remained in two groups, the seniors to one side of the bewildered coach, and the others on the other side. They politely cheered for the other competitors and acted as if nothing was amiss.

Much later, as the freshmen girls' nerves were getting the better of them, the final team had finished and the judges were busily tallying the scores. Occasionally, a freshman would look over at the seniors, but the older girls were keeping their focus straight ahead or on their phones.

Finally, the winners were announced with the top two schools moving on to represent the region at the state finals a month later. The seniors held one another's hands in death grips while the others crossed themselves or held their breath.

They came in second.

Everyone, freshmen, sophomores, juniors, and seniors alike shrieked and rushed the floor to dance around the trophy. They rushed back to the sidelines, getting high fives from parents and a big bear hug from the coach.

It wasn't until a little later, the team huddled in the lobby before boarding the bus.

"What do you want?" Coral repeated.

"Détente," Paige said.

Coral blinked.

"Oh, look at you using your big Model UN words," Yasmine teased.

"We want the bullshit to stop," Madison said. Everyone, including the other classes, were nodding in silent affirmation. "We want the state championship. Your routine is the better one and we'll win with it."

"But only if you knock the bullshit off," Yasmine said.

Isabelle stepped forward and caught the seniors' attention. "They're good. As good as advertised so why are you chasing them away? *We* need them, not for your victory lap, but for the rest of us *next* year. So, get your heads out of your asses and make this work."

Demona looked at Eleena, who shared a glance with Coral, before all heads turned to Lisanna. There was a long moment of silence, everyone ignoring the background noise of parents and competitors filing out.

Lisanna let out a breath, deflating along the way. "We'll make it work."

To their credit, the freshmen didn't make a display out of their victory but instead, silently hugged one another and then threw their arms around the sophomores and juniors. Tentatively, Coral and Eleena joined the scrum, followed by Demona.

Lisanna watched them, not quite joining in but not saying a word. She played a long game and there would be time after the championships. Her work was not yet done.

What Do You Want from Me, I'm Old
A Tale of the Four Septuagenarians
of the Apocalypse

Keith R.A. DeCandido

It was a beautiful spring day, the first really nice day of the year. The sun shone over the Bronx, but the temperature was only in the mid-sixties, and there was no humidity.

Andrew Corvin was already sitting on one of the two benches outside the bodega on the corner of Bainbridge Avenue and E. 205th Street, when Thomas Legg and Lorraine Anderson arrived, wandering down Bainbridge. Andrew was wearing a hooded sweatshirt over a green button-down shirt. Lorraine, whose pink cardigan hung loosely over her slight frame, headed toward the bench, while Tom moved toward the bodega entrance, removing his hands from his denim jacket to open the glass door.

"You're not getting anything?" Tom asked.

"You know I can't eat anything in there. It's all full of preservatives. You want me to break out in hives?"

Tom chuckled. "You're so skinny, the hives wouldn't even know where to break out." With that, he went inside.

Lorraine made a grunting noise as she sat down next to Andrew. "You doing okay?" she asked him.

Andrew just shrugged.

Raja Thiagarajan approached from around the corner on 205th, sneezing as he did so.

Wincing, Lorraine said, "You're not sick again, are you, Raj?"

"It's probably just allergies," Raja said weakly, followed by a raspy cough.

Pointing at the second bench that was on the other side of the bodega's door, Lorraine said, "Sit over there."

"Fine." Raja sat down, took a handkerchief out of his windbreaker pocket and blew his nose loudly into it. "I still think it's just allergies."

"Maybe it is, but if you're not sure, I don't wanna get sick," Lorraine said testily.

Tom came out of the bodega then, holding a paper bag spotted with grease and a bottle of water. "Can you believe they're charging two bucks for a bottle of water? It's just water! I can get it outta my tap! Well, I mean, long as I got a purifier thingie attached to it."

Lorraine chuckled. "Purifier thingie?"

Tom took a seat next to Raja. "Y'know that thing they put on the faucet to make the water clean."

"Seems to me that's why they sell it in bottles," Raja said. "If the tap water isn't to be trusted."

"Besides," Lorraine said, "you did go ahead and buy it."

"Exactly!" Raja said before he sneezed.

"Bless you," Lorraine said.

Wiping his nose again with the handkerchief, he said, "Supply and demand. You're demanding it, so there's supply."

"That's the stupidest thing I ever heard," Tom said as he pulled his breakfast sandwich out of the bag. It was laden with egg, cheese, bacon, sausage, and possibly some other meat. "Anyhow, I just needed something to wash down this thing."

"Why not coffee?" Lorraine asked.

That elicited a snort from Andrew.

Tom had already taken a bite of his sandwich, but he continued to talk with his mouth full of bread, dairy, and meat. "First of all, have you had the coffee in there? Pretty sure they filter it through a pair of filthy underwear."

Raja grinned. "And secondly, do you *want* him to be *more* hyper?"

"Good point," Lorraine said, pointing a celebratory finger at Raja.

"Both of you can kiss my wrinkled ass." Then he looked at Raja. "Not you, at least not until your nose faucet gets turned off."

"Nose faucet?"

Lorraine smiled. "That's what he uses to smell his purifier thingie."

Tom sighed and focused on his breakfast sandwich.

*****

On the hottest day of the summer, Tom and Raja were walking down Bainbridge from Montefiore Hospital. Tom had his weekly dialysis at the same time that Raja was meeting with his GP to ascertain if his latest malady was life-threatening. They were both wearing white t-shirts, and Raja's was drenched in sweat. Tom was wearing shorts, his knobby knees exposed to the world.

"Look," Tom was saying as they approached the bodega, "Joe DiMaggio and Babe Ruth were fine at the time, but nowadays? They'd get their asses handed to them. In their whole damn lives, the Yankee Clipper and the Sultan of Swat never once faced nobody who could throw a ball more than ninety miles an hour. I mean, Walter Johnson, they called him the Big Train 'cause he threw faster'n anyone, and he didn't hardly crack ninety. I mean, I saw a game yesterday, guy threw a ninety-five-mile-an-hour *sinker*. How the hell does anyone throw a *sinker* ninety-five?"

Raja blew his nose. "I was just saying that I wished I could've seen Joe DiMaggio and Babe Ruth play, that's all. For that matter, I wish I'd seen Josh Gibson play."

Andrew was already sitting on the bench when they got there. "You doin' okay?" Tom asked him.

In response, Andrew simply shrugged.

Tom and Raja sat down on the other bench. "I still think those old baseball players are crap. People are stronger now, faster, and medicine's better."

"If medicine is better," Raja said, "why am I always sick?"

Lorraine chose that moment to cross the street and approach the bodega. "If medicine wasn't better, you'd probably be dead." She was holding her cell phone in her hand, and put it in the pocket of her pink cardigan before she sat down next to Andrew.

Raja chuckled. "Fair point." Then he sneezed.

"Bless you," Lorraine said.

Tom was staring incredulously at her. "How can you wear a sweater in this heat?"

"I don't know, I'm chilled."

"Maybe try eating something?" Tom asked.

Raja said, "I think you've actually lost weight."

"Nah, she ain't got nothin' to lose."

Lorraine sighed. "I just got a call from my allergist. Turns out I'm allergic to mushrooms now, so I can't even eat half the vegetarian meals out there."

"Why not eat fish?" Raja asked.

Tom stared at him. "Don't you remember nothin'? She developed *that* allergy two months ago. An' poultry six months ago. An' red meat last year."

Wincing, Raja said, "I'm sorry."

Waving him off, Lorraine said, "It's fine, it's totally fine. I can always eat tofu."

"Oh, please." Tom threw his arms in the air. "What is it with you people and tofu?"

Lorraine gazed askance at Tom. "You people?"

"Humanity. Tofu is plastic food."

Raja sighed. "Tofu is completely natural, Tom."

"I tasted it once, and ain't no way that shit is natural."

Andrew turned and shot Tom a look, emitting a slight growl.

Holding up both hands, Tom said, "Excuse my French, Andrew."

Looking away, Andrew folded his arms over his sweat-drenched polo shirt and just sneered.

Raja sneezed again.

"Bless you," Lorraine said.

*****

It had been raining for three days straight in August. On the fourth day, it was still cloudy, but cool and dry, finally.

Lorraine went into the bodega, pausing to say hi to Andrew, who was sitting there like usual. He grunted in reply.

Inside, she waited on-line behind a woman who couldn't decide what brand of cigarettes to buy and two kids who insisted that they were twenty-one and old enough to buy the beer. Edward, the old man behind the counter, sighed with relief when he saw it was Lorraine. "Finally," he said, "a *reliable* customer."

"Sorry this is all I'm buying," she said, putting the granola bar down on the counter and then rummaging through her purse for some cash. "It's about all I can safely eat these days."

"No worries," Edward said as he rang her up.

After paying Edward, Lorraine went outside to see that Raja and Tom had joined Andrew on the benches.

Raja was wrapped in a winter coat and a blue sweater, teeth chattering. "What are you eating?" he asked.

"A granola bar. What are you wearing? It's not *that* cold."

Tom jerked a thumb at Lorraine. "And that's Miss I'm Always Chilled talkin'."

"It's fine, it's just a fever, it'll break soon."

"Y'know," Tom said, "there was some kinda community meetin' the other night. I went, and someone said we need a senior center in the neighborhood. Said this bench was the closest we had to one. Can you believe that?"

"Well, we do keep coming here," Lorraine said.

"Don't get why," Tom muttered. "I mean, it's stupid. We gotta have somewhere better to be."

They all looked at each other. "I don't," Lorraine whispered.

"I see my doctors fairly regularly," Raja said weakly.

Andrew just shrugged.

*****

On the first day of autumn, Tom was sitting with Andrew, both men wearing long-sleeved button-down shirts and khakis. It was a sunny, cloudless day; Andrew wore a Yankees cap, while Tom was wearing sunglasses.

Raja walked up to the bodega wearing a charcoal suit.

"What're you all dressed up for?" Tom asked belligerently.

Raja just stared at both of them in disbelief. "Today was the viewing for Lorraine."

"Oh, right. We'll be at the funeral tomorrow. I just fuckin' hate viewings."

Andrew snarled.

"Pardon my French, but sayin' that I just hate 'em don't really express how much I despise the damn viewings. Especially the way everyone talks. 'Oh, she looks so good.' No, she doesn't look *good*, she looks like a goddamn waxwork dummy, and besides which, she's *dead*."

Raja was about to say something in response, but he sneezed instead.

He was disheartened that he would never hear Lorraine bless him after he sneezed again.

Tom, of course, was still ranting and raving. "The worst is how she died. Eating some fucking yogurt—pardon my French," he added quickly to forestall Andrew's displeasure.

"I thought they labelled items for people with food allergies."

"Oh, sure, *technically* it was labelled. Little tiny pink letters on a little tiny white background that said it had almond flavor. Which meant almonds, which meant anaphylactic shock for Lorraine. Somebody should sue."

"I don't know who," Raja said as he sat down and blew his nose.

Tom took his sunglasses off to scratch his nose, and only then did the other two see the cut under his left eye.

"What happened to you?" Raja asked, aghast.

Smirking, Tom said, "You should see the other guy."

"The other guy is probably perfectly fine."

Tom sighed. "Well, yeah, but he shouldn't'a took my seat on the bus. Jerk was askin' for it."

"So you picked a fight over a bus seat?" Raja sneezed. "Why didn't you just sit somewhere else?"

"It was a crowded bus. Little snot shoulda let the elderly have a seat. Even says so on the damn buses."

"You know they have cameras on buses, yes? What if the police were called?"

"Everybody on that bus was on my side, you can bet on that."

Raja sighed. "If you say so." Then he sneezed again.

*****

The Tuesday after Thanksgiving was unseasonably warm. But nobody was sitting on the bodega bench for most of the morning, because that was the day of Tom's funeral. He burst a blood vessel while arguing with someone in Target on Black Friday.

After the funeral, Raja went to the bodega to find that Andrew had beaten him there. Both men were in suits, Raja wearing the same one he'd worn to Lorraine's viewing.

"How are you feeling, Andrew?" Raja asked.

Andrew just shrugged.

*****

The weather turned cold after that. Every day, Andrew wore a green sweater and flannel-lined pants under a fleece-lined coat. Raja wore a flannel-lined trench coat over whatever he wore—it was always closed tight, and he was shivering and sneezing.

A nasty December blizzard hit mid-month, but then the next day it was in the fifties and all the snow melted.

Raja didn't show up to the bodega that day. He stayed home, his fever having spiked. He died in his sleep that night.

Andrew continued to sit outside the bodega until it got too cold to sit outside.

*****

In the spring, Louie and Bernadette came sauntering up to the bodega, only to see Andrew already sitting there. "How you doing, Andrew?" Louie asked.

Andrew just shrugged.

Anna exited the bodega carrying a brown paper bag, and sneezed before she could greet the other two.

"Gesundheit," Bernadette said.

Louie kept moving toward the entrance, while Bernadette sat down next to Anna. "You're not coming in?" Louie asked.

Shaking her head, Bernadette said, "I'm not really hungry."

Sighing, Louie sat down next to Andrew. "Fine, I won't get anything either."

"What did you get?" Bernadette asked Anna.

"Just some DayQuil so I can get through the day."

Louie shook his head. "Great, another slave to the pharmaceutical-industrial complex."

Anna rolled her eyes. "There he goes again."

Bernadette snorted. "Why do you think I sit next to you instead of him?"

Ignoring them, Louie continued ranting. "It's all just so much bullshit. The human body—"

Andrew elbowed Louie in the ribs.

"Sorry for my language, Andrew. Anyhow, it's *nonsense*, 'cause the human body can heal its own damn self. How do you think humanity survived before drugs?"

"Mostly?" Bernadette said with a smirk. "They were dead by the time they were forty…"

"Yeah, well, I'm gonna live forever, you watch. I keep myself pure of garbage."

Andrew looked over at the other three and snorted. "I doubt it."

Four Entrees

James D. Macdonald

Orville Nesbit, LLD, PhD, JD, etc. etc. (although he did not use any of the initials on either social or business correspondence, rather styling himself "Gent." on those occasions where something absolutely had to be used), stood on his porch in the warmth of a June morning in 1939, turning over the Special Delivery letter in his hands. The postman's whistle had summoned him from his study to accept it, and now he held it, wondering whether he should open it. This letter bore all of the abbreviations that he rated after his name: half-a-dozen earned degrees, another half-dozen honorary, all written in blue ink in a tiny, precise hand.

"This," Orville said, addressing both the letter and the rose bushes that flanked the porch stairs, "had better contain a check," before retreating back inside his house. He placed the letter on the walnut stand beside the front door to allow himself space to shuck off the hunting jacket he had donned in honor of the postman and resume his dressing gown, before retrieving the letter and the silver-and-ivory letter-opener that lay beside it. The silver would protect him from evil, at least at a basic level, while the ivory would reveal more mundane poisons. Or so the theory ran.

The envelope did not contain a check. Or a letter. Or, indeed, anything to match the neat hand-lettering of the envelope. It held a card, printed, with words *Côte d'Hôtel* at the top and *prix fixe* at the bottom. Between lay a list of delicacies: *Timbales à la Rothschild, Hors d'oeuvres assortis, Ris de Veau cheron....* The reverse of the card had the address of a hotel on the Blue Coast of Spain, with a drawing of an edifice, presumably the hotel itself. All was in raised ink engraving. The paper was cream-laid, quite stiff, with a linen finish. Orville found the effect both gauche and oddly fascinating.

A second glance at the menu revealed a time and a date, barely a week hence, written in the same blue ink and delicate hand that had graced the envelope.

Orville cast the card aside and returned to his study, and to his newspapers, to his scissors and paste-pot, and the endless clippings of odd things for his leather-bound notebooks. If someone desired his presence, he preferred more direct means. They could make an appointment. In any case, the date was impossible.

The afternoon post brought a more conventional invitation. A certain rich widow (verified in the Social Register) requested that he visit her in Florida, bringing Tarot cards, to do a reading for her. She mentioned some of his other clients, and noted that she was prepared to pay whatever fee he thought reasonable. This note did include a check for a retainer. He scanned the schedule in his pocket diary and discovered that he was in fact free (as, sadly, he was for every day of the coming fortnight), and prepared a telegram to the effect that he would call in the afternoon, two days hence. He scheduled his railway passage, and packed. The process would have been quite a bit easier had he left it to his man, but Orville did not have anyone in service. The inconvenience of doing everything for himself was more than recompensed by the convenience of not explaining his comings, goings, or work, to anyone at all.

The next day found Orville—in a linen suit, suitcase in hand—at Penn Station, New York, in plenty of time to catch the Silver Meteor. He took a seat in the observation car, and settled in to read Haverstock's definitive *A Compendium of the Heresies of Asia Minor*. Soon enough the diesels throbbed to life and the streamliner departed.

Not much south of Newark, Orville heard a feminine voice saying, "Excuse me, sir, is this seat taken?"

He looked up from a discussion of monophysitism to see a woman in a smart white cotton suit, white gloves, and a white cloche draped about with a veil that softened and obscured her features. "No, Madam," he replied. "It is not taken."

Without another word, the young lady, who was scarcely out of her teens, sat. Orville had scarcely returned to his book, however, when she spoke.

"I regret to inform you," she said, "That there is no elderly widow awaiting you in Jacksonville."

Orville said nothing; the girl knew too much of his business, perhaps, but he was intrigued. Unusual events were ever his downfall, a fact which he acknowledged and in which he inwardly rejoiced. Remaining silent prompted the other person to speak, to fill the silence. Soon he was rewarded.

"You may call me Nelly Bly," she said. "And I am in need of a traveling companion."

"Not your real name."

"No. Not my real name." She had a touch of a foreign accent, Orville thought, though he could not exactly place it.

"If you agree, we will depart this train when it stops in Baltimore, at six this evening. You will be my uncle; for it is not right for a person such as myself to travel unaccompanied. You will, I promise you, be handsomely recompensed. If you do not desire to come with me, well, the check you got in yesterday's mail is quite valid and will pay for your time and this little journey."

"And if I were to accompany you, where would we be going?"

"Spain. You have seen the hotel's card."

"My duties?"

"To guard my virtue."

"That is all?"

"Other circumstances may arise which I cannot now anticipate. I have utmost faith in your abilities."

Orville hesitated, and turned back to his book.

"*Handsomely* recompensed."

He placed a bookmark in the *Compendium*, shut it, and laid the book aside on the seat between them.

"If you would indulge me," he said, and reached into his inner pocket on the left side of his jacket. He pulled out a velvet bag threaded with a golden cord, opened the bag, and removed a Tarot pack. "Was asking me to bring Tarot part of the ruse, or is it an actual necessity?"

Miss Bly did not answer.

"Please indulge me by taking the cards, and giving them a mix," he said. She reached out, but Orville stopped her. "I would prefer that you touch them with your bare flesh. If you would be kind enough to remove your glove?"

Miss Bly did so, while Orville held the pack casually in his hand. She put her gloves into her clutch, then reached out and took the Tarot. She gave them an overhand shuffle with precision and skill; Orville noted that she did not wear an engagement ring or wedding band.

"Now cut the pack three times to the left, with your left hand, and turn over the top card."

She did so; the card revealed was the three of swords, reversed.

"Very well, Miss, I will take your commission."

"Thank you," Nelly said. "There is something else you need to know. There is a gentleman, who is traveling under the name Colley Cibber. He stole a march on me and managed to depart on the *Queen Mary*, and hopes to be on the Continent well before me. He will be docking tomorrow, or the day after. You will know him by his great height and, unless he has shaved it, spectacular mustache. I would prefer not to meet him until I can do so on my own conditions."

"Your loving uncle, protecting your virtue...?"

"Exactly. One more thing." She reached up and unbuttoned the top two buttons of her shirtwaist. Reaching into the gap, she found a golden chain and pulled it forth. Hanging from the chain, set in silver, was a large blue sapphire. Nelly handed the gem across to Orville, then buttoned up. "Please keep it safe."

"I find your faith in me touching."

Not looking back at him: "It's cursed."

*****

Straight up at six o'clock the Silver Meteor pulled into Baltimore. Nelly rose and, with Orville following, walked out onto the platform. Miss Bly's suitcase, a small one, was waiting by the baggage car. Orville's was nowhere to be seen

"It will be in Left Luggage in New York when you return," Nelly said. Then, "We'll replace your kit when we arrive in Marseilles. Could you take my bag?"

The two made their way to the street, and hailed a cab. "Harbor Field," Miss Bly said, and settled down for the ride.

Arriving at the airfield, Orville again took Nelly's suitcase. As they walked to the terminal, he said, quietly, "Don't look around right now, but the fellow getting out of that cab, wasn't he five seats behind us on the Meteor?"

"Yes. His name is Ransome, and he's dangerous."

"What does he want?"

"To stop me; to get the gem; nothing good."

"This is the part where I defend your virtue?"

"Yes."

"Take your suitcase. As soon as we go through the doors, make a quick turn to the right and get up against the wall."

The glass-and-brass doors of the air terminal were approaching. Nelly went in, as Orville held the door for her. He paused then as Nelly vanished inside, allowing Ransome to get nearer. The man slowed, but Orville turned and stepped up to him, striking him on the forehead with the heel of his hand while saying, "Sleep."

Ransome stopped; his eyes drifting closed, swaying like a tree in a heavy breeze.

"You can't find them. You can't see them. Take lodging and go to sleep. Have pleasant dreams. Wake in the morning, refreshed, and not remembering anything after you left the train."

Orville grasped Ransome by the lapels and brushed his hands over the man's coat. He dipped his hand into Ransome's pocket and retrieved a passport, which he placed in his own pocket beside the Tarot cards. Then he tapped Ransome on the shoulder, said "Wake!" and stepped back.

Ransome shuddered, blinked rapidly, and looked around. His eyes went right past Orville; Nesbit had to step rapidly back to keep Ransome from walking into him as he started back toward the terminal.

Orville followed him, then broke off to go to the right to where Nelly was standing against the wall, her suitcase beside her.

"What did you just do?" Nelly asked, breathlessly.

"Mesmerism," Orville replied. "The human mind has strange depths, Miss Bly; my studies have taken me perhaps a bit beneath the surface to see what lies below. In any case, something that had been concerning me has been resolved; I now have a passport." He took out the document and flipped it open. "Ransome?" he said. "According to this his name is Heinrich Ostermann. That's his photo."

"Names are such bothers," was all Nelly said. "I have two tickets reserved on the *Yankee Clipper*. Come along."

"You were that confident that I'd accompany you?"

Nelly nodded.

"Shall I fly as Ostermann?"

"That... would have a certain charm."

Soon enough boarding was called and, together with dozens of other passengers, Nelly and Orville walked across the sponsons as the giant flying boat rocked at its moorings. Smoothly they taxied out into the harbor, then with a roar of the mighty engines, took off to the northeast.

Soon after the aircraft leveled, Orville turned to Miss Bly and asked, "Would you like to accompany me back to the dining room? And while we're there I was hoping you would tell me exactly what is going on here."

"There's nothing much to tell," Nelly said.

"Try me. If there's really nothing to tell, then I'll tell you stories. Would you prefer the Werewolf of Luga, or the Rain of Worms in Guildhall?"

"Whichever goes best with an unassuming wine."

They walked aft to where the cold buffet was being served, and took seats at one of the tables. "To begin," Orville said, "Are you aware that Ostermann, or Ransome, or whoever he is, was carrying a gun?"

"I didn't know, but I'm not surprised. He is trying to obtain that gem, the Hohenstaufen Sapphire, and will stop at nothing. All that his masters ask is that he be discrete about it."

"You weren't discrete about it. You showed it to the whole train when you pulled it out of your bosom."

"Well, I had to make sure he knew I had it," Nelly said.

The steward in his white jacket came by with wine and filled both their goblets. Nelly pulled back her veil to nibble on bruschetta. The aircraft droned on as the light outside the large circular portholes grew dark with the approaching night.

"Forgive me," Orville said, "but could I beg your indulgence?" He pushed aside his plate laden with truffle macancini and beef in horseradish cream to make a clear space on the table. He fetched out the bag with his Tarot cards, ran through them, and placed the three of swords in front of him. "Please be so good as to give these a mix; exactly as before. Cut them three times to the left."

Nelly did as he asked, though her mouth was twisted into a quizzical expression. Orville dealt out six cards around the single three of swords: one above, one below, two the left, two to the right. Then, beginning at the top, he turned each one face up, proceeding counter-clockwise around the spread. He examined the pictures: Temperance, the Magician, Ace of Wands, the Hermit, the Lovers, Knave of Pentacles. Then he returned the cards to the pack, gave them a quick shuffle, and returned them to the pouch and the pouch to his pocket.

"Aren't you going to tell me what they mean?"

"No," Orville said. "That wasn't for you—it was for me." He dipped a bit of cold roast beef into the horseradish and raised his fork to his lips. "Shall we prepare for sleep? Tomorrow will be a long day, I fear."

While the passengers had been at dinner, the stewards and stewardesses had converted the seats to bunk beds. Orville swung himself into a lower, but did not immediately close his eyes. Instead he pulled the Hohenstaufen Sapphire from his pocket and held it in a beam of light that entered through a gap in the curtains from the main cabin. He gazed into its depth, and let the sparkling light guide his thoughts. The images he saw were of smoke, though they might have been mere reflections. At length he put the chain around his neck, turned his back to the cabin, and fell into a dreamless sleep as the engines droned outside.

*****

The flight to Marseille Provence Airport was scheduled to take twenty-nine hours, considerably faster than a steamship but, Orville thought, significantly slower than a telegram. He fretted that police would be waiting for him to ask about a stolen passport. When he asked Miss Bly, now turned out in a stylish navy-blue summer-weight blouse and skirt, topped with a beret with a black veil, as they chatted over breakfast in the dining room while the stewards converted the bunks back into seats, she merely smiled and told him not to concern himself. Ransome, she informed him, was hardly the man to go to the police, and regardless, the matter was "arranged." Orville was feeling rumpled, unwashed, and quite discommoded. He completed his reading of *Heresies* by lunch and was reduced to examining the magazines in the lounge. Shortly after a snack service, the aircraft began its descent, skimming across the water, then pulling up to the dock to disembark the passengers with the sun still half-an-hour above the horizon.

"I would like," Orville told Miss Bly, "to be indoors before dark."

"Why is that?"

"You hired me as an expert. This is my expertise."

"I hired you to be my uncle."

"Neither you nor I believe that," Orville said, picking up Miss Bly's suitcase and carrying it with them as they made their way to the arrivals hall. "If you had merely wanted an older male to accompany you, there are hundreds—thousands—you could have found with far less trouble and expense. Why me? I think we both

271

know. Now let us find a hotel, or do you already have one in mind?"

Nelly looked at him suddenly, sharply, but said nothing. Rather she led and he followed to the customs benches.

"No luggage, Monsieur?" asked the *Agent des Douanes*, a bored expression on his face.

"Lost in transit. I'm sure it will catch up with me," Orville said, quite truthfully. The man responded by stamping Osterman's passport and handing it back to Orville.

Orville met back up with Nelly in the grand atrium of the airport terminal. A taxi to *Escale Oceania Marseille Vieux Port* put them on the street in front of that edifice after the sun was down but before the sky was dark. Miss Bly, it seemed, had two adjacent rooms on an upper floor for herself and her uncle; the rooms had a connecting door. She said, to the concierge, "Send up dinner in one hour; send up a tailor now," before they went up, a bellboy carrying that single suitcase.

The rooms were small but well appointed. A few minutes later a knock at his door revealed a small, dour man with a cloth measuring tape hung about his neck. The tailor looked at Orville, Orville looked back, the man, by means of gestures, asked Orville to stand on a footstool while he made various measurements, then departed as silently as he had arrived.

No sooner had the tailor departed than the inner door opened and Nelly entered. She didn't close the door behind her.

"Please, sit," Orville said, lowering himself to an armchair even as he spoke. Nelly handed Orville a new passport, this one in the name of John Rodgers but with Orville's picture in it, and held out her hand for Ostermann's passport. She tucked it into her clutch purse.

"Looks as good as genuine," Orville said, examining Rodgers's passport, running his thumb over the picture with its embossed seal.

"Marseille has been a smuggler's port since Roman times," she replied. "If such things are not available here, they are not available anywhere in the world."

"Why don't you ask your friend to join us?" Orville said, quietly.

Nelly looked up, startled. "What?"

"There is no other reason for you to leave the door ajar," Orville said, "except to allow someone to eavesdrop. So: why not ask him or her to join us? It would be more convivial."

"Just as you say," Nelly said. "Colley, would you please come in?"

A rustle of movement, and a tall man, of nearly skeletal thinness, entered the room through the connecting door. Just as promised he wore a handlebar mustache of heroic proportions. "Colley Cibber, I presume?" Orville said, rising and offering his hand.

"At your service," the fellow replied, clasping Orville's hand in both of his own, while at the same time nodding his head.

"Please, join us." Orville pulled out a chair from the table and swept his hand toward it before resuming his place in the easy chair. He turned then to face Miss Bly. *A time and place of my own choosing*, he recalled the young woman saying. He supposed this was it.

A knock sounded at the door. "*Entrer!*" Orville called out. The door swung open and a waiter pushed in a cart over which a white cloth was laid. He brought it to the table, removed the cloth and folded it over his arm, then proceeded to lay out a series of dishes, each with its own cover which he removed and stacked on the lower level of the trolley. The smell, Orville though, was divine, particularly compared with the snack service on the *Clipper*. The last item was a tall white candle in a silver holder which the man placed in the center of the table, then lit with a long wooden match. Colley pulled a banknote from his pocket and slipped to the man, who nodded, and backed from the room, pulling the trolley with him. The door snicked closed.

"Don't hold back on my account," Orville said, gesturing toward the table. "When do we expect Ransome to join us?"

"I had a very confused cable waiting for me when I docked," Cibber said. "I could make neither head nor tail of it, save only that he would be joining us as soon as he could. I expect we'll see him down in Spain."

"Miss Bly?"

"Yes?"

"Would I be wrong is guessing that your name is Europa?" Orville sprang from his chair and cast a pinch of dried and powdered herbs from between his fingers into the flame of the candle. The flame exploded into a ball of fire. Orville whirled and shouted into Cibber's face, "In truth thou art Asmodeus!"

Colley Cibber started back and cried, "Even so!" but as he spoke he was transforming into a large dog with wide whiskers. Orville took another pinch of herb from his pocket into the candle flame and said, "*Exorcizo te, creatura in forma canis! In nomine Patris et Filli et Spiritu Sancti, Amen!*"

The dog that had been Colley Cibber ran yipping through the door that connected the two rooms. "What—what was that?" Nelly asked, her voice shaking.

"That was me protecting your virtue," Orville replied in a reasonable tone of voice. "It's what you hired me to do. Perhaps you did, or perhaps you didn't, notice that you were about to break bread with a demon." He took a seat at the table and speared a pork chop with a serving fork. "Oh, the fire? That was sage that I filched from the buffet table last night. They had a branch of it laid on the cold-meat tray as a garnish. Sage purifies and protects." Orville began to slice up his pork chop. It was creamy-soft, moist, and toothsome smelling. "But I asked if you were Europa," he continued. He took a bite of the pork and chewed it daintily. "Are you?"

Nelly looked down at her hands, twisting her napkin. At last the word "Yes" escaped her lips.

"I thought as much." A different voice, from the balcony. Ransome stepped into the room.

"How? Nelly asked.

"I travel fast."

Ransome: "You are Death?"

"No, nothing so gauche. The fellow, Ostermann, was genuinely a fellow named Ostermann whom I had hired." Here Ransome gestured toward Nelly in a sweeping hand motion that took in Orville. "Just as you hired a—what is it the Americans call them – ringer. I am Betrayal." Ransome looked sharply at Nelly. "And you have been betrayed. You are not just Europa. You are Decadence."

"Please, join us," Orville said, gesturing toward the empty seat. "The demon who just left us would be Despair. But aren't there supposed to be four of you?"

"There are four," Ransome replied, sitting and pouring some wine into a stemmed glass. "Four of us." He swirled the wine and drank. "You are Selfishness, Mr. Nesbit."

"I am miffed," Orville said. "I would have hoped I would be Pride."Together we four will bring ruin upon Europe, very soon. But we will not bring about the last days. Another time," Ransome concluded.

"Then there is no need for us to continue on to Spain; our business there is done," Nelly said. "Mr. Nesbit, your fee will be found in your bank account when you return home, listed as a wire transfer from Europe. I trust that will suit?" She did not smile at him.

"No, I'm not about to return home," Orville said, sipping wine in his glass and taking another bite of the pork. "At least, not yet. I have my own appointment in Samarra. Yes, the fee will be adequate, but first I will see the farce through to its conclusion.

You were going on to Poland next, were you not?"

"If not Pride certainly Smugness," Nelly said. Then, "Yes. Poland."

"Please fetch Despair. Let him keep his canine form, for now, and see he is well leashed. Miss Bly, I will accompany you, and guard your virtue. Just as you asked."

"Why should I... we allow any such thing?" Nelly asked, her voice low and tone dangerous.

"Because I still carry the Hohenstaufen Sapphire. Now I suggest we retire for the night and get such rest as we may. Tomorrow, we will dine elsewhere."

Prepocalypse Now

Dayton Ward & Kevin Dilmore

No one ever bothered to write down for any sort of official record how the world ended. It was left to regular people, those struggling to survive in the hellish reality which was all the life they would ever know, to remember the past in the hopes of informing the future. It's because of their heroic efforts that we now know how the end of the world came to be.

As one might expect and as with all earthly tales of chaos, wanton destruction and mass extinction, our story begins in Florida, with one man....

To Eric Lowmiller, the scene around him seemed drawn from the very depths of hell itself. Fire rained down from the sky, illuminating the darkened community that was his lifelong home of Land O' Lakes. When the power failed with no indications of its return, people emerged from their houses and trailers to investigate. In the streets sat abandoned cars, their owners wandering aimlessly as if seeking any explanation for the alarming situation. Standing on his front lawn, Eric watched a passenger jet halt its rise toward the burning clouds after taking off from Tampa International Airport and roll to its left before plunging headlong to the ground. The plane disappeared in an expanding fireball perhaps a mile to the east.

Holy shit.

That thought repeated in Eric's mind as he ran toward his back yard and the bunker installed there. Built by his grandfather in the 1960s when everyone feared nuclear annihilation, it lay buried beneath the soil behind the house, invisible save for a concealed metal hatch similar to those found on submarines. The shelter had fallen to neglect and disrepair by the time Eric inherited it along with the house and surrounding property following his own father's death. Spurred by the certainty of a New World Order one day coming to enslave them all, he had improved the bunker. Expanding and updating it, he also increased its fortifications and ensured its cache of supplies remained fresh and ready.

On this day, all of Eric's preparations appeared vindicated.

As he rounded his house's back corner, Eric was surprised to see the bunker's door already open, pushed up and to the left out of its reinforced frame. Standing next to the entrance was his cousin, Bowley. A mop of unruly brown hair framed his round, puffy face, and Eric noted what looked to be mustard stains on the other man's dingy gray T-shirt. His eyes were wide with fear as he took in the crimson sky overhead and gestured in frantic fashion toward Eric.

"Come on, man! Get your ass inside!"

After breaking up with his girlfriend and moving home from Chicago, Bowley had been living on Eric's couch for the past six months. Although that, along with a seemingly endless string of annoying habits, had long since worn on his nerves, Eric was still relieved to see his cousin had made it to the bunker.

"What about Josh?" Eric asked. His best friend since high school, Josh Ward was closer to him than most of his own fractured, dysfunctional family. If the end of the world was coming, he certainly wanted Josh by his side to face whatever might come next.

Bowley gestured toward the bunker's open door. "He just got here and he's already inside. There's some—"

A nearby explosion, far too close for Eric's comfort, made him and Bowley flinch and cut off whatever his cousin was going to say. The sky's red tint was deepening with every passing moment. Following Bowley into the bunker, Eric pulled the heavy door with him as he descended. The door slammed shut and he engaged the locking bolts that ensured the airtight hatch could not be opened from the outside. Around him, battery-operated lights illuminated the narrow stairwell leading down to the bunker's main level.

In the confined space, the sound of Bowley's gut-wrenching fart echoed off the metal walls and it took only seconds before a foul stench assaulted Eric's nostrils.

"Holy fuck, dude." Eric waved the air around his head. "You couldn't have done that shit *outside*?"

Working his way down the steps, Bowley grunted. "Sorry, man."

The malodorous evidence of his cousin's gastric transgression followed them to the bottom of the stairs, where Eric noted the shelter's main lights were on and a slight breeze wafted through the compartment. He also was relieved to see Josh emerging from the short passageway leading to the area set aside for the generator. Tall and lanky, his friend had to duck to pass through the squat doorways separating the bunker's sections.

"Hey, bud," said Josh, hooking a thumb over his shoulder. "Just fired up the generator. Everything's working great. Exhaust vent's working, and so are the ones bringing in fresh air. We're set."

Eric nodded. It was Josh who had created the venting system to channel the fumes from its diesel engine away from the bunker. His skills as a handyman at the local retirement home had proven invaluable while helping Eric to improve the shelter's features.

"Thank god you put an air conditioner down here, too," said Bowley. Overweight and not at all suited to the humidity that defined the Florida climate, he was out of breath and sweating. Leaning against a nearby wall, he looked first to Josh then Eric. "So, what do we do now? You think somebody's bombing us?" His voice shook as he spoke.

Eric shrugged. "Fuck if I know, but it wouldn't surprise me. Do we know if MacDill is still there?" MacDill Air Force Base in Tampa, thirty miles south of Land O' Lakes, was home to a handful of important United States military command organizations and tactical aircraft squadrons. In the event of a full-scale conflict that included the exchange of nuclear weapons, the base would be a primary target.

"Haven't heard," replied Josh. "But we'd know by now if they'd hit it, and I didn't see any mushroom clouds to the south before we came down here and found Bowley."

It took a second for Eric to register the last part of that comment, but then it clicked and his eyes narrowed as he regarded Josh.

"We?"

"He means me."

Turning toward the new voice, Eric felt his jaw slacken as he beheld the woman standing in the open doorway leading to the bunker's pantry. Dressed in jeans, boots, and a green military-style jacket, she wore her dark hair stuffed up under a red trucker's cap. She was eating a granola bar, and Eric looked past her to see she had been rummaging through the food stores packed into the compartment. Glaring at Josh, he hooked an accusatory thumb toward the woman.

"Who the hell is this?"

Josh's expression turned squeamish. "I ran into her outside, when everything started going crazy."

"You ran into her outside." Eric eyed the woman again. "And you just fucking brought her down here like a fucking lost puppy or some shit?"

Bowley said, "Eric. Come on, man. He should have just left her out there?"

"Yeah, Eric." The woman's tone was laced with mocking contempt. "What did you expect him to do?"

Turning to her, Eric scowled. "You're giving me attitude inside *my* fucking shelter, while eating *my* fucking food?" He looked back at Josh. "Do you even know her name?"

"Melissa," answered the woman. "Melissa Healer." She waved the half-eaten granola bar in her hand. "Nice to meet you."

Josh shrugged. "Melissa Healer. As in healing? That's a good sign, right?"

Shaking his head, Eric blew out his breath. "Like the sign around your neck that says, 'I'm a fucking gimp,' Josh."

"I don't think we're supposed to say that, Eric," said Bowley.

"It's my fucking shelter, Bowley! I'll say whatever the fuck I want." Eric pointed at Melissa. "I'm sorry Josh chose you to be his doomsday date, but I didn't prep this place to handle four people. I'm not kicking you out until things calm down outside, but after that you need to find your own hole to hide in."

For the first time, Melissa smiled. "Josh didn't *choose* me, Eric. *I* chose *him*, and he brought me to you and your cousin. That works out pretty well for me, since I needed three helpers for what comes next."

Trying to decide if she was crazy, Eric asked, "And what exactly comes next?"

"The End Times." She gestured toward the stairs leading to the bunker's main door. "Out there? Ground zero for Armageddon, Eric."

Bowley asked. "What? Wait, do you know about what's going on outside? What's causing it?"

Looking at him the way a convenience store employee regards

a customer holding up the line while trying to buy lottery tickets, Melissa replied, "I know exactly what's going on. *I'm* going on outside, Bowley. Everything you saw, everything happening right now while you cower down here in your little bunker, is me. I caused that. *All of it*, and everything that's still to come."

Silence enveloped the room as the guys absorbed this. Eric was the first to give in, a cynical laugh escaping his lips.

"So you're the one bringing fire, and causing planes to crash, and whatever else is happening." He eyed her with disdain. "What exactly is happening?"

Melissa smiled again. "I already told you. The End Times, Eric. Painful sores. Waters turning to blood. Fire from the heavens… wait, I already started that one. Perpetual darkness. Drought. Earthquakes. Whatever you can think of, if it sounds like a shitty time for everyone, it'll probably be in the mix somewhere."

"I've read the Bible," said Josh. "I don't remember anything about the end of the world starting in Florida."

"This place is primed for an Apocalypse. Alligators living on golf courses? Pythons sneaking into washing machines? Limp Bizkit?" Melissa shrugged. "To be fair, that last one is more than enough to justify all of this."

Everyone was silent for a moment. Bowley and Josh both sported expressions of confusion and disbelief Eric was sure mirrored his own before he finally said to Melissa, "Okay, let's pretend for a moment you're not completely full of shit. Why do all of that?"

"It's my whole reason for being, Eric." Chewing the last bite of her granola bar, Melissa wadded up the empty wrapper and tossed it toward a trash box. "I was created for the sole purpose of bringing down an Apocalypse that totally rocks the house. This isn't even my first one. I've been doing this sort of thing for eons, on planets across the universe." She leaned closer. "But I have to tell you, this is the one I've been waiting for. How am I doing so far?"

Before Eric could answer, she raised her right arm, fingers extending to point at him. A bolt of swirling black energy shot from her hand. Eric felt something slam into his chest, followed by a sudden warmth coursing over his body.

"Holy shit!" It was Bowley, crying out in alarm as a similar burst of energy struck him. Eric saw Josh try to duck the bolt aimed at him but the beam found him.

Whatever hit Eric reached his face, blocking out the lights and everything else. His eyes burned. His skin tingled. The sensation moved into his mouth and down his throat. Ears rang with a sudden high-pitched whine. His every nerve ending seemed aflame, and just when he thought he might pass out from the pain, the assault faded. The tingling was gone, the whine in his ears dissipated, and his vision returned.

"What the *fuck* just happened?" It was Bowley, stumbling backward until he collided with the wall. His hands went to his face. He was sweating and his breathing was ragged. Next to him, Josh was in a similar state.

Eric glowered at Melissa. "What did you do to us?"

"I'm fucking starving, you guys." Pushing himself from the bunker wall, Josh was gripping his stomach. "It hurts. I don't under—"

Without warning, his mouth opened, stretched, elongated into a hideous, undulating maw of deep, bottomless black. A heavy, mournful wail erupted from his face, echoing inside the shelter, and in response Eric heard a series of rumbles and clatters from the pantry. Then Bowley screamed as canned goods, packages of freeze-dried food, bottles of water—all of the food stored in the bunker—flew from shelves and cabinets straight into the abyss that was Josh's open mouth. Eric felt the rush of air as it all flew past, disappearing into his friend's face.

"Fuck, Josh!" was all Eric managed, turning to Melissa for explanation.

"Say hi to Famine." Melissa smiled. "He's going to gnaw through whatever food we happen across when we go touring the devastation."

Feeling his anger rising, Eric pointed at her. "Get out. Get the *fuck* out of my bunker. I don't care who you are, I want your ass gone. I—"

His hands began to pulse and vibrate. Light appeared from under his skin, highlighting the bones of his fingers. Seconds later the shelter was filled with the sounds of buzzing, scratching, and skittering and he looked up toward the ceiling vents to see swarms of insects—flies, mosquitoes, bees, wasps, anything that flew and irritated the shit out of him—emerging from the protective grills.

"Rats!" Bowley yelled, doing his best to leverage his bulk onto a folding chair. He succeeded in breaking it before Eric saw the first of dozens of rats entering the main compartment.

"From where?" Eric shouted. "How the hell did they get inside?"

Examining her fingernails, Melissa replied, "You summoned them. I dub thee Pestilence, my dude."

As if to punctuate her statement, Josh's face contorted again to form that revolting maw, and the rats and bugs began sailing in his direction.

"Get me the fuck out of here!" cried Bowley.

Whatever he might have said next was cut off as his face turned a brilliant crimson and an immense gout of fire spewed from his mouth. Bowley twisted his head from left to right, flame surging from his face and enveloping the room. By the time he managed to close his mouth and arrest the blast, anything flammable in the entire compartment was burning, filling the air with smoke.

Eric heard Melissa laugh, and when he turned to her it was to see her climbing the steps toward the bunker's hatch.

"Fire?" he shouted after her as she disappeared from view.

"Now you're catching on," her voice filtered down the shaft. "Let's go. We're just getting started."

*****

And it came to pass that the Florida men stumbled out of their now befouled bunker and into a world very much changed from the one in which they had lived. A blood-red moon dominated the sky in a proportion greater than any of them ever had beheld. Punctuating the blackness was the occasional fiery ball of molten rock, streaking across the night sky to land explosively in the distance. Flames licked upward from treetops and roofs alike, spewing black smoke into a sky that swirled in the moon's brilliant red light. Accompanying these sights was a cacophony of screams, crashes of glass and metal and low rumblings that sounded as if the Earth itself was heaving.

Bowley surveyed the destruction, feeling the heat of flame on his face and smelling the singe of vegetation and lumber. He paused a moment as his mind processed the world's simultaneous assault on all of his senses then did his best to articulate his most heartfelt response to it all.

"Kick ass."

"That's your takeaway, you fat fuck? 'Kick ass'?" Eric shoved Bowley aside and spun around to face them all. "What are we supposed to do now? You torched my fucking bunker. And look, the whole town is on fire! We got nowhere to go!"

"You have *everywhere* to go." Melissa gestured around them. "This town—this *world*—is yours for the taking. Now's your chance to show these people that *you* are the chosen rulers of all you see."

Releasing a single breathy laugh that could have been mistaken for a cough, Bowley set off toward the street in front of Eric's house.

"Cool."

*****

Bowley's abrupt departure snapped Josh's gaze from the devastation surrounding them.

"Hey, where's he going?" he asked no one in particular. Realizing his voice was too soft to carry over the din, he shouted. "Hey! Bowley! Where you going, man?"

Continuing his shuffle down the center of the empty street, Bowley shouted over his shoulder. "Later, losers."

"You can't just...." Josh let his voice trail off then turned to Melissa. "He can't just leave like that, can he? Aren't we supposed to work together?" Not that he was particularly concerned about Bowley's well-being, but he assumed they along with Eric and Melissa would basically be the hell-spawned version of the Fantastic Four or something—without the cool clubhouse and uniforms, anyway.

Melissa crossed her arms, staring at him. "It's really up to you at this point."

Her gaze made Josh feel a gnawing in the pit of his stomach. It was a new wave of the sensational hunger he had experienced in the bunker. He winced at the fresh memory of having eaten— *inhaled*—more food than he ever should have had the capacity to consume. Those recollections were fleeting, swept aside by a renewed and overwhelming urge to eat.

Josh started running after the lumbering Bowley.

*****

Watching his departed bunker buddies moving off down the street, Eric turned to Melissa. "What the fuck? Do I go after them now?"

"What do you want to do?"

"I mean, I dunno. I was just fine down there until they all fucked it—"

"*Lowmiller!*"

284

Eric looked in the direction of the shout to see a half dozen people marching up the street toward him. Leading the pack was a middle-aged man he had seen around before but whose name he had never bothered to learn.

"Go home, assholes!" he shouted at the pack.

Eyeing the group, Melissa asked, "Who are these people?"

"Fuckin' neighbors."

"Lowmiller!" the man shouted again. "Farnsworth here says you've got food in a bunker, and as president of the homeowners' association, I expect you to share it with the neighborhood."

Melissa smirked at Eric and made a small flourish with her fingers. "You just going to take that?"

Eric's eyes widened and he smiled, struck by the greatest idea he had conceived in all his years. Energy tingled up his spine, spreading across his body.

"Nope," he said. "I'm not taking any of it." Raising his arms, he cupped his hands as if scooping up an offering to the gods. "You want food? Eat *this*, you HOA fucks!"

The air between Eric and his approaching neighbors filled with uncounted flying, buzzing locusts that seemed born of the wind itself. They swarmed and pelted the neighbors, popping on impact like overripe grapes and leaving inflamed welts.

Also heeding Eric's silent call, hordes of rats large and small squealed and scurried from the street's storm drains, rushing at the neighbor's feet to bite at their ankles. The men and women shrieked as every step brought their foot on top of a feral, writhing rodent.

When Eric laughed again, his voice boomed from his mouth more guttural and reverberant. What was happening to him? He felt rush of empowerment against everyone in this shithole neighborhood who for years told him what he could and could not do with his roof and his tool shed and his boat trailer and his landscaping. Now he could let them know once and for all just what he thought of their Halloween decoration rules and their lame-assed Christmas block parties. Finally, he had the upper hand.

And all these motherfuckers are gonna pay.

"Ruuuuuuun!" Eric shouted as he ran into the cloud of locusts and swarm of rats, chasing his neighbors back down the street from whence they came.

*****

Josh's hunger brought him down the street to a mom-and-pop convenience store. As soon as he swung open the plate-glass doors, his nose was filled with the distinctive smells of various snacks and treats: microwavable burritos, rotisserie hot dogs, candy, potato chips, and snack cakes. He relished the aroma of each item, sweet or savory and regardless of whatever plastic wrapper or foil-lined tube or aluminum can contained it. Driven by ravenous need, he stormed in, bellowing like a wild beast. His unearthly howls were like nothing Josh had heard or even imagined, and particularly not from his own mouth.

"I...*hunger*!"

A pair of young skateboard punks pressed their backs against the slush machine at Josh's outburst. "What the eff, dude?" the taller one shouted back as he clutched his board along with a bright red frozen drink. "Like, just get a Slim Jim or something and shut up."

Josh howled at the gnawing in his gut, the pain feeling as if it might burst forth from his body as a separate malevolent being. There was only one way to satisfy his need.

"No one eats but *meeeeee*!"

He felt his mouth opening again. Jaw aching from the impossible, inhuman contortions, he turned toward the teens. The tall kid's drink flew from his hand into the coal-black maw that widened to cover every inch of Josh's face, followed by entire shelves of food and snacks. All of it flew through the air and into the maw that was his mouth. Refrigerated cases emptied their contents to be swallowed by Josh. It took only seconds for the store's entire stock of edible wares to disappear into his mouth, save for several packages of plant-based hamburger patties and a rack of Corn Nuts.

Fuck that shit.

His lanky frame showing no effects of all the food he had consumed, Josh staggered out of the store. Already he was feeling the familiar sensation of hunger. He needed more food. He gasped, catching sight of a lone building surrounded by a freshly striped parking lot across the street from the convenience store, and he smiled as his gaze settled on the glowing signage of an iconic yellow bell. Rushing across the street, Josh burst into the restaurant.

"I...*hunger*!"

*****

Not far from the convenience store, a Toyota Rav4 exploded moments after being bathed in belched flame. Bowley chuckled as he surveyed the dozen torched vehicles around him. Wiping a line of drool from his chin, he felt genuine satisfaction at what he had accomplished with his newfound talent. Nothing was safe. As with the cars, he directed flaming burps at hedgerows, trees and lawns. Bowley even torched an opossum that peered from a storm sewer, an act that made him laugh until he farted.

It was the fart that gave him one of the few self-inspired ideas of his life.

Rather than aim his mouth at a parked pickup truck, Bowley decided to spin around and squat toward it. He screamed as hellfire erupted from his ass, engulfing the truck. Howling with laughter, he pitched forward and face-planted into the street, baring his cheeks to the world through the singed hole that was the seat of his pants.

"Did ya see that?" Bowley yelled to no one as he rolled over and got to his feet. "Ass-blasted! Hoo-whee! Shit!"

Motivated to wreak more havoc with the power of his own flatulence, he turned his attention toward a new target. A smile crept over his face as he approached a building he had frequented for lunches and dinners over much of his life—meals that never treated his gastrointestinal system with the respect that he felt it rightly deserved. Arriving at his destination, Bowley stopped and beheld his nemesis.

"Taco *fuckin'* Bell. It's payback time, bitch!"

Turning his now bare ass toward the restaurant, he felt energy surging through him as a torrent of flame erupted from within him and blew through the building. Patrons who had sheltered in place now bolted outside, some of them aflame as they fled in various directions.

Then Josh stumbled from the wreckage, singed but uninjured, in a daze of disbelief until he set eyes on Bowley.

"What the hell, man!" he shouted. "I wasn't done eating!"

Bowley started to laugh but froze as a new sensation gripped him. He could tell Josh also felt it. Indeed, all of the people around them appeared to freeze in their tracks. Something rang in Bowley's ears, a high-pitched whine that compelled him to turn away from the ruined restaurant.

"Gotta go," Bowley said even as Josh walked past him. Around them, dozens of people moved with them, with more emerging from nearby buildings and homes to join the growing pack. Bowley and Josh led the procession, with everyone walking silently amid the glow of burning cars and trees toward Eric's house.

As they neared, they recognized Eric walking toward them. Even more people kept pace behind him. Bowley broke the silence with a soft exclamation as he pointed toward Eric's place.

"Holy shit."

*****

Eric looked to see Bowley pointing at Melissa. She floated a dozen feet above the ground, arms extended from her sides as if she were balancing on a wire. White light emanated from her chest, expanding to engulf her body. As the light faded, she now appeared before the assembled throng as a robed skeletal spectre.

Then she clapped her hands together.

In that moment, everyone howled in agony before they exploded, disappearing in clouds of blood and bone. Only Eric along with Bowley and Josh were spared, unharmed beyond being spattered head to toe in gore.

"Not cool, man," Bowley said.

"Definitely not cool!" Eric shouted as Melissa slowly returned to the ground and resumed her human appearance. "What the fuck was that?"

"What the fuck do you think it was?" she replied calmly. "I am Death. That is my purpose. That is the reason for everything you see happening around you."

Josh wiped his hand against his shirt, then brought it to his face to sweep away bits of flesh and blood from his mouth. "So how many people are you planning to blow up like that?"

"All of them."

"Like, all of them in Land O' Lakes?"

"No, Josh." Melissa shook her head. "*All* of them...on the planet. Everyone dies. It's the Apocalypse. That's how this shit works."

"We're killing *everyone*?" Eric asked. "How long is that gonna take?"

"You have somewhere to be?"

Gesturing to Melissa, Bowley said, "Hey, guys. If we kill *everyone*, then the only girl left on the whole planet is gonna be *her*."

Silence settled upon the men as realization dawned. They

traded glances. Josh took a backed few steps away from Bowley. Eric squared his stance, feeling his hands clench into fists.

"Hey," said Josh. "I saw her first."

Melissa sighed loudly. "*Really?*"

"You missed your shot, dumbass." Eric raised his arms and the air filled with locusts and flying cockroaches. Josh instinctively opened his mouth wide, the sucking maw spreading across his nose and eyes. Every pest that Eric summoned to overrun Josh was sucked into his featureless face, even the rodents that scurried up to heed Eric's call.

"You can't eat them all, fuckface!"

"I...*hunger*!" The maw added hellish undertones to Josh's voice, which sounded even more hideous once he started screaming.

Eric howled in reply and kept feeding vermin into the face-sized void until he felt his feet lifting from the ground. Bowley had grabbed him by his collar and belt, and shoved him head first into Josh's maw of famine. The act knocked Josh off of his feet and the two collapsed in a heap. Before either had his wits about him long enough to stand, they got blasted with a white-hot jet of fragrant fire from Bowley's ass. He hunkered down over the men and shat fire until the two were incinerated completely and irredeemably.

*****

Smoke still wafting from the ashen remains of his friends, Bowley turned to find Melissa staring at him.

"The only way any of you could be harmed was if you decided to harm each other," she said, "and you just couldn't help yourself."

Bowley shrugged, feeling the first ache of desire now that Josh and Eric were gone and it was just him and Melissa. "We don't need them. It can just be you and me."

"There must be four! Now I have to start all over!" She waved her hands before her and Bowley's eyes widened as he felt his face tightening. He reached up to find his mouth completely missing, replaced by smooth skin. Another sensation made him reach back to feel for an ass crack that was no longer there. His stomach began to rumble and swell, and he was overcome by the urge to belch fire, fart fire, anything to vent the noxious gas from his body. With no place for it to go, his stomach split open, disgorging his innards on the ground before him. His strength and consciousness ebbing, Bowley's final act was to collapse into his own entrails with a wet and unceremonious plop.

Surveying the carnage with a shake of her head, Melissa muttered to herself as she walked away and into the night, backlit by the fires that continued to rage.

"Idiots. I knew I should have stuck with women."

*****

And so began the end of the world as we knew it. We the descendants of those who survived Death's march across the planet will likely never fully understand her reasons for visiting such wanton destruction on humanity, let alone why she chose to bestow mercy upon a precious few. Did we suffer her wrath because of our own selfish hubris, failing to live in peace and harmony with our brothers and sisters while we chased avarice, gluttony, and other sins of flesh and soul? Perhaps her act of benevolence is our final opportunity to seek redemption. We wait with hope for a brighter future.

But I'm still stocking my shelter, and none of you fucks are invited.

Live, Laugh, Apocalypse
A Tale of the Four Karens of the Apocalypse

Patrick Thomas

Diners had avoided the tables around the party of eight as if their lives depended on it. Perhaps it did.

Death's wife cleared her throat and three Horsemen squirmed in their seats as even the Grim Reaper grew paler.

"We need to discuss our second honeymoon," Karen said.

"With all of us going together," said Karyn. Famine ignored his meal to gaze lovingly at his wife as she ate. She tried not to grimace at the inferior quality of her lamb salad with Fregola. She could have made better half-awake and sick with Caren's worst hypochondriac symptoms.

Always eager for a spirited discussion—what others would consider an argument—Kyrin, War's wife, pointed out, "Technically, we never had a first honeymoon. We got married on a Saturday night in Vegas and had to check out on Sunday. We spent most of that time sobering up after realizing we'd gotten married."

With a sound like a coffin lowering into a grave, Death sighed. Hearing it, a couple at the nearest occupied table threw their forks down along with a pile of money and sprinted for the door.

"We can't."

"Why not? Aren't I worth it?" At times, Karen scared people—mostly managers—more than her husband did. The mix of her unhappy face and righteous indignation was enough to give even the Grim Reaper pause.

"It's not a question of worth, my dear. Death is simply not allowed to take a holiday."

"Nor are Famine, Pestilence, or War," pointed out Famine, looking emaciated under his baggy clothing.

"Besides, this is the end of flu season. I'm swamped," Pestilence said, wiping his nose on his napkin. The cloth turned green and seemed to be moving.

"So fewer people get sick. What's the big deal?" Kyrin said.

Pestilence pointed a deceptively clean-looking fork at the wife of War. If it wasn't scrubbed thoroughly in scalding water, it would start an outbreak of botulism. "I am an artisan. This year's strain was totally unexpected and the flu shots are less than ten percent effective."

"Don't you pick on my husband because he's doing a great job," scolded his wife, Caren.

"Thank you, dear," Pestilence said.

Caren smiled. "But I still think you gave *me* the flu." Pestilence shrugged, knowing that he had made his wife immune to all disease and that it was pointless to argue when she went into hypochondriac mode. "And work isn't an excuse for us not to get a honeymoon."

"But we're the Four Horsemen of the Apocalypse. We have responsibilities," Famine said.

"You also have responsibilities to your families. Which is more important—your wives or your jobs?" Karen said.

The Four Horsemen of the Apocalypse were ageless incarnations of the vast powers of the universe itself, so none of them were stupid enough to answer that question directly. They had learned their lesson the time Karen asked if her jeans made her butt look fat.

They exchanged glances until Death realized the other three Horsemen were looking at him. After all, it was his wife who'd asked the question.

The Grim Reaper turned as pale and green as his horse, Ashy.

"Karen, dear, it's not as simple as that. We literally are our jobs and while we each take our vows to our wives seriously, we also have responsibilities that date to before the Big Bang. I'm sure we can figure out a way to steal a day or so, but there's simply no way that all of us can take a week off at the same time. Reality would start to crumble."

"When we met, you were on vacation," Karen countered.

"Technically, no. We were clocked out from our duties for less than eighteen hours. We can all take off a few hours every day without damaging the universe. Why don't you four go ahead of us and we'll join you every night, the same as if we were at home."

The Four Horsemen exchanged glances and grins all around, stopping short of high-fiving in front of their wives. Death had done it again and come up with a reasonable solution.

With all their power and millennia of experience, the Four Horsemen should've known better. The Karens also exchanged a look that contained no smiles.

Together the Karens curled their lips, crossed their arms, and did a head shake with synchronization that'd make any boy band jealous.

"Unacceptable," Karen said.

"I'm not going to explain to my mother why I haven't got a honeymoon," Caren said. "Not again."

"All my friends got at least a week," said Karyn.

"My cousin Rachel married an accountant and they had a month-long cruise of the Mediterranean. How am I going to explain that my husband can barely give me a day trip?" Kyrin said.

"But you can go for as long as you want and we'll join you when our workday is done," War said.

"Oh really?" Kyrin tilted her head to glare up at her burly husband. "Why do you want us gone all of a sudden? Planning on having some hussies over while we're away?"

"Why would we do that?" War was sincerely confused. The Four Horsemen had no intention of cheating on their wives. In fact, there were times they questioned the wisdom of having wives at all, but as primordial incarnations, they were bound by their drunken vows far more than any mortal would be.

"Why would any man?" Karyn asked.

Famine threw up his hands and shook his head. "I have no idea."

Karen raised a hand and the other three Karens fell silent. "Bottom line, what has to happen for us to get our honeymoon with the four of you present the whole time for at least a week?"

"It can't happen," War said.

"I mean, unless the Apocalypse had occurred," Pestilence said.

Knowing his great sense of humor, the other three Horsemen laughed at the joke, but the Four Karens didn't share a single chuckle. Their hive expression was the offspring of a smile and a smirk.

It was a look which, had the four husbands of the Apocalypse been paying better attention, would have sent chills up their immortal spines.

*****

"Are we sure this is a good idea? If the world ends, won't all the good resorts be closed?"

"Karyn's right," Caren said. "What's the point of a honeymoon if we can't get spoiled? Don't we need the little people alive to give

293

us massages, drinks, and mani-pedis? We can do for ourselves without leaving home."

Much to the chagrin of the Karens, the Horsemen hadn't given in to the idea of having maids, cooks, and pool boys. Especially since only Karen had a pool.

"You'd think the Apocalypse means that everyone dies, but that's not the way it works," Karen said. "I talked to Grimmy. Turns out, it's all outlined in the Book of Revelation in the Bible."

Caren squealed. "I have a Bible at home. It used to be my grandmother's."

Kyrin rolled her eyes. "We all have Bibles."

"But have any of you actually read them?" Karen asked with a knowing smile.

The other three Karens looked at each other sheepishly.

"Yeah, sure," Caren said. "Well, not really, but once I read parts because I thought I had leprosy." In reality, she had splattered some tomato soup on her skin. "Sometimes I listened in church. I know begat means they had sex."

"I much prefer to watch my religion," Karyn said, "you know the movies about Jesus, Charlton Heston in *The Ten Commandments*, how Rudolph saved Christmas."

"I've been meaning to, but I've been so busy," Kyrin said. "But we all know you haven't read it either. If it don't have some shirtless hot guy and a slut on the cover, you'd never pick it up."

"That's a great idea," Caren said. "They should put a hunky Jesus on the cover of the Bible with Mary Magdalene in some slinky Bibley outfit. Wasn't she a hooker? Plus, Jesus was all ripped and the son of God? You can't tell me she didn't try to hit that at least once. *We* should look into making a hot Bible. Everyone's got their granny's but you never see anyone buying a new one. We can do different editions for the Old Testament like *Fifty Shades* with Adam and Eve getting busy and then her cheating on Adam with that snake."

"I'd read that," Kyrin said.

"We'll circle back to the sexy Bible after we get our honeymoons," Karen said. "And Kyrin's right. I never bothered to read the Bible until last night. Well, not the whole Bible, just the Revelation part. It's supposed to outline the end of the world and let me tell you whoever wrote this thing did a piss-poor job. He'd never make it on Twitter. He just drags everything out instead of getting to the point. I had to take notes. The first misconception about the Apocalypse is not everybody dies. One hundred and forty-four thousand holier-than-thou types go straight up to heaven."

"*I* want to go to heaven." Karyn's voice turned into an annoying whine.

"Apparently, that doesn't matter because these holy rollers don't bother to take anybody else." Karen rolled her eyes.

Kyrin said, "I hate people like that who think just because they do the right thing and follow the rules, that they should get what's coming to them. What about the rest of us? Why should we suffer because we're not uptight like them?"

"Exactly. And there's a lot of blah blah stuff, but what it boils down to is when our hubbies ride out into the world to do their thing it kicks off the Apocalypse. Due to my husband's excellent work," Karen bragged, "two-thirds of the Earth's population dies when heaven and hell throw down."

"Now wait just a booger-picking minute..." Kyrin used to say "cotton-picking" until someone pointed out to her at length that the phrase originated back when slaves had to pick cotton. Kyrin hadn't known that and actually apologized, much to the surprise of the person lecturing her. Kyrin thought slavery was wrong and would tell anyone who would listen how she could relate because, back when she was growing up, her parents made her do chores and didn't even pay her. If you're going to have people serve you, you should at least pay them. In solidarity with her slave brothers and sisters, Kyrin stopped using the phrase and made up one of her own. "Your husband may be the leader of the Four Horsemen, but he couldn't do his job if our husbands didn't do theirs. Without War, Pestilence, and Famine there wouldn't be many people dying, would there?"

Karen smiled, took a deep breath, and counted to five. She loved the other Karens like sisters but it annoyed her when they showed their insecurity like this. True, their husbands had big jobs but, in the end, they all just really worked for Death. Sure, the guitarist, the bass player, and the drummer in a band were important, but not as much as the lead singer was. At the end of the day, they all knew her husband was the star, which of course made her the most important wife. And as good as it might feel, she didn't need to hurt their feelings by pointing out the obvious. At least not today.

"Of course. The problem is our husbands are so happy being married to us that they've become slackers, too worried that the Apocalypse will end their wedded bliss. The way I figure it, the third who survive will still need to work so we'd be able to have them wait on us. And it will be easier to get reservations. Plus, we wouldn't have to worry about keeping the whole Four Horsemen thing a secret because it would already be out in the open and all the survivors would look at us like we're movie stars."

"Like that lawyer lady no one knew about until she married George Clooney," Karyn said.

"Exactly. So, it's up to us to do their jobs for them. We should start by making a vision board and brainstorming ideas to get more people to fight, get sick, go hungry, and ultimately die so we can get the Apocalypse over with and have a honeymoon for the ages."

*****

The Karens worked hard, using social media bots to push the anti-vax agenda, making their own essential oil company which claimed to have the cures for everything from constipation to the black plague (as long as nobody read the fine print which said the oils were not intended to actually treat any known disease).

But it wasn't helping the end of the world happen any sooner.

"I was doing some more research on the Apocalypse," Kyrin said.

Caren's jaw dropped. "You've been reading?"

Kyrin laughed. "Get real. I've been streaming Apocalypse movies. You know what they all mention that we haven't addressed?"

"Torturing baristas who get our orders wrong?" Caren said.

"Getting salespeople fired because they won't look in the back room again for the shoes we want?" Karen said.

"I like the energy, but no. They all feature the Antichrist who triggers things so our boys can ride out."

"Then we need to give this Antichrist a kick in the pants," Caren said.

"How do we get ahold of her?" Karen typed on her phone. "Google is not giving me anything by way of name or phone number. And whose auntie is she?"

"It's A-N-T-I, not auntie and that's the problem. No one seems to know who *he* is."

"I do," Karyn said.

The other three turned towards her.

"You know who the Antichrist is?" Karen asked.

She nodded. "His name is Billy Damien."

"How do you know this?" Kyrin said.

Karyn opened her purse and pulled out a bright blue envelope.

"Because I brought a card for all of you to sign for his birthday this Saturday."

The heads of the other three Karens tilted in confusion.

"Our sweeties work with his dad. Famine asked me to mail a card. I figured all of you could sign and chip in twenty-five bucks for a gift card."

"I have a better idea. The boys will be busy watching some dead guys playing football Saturday so let's deliver it in person."

*****

"Are you sure it's okay to crash his birthday party?" asked Karyn. "People might notice we don't belong."

"Nonsense. Classy ladies like us fit in anywhere. If they notice, they'll surely invite us to stay," Karen said.

"I'm a bit more worried about what our husbands will say if they find out that we took their horses without asking permission," Caren said.

Karen rolled her eyes back and waved her hand dismissively. "We didn't take them—we borrowed them. Borrowing your husband's car, or in our case horse, is one of the perks of marriage."

"I'm not sure the boys will agree. After all, cars aren't supernatural entities that can fly across the country so fast they make jets look like turtles," Kyrin said.

"Which only proves my point. The Antichrist's house is over a thousand miles away. There's no way we could have gotten there on time, even by plane," Karen said.

"But we don't know what time the party is," Karyn said.

"Or if there even is one," Kyrin said.

Karen rolled her eyes again, this time leaning her head back and chuckling. "This guy, Billy Damien, is the Antichrist, the most powerful guy on the planet. There's no way he's not having an epic party. It'll probably make our weekend in Vegas seem like a night in a convent by comparison."

The other three Karens exchanged a look of resolve, simply accepting the fact that, like always, they were being swept along in Karen's wake.

GPS worked wonderfully in a car but when one is high above cell towers on a flying horse, it wasn't so efficient. It took several tries dropping back down to reconnect their cells to find the house.

Leaving the four horses of the Apocalypse tied to a lamppost, the Karens approached a modest suburban home.

Karyn checked the address on the envelope versus the one on the mailbox. "It matches up."

"Let's do this." Karen sashayed to the front door and the other three followed her.

She rang the doorbell, then whispered over her shoulder. "Remember to blend in with the crowd."

They waited, but no one answered the door.

Kyrin eye-rolled. "Must be a really great party."

"Isn't it awful quiet for a wild party?" Karyn put her ear to the door. "I hear video games."

Karen's worry turned to annoyance and she leaned on the bell repeatedly, until finally, the door opened, revealing a scowling stout man in a very average suit.

"What do you lot want?" the man demanded.

The Karens exchanged a look. This guy didn't look much like someone destined to destroy the world.

"Must be the butler," Karen concluded.

"Do people even have butlers anymore?" Karyn said.

"If the Antichrist wants a butler, I'm sure he has a butler," Caren said.

"Take us to the birthday party," Karen said.

"There's no birthday party. Leave before I call the police."

Kyrin laughed. "We're the ones who call the police on people, not you."

"Step aside, Jeeves." Karen bulldozed her way between him and the door. "And feel free to call the cops if you want. We'll just have to tell them that it's the Antichrist's birthday."

The portly man became pale. "How in the world could you know about Billy?" He looked past the Karens onto the street. "Is that rain? The weather reports said it would be sunny. Wait, did that black horse just eat our fire hydrant?"

The Karens didn't answer as they had already spread out to search the house while screaming, "Billy!"

A woman dressed like a housewife in a 1950s sitcom, complete with apron, stepped out. "What are you doing in my house? And how do you know my son?"

"He works with our husbands," Karyn said.

"That doesn't make any sense. Billy doesn't have a job."

"Obviously the Antichrist wouldn't have a normal job," Karen said and the woman in the apron went as pale as the stout man, who at the moment was struggling to shut the door against a red horse that was pushing to get in.

"Are you guys looking for me?" came a soft voice. They turned to stare at a little boy holding a game controller.

Karyn dropped to one knee. "We're not looking for you hon, we're looking for Billy Damien."

"That's me."

"But... you're just a kid," Caren said.

Karen realized she may have miscalculated. "Billy, is today your birthday?"

The boy smiled. "Yes. I'm eight."

The Karens exclaimed, "Oh boy."

"Billy, we're here to discuss starting your destiny soon. Today even," Karen said.

The woman in the fifties housewife getup leapt to cover the boy's ears. "He doesn't know about any of that yet."

Karyn sighed. "I don't think we're getting a honeymoon for a long time."

Undeterred, Karen jutted out her jaw and put her hands on her hips. "I want to speak to your manager."

"I'm his mother. I don't have a manager."

"She means his father," Kyrin said.

"I'm his father," screamed the portly man just as the red horse spun and back kicked the door, slamming the balding man onto his rear end, the door falling on top of him.

Billy pulled the hands away from his head. "My stepfather actually. My real dad has a very important job so I don't get to see him often."

"Is he coming today for your birthday party?" Caren asked.

Frowning, Billy shook his head. "No. I'm not having a birthday party."

That flabbergasted the Karens.

"Why wouldn't you have a birthday party?"

"I'm not allowed."

The Four Karens glared at the boy's mother.

"His father has forbidden us to celebrate anything, even holidays and birthdays."

Karen stroked her chin and did her best to hide a grin. "So you're saying you won't call his father, the same father who's not coming to his forbidden birthday party?"

The stereotype of a fifties housewife crossed her arms and nodded. "That's right."

"Hey Billy, guess what? We're throwing you the best birthday party that anyone's ever seen."

"Oh yeah!" Billy cheered.

"You can't barge into our house and throw our son a birthday party against our wishes."

"Watch us," Kyrin said.

"Honey, call the police," the mother said.

The portly man pushed the broken door aside and stood. "But dear, they said they would tell them about..." He pointed to the boy. "You know."

The housewife's eyes narrowed as she rolled her dress sleeves above her elbows. "If I have to, I'll kick you all out myself."

As the woman charged towards Karen, the wife of Death whistled and the pale green horse trotted past where the front door had once been. "Ashy, take Mrs. Damien into the backyard."

The horse bent his neck to chomp on the back of her dress and pick her up like he was carrying a kitten. As horses were notoriously lacking in opposable thumbs, no one was terribly surprised when the horse reached the back of the house and they heard a crash instead of an opening door.

"Billy, text your friends and invite them over," Karen said.

Billy looked at the floor, his face a pale pink. "I don't have those kind of friends."

"Then call your classmates and your neighbors," Karen said. "Karyn, I need you to bake a cake."

Famine's wife grinned. "I was hoping you'd say that."

"Caren, hire some sort of children's entertainment. A magician or a clown."

"How about pony rides?"

Karen turned to watch as Famine's black horse chewed on the banister, Pestilence's white horse laid down on the couch and turned on the TV, and War's red horse tried to use his hooves and mouth to operate a game controller for a first-person shooter videogame.

"We've got that covered."

*****

A clown was soon on the way, as were a dozen pizzas and soda.

The meager guest turnout disappointed the Karens—a mere three boys and two girls. However, Billy was thrilled because he didn't realize he had so many friends. Being eight, he didn't understand that four of those kids were dropped off by parents thrilled to get a few hours of free babysitting.

Only Tiffany, the girl next door, was excited about coming. Despite having ridden the school bus together since kindergarten, she'd never been invited over. Being blissfully ignorant that Billy was the Antichrist factored into that enthusiasm significantly.

The clown, Mr. Balloony, put on a slightly above-average performance, with a mix of pratfalls and magic tricks. All of the children got a balloon animal. Tiffany asked for a swan. Billy wanted a three-headed dog that spit fire. Without raising a painted eyebrow, Mr. Balloony made a regular balloon dog, took another balloon wrapped around the neck, and added two more heads before proceeding to tie orange balloons to the mouths of each head. Karyn was so impressed she asked for a fire-breathing pink flamingo.

Had Mr. Balloony simply closed his act with a bow and left then, things would've gone much differently for him. Instead, he "milked" a balloon cow into a bucket and then threw the contents at Tiffany. She wasn't splattered with milk, of course, but instead covered in glitter.

A shrink would've blamed her shrieking on all the evil clown images children were exposed to, but Billy didn't care about any of that. He considered his bus seatmate his best friend and became furious that Tiffany was upset.

Billy grabbed Mr. Balloony by the collar of his neon jumpsuit. The clown was a professional and stepped back, expecting to break the eight-year-old's grip. Instead, Billy yanked the children's performer down to his knees. The jumpsuit became significantly moister when the clown noticed that the little boy's eyes were on fire.

"You are a very bad clown. Apologize to Tiffany."

Normally, Mr. Balloony would politely correct a child's poor manners, but the blaze on the boy's face had convinced him that normal things didn't apply here.

"Tiffany, I'm very sorry. It was meant to be funny, not scare you."

Tiffany sniffed then nodded her forgiveness.

"Now leave!"

Mr. Balloony may have been terrified, but he wasn't about to get stiffed for a performance. "Just as soon as I get paid."

Billy's response was an evil smile. The selfsame psychologists who would've blamed Tiffany's fright on exposure to clown images would also point out how wrong it was to describe anything about a child as evil, but they weren't staring into twin vortexes filled with flames dancing to the tune of human misery.

Money forgotten, Mr. Balloony tried to flee but Billy wouldn't let go until the jumpsuit, whose label proudly proclaimed that it was flame retardant, burst into a ball of fire and ash.

Now in neon yellow boxers, Mr. Balloony bolted screeching from the backyard. He had no intention of ever stopping. Even the orders to get on the ground shouted by police officers an hour later couldn't convince him to change his plans. Sadly, one of the officers suffered from coulrophobia, better known as fear of clowns, so when he saw the neon underwear wearing man with white face paint, his mind demanded he taser Mr. Balloony. Repeatedly.

The clown later woke up heavily medicated in a psychiatric ward.

Released a few weeks later, he had to find a new career. The clown now had severe pedophobia—fear of children—so Mr. Balloony found himself a far less stressful job as a bomb technician.

*****

The pony rides were a challenge. After hearing the Karens' plan, the horses flew onto the roof and refused to come down. They'd ride into the Apocalypse without blinking, but let a child ride on their back? That was a hard no.

Finally, a trail of pizza tricked Ravenous, Famine's black horse, down onto the lawn where they put Piers, one of the boy guests, on his back.

Karyn was busy finishing the birthday cake, so Kyrin led Ravenous around by the bridle. Thanks to her husband's wedding gift, the bride of War couldn't be harmed by any weapon, which in this case included horse teeth. After two laps around the yard, the other girl, Nina Semjonous, got on next.

Partway into the second lap, Karyn stepped out of the back door with a candle-adorned cake while singing happy birthday.

Kyrin joined in, clapping her hands at the end of the song and letting go of Ravenous's bridle.

Sensing freedom, the black horse leapt into the air as swift and quiet as a falling star.

At first, Nina was thrilled to be riding a flying horse until it sunk in that Ravenous wasn't returning to the party and the girl had no way to control the animal. In a blink, girl and horse disappeared over the horizon, barely missing some geese and a 747.

Kyrin completely forgot about the horse and rider and got in line for cake.

*****

The mother and stepfather of the Antichrist marched onto their deck smirking, followed by a man who made professional wrestlers seem puny.

Billy plopped a piece of cake on Kyrin's plate, then rushed straight at the newcomer.

"Dad! You made it!"

The scowl etched into the big man's face vanished, replaced with a smile as he knelt to hug the boy.

"Happy birthday, Billy."

"Thanks, Dad. And thanks for letting me have this awesome party. This is the greatest day of my life!"

The big man stood and mussed the boy's hair while scowling at the four women. "I'm going to thank the party planners personally." The big man motioned towards the side of the house. "Ladies, won't you join me?"

"You bet your goddamn ass we will," Karen said.

Karyn elbowed her in the side and motioned with her eyes toward Billy and his friends. "Language. There're kids around."

"Right," Karen said. "You bet your gosh-darn ass we will."

"You four have no idea with who you're messing," the big man said.

"Want to bet?" Karen said.

"You want us to guess your name?" Kyrin said.

"Honestly, I expected horns," Caren said.

Karyn bent over to stare at the man's buttocks. "I can't see your tail. Do you tuck it into your underwear? And do you wear boxers or briefs?"

The big man blinked twice, flummoxed to the point where horns did appear on his head, but his pants stayed on so the tail question went unanswered. "You know I'm the Devil, yet still disobeyed my orders regarding my son? You must be a whole new kind of stupid never before seen upon this wretched world."

"Look, we're just trying to bump up the Apocalypse here. We mistakenly thought Billy was an adult. Then we found that the poor kid wasn't having a party. What kind of a monster doesn't let an eight-year-old kid have a birthday party?"

The horned man chuckled. "Hello. Devil here. There are reasons I didn't want him to have a party."

"Or apparently any fun," Karyn said.

"For him to do his job and end this wretched world, he must rebel against *everything*. If he's just given whatever he wants and is deliriously happy, what reason will he have to destroy the Earth?"

Kyrin said, "Actually, as Karen mentioned, that's kind of why we're here. Is there any rule saying Billy has to wait until he's grownup before starting the Apocalypse?"

"Because we'd like to get things moving on that front as quickly as possible. Today if you can squeeze it in, but definitely by the end of the week," Caren said.

"What Satanic cult are you guys from again?" the Devil asked. "I've told those guys they need to screen members better. Psychotics are fine but wackos bring down the brand."

"I'll have you know we're Christians," Caren said.

"Except we really don't go to church except maybe on Christmas and Easter," Karyn said. "But we are going to redo the Bible with sexy covers."

"What's the deal here, horn-boy? Are you going to be able to get the Apocalypse up and running by Monday or do you need more time?" Karen said. "We need you to drop everything else and focus on this."

The Devil laughed, then realized he was the only one. "You're serious? The Devil doesn't take orders from humans. I'm going to destroy the four of you."

"Nope, you're not. If you can't handle this, we need somebody who can, so kindly get your manager," Karen said.

"You make demands of me? So you're suicidal too."

"You can't kill me," Karen said.

As the Devil smiled, his incisors grew into fangs. "I wouldn't place too much faith in the rules that I can't kill. Oh, they make it difficult, but they go right out the fifth circle when someone gets up in my business."

"No, I don't mean you won't. You *can't*."

"Hope you left a will." The Devil snapped his fingers, but Karen was still standing. He did it again and she didn't fall. He looked at his hand, then snapped three times in rapid succession. Squirrels fell out of nearby trees and birds dropped from the sky. "Why aren't you dead?"

"I can't die. Now about that manager."

"I'm not calling..." The Devil pointed a finger up at the sky. "...Him just because you asked me to."

"You better. Do you know who my husband is?"

"No, but I'd like to so I can share the torment I have planned for you with the idiot dim enough to make you his bride."

Ashy chose that moment to leap off the roof of the house and trot over to nuzzle Karen's hand. The Devil recognized the pale green horse and grimaced. "Oh no!"

"Oh yes."

"What did the rest of the horsemen say when this happened?"

"They said 'I do' to the rest of us." Karyn and the other three Karens held up their left hands to show off their wedding bands.

The Devil facepalmed. "They made it all the way from the Big Bang without getting hitched. Why ruin it now?"

"So about..." Kyrin said, but the Devil turned his palm towards her.

"Do the boys know what you're doing?"

Caren shook her head. "It's a surprise so we can all go on a honeymoon because until the Apocalypse happens, they can't take an entire week off."

The Devil blinked. "Let me get this straight. The four of you are willing to destroy the world decades early so you can go on *vacation*?"

The Karens nodded.

"Maybe I misjudged the boys. You're my kind of people." The Devil pulled out his cell. "Grim, Lucifer. Yes, of course, I ordered the game on dead-per-view but I couldn't finish watching because four crazy women crashed my kid's birthday because they want to start the Apocalypse ahead of schedule." The Devil smiled and covered up the mouthpiece. "Death's saying those people sound like lunatics." The Devil took his hand away. "I'd most certainly agree, especially since they married the four of you... Yep, your wives are at my kid's house. No, I don't think you'll be here in five minutes. They have your horses."

*****

"Karen, you've got some explaining to do," the Grim Reaper said.

And explain she did.

"What it boils down to is this—we spent the last few million years planning the Apocalypse," the Devil said. "Changing the

305

timetable at this late date is simply not going to work. I get the distinct impression that these four ladies are very stubborn. I don't have the time or the energy to deal with them bothering me for the next few decades—especially after you four shared the powers of your aspects with them. Something needs to be worked out so they leave me alone."

Much yelling ensued.

"Enough! How bad are you if the Devil has to act as your marriage counselor? Ladies, you've already been told that the Four Horsemen of the Apocalypse cannot take a week off from their duties. At least not at the same time. What if three Horsemen cover for the other while he goes on a week-long honeymoon?"

Karen stomped her foot. "We wanna go *together*!"

"And I want to rule the universe. Neither is happening. How about I sweeten the deal and pay for all four honeymoons?" The Devil ate some cake. "This is sinfully delicious. Karyn, you simply must give me the recipe."

"I'd be happy to."

Karen squinted. "So totally free?"

The Devil nodded.

"No matter how exclusive or expensive?"

"I'll book everything myself."

The Karens huddled.

"I'd miss you guys but I want to go where Kanye and Kim went."

"I wanna go to this place that charges half a million a night."

They turned around. "Deal."

After Famine snagged a piece of his wife's cake, the four horsemen and their brides returned home. The Devil stayed to spend time with his son.

And Nina was found safely five hundred miles away by a local fire department at the top of the tree Ravenous had dropped her in.

We Got the Beat

Russ Colchamiro

In the grand scheme of the universe, fifty-six asteroids soaring through the cosmos, each roughly the size, density, and configuration of a CPAC convention, and another few hundred particles only a fraction that size, would not have made the morning news. And they didn't.

Their points of origin and unconventional orbits were unknown, but in the course of time, theories would abound. Partially because the irradiated bodies hurtling through the far reaches of space vibrated with a particular cadence those sensitive enough to appreciate could feel but not yet articulate. And also because those very same asteroids were on a direct and violent collision course with Earth.

But mostly it was the cadence thing.

Such that Charlotte Zara watched curiously, and perhaps sadistically, as a dozen townsfolk pedaled swan-shaped paddle boats across the glistening reservoir in West Orange, New Jersey, wondering if the end times had finally come.

While an orange sun settled at dusk behind the distant trees lining Pleasant Valley Way, she neither feared nor clamored for the destruction of all life as she knew it. As an eleven-year-old, she'd experienced unfettered joys and sorrows of childhood, doing her best to navigate her shifting place in a community constructed of rules and regulations she struggled to understand and determined by grownups who seemed equally confused and were, apparently more often than they were prepared to admit, batshit crazy or just too dumb, numb, or bummed to notice.

Her middle-class suburban community in Essex County ten minutes west of Newark was populated with lawn signs declaring *Hate Has No Place Here*, *Stop Asian Hate*, and *Black Lives Matter*. Charlotte wasn't sure why those sentiments needed to be displayed on mini billboards, as to her it was self-evident that the color of one's skin wasn't what defined a person's worth, but rather how they treated others and carried themselves.

In her experience, limited as it may have been, color, ethnicity, and gender identification were utterly irrelevant, because most people sucked big honking farts regardless. It was simply a matter of degree.

But she was told often and intensely, by her own parents, that being white meant she didn't understand what it meant not to be white, and that because she didn't understand the life experience of someone born with darker hues, she needed to be constantly reminded that actually being white meant she had an obligation to never forget she had, and would continue to have, opportunities and choices people with different skin tones often did not.

It's not that Charlotte didn't believe her parents. But they seemed to be working way too hard to drive home that point when neither of them had a single friend who wasn't white, as if she was supposed to be living up to an ideal her parents desperately wanted to believe they were living up to themselves, but clearly were not.

There was also a bombardment of noise about people being woke, or too woke, or not woke enough, when all Charlotte wanted, as she entered her tween years, was to take a long and glorious nap.

Grownups yelled constantly about people wearing masks, or not wearing masks, or wearing them incorrectly. Not to mention the overwhelming sentiment that the citizens of America, if not the entire world, were going to finally beat each other into bloody stumps in the name of—well... she wasn't exactly sure what—until no one was left to clean up the mess.

The Jews were probably to blame anyway. They got blamed for pretty much everything else, although no one she knew had been able to explain why. Apparently, they were too *Jewy*, whatever that meant.

As long as people left Charlotte out of whatever was twisting their nerps, she was happy to let any and all nonsense unfold as it would. So, when the first wave of orange-tailed meteorites soared across the darkening sky and pelted the reservoir, she shrugged.

Only a year into her music class (she descended from a long line of drummers, and nothing was going to stop her from continuing that tradition), Charlotte recognized the rhythm of those pellets, in classic 4/4 time.

Sitting cross-legged on a swath of grass, she felt the rhythm in her soul, the hard-hitting stroke of Cindy Blackman Santana, the power-blasting drummer who backed Lenny Kravitz's band.

Whereas in most pop and rock songs the bass drum and snare drum were played in alternating beats (bass *and*, snare *and*, bass *and*, snare *and*), Charlotte was grooving to her favorite drummer pound the bass and snare simultaneously, kicking off the opening riff of *Are You Gonna Go My Way*:

Snap and, snap and, snap and, snap and

With each snap into the water, the meteorites released a hiss of steam. Much like the rock songs Charlotte so loved, they brought the heat.

Surrounded by a massive tree line separating the town's reservoir from Turtleback Zoo and the kiddie train serpentining through the surrounding forest, the paddleboaters were confused at first, unsure what was falling from the sky. In short order, however, it became clear to all floating on the reservoir's otherwise placid waters that they were sitting swans, er, ducks and should probably get the fuck out of there.

"Mr. Swanson!" Charlotte called out to her school's music teacher who, while blessed with excellent timing and a gift for instruction, had a lousy sense of direction.

Flustered, he replied anxiously, "Kinda busy!"

"I know! But the beat on the water...!"

Ducking meteorites, he was pedaling as fast as he could, his face red and sweaty. "What about it?" His wife was pedaling, too, although her efforts didn't seem to be helping.

Charlotte bopped her head in rhythm to the drum track. "It's kinda rad!"

"Can we talk about this later?"

Charlotte looked up into the darkening sky, streaked with meteorites. "I don't think so!"

"Why?"

"You're pedaling in the wrong direction!"

Like most adults she knew, Mister Swanson did not appreciate being corrected by a child, particularly in front of his wife. "I know what I'm doing!"

Only he was, in fact, moving farther away from the dock, into the center of the reservoir, rather than toward it. While in full-blown panic, he took a golf ball-sized meteorite flush in the face, knocking his head clear off his shoulders, converting his torso into a headless, squirting fountain.

Covered in her husband's blood, his wife sat in befuddled silence next to him there in the white swan-shaped boat until the shock wore off just enough that she began screaming at a decibel rarely emitted by human voice.

One by one meteorites capsized each of the paddleboats and the townsfolk in them until the reservoir looked to Charlotte like the top of her fish tank less than a week after her mom had set it up—a body of water littered with dead bodies.

But as with all great rock beats, she felt the propulsive rhythm of those bruising meteorite snaps drawing her in, to a specific destination she saw in her mind's eye as clear as she saw Mr. Swanson's decapitated corpse bobbing in the reservoir among the other floaters.

She would find her way to the two towers. And when she arrived, there and only there, the final beats would play.

*****

Like a metallic dragon thrust from its decrepit cave, the 7 train roared along the elevated subway tracks past the 74th Street stop in Jackson Heights, a multicultural neighborhood in the northwest region of Queens, New York.

With the city out of quarantine, although still not out of the woods, the daily carnival along Roosevelt Avenue was in full effect. The neighborhood's main thoroughfare was choked with cars, cabs, trucks, buses, and thousands of walking, biking, and scootering residents, half of which had emigrated from other countries.

So as they starting keeling over, one by one, having instantaneously, unexpectedly starved to death, there were no calls of bigotry, racism, or cultural genocide. White, black, brown, olive, and every shade in between, bodies dropped indiscriminately.

"Holy shit, Esai. You seein' this?"

Fifteen years old, Esai Dominguez studied a fallen mother who, within seconds, shriveled from plump to tragically emaciated, then slumped over a beat-up double stroller. The twin toddlers strapped into the padded seats suffered the same fate, their eyes open and hollow.

Esai twirled a drum stick between his fingers. An experimental percussionist, he took his sticks everywhere. Conduits of expression, they kept him calm, helped him think. He turned to his cousin, Christina. Wearing a navy-blue Yankees baseball cap with the interlocking NY logo on the front, she thumbed the silver cross dangling around her neck, then kissed the holy symbol.

Esai wiped sweat from his brow. "There's a lotta great drummers, cuz, but you know... Sheila E.'s still my hermosa. She got skills, she got faith. And most of all... she got *rhythm*."

"No offense, cuz, but don't start with that Sheila E. *mierda* right now. Look around, yo! They're dead! Like zombies, but, you know... dead! What the fuck?" Christina leaned forward in disbelief, the dead boys' eye sockets so caved in their faces appeared more alien than human. "I'm gonna be sick."

While Christina splattered on her open-toed sandals, Esai looked on as motor vehicles of every kind haphazardly crashed into one another, a yellow cab plowing through the front window of the local McDonald's and the bodega next door.

Sirens wailed. Horns blared. Glass shattered. Voices gasped and screamed. The streetscape was coming alive with death.

Esai closed his eyes. In his mind's eye he saw rough currents. He saw massive cables. He saw plumes of smoke, blazing fires, and a trail of dead bodies. And he saw the two towers.

"Every moment has a rhythm, cuz. Every breath, every motion. Maybe you don't hear all the notes, but if you listen... if you really *escucha*... there they are. Even when you're still. A rest is just a note you don't play. Sounds... silence. Sounds... silence. It's the music of the world. It's the music *de la vida*."

A half block away beneath the elevated train trestle, like an urban banshee another string of subway cars screeched metallically, then veered off the track, demolishing a row of storefronts, killing everyone in its path. The force knocked Christina to the sidewalk. But Esai just stood there, twirling his sticks.

"And the music of *muerte*."

Disintegrating in real time, Christina fell over, another emaciated body. Close to death, but not quite. She reached out with her tiny, shriveled hand. "Cuh... cuz. *Lo que está sucediendo?*"

Esai was well aware of the carnage surrounding him. Nothing he could do about those who were already dead. Drumming had always been his love. But now, at long last, he knew for certain what he'd always felt but had failed to fully embrace because those around him, jealous of what made him shine, had done their best to neuter his passion, challenging his resolve.

Drumming was his true calling. It was time to own it. "Know why I love Shelia E.?"

Facefirst on the concrete, unable to even crawl among the urban graveyard, Christina could barely speak. A single tear, the final drop of fluid her body could secrete, puddled on her cheek. "Nuh... no."

Esai offered a satisfied smile. "Because she's got *style*, cuz. She played with *Prince*! Whoo! Don't get me started on that. And she's still out there doing her own thing. Because for her, playing drums isn't just about holding a beat, about being the backbone of a song. It's about taking you on a *journey*! Showing the world she's still *alive*. She's knows R&B, Latino, pop, rock, and funk. She can play *anything*. But whatever she's playing, she never holds back. Every step we take, every breath we breathe, somebody somewhere's telling us where we can go and where we can't. Who we are, who we should be, and what we're about. They tell us what we should think, who we're allowed to love, and who we're supposed to hate."

In her final throes on the sidewalk, Christina convulsed so hard her neck snapped.

"Shiela E. doesn't care what anybody says, cuz. She hits those skins, rides those cymbals like she's trying to set us all *free*."

Cracked open by a crashed Entenmann's delivery truck, a fire hydrant spewed an arch of flowing water down the boulevard of fallen corpses.

"You can only fuck with the world for so long, cuz. And you can only fuck with it so hard. I hear the beat. I feel it *en mi alma*." Esai twirled his sticks again, then like a seasoned gunslinger, slipped them seamlessly into his back pocket. "The two towers are calling me, cuz. Sorry you can't make it. But I'm on my way."

*****

Recently orphaned, Tanya King had long been fascinated with the design, theory, and construction of bridges. Not just because her mother, Monique, had been a passionate and in-demand architect until her untimely death earlier that morning, but because those very structures were, by their nature, intended to physically bring people together, or allow them to escape, explore, or travel far beyond the confines of their immediate circumstances.

The Ponte Vecchio medieval bridge over the Arno River in Florence. The gothic Charles Bridge crossing the Vltatva River in Prague. The Si-o-se Pol bridge in Isfahan, Iran. The Stari Most bridge crossing the Neretva River in the city of Mostar in Bosnia and Herzegovina, built by the Ottoman Turks in 1566. The Brooklyn Bridge. The Golden Gate.

But as the remnants of humankind gathered for the great

reckoning, Tanya was drawn by the thrumming, unpredictable beats of Keith Moon—The Who's famous drummer—to the two massive towers she'd been dreaming about for weeks.

Tanya's father Boyd, who died years ago in a drunk driving accident while on the southbound lane of the West Side Highway, on weekends had served as backbone of Pinball Wyzard, a semi-popular cover band playing The Who's classic hits and some of their deep tracks.

Much like Keith Moon himself, Boyd was a wild, enthusiastic stickman who also drank and snorted cocaine to, among other reasons, get a rise out of anyone who couldn't believe he'd be willing to push the bounds of manic fun quite that far.

So as dynamite exploded within nearly every residential and commercial building along Manhattan's West Side, starting at Battery Park City in Lower Manhattan all the way north through Hell's Kitchen, Harlem, and up to Washington Heights, Tanya knew exactly where to go.

Especially as the nitroglycerin-based explosives had been placed only in toilets.

A rampant prankster in his day, Keith Moon was notorious for setting off tiny bombs in hotel commodes, because it was a good laugh. And maybe it was.

Nevertheless, the exploding toilets Tanya still heard rumbling throughout Manhattan resulted in epic amounts of water spewing through windows, pipes, and doorways, setting off electrical fires and blackouts, and thus widespread panic.

The mayhem had already killed tens of thousands, including Tanya's mother. As the only Black and transgender executive in the architectural firm she joined before almost everyone else who worked there, Monique had been preparing for her first day as a full partner, the last of the senior members to reach that lofty position. That during her fourteen years with the firm she had outperformed and generated more revenue than every other partner, who all happened to be cis-gendered, or at least publicly identified as such, was of course sheer coincidence.

Yet while squatting on the toilet doing her morning business, the dynamite exploded in the tank behind her. The blast left Monique pinned to the bathroom floor of her third-floor apartment on West 63rd Street, bleeding through the floorboards, as toilet paper shreds and ceramic dust floated in the air like confetti.

Had Tanya not been hunting under her bed for her not-so-secret stash of medical-grade THC gummies, she would have been killed as well.

Toilets continued to explode around the entire perimeter of Manhattan until Tanya realized that grieving for her mutilated mother in real time was pointless. The dream Tanya been having wasn't just about the two towers. It was the expanse between them. And who, at long last, was poised to gather there.

The final horseman was coming.

*****

The double-decker George Washington Bridge spanned the nearly five thousand feet over the Hudson River between Manhattan and Fort Lee, New Jersey, with the lushly forested Palisades to the north and Union City, Jersey City, and Hoboken to the south.

Sites on both sides of the river had, back in 1776, served as fortified positions by General George Washington and his forces as they attempted, unsuccessfully, to fight off the Brits. The bloodshed during those ruthless attacks nearly turned the river—at the time as crystal clear as the Caribbean Sea—beet red.

Fitting, thought Manoop Bhutani, who at sixteen had been practicing his drums day and night, making sure he got the timing just right, much to the chagrin of his father. Doctor Bhutani was an anesthesiologist at Columbia Presbyterian Hospital, a medical facility less than a quarter mile away, where Manoop was born.

"Father wanted me to become a doctor like him," Manoop said as thousands marched onto the upper and lower bridge expanses from both sides of the river. "'Manoop,' he said to me many, many times, 'I did not come aaallll the way to America for you to bang your silly sticks on a drum. You must work very very hard to become a doctor. You must earn your reputation and your place. The family is counting on you. The life you have is yours, yes, but not yours alone. You owe that life to every Bhutani who came before you, including me and your mother. We gave up our friends and family in Calcutta so that you could ensure future generations of Bhutanis would thrive in America.'"

Charlotte rolled her eyes. "Guilt trip much? That's heavy."

"Muy pesado," Esai concurred.

"My mom was like that too," Tanya said. "But now she's dead. She got shit for having the conversion surgery. She got shit for living her truth. She got shit for adopting me. And she got shit for not taking shit. All those years working twice as hard as everyone else just to earn half what they got... it was all for nothing. I told her it wasn't gonna matter. But she said it wasn't about them. It was about her. It was about us. About integrity."

Charlotte gazed into the sky, first facing south, as the Hudson River curled around the tip of the island, then west toward her native New Jersey. Hundreds of thousands of survivors trundled painfully toward the bridge, half of them collapsing along the way.

Although she lived only twenty miles from where they stood, she hadn't until then realized how closely they were all connected despite feeling so far apart.

Not that it mattered. Time was running out.

Tanya continued. "You have two options, my mother said. Fight for your place with every last breath or give up and accept your fate at the back of every line. But whichever path you follow, if you don't make the choice yourself, others will make it for you. And if you do that, you got nothing to complain about, because you allowed it. Nobody ever said life was gonna be easy, fair, or just. In fact, we're told every day, in almost every way, that most of us don't matter, no matter where we come from, what we look like, or how we hard we try. My mom wanted her life to be based on merit, but she said it almost always came down to just two things: money and power. It's good to have one, she said, but it's better to have both."

Gathered on the upper level of the George Washington Bridge, the four junior drummers, one each facing north, south, east, and west, looked out at the fallen bodies strewn across the streets and floating in the river, as half of Manhattan and New Jersey burned in torrents of orange and black flame.

"Sure don't matter now," Charlotte said.

"Nope," Tanya said.

"No importa," Esai said.

In an alternating sequence with the exploding toilets and destruction they inflicted, the comets Charlotte first encountered in New Jersey were now taking out rows of multimillion-dollar brownstone apartment buildings along Riverside Drive.

"Father often told me about the stages of anesthesia," Manoop said, a couple of hundred feet above the rough and dangerous currents below. "First is the induction stage. You are given medication until you sleep. Nowadays, the anesthesia is so strong, you're out before the count of four."

The four junior drummers clacked their sticks together and counted aloud, "one, two, three, four..." as if kicking off a rock song. With their sticks, they shared common ground.

"It's been happening to us," Esai said. "The warnings were clear. Jim Morrison sang it in 'Roadhouse Blues'. The future's uncertain and el final siempre está cerca."

"Huh?" Charlotte said.

Tanya translated. "The end is always near."

*****

The scalding sun beat down on the remaining survivors as they slowly marched toward the George Washington Bridge. Half had starved to death along the way, literally dropping in place. And like the true bastion of inclusion that it is, Death did not single out any race, creed, color, religion, age group, gender, or economic status.

Death proved itself the bastion of inclusion.

Charlotte twirled her sticks. "Kinda fucked up out there."

"Ya think?" Tanya said.

"Si," Esai said. "I kinda do."

Manoop closed his eyes, breathed in. Yes, he smelled vomit and urine and fecal matter and salt and fire and toxic fumes. But in the quiet of his mind, in his very self, among all that death, something else came alive. "The beats," he said. "The rhythms. You feel that?"

The four junior drummers gently rocked in place, falling into the percussive rumblings in the wind.

The survivors, some masked, some not, who had walked for miles in fear and desperation as bodies fell all around them, had nearly filled up the bridge's upper and lower decks. From all stations of life, what was left of it, the survivors sought an end to their suffering.

"We made it!" cried a woman in tattered clothes, who began weeping uncontrollably. A dirty cloth mask hung from one ear.

"Thank Christ," said another man in a tattered two-piece suit, who'd been beaten half to death but made it to the bridge nonetheless.

Said an older woman, "We are the chosen ones. God brought us here."

The sky rumbled. Lightning crashed. Through dark, lumpy clouds stretching toward the horizon, a patch opened.

Initially appearing like tiny birds, one, then two, then three winged beasts appeared from that opening, piercing the membrane of existence itself. As the beasts drew nearer, the beats the survivors felt, the rhythms, grew louder, clearer, and more propulsive, resonating in the hearts and souls of all who congregated.

Esai had been waiting for this moment. "It's them. Los Cuatro Jinetes."

"The Four Horsemen," Charlotte said.

Tanya squinted. "Are you sure? There's only three."

Closer and closer the creatures soared on the grace of glorious wings, until it became clear they weren't birds at all.

Perched on individual, winged risers, Cindy Blackman Santana and Keith Moon sat on drum stools, behind custom configured drum sets, while Sheila E., on her own winged riser, stood behind her snare drum.

Charlotte looked upon the drummers. She then asked a question, not because she thought it reasonable, but because she wasn't sure what else to do. "Are you here to save us?"

Cheeks puffed out in his prankster pose, Keith Moon guffawed. He took a hearty swig from a bottle of Jack Daniels. "Bollocks to that, mate! We're here on the piss!" He pounded the drums and cymbals in his manic, swooshing style, like a skier barreling down the slopes. Massive soundwaves thrust over the river, demolishing most of downtown Hoboken. Victorious, he snorted a line of cocaine off the ride cymbal. "Time to fuckin' party!"

Dressed in black flowing robes, dotted scarf, teased hair, and large hoop earrings, Sheila E. shook her head. "Keith, we talked about this. Well, we would have if you had showed up for rehearsal."

"Sorry, mate. But I forgot to smash the telly in a few hotel rooms. Had to go back and give 'em a good kickin'!"

"Quiet!" Cindy Blackman Santana demanded with a thunderous snap of the bass drum, powerful enough that it knocked half a million survivors back two feet each like fallen dominoes. Behind black sunglasses, she spoke truth. "He's coming. He's here."

The sky grew darker, more ominous. Lightning bolts flashed against a purple sky. Thunder rumbled. Fires burned.

Charlotte reached to her chest. "The beat. The rhythm. It's getting stronger."

"I feel it too," Tanya said.

"Tambien," Esai said. "But who?"

Cindy Blackman Santana, Sheila E., and Keith Moon raised their arms, pointing their drum sticks to the heavens. "The Professor," they said in unison.

A die-hard Rush fan, it was Manoop who spoke his name aloud. "Neil Peart. The greatest of all."

Head adorned in a black skullcap, Neil Peart rode down on his winged riser, replete with a thirty-seven-piece drum set, including snare drum, double bass, multiple tom-toms, cowbell, and two dozen cymbals. "Love and life are deep, my friends. But you have chosen death."

Desperately holding back a laugh, Keith Moon took another swig of Jack Daniels. "A bit apocalyptic there, mate, no?"

"Keith," Sheila E. said. "It *is* the apocalypse."

"Really? Fuuuuuuuck. I thought this was just the soundcheck. My bad."

In black leather, Cindy Blackman Santana glowered. "You waste time blowing shit up, you're gonna miss a few memos."

Keith Moon giggled.

"Each microcosmic planet is a complete society," Neil Peart said. "And the universe is vast. You were given a choice. To value the life you were given or tear yourselves apart."

The first woman who had arrived at the bridge felt the hand of her only daughter slip from hers, the child dead of starvation. "We did the best we could. But the systems, the governments. They put us in cages we couldn't see, with locks we can never open. So few have so much, and the rest of us…"

"All the world's indeed a stage," Neil Peart said, "and we are merely players."

"But why is this happening?" the woman asked. "What have we done?"

Keith Moon guffawed. "Haven't you paid attention, mate? You fucked yourselves good 'n proper. Air? Polluted it. Food? Wanked it. Nature? Raped it. You were so busy pointing fingers at each other you didn't stop the evil bastards from shagging the whole world! Which is what makes them such evil geniuses. They get you all riled up, fighting each other so they can steal your shit right in front of your faces, when really, there's plenty to go around. Don't get your knickers in a twist because the world's gonna end. You had your chance."

Neil Peart held out his drum sticks like conductor's wands. "Don't be so harsh, Keith. We are only immortal for a limited time."

"That's some Tom Sawyer shit right there," Cindy Blackman Santana said. "Mean, mean stride. Mean, mean pride."

"And yet... judgment day has arrived," Neil Peart said. "From across the vast reaches of existence itself, from places we cannot fathom, a message has been sent."

Manoop turned to him. "Is that what I've been feeling? The message?"

Esai tapped his chest. "Sí. En mi corazón."

Tanya still didn't understand. "What fucking message?"

"Rocks," Cindy Blackman Santana said. "Big muthafuckin' rocks."

"Wait," Charlotte said. "You mean... the meteorites? That's why they're falling?"

Keith Moon giggled again, clapping his hands like a butterfly flapping its wings. "Not just meteorites. Asteroids."

Sheila E. began double-sticking on her snare drum. Tack-ah-tack-ah-tack-ah-tack-ah-tack-ah. "Neil. It's time."

He nodded. "And so it is."

"No puedos!" Esai cried. "You can't. We came!"

Sheila E. increased her rhythm, the drum sticks flickering with wondrous skill. "As long as there is life there is beauty and there is pain. Whether you view the waking times as a gift or a burden is entirely up to you."

Like his fellow junior drummers, Esai had gone into shock as the world crumbled around them with apocalyptic fury. There was no other way to heed the call. And the call, at last, was loud and clear. "It's neither, it's both! But at least it's mine. And I don't want it to end!"

Sheila E. offered a compassionate nod. "I'm afraid it's too late, dear. If only you all had acted sooner."

It was thus decreed. The Four Drummers of the Apocalypse all spoke in their percussive language, with drums and cymbals, finalizing the end of the world. Meteorites plunged. Starvation washed over the city like a fast-acting virus. Toilets exploded. Building fell. Fires raged. Rats scurried in droves.

The end time was upon them.

Meditating on his father's many sacrifices and encouragement to put family above self, it was Manoop who acted. Vibrating his sticks on the bridge's metallic beams, he initiated a drumroll with unwavering precision, much like his hero Neil Peart, the human metronome.

Charlotte joined him, her stick work not as precise, but with thunderous beats. Then Esai turned to Sheila E., stared out over the Hudson River, and added his Latin rhythms. Tanya unleashed a wild barrage of drum fills.

Individually they produced beats, but in tandem they created rhythm, fortified in strength. Targeted soundwaves pulsed into the sky, neutralizing meteorite fragments before they assaulted the Earth, turning them into dust.

Once the survivors realized what was happening, they started to chant.

"Drum-mers! Drum-mers! Drum-mers! Drum-mers!"

Chanting faster and faster until the four junior drummers picked up the cadence, pounding their sticks faster, faster, and faster still, taking out one meteorite after another.

"They're doing it!" a survivor said. "We're saved!"

Until a massive meteorite split the Empire State Building in half, toppling Herald Square, Korea Town, and the Seventh Avenue entrance to Penn Station. And though they couldn't see it from the bridge, a meteorite knocked the head clean off the Statue of Liberty, sinking it into New York Harbor, overturning four barges.

Neil Peart gazed out over the Hudson River, the city, and the Earth itself, and then to the four junior drummers—the four disciples—who heeded the call. And then he did what he did best. He beat on his drums and cymbals at a frequency no other drummer in human history had been able to replicate. Force, precision, and repetition.

Following his lead, Sheila E., Keith Moon, and Cindy Blackman Santana turned their sticks upon their drums, directing their power into the heavens.

Acting as a battalion of anti-ballistic gun turrets, the Four Drummers of the Apocalypse blasted the equivalent of bullets, rockets, and bombs at the biggest of the hurtling asteroids. The fragments broke in half, then again, until only two were left, each massive rock still large enough to create a fifty megaton explosion upon impact.

Cindy Blackman Santana adjusted her sunglasses. "I got this." With a ferocious pound on her drums, she launched a soundwave so massive, deafening, and intense that in a single blast it obliterated one of the two remaining asteroids into thousands of pieces.

Sheila E., with her fusion-style drumming, shattered those fragments into dust, while Keith Moon took out whatever pieces were left.

Except for the largest asteroid of all.

"Students," Neil Peart said. "Put aside the alienation. Get on with the fascination."

"Catch the spirit," Manoop said. "Catch the spit."

Neil Peart and his disciples thrummed their arms, calling upon ancient forces into the darkening sky. The junior drummers all discovered within themselves a power, stroke, confidence, and pulse they had never been able to access—or knew existed.

Their collective soundwaves chiseled away at the soaring asteroid, shaving off its outer edges. But the inner mass was still enormous.

Drummers and survivors alike, everyone knew only the One could strike the final blow.

Neil Peart adjusted his skullcap. Breathed in, breathed out. In an awesome display of his power, synced with incomprehensible speed, technique, and surgical accuracy, he manipulated his sticks and double bass drums.

The ground shook. The sky rumbled.

Such that the greatest drummer known among Heaven and Earth pummeled the asteroid with soundwaves, like a rail gun with unlimited ammunition, until that enormous, life-cratering rock was reduced to ash.

The skies began to clear. Lighting ceased. The survivors did not cheer in victory, nor expel sighs of relief. They were just there, left among the ruins.

The Professor smiled and nodded. "Live in the limelight, my friends. The universal dream."

On his winged riser, Neil Peart left the bridge, soared over the city toward the heavens, and finally disappeared through the membrane. Wordlessly, Cindy Blackman Santana did the same.

Sheila E. smiled, neither a gesture of sadness nor joy. She ran a gentle hand under Esai's chin. "Good luck, children." And then she too, like the Lorax, was gone.

The four junior drummers looked to the burning ruins all around them, to each other, then to Keith Moon, left to consider their fates.

Tanya asked what they were all thinking. "So, Keith... what do we do now? Like my mom tried to teach me, do we keep fighting the good fight? Or do we throw it all way?"

The Who's former drummer did another line of coke off his hi-hat cymbal, grinned, then on his own winged riser, soared back toward the membrane.

"How the fuck should I know, mate? I just work here."

The Four Course Men

David Gerrold

It was time to begin.

The Chairman strode into the room without acknowledging the existence of any of the others. He went directly to the head of the table. He stood quietly for a moment, studying his fingertips on the polished obsidian surface. Finally he raised his eyes and looked around slowly. Every place was filled. Everyone stood at respectful attention, silently waiting. He nodded his satisfaction, then took his seat without ceremony.

The various division heads waited respectfully until he had settled himself, then took their seats around the table as well. Rows of chairs lined the walls around them for the heads of the assorted subdivisions; every chair was filled.

A single pitcher of ice water and a small glass marked the Chairman's place. He filled the glass halfway, took a polite sip, replaced it on the table, cleared his throat, then looked to the men in the room. "Well, I suppose you're wondering why I asked you all to be here today." Then, with the barest hint of a smile, he added, "No, probably not. You've all been expecting this for a while, haven't you? Right. Well, we're all here. So let's get right to it.

"This special meeting of Omega Corporation, LLC. is now in session. Let me note for the record that all four Division Chiefs are present: War, Famine, Pestilence, and Death. Welcome gentlemen."

He indicated the rows of deputies in the chairs around the walls. "Media, Ideology, Hysteria. Fear and Anger. Deceit, Discord, Despair. All of you. Exemplary work. And of course, we cannot overlook the enormous contributions of Ignorance."

He turned his attention back to the whole room. "But quite frankly, none of it has been enough." He paused, allowing his words to hang in the air, allowing the impact of their meaning to be felt. He lifted a hand to stop anyone from protesting. No one would, of course, but the gesture was necessary if only for dramatic effect.

"This is no one's fault, this is not a time for accusations or recriminations. The responsibility is entirely mine. Events have moved much faster than any of us could have predicted. Human beings are marvelously inventive, it's what makes them so delightfully delicious—but at heart, they remain stubborn, selfish, and cruel, so even though circumstances have evolved, our mission has not.

"If we are to remain relevant, we need to reexamine and refocus our efforts. As most of you know, we have hired several independent agencies to determine where we can most profitably invest our future efforts. The goal is complete effectiveness in every arena.

"Toward that end, we have the United Nations studying the specific causes of war, we have the World Health Organization and the Centers for Disease Control reporting back to us on plagues, and Greenpeace has accepted a healthy donation to report on global climate disruption as a cause of famine. And even though lifespans now extend more than twice what was experienced in the recent past, Death still remains a constant presence.

"We have their latest reports, and the information is both enlightening and disturbing. Even though the work is far from complete, the trends that we suspected are already becoming obvious." He spread his hands wide, as if to include everyone in the room. "There is no question that we have been very effective in the past, and perhaps our long history of successes have lulled us into a sense of complacency and comfort.

"To be blunt—the best methods of the past will be irrelevant in the future. If we are to continue to be effective, we have no choice. We will have to restructure. We will have to invest our energies into new arenas. This is neither good news nor bad, it is merely a test of our commitment."

He looked around the table. "Let me get into some detail here. This will take some time, but it's necessary for a more complete understanding. I'll start with one of our most effective divisions, War.

"War has been the leader in more disasters than I can list. War was here even before Omega. War got his start with insects, worked his way up to primates, and was instrumental in the very beginnings of this corporation. We would not be here were it not for War and our debt to him and his work is enormous. War has made great contributions to all of our separate divisions and all of our divisions have contributed to his efforts in return. So thank you, War."

The Chairman waited for the polite applause to fade. He took a quick sip of water. "The last few thousand years in Europe have been spectacular. And Asia as well. The advances in technology, catapults, crossbows, cannons, machine guns, aerial bombing—magnificent. The twentieth century was an unparalleled achievement. Two world wars and a smoldering aftermath in Korea, Vietnam, Afghanistan, no question but that War outdid himself. But nuclear weaponry made War so horrible that humans have recoiled in horror. Where once War could have run up a score in the tens of millions, now it takes as much effort even to reach a few thousand. War is no longer a daily presence. For most of humanity, he has been reduced to a distant annoyance."

War remained expressionless, but his folded arms betrayed his discomfort. The Chairman looked directly to him. "I know that this is upsetting to hear. But you and I are old friends and our friendship is based on partnership as well as affection. I would not betray that friendship by giving you anything less than an honest evaluation of our situation. Your work is still relevant, more than you might realize. As a continually looming possibility of apocalyptic disaster, you are now the kind of threat that humans use to terrify themselves. You are a cultural icon."

War shook his head. "With all due respect—considerable respect—I disagree." He stood up, a rare breach of etiquette, almost a confrontation. He rose to his full height, because he was after all War. "I am not an icon. Mickey Mouse is an icon. Coca-Cola is an icon. What I create is elemental."

He spoke with deliberate resolve. "They called World War I 'The Great War.' When I surpassed that effort with World War II, they called the participants 'The Greatest Generation.' Humans respect me, they fear me—and they invest billions of dollars a year to be ready for my next great effort. Yes, their technology has become formidable. It needs to be. We cannot create an apocalypse without apocalyptic machineries."

"Please sit down," said the Chairman. It was not a request. War met his gaze with ill-concealed resentment. For a moment, the two were locked in silent conflict. Then War sat down stiffly.

The Chairman took a deep breath. "What you say is true. There is no question of that. But all of that is the past. And it assumes that the goal of Omega is a final annihilation. As glorious as another World War might be, the ultimate result would be a world so fractured, so devoid of humanity, that our efforts here would be irrelevant.

"As difficult as this is to hear, it is necessary that you accept it. You remain important, War, but your role has changed. Perhaps icon was the wrong word. Perhaps there is no word to describe your new role in human consciousness. Humans now spend billions of dollars every year to create IMAX illusions of destruction. They have invented euphemisms like kaiju and aliens and super-villains, but the intention is the same—a justification for hatred. They have created an entire industry that does nothing but create vicarious devastation as a two-hour adventure. They wallow in it. They enjoy it. And it serves their need for hatred."

War folded his arms. "I am not an entertainment."

"No, you are not. You are a way of being. You are elemental. And as an elemental, you are much more important. Our long-term goal has always been the creation of a state of permanent apocalypse. Your successes with the world wars were admirable, but in the aftermath, humans created first the League of Nations and finally the United Nations, specifically to prevent the possibility of a third world war. Yes, you were successful, but you were too successful. Humans are so afraid of another global outbreak that they have been working desperately to prevent it. And they have been effective enough to reduce your efforts to very small arenas. That is your real victory. They think about you every day. The billions they invest are intended as prevention. They are so terrified of you that the entire focus of their global political stance has been prevention. Everything they do in the name of cooperation and community is about prevention. Even as you remain unexpressed, what you represent remains a permanent threat. The little flurries that you have stirred up—in Afghanistan, in the Mideast, and elsewhere—those are necessary reminders that they must not forget you ever."

War remained unconvinced, his expression was unchanged, but he said nothing.

The Chairman decided not to pursue it. "Your feelings are understood," he said. "And you are not alone. You will see that as we proceed."

He turned his attention to his left. "Pestilence, it has not escaped our attention that you have been a tireless worker. You have shaped human history as definitively as War."

Pestilence shook his head. "I wish I could take all the credit, but I cannot. Humans themselves are responsible. They have been the most effective partners in these efforts, all the way back to their own beginnings. When they built cities and ships, they created their own reservoirs of disease and avenues of transportation. It was a simple matter to use their efforts to achieve my own accomplishments."

"And that is your victory. Throughout history, you have been creative in using their own machineries against them. When we consider how well the Black Death spread, for instance. And when we look at the more persistent afflictions—smallpox, cholera, polio, malaria, measles, and various forms of the flu, some of which have been deadly—we cannot help but marvel at your inventiveness. AIDS was a particularly clever scourge. You bring illness into every human activity. But—"

The Chairman hesitated. This was not going to be easy. But it had to be said.

"Unfortunately, your situation is much like that of War. The humans have invested billions in treatment and prevention. In just the past century, they have severely limited your effectiveness. Even your success with Covid could not have happened without the help of Media and Ignorance. And while we all had high hopes that you might repeat your successes of 1918, humans surprised us. They developed several effective vaccines in less than a year. Even Ignorance cannot prevent the spread of that kind of knowledge. Ignorance can slow it down, but cannot stop it.

"Pestilence, you have been so effective in the spread of disease that you have alerted humanity to investigate and eradicate your most terrible threats. Humans have come to regard their relationship with you as a specifically focused war. And as with War, humans have become inventive enough to create specific countermeasures."

Pestilence nodded reluctant agreement. "Yes. Humans are inventive. I had hoped that their inventiveness would create new opportunities, and to some extent, yes—air travel for instance. And conventions and cruise ships. But the humans are getting much better motivated in their campaigns against disease. The more inventive they became, the more inventive I became as well—but now that relationship has reversed. Their advances in technology have given them tools to investigate and understand. I am not defeated, no. I will never be defeated. There are eight billion opportunities, eight billion possibilities—but yes, without Ignorance, the job will be far more difficult."

The Chairman nodded. "Thank you for your candor. And your commitment as well. You are powerful. There is no question of that. You should take comfort in the billions that they spend on research, on treatment, on prevention, even on cures. All of that is a well-earned recognition of your effectiveness, your ability to terrify. Your role has been changed, but it has not been diminished."

Pestilence accepted the acknowledgment, but said nothing.

"Famine," said the Chairman. He looked down the table where Famine sat quietly, hands folded in his lap. "You have a truly difficult job, made all that much harder in recent years. Where you used to follow in the wake of War and Pestilence, now you must often travel alone.

"In 1975, the population of the Earth was four billion. Two-thirds of them went to bed hungry. Today, the population approaches eight billion, and only half of them go to bed hungry. Consider the numbers. In 1975, 2.7 billion humans were without sufficient food. Today, it's four billion. One could argue that Famine now starves an additional 1.3 billion humans.

"Under any other circumstances, that would be considered an astonishing accomplishment. But while Famine has gained 1.3 billion, the humans now have more than four billion on their side of the equation. By reducing the ravages of War and Pestilence, by improving their farming methods, their processing of perishables, their greater efficiencies of transportation, they have changed the equations of starvation.

"But, at the same time, the continuing deforestation of the Amazon, the increased production of pollutants and carbon dioxide, the acidification of the oceans—that will eventually produce significant climate change. The effects will be disastrous. So even though the current numbers might seem disappointing, you are still maintaining yourself as a global presence and there is some comfort in that, but at the same time, we have to acknowledge that unlike War and Pestilence, you have an unwitting partner in the human race. More than you, they are creating their own disastrous consequences."

Ashamed, Famine said nothing.

Finally, the Chairman turned to Death. "Hello, Darkness, my old friend. We've come to talk with you again."

Death grinned at the reference. Death grinned at everything. Death was incapable of not grinning.

"The news is not good for you either, I'm afraid. A century ago, a human being in good health might expect to reach the age of fifty or sixty. Today, the general life expectancy is eighty years, and many humans are living well beyond that. A person living a full hundred years has become commonplace. The humans have delayed the final call by a full score of years and they are on track to further postpone the last appointment. It is not just that War and Pestilence and Famine have been inhibited—it is their own inventiveness at work here." The Chairman raised a hand as if to object to his own assertions. "Yes, you can argue that the humans have merely delayed the inevitable, but even that delay represents a failure.

"In the past, humans died young, before they could reach their full potential, before they could complete their work, before they could pass on their knowledge and experience to the next generation. Today, far too many are living long enough to achieve levels of mastery in their specific arenas. They have so much more time to gain experience, to discover and explore, to learn, and to use that knowledge to increase their achievements. The ability of humans to invent and design and build has been expanded by several orders of magnitude—and in no small part because Death has been deferred."

The Chairman looked around the room. "War has been reined in, controlled, even tamed. Likewise, Pestilence no longer has the freedom of the past. Famine's gains are pale in comparison to humanity's. And even Death has lost much of its power. And that finally brings me to the purpose of this gathering. We cannot continue as we have done in the past. Humanity has learned, is continuing to learn, how to mitigate our most aggressive efforts. Based on the evidence, based on the work of the study groups we have commissioned, this increase in their effectiveness is only going to continue. Therefore—"

The Chairman paused, looked around the room. His gaze was severe. "We have no choice. We are going to restructure." He held up a hand to forestall any words of dismay or objection. There were none, of course. There never were. Nevertheless, the gesture was necessary.

"Yes, we must acknowledge that we have experienced enormous successes. We can be proud of that. But the circumstances have evolved dramatically. What worked in the past is no longer effective in the present, and we cannot expect that it will be again in the future. We must restructure.

"War, Pestilence, Famine, Death—you will always be the grandmasters of the apocalypse. And nothing we do or say here can ever diminish the impact of your work throughout the millennia. You will always be known as the elements of apocalypse. But because humanity continued to survive despite War, Pestilence, Famine, and even Death, they have learned that apocalypse was no longer an end to be feared, but merely a circumstance to be endured."

The Chairman finally smiled. "And that, my colleagues, my friends, is our future. They have changed their conversation about apocalypse. We cannot fight that conversation, we cannot fight their inventiveness, nor their technology, but … we can use it ourselves.

"There is precedent for this. They drew borders. War used those borders as justification. They built cities and ships. Pestilence used those as reservoirs and vectors. They planted monocrops. Famine sent blight. And Death used everything they ever created against them. So now that they have changed the nature of their communities, let us change as well to take advantage of the circumstances.

"I give you this thought. Apocalypse is no longer an achievement, it is no longer a goal—it is a context. Let us create it as a continuing state of existence. Let us use the humans as the masters of their own despair. Let them invent—we will use their inventions against them.

"War, you have the expertise for this challenge. You will turn your attention to the political arenas. There, you will push tensions to the breaking point. They will resist, of course—but they will have to invent other ways of fighting without resorting to open violence. The result? They will sacrifice the joys of cooperation for the savagery of competition—and their economies will be the new battlefields. That will be where we will create the greatest havoc.

"Pestilence, you have the greatest of all opportunities. New communities to serve as reservoirs, new vectors of transmission. The digital world is the most fertile domain you will ever have. You will spread viruses from one computer to the next, traversing the world at light speed—you will spread malware throughout the global network, taking down whole communities in a single instant.

"Famine, your commitment is tireless. Your task has always been deprivation. You are fortunate that humanity has become your partner in this effort. Your challenge shall be to encourage them to even greater success. Let them starve themselves with processed foods of all kinds—imitation protein, imitation sugars, imitation flavor. Let them drown in all the different chemicals they use to simulate nourishment. The more they distance themselves from the ground that sustains them, the weaker they will become, the more they will become prey for illness and lingering death.

"Death? You need no new challenges. You are the patient one, the ever-present watcher. You are the visitor who whispers in the night. You are the ground of being, the foundation of everything we do here. All of us are ultimately at your service. But if it amuses you, then wield your scythe like a scalpel. Take down their heroes, their stars, the ones who inspire them to greatness. Take down their peacemakers, their healers, their planters and artisans. Take down their best and leave them their worst. Doing that will prepare the field for everyone else in this room."

The Chairman helped himself to another glass of water. This time he drank deeply. He took a deep breath, looked around the room, and continued. "But I shall now ask the four of you to take on a new set of responsibilities. By this declaration, the four of you are now elevated to grandmasters of the apocalypse. You shall serve as my special deputies. You shall not only advise and consent, you will supervise the activities of our four new horsemen."

For the first time in the meeting, a wave of reaction swept through the room, impossible to gauge. Each reacted in their own way. The Chairman ignored it.

He pointed first to Media.

"Media, you shall ride a white horse. You shall create a billion voices all chattering at once. You will bury every golden nugget of information under a mountain of advertisements and distractions. Media, you shall become an avalanche of noise, depriving humanity of the ability to connect and function as a global community.

"Ideology, you will ride a dark horse and you will ride with Media. The two of you will have no shortage of deputies. Hope, the last curse out of Pandora's box, will be your voice. Deceit will be your ally. Discord shall follow in your wake.

"Hysteria, you will ride a red horse. Fear and Anger will serve under you. Religion and Nationalism will also make themselves available.

"And finally, Ignorance. You have served War and Pestilence and Famine well. You have proven time and again that there is little that any of us can accomplish without you. Your job has been the hardest of all because humans are by nature curious creatures. They are explorers and adventurers. It takes commitment to remain ignorant. But that commitment can be instilled by Fear and Anger. It is fed by Deceit and Discord. It is a result of being overwhelmed by information. So you must be an ally of Hysteria, Ideology, and Media. You shall ride with them on a horse of many colors, because Ignorance knows no boundaries."

The Chairman took a deep breath. "There is work to be done. Let us begin. Let us prey.

"Gentlemen, give us this day, our daily dread."

THE BONUS STORY
OF THE APOCALYPSE

When we ran the Kickstarter for **The Four ????
of the Apocalypse,** *one of the bonus rewards was
to have a custom story written for you by Aaron
Rosenberg. That bonus was purchased by Kathleen
Hannon, who requested the Four Crazy Cat Ladies
of the Apocalypse, and also asked that the late great
Betty White be a part of the story. Kathleen gener-
ously gave her consent to have her custom story also
appear in the anthology itself, so as a special bonus,
here's "Putting Doom on Paws."*

Putting Doom on Paws

Aaron Rosenberg

*For Betty White, who graced us with her wit,
wisdom, and warmth*

Maureen was sipping her coffee when Katie burst into the kitchen. "Oh, Maureen," the slender middle-aged blonde declared, flitting over to the table and shoving a large and slightly mangy brown and gray cat in her friend's face. "Look who I just found outside! Isn't he darling?"

The furball regarded Maureen with some trepidation, which she shared. "Well, honey, I don't know," she started, lowering her cup—and the big, striped cat took that opportunity to lean in and lick her nose. Maureen couldn't help it. She giggled. The cat purred in response, his yellow eyes fluttering closed slightly, and she sighed. "Yes, I suppose he is," she admitted despite herself.

"Oh, good, we can keep him then!" Katie said, beaming. "Thank you, Maureen! I think I'll call him Dusty!"

She was still standing there nuzzling the hefty feline when their third roommate, Stacy, entered the room. "What, another one?" she asked, spying the cat in Katie's arms. But, even though she was careful to keep the frown on her face, she still scratched the furry beast on its head as she took one of the other chairs with a sigh of relief. "Ah, that's better."

"How are the preparations going?" Maureen asked, returning to her coffee. She just couldn't be expected to be fully awake until she'd had at least her third cup!

"Fine, fine," Stacy answered, absently reaching down to pet another cat that was currently winding around her ankles. Two more were tussling beneath the credenza in the corner, and a fifth was perched on the counter by the sink, swatting the water dripping from the faucet and then delicately licking her damp paw. "We'd probably be a lot farther along if we had a bit more room here—

and a few less critters," she pointed out archly, eyeing both the cats and Katie, who ignored the jab. After all, she already knew that Stacy didn't really mean it—beneath that tough New York exterior she was just as cat-crazy as the rest of them.

Their final roommate joined them a few minutes later, a black cat draped over her shoulders and a pair of mackerel tabbies batting at her ankles as she walked. "Stop that," she warned, "before I make you into slippers!" The cats ignored the threat, well aware the tiny older woman didn't mean it, but they did at least wander off to find other amusements as Beatrice joined her daughter and friends at the table. The coffeepot was still sitting in the center, half full, and she poured herself a cup, adding liberal amounts of cream and sugar from the containers set out there for that purpose. The rich aroma nearly masked the ever-present smell of cat. Nearly.

"Almost there, girls," Beatrice declared, pushing her large glasses back up her nose, the chain that held it in place fluttering against the back of her neck and causing the cat there to swat at it lazily. "Then we can do away with all this, once and for all." She frowned, tugging the glasses off and examining them before restoring them. "I won't miss these, that's for sure! Who ever heard of a demon with poor eyesight? And cataracts—I'm sure we're supposed to give those to other people, not get them ourselves!"

"Well, there are plenty of things I'll miss," Maureen replied, taking another sip in her typical lady-like fashion. "This is one of them." Her eyes twinkled as she added, "Most of the others have to do with toms—and I don't mean the four-legged variety!"

"Oh, you're terrible!" Katie told her, but giggled as she said it. She finally dropped into the final chair around the table, her latest acquisition still clutched to her chest. "What do you think, Dusty?" she asked the purring creature. "Will you like it down there? You'll never get cold, that's for sure!"

"Katie, don't be silly," Stacy scolded. "You know perfectly well he can't come with us." As usual, a faint scowl sat upon her face. It was her default expression.

Their roommate, however, looked shocked—also a common sight. "Whatever do you mean?" she demanded, cuddling poor Dusty even closer. "Just because he's only been part of the family for a few minutes doesn't mean we can leave him behind! That'd just be cruel!"

"It's got nothing to do with tenure, you ninny," Beatrice snapped. "None of them can go Down Below! They'd roast in an instant!" For a second, a look of concern crossed her wrinkled face, but she quickly schooled her features back to their usual fierce glare, which was a smaller, older version of Stacy's.

"What?" Now Katie actually let Dusty drop into her lap as she regarded her three closest friends and partners. "None of them? What about Alexander?"

"No," Maureen replied, brushing her hair back with one well-manicured hand. She'd made sure to look her best for their upcoming big day.

"Thirsty?" Katie asked next.

The other three all shook their heads.

"Maji?" their friend continued, undeterred. "Shadow? Bugsy? Buddy, Little Mama, Blackie, Smokey and Smokey 2? How about Stubby? Big Boy? Willie, Tummie, Finnegan, Iggy, Willow, and Boo? And Marisol—surely Marisol can come with us! She was our first!" The black cat adorning Beatrice's narrow shoulders lifted her head at the sound of her name and uttered a plaintive little meow that sounded very much like *Yeah, what about me?*

"No no no!" Stacy told her. "None of them! Not a single one! Not even dear, darling Marisol!" Her hands rose, as if of their own accord, to scratch the black cat her mother carried, but she snatched them back a moment later, folding them on the table in front of her instead. "We can't bring any of them!" she insisted, striving to keep her eyes on her friend's stricken face rather than on the imploring little feline. Though, honestly, she wasn't sure that was any better.

"I—" For once, Katie was speechless.

It didn't last.

"I don't think I like that," she declared, crossing her arms over her chest, her usually sunny face set in a stern frown. "No, I don't think I like it at all."

"Dear." Maureen reached out and rested a comforting hand on her friend's arm. "You know it has to be like this. Beatrice is right. They would fry like bugs in a zapper if we tried bringing them down there with us. This is the only way."

"Oh. *Oh!*" Katie's eyes went wide. "So we're leaving them up here to protect them?" Maureen nodded, though warily, because once Katie got going you never knew which way she was headed, only that it was nigh impossible to stop her. "I see." Katie bent over to nuzzle Dusty, who seemed confused about all these strange goings-on. "Don't worry, dear," she reassured him. "You can stay right here with all your new brothers and sisters instead. And we'll come back up to visit all the time."

"Um, Katie . . ." Stacy began, shaking her head, but as was often the case her mother got there first.

"We're not coming back up, dummy!" Beatrice snapped, slamming one wizened fist down on the table. "Nobody is! And even if we did, there wouldn't be anything here to come back *to*! That's the whole point of what we're doing! They don't call it a Doomsday device because it's gonna poop out a whole bunch of flowers and chocolates!"

"Well, sure, I know that." Katie gave a little laugh. "Everybody knows *that*! It's going to rain down the fires of Hell upon all the Earth, just like it's supposed to." She paused, glancing at her friends. "But only on the people, right? It won't hurt any of the animals."

Stacy leaned over and rested her forehead on the cool surface of the table, just for a second, before straightening up again. She'd been a teacher up here for years, she knew how to deal with slow students. Katie, however, was a special case, even for her. "No, Katie," she explained slowly and carefully. "Not just the people. Fire isn't that selective, and hellfire is even worse. It's going to...." Here even her strong resolve faltered, and she glanced at the other two for help.

"It's going to blanket the whole world, sweetie," Maureen supplied. "Every last bit of it." Which is why she'd needed to make sure she'd been to see both Juliette and Mario one last time. Nobody did a mani-pedi or a blowout like they did! And, soon, nobody *could*.

But Katie was still shaking her head. "No, I know that," she insisted. "But I thought it would only . . . you know . . . hurt the people. And the buildings. And those awful overpasses that block the view and let cars drive overhead and shower you with their exhausts, ugh! The animals, though . . ."

"Cooked," Beatrice told her with her usual candor. "Flesh to fricassee in three seconds flat. The whole world's about to become one big oven, and when we're done, there'll be nothing but cinders." Marisol mewed at that, and she reached up to pat the cat, as if that would somehow do any good.

Katie's frown had only deepened. "We can't do that," she said, softly at first but her voice building in strength and volume with each word. "We can't, we simply can't!" The look she gave her friends was half glare and half plea. "How can we? Think of all the dogs and birds and dolphins and turtles and bears and penguins and—"

"Penguins *are* birds," Stacy pointed out, her teaching instinct kicking in, but she only got a scowl in return.

"We're talking the end of the world here, Stacy!" Katie scolded her with a ferocity that set the taller woman back in her seat. "Do you really think now is the time for a lesson on taxonomy?" She studied each of the others in turn. "Think about all of them, girls! Think about the *cats*!" Spreading her arms wide, she took in all the felines currently roaming about them, and the many more curled up in various spots throughout their cozy little house, and all the others out there walking the streets or prowling the alleys or simply sleeping or playing in different homes all around the world. "How can we do that to all the cats?" she repeated more softly, her eyes shining with unspent tears, her lower lip trembling but her head held high. "We can't!"

It was Maureen who broke first. "Oh, girls, I think she may be right!" she wailed, laying her hands flat on the table, fingers splayed, coffee forgotten for the moment. "I don't think I could incinerate all the poor little kitties like that!" Willow hopped up into her lap as if to prove the point and Maureen scooped the little calico up, cradling her close. "I just couldn't!"

"But that's what we're here for!" Beatrice argued. "It's what we've been slaving away at, all these years!" Her words faltered, however, when Marisol gently headbutted her cheek, and her glare softened as the black cat purred in her ear. "I mean . . ."

"Oh, Ma." Stacy had held out the longest, but even she was clearly affected by the felines each of her roommates held. Maji and Thirsty stalking over and rubbing up against her legs, purring in perfect counterpoint, sealed the deal. "Well, fine." She threw up her hands. "So what are we gonna do, then? They're counting on us, you know. There's a timetable and everything!"

"We'll have to stall," Maureen declared, her words muffled as they emerged from behind Willow's spotted head. "We'll come up with some excuse."

"Yeah, what, that our cats ate the wires?" Beatrice demanded. "Like they're gonna fall for that!"

"Oh, they might," Katie replied, a small smile now playing on her lips. "If we tell them these are big cats, jungle cats. Lions and tigers and panthers and all that."

The "Oh, my" slipped from Stacy's lips before she could stop it, but then she shook herself. "Come on, really?" she argued, glancing at the cats all over them and the rest of the kitchen. "Who's going to believe that? Even Stubby and Little Mama and, yes, Dusty aren't much more than knee-high to a panther, let alone a lion or tiger!"

Katie laughed, her eyes alight now with far more than tears. "Not yet," she agreed. The light grew, and slowly answering glows appeared in each of her friends' eyes as well as her crazy idea somehow infected them all. "All together, now," she whispered, and the room itself began to take on a golden hue, filling with light that outlined each and every cat present and seeped out under the swinging door to find the rest of their brood.

And, slowly, in that glow, Dusty and Marisol and the others began to grow.

It was subtle at first, the black cat's weight pressing down just that much more on Beatrice's shoulders. But then her paws were dangling halfway down the chair back, the tip of her tail swaying rhythmically across the floor. Finally Marisol hopped down, eliciting a small sigh from her former perch, as the cat's head was now level with the tabletop itself. Dusty and Willow had also settled onto the floor, and all three of them were now enormous, as were the other cats around the room. The space suddenly seemed a good deal smaller, and the smell of fur and feline significantly stronger.

Katie, however, was clearly thrilled as she surveyed their handiwork, the glow in her eyes fading back to its normal gleam of mere human enthusiasm and good cheer. "There!" she stated happily. "We'll let them go to town on the device for a bit, and then we'll call it in. It'll take us months to fix it again! Years!"

"Longer, if some of those parts become hard to find," Stacy agreed slowly, thinking it through. "Why, we could put this off indefinitely."

"I'll make a few calls," Maureen stated, rising to her feet. "Let the boys know that, next time we ask for things, they're to be mysteriously out of stock."

"I'll go supervise the destruction," Beatrice offered, standing as well. She gave them all a crooked little grin. "Tearing it apart's actually gonna be a lot of fun—I might have to get in there and do a little clawing myself!"

Stacy regarded their friend with new respect as the other two exited. "And what about you, Katie?" she asked, still trying to adjust to this strange new paradigm. "What are you going to do now?"

"Oh, that's easy," Katie answered with another little laugh. "I'm going to go to the store. We're going to need a whole lot more tuna—and some really big new litter boxes!"

She skipped out, and Stacy contemplated that, imagining a full score of tiger-sized cats and the resulting stink they'd make.

"Maybe we should've burned it all down after all," she muttered, pushing her chair back and getting up. Behind her, Thirsty let out a little chirp and headbutted her, which nearly sent her flying.

"No, don't worry, dear," Stacy assured the enormous Persian, scratching her under the chin. "I'm just saying that. We won't let anything happen to you."

Then, with the big cat trailing behind her purring, she headed into the living room to help demolish the device they'd been planning and building for the better part of eternity.

Hell was way too hot in the summers, anyway.

Please be advised that ALL the animals of any kind mentioned—earth animals or otherwise—were treated with the utmost respect and dignity during the writing of this story. So were the people—regardless of race, gender identification, sexual orientation or identity, religious preferences, and country—or plane—of origin.

THE AUTHOR BIOGRAPHIES OF THE APOCALYPSE

Award-winning author, editor, and publisher **Danielle Ackley-McPhail** has worked both sides of the publishing industry for longer than she cares to admit. In 2014 she joined forces with Mike McPhail and Greg Schauer to form eSpec Books (www.especbooks.com). Her published works include eight novels, *Yesterday's Dreams, Tomorrow's Memories, Today's Promise, The Halfling's Court, The Redcaps' Queen, Daire's Devils, The Play of Light*, and *Baba Ali and the Clockwork Djinn* (written with Day Al-Mohamed). She is also the author of the solo collections *Eternal Wanderings, A Legacy of Stars, Consigned to the Sea, Flash in the Can, Transcendence, The Kindly Ones, Dawns a New Day, The Fox's Fire, Between Darkness and Light*, and the nonfiction writers' guides *The Literary Handyman, More Tips from the Handyman*, and *LH: Build-A-Book Workshop*. She is the senior editor of the *Bad-Ass Faeries* anthology series, *Gaslight & Grimm, The Side of Good/The Side of Evil, After Punk*, and *Footprints in the Stars*. Her short stories are included in numerous other anthologies and collections. She is a full member of the Science Fiction and Fantasy Writers Association.

In addition to her literary acclaim, she crafts and sells original costume horns under the moniker The Hornie Lady Custom Costume Horns, and homemade flavor-infused candied ginger under the brand of Ginger KICK! at literary conventions, on commission, and wholesale. Danielle lives in New Jersey with husband and fellow writer, Mike McPhail and four extremely spoiled cats. Find out more at www.sidhenadaire.com

Derek Tyler Attico is a science fiction author, essayist, and photographer. He won the Excellence in Playwriting Award from the Dramatist Guild of America. He is also a two-time winner of the *Star Trek: Strange New Worlds* short story contest ("Alpha & Omega" and "The Dreamer and the Dream") published by Simon and Schuster. His short stories appear in *Turning the Tied* and *Double Trouble: An Anthology of Two-Fisted Team-Ups*, both from the International Association of Media Tie-In Writers, *Thrilling Adventure Yarns 2021* from Crazy 8 Press, the NASA Exoplanet Science Institute at Caltech, and others. His essays appear in print from *Star Trek Magazine* and ATB Publishing. Derek is also a contributing writer for the *Star Trek Adventures* tabletop role-playing game and a role-playing game designer. With a degree in English and History, Derek is an advocate of the arts, human rights, and inclusion. Derek can be found at DerekAttico.com and on Twitter @Dattico.

Adam-Troy Castro made his first non-fiction sale to *Spy* magazine in 1987. His books to date include four Spider-Man novels, three novels about his profoundly damaged far-future murder investigator Andrea Cort, and six middle-grade novels about the dimension-spanning adventures of young Gustav Gloom. Adam's works have won the Philip K. Dick Award and the Seiun (Japan), and have been nominated for eight Nebulas, three Stokers, two Hugos, one World Fantasy Award, and, internationally, the Ignotus (Spain), the Grand Prix de l'Imaginaire (France), and the Kurd-Laßwitz Preis (Germany). The audio collection *My Wife Hates Time Travel and Other Stories* (Skyboat Media) features thirteen hours of his fiction, including the new stories "The Hour In Between" and "Big Stupe and the Buried Big Glowing Booger." In 2022 he came out with two collections, *The Author's Wife vs. The Giant Robot* and his thirtieth book, *A Touch of Strange*. Adam is an Author Guest of Honor at 2023's World Fantasy Convention. Adam lives in Florida with a pair of chaotic paladin cats.

Russ Colchamiro is the author of *Crackle and Fire, Fractured Lives*, and *Hot Ash*, the first three novels in his ongoing sci-fi noir series featuring hardboiled private eye Angela Hardwicke. He is currently working on the fourth Hardwicke novel. A member of Crazy 8 Press, Private Eye Writers of America, and board member of the Mystery Writers of America New York Chapter, Russ is also the co-author and editor of the noir novella collection *Murder in Montague Falls*, editor of the sci-fi mystery anthology *Love, Murder & Mayhem,* has contributed short stories to more than fifteen anthologies, including various Hardwicke mysteries, and is the author of the sci-fi adventure novels *Crossline, Finders Keepers, Genius de Milo*, and *Astropalooza*. Russ also hosts his popular *Russ's Rockin' Rollercoaster* podcast, interviewing a who's who of science fiction, crime, mystery, and horror authors. He lives in Northern New Jersey with his wife, two ninjas, and black lab, Jinx, who may be an alien herself.

Peter David is a prolific author whose career and continued popularity spans more than three decades. He has worked in every conceivable medium: television, film, books (fiction, nonfiction, and audio), short stories, and comic books, and acquired followings in all of them. In the literary field, Peter has had over forty novels published, including numerous appearances on the *New York Times* bestseller list. *Publishers Weekly* described him as "a genuine and veteran master." Probably his greatest fame comes from the high-profile realm of *Star Trek* novels, where he is the most popular writer of the series, with his title *Imzadi* being one of the bestselling *Star Trek* novels of all time. He is also cocreator and author of the bestselling *New Frontier* series. A partial list of his titles includes *Q-Squared, The Siege, Q-in-Law, Vendetta, I, Q* (with John deLancie), and *A Rock and a Hard Place*, plus such original science fiction and fantasy works as *Knight Life, Howling Mad*, the Psi-Man adventure novels, *The Camelot Papers, Artful*, and *Pulling Up Stakes*, and the three *Babylon 5 Centauri Prime* novels. He has also had short stories appear in such collections as *Shock Rock, Shock Rock II, OtherWere, The Side of Good/The Side of Evil*, and *Bad Ass Moms*, as well as *Isaac Asimov's Science Fiction Magazine* and the *Magazine of Fantasy and Science Fiction*, and in the shared-world anthology series *Pangaea* and *Phenomenons*.

Peter has written more comics than can possibly be listed here, remaining consistently one of the most acclaimed writers in the field. His resumé includes an award-winning twelve-year run on *The Incredible Hulk*. He has also worked on such varied and popular titles as *Supergirl, Young Justice, Soulsearchers and Company, Aquaman, Spider-Man, Spider-Man 2099, X-Factor, Star Trek, Wolverine, The Phantom, Sachs & Violence*, and many others. He has also written comic book related novels, such as *The Incredible Hulk: What Savage Beast, Fantastic Four: What Lies Between*, and *Wolverine: Election Day*, and co-edited *The Ultimiate*

Hulk short story collection. His incredibly popular opinion column "But I Digress..." ran in the industry trade newspaper *The Comics Buyers Guide* for more than two decades, and was collected in two trade paperback editions. Peter is the co-creator, with popular science fiction icon Bill Mumy (of *Lost in Space* and *Babylon 5* fame) of the Cable Ace Award-nominated science fiction series *Space Cases*, which ran for two seasons on Nickelodeon. He has also written several scripts for the Hugo Award-winning TV series *Babylon 5*, and its sequel series, *Crusade*, as well as the animated series *Roswell, Ben 10*, and *Young Justice*. He has also written several films for Full Moon Entertainment and co-produced two of them, including two installments in the popular *Trancers* series as well as the science fiction western spoof *Oblivion*, which won the Gold Award at the 1994 Houston International Film Festival for best Theatrical Feature Film, Fantasy/Horror Category. Peter is a founding member of Crazy 8 Press, the internet publishing venture launched in 2011.

Randee Dawn is a Brooklyn-based entertainment journalist whose funny fantasy debut novel, *Tune in Tomorrow*, was published in 2022 by Solaris. She's a former editor at *The Hollywood Reporter* and *Soap Opera Digest*, and these days covers the wacky world of show business for *Variety, The Los Angeles Times, Emmy*, and Today.com. Dawn's obsessive love of all things *Law & Order* led her to appear in one episode and later co-author *The Law & Order: SVU Unofficial Companion*. Her short fiction has appeared in numerous anthologies and online publications. Once a month she can be found hosting Brooklyn Books and Booze at Barrow's Intense, and when not writing she's focused on her next travel destination and hangs out with her wonderful, funny husband and fluffy Westie. She has a weakness for mangoes. She can be found at RandeeDawn.com

Keith R.A. DeCandido has been in his career an author, editor, critic, podcaster, library worker, gallery curator, TV personality, Census worker, musician, and martial artist. He has edited more than a score of anthologies (both publicly and behind the scenes), including several in the media universes of *Star Trek, Doctor Who*, and Marvel Comics, as well as the 2023 anthology *Double Trouble: An Anthology of Two-Fisted Team-Ups* (co-edited with Jonathan Maberry). He has also written sixty novels, a hundred short stories, fifty comic books, and more nonfiction than he's comfortable counting. Recent and upcoming work includes the fantasy novels *Phoenix Precinct* and *Feat of Clay*, both part of ongoing series; the *Resident Evil* comic book *Infinite Darkness: The Beginning*, a prequel to the Netflix animated series; the *Star Trek Adventures* role-playing game module *Incident at Kraav III* (with Fred Love); the urban fantasy short story collection *Ragnarok and a Hard Place: More Tales of Cassie Zukav, Weirdness Magnet*; short fiction in *Star Trek Explorer* magazine and in the anthologies *Weird Tales: 100 Years of Weird*, *Sherlock Holmes: Cases by Candlelight* Volume 2, *Three Time Travelers Walk Into...*, *Joe Ledger: Unbreakable*, the *Thrilling Adventure Yarns* series, the *Phenomenons* shared-world superhero series created by Michael Jan Friedman, and *The Good, the Bad, and the Uncanny*. He and Wrenn Simms formed WhysperWude LLC in 2021, for which *The Four ???? of the Apocalypse* is their inaugural publication. Find out less at DeCandido.net.

Kevin Dilmore has partnered with author and best pal Dayton Ward for more than twenty years on novels, short fiction, and other writings chiefly in the *Star Trek* universe. Look for their newest collaboration, *Iron Man: Tony Stark Declassified*, in November 2023 from BenBella Books. As a senior writer for Hallmark Cards, Kevin has helped create books, Keepsake Ornaments, greeting cards, and other products featuring characters from DC Comics, Marvel Comics, *Star Trek*, *Star Wars*, and Hallmark properties including Rainbow Brite. A contributor to publications including *The Village Voice*, *Amazing Stories*, and *Famous Monsters of Filmland*, he lives in Kansas City, Missouri.

Mary Fan is a sci-fi/fantasy writer hailing from Jersey City, New Jersey. She is the author of the *Jane Colt* sci-fi series (Red Adept Publishing), the *Starswept* YA sci-fi series (Snowy Wings Publishing), the *Fated Stars* YA high fantasy series (Snowy Wings Publishing), the *Flynn Nightsider* YA dark fantasy series (Crazy 8 Press), and *Stronger Than a Bronze Dragon*, a YA fantasy (Page Street Publishing). She is also the editor of *Bad Ass Moms*, an anthology from Crazy 8 Press. In addition, Mary is the co-editor (along with fellow sci-fi author Paige Daniels) of the *Brave New Girls* YA sci-fi anthologies, which feature tales about girls in STEM. Revenues from sales are donated to the

Society of Women Engineers scholarship fund. Her short fiction has appeared in numerous anthologies, including the *Thrilling Adventure Yarns* and *Phenomenons* series (both from Crazy 8 Press), *Mine!: A Celebration of Liberty and Freedom for All Benefitting Planned Parenthood* (ComicMix), and *Sing, Goddess!* (Snowy Wings Publishing). Her non-writing activities include singing (including opera!), aerial arts, and kickboxing. Find her online at www.MaryFan.com.

Michael Jan Friedman is the author of 81 books of fiction and nonfiction, nearly half of them set somewhere in the wilds of the *Star Trek* universe. His first book, *The Hammer and the Horn*, was published by Questar, an imprint of Warner Books, in 1985. In the next couple of years, he wrote *The Seekers and the Sword* and *The Fortress and the Fire*, completing what has come to be known as the Vidar Saga trilogy, as well as the freestanding novel *The Glove of Maiden's Hair*. In 1992 Friedman penned *Reunion*, the first *Star Trek: The Next Generation* hardcover, which introduced the crew of the *Stargazer*, Captain Jean-Luc Picard's first command. Over the years, the popularity of *Reunion* spawned a number of *Stargazer* stories in both prose and comic book formats, including a six-novel original series. Friedman has also written for the *Aliens*, *Predator*, *Wolf Man*, *Lois and Clark*, DC Super Hero, Marvel Super Hero, and *Wishbone* licensed book universes. Eleven of his book titles, including the autobiography *Hollywood Hulk Hogan* and *Ghost Hunting* (written with SyFy's Ghost Hunters), have appeared on the prestigious *New York Times* primary bestseller list, and his novel adaptation of the *Batman & Robin* movie was for a time the #1 bestselling book in Poland (really).

Friedman has worked at one time or another in network and cable television, radio, business magazines, and the comic book industry, in the process producing scripts for nearly 180 comic stories. Among his comic book credits are the *Darkstars* ongoing series from DC Comics, which he created with artist Mike Collins, and the *Outlaws* limited series, which he created with artist Luke McDonnell, as well as tales of Superman, Batman, Green Lantern, Flash, Deadman, Fantastic Four, and the Silver Surfer. He also co-wrote the story for the acclaimed second-season *Star Trek: Voyager* episode "Resistance," which guest-starred Joel Grey.

As always, he advises readers that no matter how many Friedmans they know, he is probably not related to any of them.

David Gerrold's work is famous around the world. His novels and stories have been translated into more than a dozen languages. His TV scripts are estimated to have been seen by more than a billion viewers. His prolific output includes stage shows, teleplays, film scripts, educational films, computer software, comic books, more than fifty novels and collections, and hundreds of articles, columns, and short stories. He has worked on a dozen different TV series, including *Star Trek, Land of the Lost, Twilight Zone, Star Trek: The Next Generation, Babylon 5*, and *Sliders*. He is the author of *Star Trek*'s most popular episode, "The Trouble with Tribbles." Many of his novels are classics of the science fiction genre, including *The Man Who Folded Himself* and *When HARLIE Was One*. His novels on ecological invasion (*A Matter For Men, A Day For Damnation, A Rage For Revenge*, and *A Season For Slaughter*) have all been best sellers with a devoted fan following. His young adult series, "The Dingilliad" (*Jumping Off the Planet, Bouncing Off the Moon, Leaping to the Stars*), traces the healing journey of a troubled family from Earth to a far-flung colony on another world. A ten-time Hugo and Nebula award nominee, David is also a recipient of the Skylark Award for Excellence in Imaginative Fiction, the Bram Stoker Award for Superior Achievement in Horror, the Forrest J. Ackerman lifetime achievement award, and was the 2022 recipient of the Heinlein Award. He was a Guest of Honor at the 2015 World Science Fiction Convention and emceed the Hugo Award ceremony. In 1995, David shared the adventure of how he adopted his son in "The Martian Child," a semi-autobiographical tale of a science fiction writer who adopts a little boy, only to discover he might be a Martian. "The Martian Child" won the science fiction triple crown: the Hugo, the Nebula, and the *Locus* Poll. It was the basis for the 2007 film *Martian Child* starring John Cusack and Amanda Peet. An accomplished lecturer and world-traveler, David has made appearances all over the United States, England, Europe, Canada, Australia, and New Zealand. His easy-going manner and disarming humor have made him a favorite with audiences.

Laura Anne Gilman's novels have been hailed as "a true American myth" by NPR, and praised for their "deft plotting and first-class characters" by *Publishers Weekly*. She has won the Endeavor Award, been shortlisted for a Nebula, another Endeavor, and a Washington State Book Award. She is currently at work on the third "Huntsmen" novel (after *Uncanny Times* and *Uncanny Vows*). She lives in Seattle with a cat, a dog, and many deadlines.

Robert Greenberger has been writing and editing since 1980, working on staff at Starlog Press, DC Comics, Gist Communications, Marvel Comics, Famous Monsters of Filmland, ComicMix, and *Weekly World News*. Additionally, he has written fiction and non-fiction in various genres for a wide range of audiences. A member of SFWA and the International Association of Media Tie-In Writers, he actively contributes to numerous books, including this fine volume. A cofounder of Crazy 8 Press, a digital book hub, he edits the *Thrilling Adventure Yarns* anthologies. When not writing, editing, or watching the New York Mets, Bob is a teacher at a private Catholic school in Maryland, where he makes his home with his wife, Deb. Find him at www.bobgreenberger.com.

Gerard Houarner fell to Earth in the fifties, where he became a product of the New York City school system, the City College of New York (when it was free) and Teachers College, Columbia University. He is currently retired, but still a Licensed Mental Health Counselor, having spent thirty-eight years in the field, from the go-go '80's on Delancey Street, in Hell's Kitchen, and in the Bronx, to the '90's and beyond in state psychiatric facilities in the Bronx, Manhattan, and the real-life equivalent of Arkham. Along the way, he's had over 300 stories published in *Cemetery Dance, Weird Tales, Indian Country Noir, Mojo: Conjure Stories*, and others, and collected in *A Blood of Killers, Visions Through a Shattered Lens, I Love You And There Is Nothing You Can Do About It*, the recent *Painfreak: Ultimate Edition*, and the upcoming *Dead Cat Omnibus*. Novels include the Max series, *In the Country of Dreaming Caravans, The Bard of Sorcery*, and *The Sting of Wonder, the Seed of Faith*. He has also served as Fiction Editor for the magazine *Space and Time* for over twenty years. His work is available through Crossroad Press and Amazon's Gerard Houarner author's page.

Gordon Linzner is the founder and former editor of *Space and Time Magazine*, and author of four published novels and scores of short stories in *The Magazine of Fantasy & Science Fiction, Twilight Zone, Sherlock Holmes Mystery Magazine*, and numerous other magazines and anthologies. He is a full member of the Horror Writers Association and a lifetime member of the Science Fiction & Fantasy Writers Association.

Jonathan Maberry is a *New York Times* bestselling author, five-time Bram Stoker Award winner, three-time Scribe Award winner, Inkpot Award winner, anthology editor, writing teacher, and comic book writer. His vampire apocalypse book series, *V-Wars*, was a Netflix original series starring Ian Somerhalder. He writes in multiple genres including suspense, thriller, horror, science fiction, epic fantasy, and action; and he writes for adults, teens, and middle grade. His works include the *Joe Ledger* thrillers, *Kagen the Damned, Ink, Glimpse*, the *Rot & Ruin* series, the *Dead of Night* series, *The Wolfman, X-Files Origins: Devil's Advocate*, the *Sleepers War* series (with Weston Ochse), *NectroTek, Mars One*, and many others. Several of his works are in development for film and TV. He is the editor of high-profile anthologies including *The X-Files, Aliens: Bug Hunt, Out of Tune, Don't Turn Out the Lights: A Tribute to Scary Stories to Tell in the Dark*, the *Baker Street Irregulars* series (with Michael A. Ventrella), *Double Trouble* (with Keith R.A. DeCandido), *Nights of the Living Dead* (with George A. Romero), and others. His comics include *Black Panther: DoomWar, The Punisher: Naked Kills*, and *Bad Blood*. His *Rot & Ruin* young adult novel was adapted into the #1 horror comic on Webtoon and is being developed for film by Alcon Entertainment. He the president of the International Association of Media Tie-in Writers and the editor of *Weird Tales* magazine. He lives in San Diego, California. Find him online at JonathanMaberry.com.

James D. Macdonald is the son of a commercial artist and a chemical engineer. Together with his long-time writing partner, Debra Doyle (daughter of a librarian and a civil engineer), he has written over thirty novels and over thirty short stories, primarily fantasy, science fiction, and horror. These include the best-selling Mageworlds series, and the award-winning *Knight's Wyrd*. When he wasn't writing, he's been an enlisted sailor, a Naval officer, an EMT, a magician, a sysop, and Santa Claus. He and Debra raised four children who have gone on to lives of their own mingling the arts and the sciences.

David Mack is the award-winning and *New York Times* best-selling author of thirty-eight novels and numerous short works of science fiction, fantasy, and adventure, including the *Star Trek: Destiny* and *Cold Equations* trilogies. Mack's writing credits span television (for episodes of *Star Trek: Deep Space Nine*), film, and comic books. He also has worked as a consultant on the animated television series *Star Trek: Lower Decks* and *Star Trek: Prodigy*. In June 2022, the International Association of Media Tie-in Writers honored him as a Grandmaster with its Faust Award. His most recent publications include *Star Trek: Coda,* Book III: *Oblivion's Gate* and *Harm's Way*, a *Star Trek: Vanguard* / *Star Trek: The Original Series* crossover novel. Mack's upcoming work includes several works of original short fiction and, in 2024, a new *Star Trek: Picard* novel titled *Firewall*. Mack resides in New York City with his wife, Kara. Follow him on Twitter (@DavidAlanMack) and Facebook (facebook.com/thedavidmack).

Megan Mackie is a Chicago-based writer. She is the author of the Amazon bestselling Lucky Devil series (urban fantasy/cyberpunk), the Dead World series (post-post-zombie apocalypse), *The Adventures of Pavlov's Dog and Schrodinger's Cat* (middle-grade science fiction), and the Working Mask series (wannabe superhero). Her other work can be found on the Yonder app, where she has published three web novels, *Cookbooks and Demons* (paranormal demon romance), *Star Courier* (*Firefly*-like speculative fiction), and *Novantis* (steampunk political intrigue with sky pirates, think *Bridgerton* meets *Black Sails*). Outside of her own series, she is a contributing writer for the role-playing games *Legendlore* and *Legendlore: Legacies* by Onyx Path Publishing and *Sirens: Battle of the Bards* through Apotheosis Studios. She also has a thing for iconic leather hats.

Outside of writing, she likes to play games: board games, puzzle boxes, RPGs, and video games. She lives in Chicago with her husband and children, two dogs, two cats, and her mother in the apartment upstairs.

Gail Z. Martin writes urban fantasy, epic fantasy, steampunk, and more for Orbit Books, Falstaff Books, SOL Publishing, and Darkwind Press. Urban fantasy series include Deadly Curiosities and the Night Vigil. Epic fantasy series include Darkhurst, the Chronicles of the Necromancer, the Fallen Kings Cycle, the Ascendant Kingdoms Saga, and the Assassins of Landria. Together with Larry N. Martin, she is the co-author of *Iron & Blood*, *Storm & Fury* (both Steampunk/alternate history), the Spells Salt and Steel comedic horror series, the roaring twenties monster hunter Joe Mack Shadow Council series, and the Wasteland Marshals near-future post-apocalyptic series. As Morgan Brice, she writes urban fantasy MM paranormal romance, with the Witchbane, Badlands, Treasure Trail, Kings of the Mountain, and Fox Hollow series. Gail is also a con-runner for ConTinual, the online, ongoing multi-genre convention that never ends.

Seanan McGuire writes things. It's difficult to make her stop, and she starts climbing the walls pretty quickly when people try, and so, in an effort to keep her from transforming into the sort of thing that isn't supposed to exist outside of horror movies, people very rarely bother to try. Her writing things has resulted in upward of seventy published novels under a variety of names, more short stories than she can count, comics, poetry, and way too much else. One day a bookshelf in her house will collapse and we will never see her again. She will return to the night air and the October wind, to blow through fields of corn and frighten sleeping children.

Seanan lives in the Pacific Northwest in a house with too many books, several thousand My Little Ponies, and an ever-changing assortment of cats, amphibians, and predatory insects. She has won multiple major genre awards, and is prone to telling people the history of the *Magic: The Gathering* universe when they hold still for too long. Find her at seananmcguire.com.

Jody Lynn Nye lists her main career activity as spoiling cats. When not engaged upon this worthy occupation, she writes fantasy and science fiction books and short stories. Since 1987, she has published over fifty books and more than 170 short stories. Among the novels Jody has written are her epic fantasy series, The Dreamland, beginning with *Waking in Dreamland*; five contemporary humorous fantasies, *Mythology 101, Mythology Abroad, Higher Mythology* (the three collected by Meisha Merlin Publishing as *Applied Mythology*), *Advanced Mythology*, and *The Magic Touch*; three medical science fiction novels, *Taylor's Ark, Medicine Show*, and *The Lady and* *the Tiger*; and *Strong Arm Tactics*, a humorous military science fiction novel, the first of the Wolfe Pack series. Jody also wrote *The Dragonlover's Guide to Pern*, a guide to the world of internationally best-selling author Anne McCaffrey's popular world. She also collaborated with McCaffrey on four science fiction novels, *The Death of Sleep, Crisis on Doona* (a *New York Times* and *USA Today* bestseller), *Treaty at Doona*, and *The Ship Who Won*, and wrote a solo sequel entitled *The Ship Errant*. Jody co-authored the *Visual Guide to Xanth* with best-selling fantasy author Piers Anthony. She has edited two anthologies, *Launch Pad* (with Mike Brotherton) and *Don't Forget Your Spacesuit, Dear!* She has two short story collections, *A Circle of Celebrations* and *Cats Triumphant!* She wrote eight books with the late Robert Lynn Asprin: *License Invoked*, a contemporary fantasy set in New Orleans, and seven set in Asprin's *Myth Adventures* universe, including the collection *Myth-Told Tales* and the novels *Myth Alliances*, *Myth-Taken Identity, Class Dis-Mythed, Myth-Gotten Gains, Myth Chief*, and *Myth-Fortunes*. Since Asprin's passing, she continued his Dragons series for Ace Books with *Dragons Deal* and *Dragons Run* and also written *Myth-Quoted* and *Myth-Fits*. Her newest series is the Lord Thomas Kinago books for Baen Books, including *View from the Imperium* and *Rhythm of the Imperium*.

Other recent books include *Moon Tracks* (Baen), a YA hard science fiction novel, the second in collaboration with Doctor Travis S. Taylor; and *Pros and Cons* (WordFire Press), a nonfiction book about conventions in collaboration with Bill Fawcett.

Over the last thirty or so years, Jody has taught in numerous writing workshops and participated in hundreds of panels covering the subjects of writing and being published at science-fiction conventions. She has also spoken in schools and libraries around the north and northwest suburbs. In 2007 she taught fantasy writing at Columbia College Chicago. She also runs the two-day writers' workshop at Dragon Con. Jody is the Coordinating Judge of the Writers of the Future contest, the world's largest science fiction and fantasy writing contest for new authors (free to enter!).

Jody lives in the northwest suburbs of Atlanta, with her husband Bill Fawcett, a writer, game designer, military historian and book packager, and three feline overlords, Athena, Minx, and

Marmalade. Check out her website at www.jodynye.com. She is on Facebook as Jody Lynn Nye and Twitter @JodyLynnNye.

Aaron Rosenberg is the best-selling, award-winning author of nearly fifty novels, including the DuckBob SF comedy series, the Relicant Chronicles epic fantasy series, the Areyat Islands fantasy pirate mystery series, the *Dread Remora* space-opera series, and, with David Niall Wilson, the *O.C.L.T.* occult thriller series. His tie-in work contains novels for *Star Trek, Warhammer, World of Warcraft, Stargate: Atlantis, Shadowrun, Mutants & Masterminds*, and *Eureka* and short stories for *The X-Files, World of Darkness, Crusader Kings II, Deadlands, Master of Orion*, and *Europa Universalis IV*. He has written children's books (including the original series STEM Squad and Pete and Penny's Pizza Puzzles, the award-winning *Bandslam: The Junior Novel* and the #1 best-selling *42: The Jackie Robinson Story*), educational books on a variety of topics, and over seventy roleplaying games (including the original games *Asylum, Spookshow*, and *Chosen*, work for White Wolf, Wizards of the Coast, Fantasy Flight, Pinnacle, and many others, the Origins Award-winning *Gamemastering Secrets*, and the Gold ENnie-winning *Lure of the Lich Lord*). He is a founding member of Crazy 8 Press. Aaron lives in New York with his family. You can follow him online at gryphonrose. com, on Facebook at facebook.com/gryphonrose, and on X (formerly known as Twitter) @gryphonrose.

Jenifer Purcell Rosenberg is an author, artist, and digital marketing consultant based in New York City. Jenifer has published work in anthologies, tabletop role-playing game manuals and journals, and a children's book they wrote and illustrated, *Alligator's Friends*. Jenifer has been a panelist and presenter at multiple conventions and trade shows, including Dragon Meet (UK), Shore Leave, and GenCon, and has taught online workshops for digital marketing and social media promotion. In their spare time, they enjoy painting, gaming, and oh, so many books.

Hildy Silverman writes in multiple genres, including science fiction, fantasy, horror, and blends thereof. In 2020, she joined the Crazy 8 Press authors collective, which publishes novels and anthologies by its membership. In 2013, her short story, "The

Six Million Dollar Mermaid," which appeared in the anthology *Mermaids 13: Tales from the Sea*, edited by John L. French, was a finalist for the WSFA Small Press Award. In 2005, she became the publisher and editor-in-chief of *Space and Time Magazine*, one of the oldest small-press genre magazines still in production, and ran it until 2018. She is a past president of the Garden State Speculative Fiction Writers and a frequent panelist on the science fiction convention circuit. For more information about Hildy, including a complete list of her published work, please visit HildySilverman.com

Wrenn Simms has worked a wide variety of jobs in her adult life, from seamstress to investment accountant to personal assistant to tax preparer to investment operations analyst/consultant to office manager to Census supervisor. In the publishing world, she has done editorial and production work for a variety of clients since 2011, including Dark Quest Books, EGZ Productions, eSpec Books, Prince of Cats, Riverdale Avenue Books, the Society for American Baseball Research, and WordFire Press. With Keith R.A. DeCandido, she formed WhsyperWude LLC in 2021, and is pleased for this anthology to be their first publication. In what passes for her spare time, Wrenn is an award-winning master-class costumer and convention organizer.

There's been a debate among certain obscure and drunken literary scholars about whether **Patrick Thomas** was raised by Cthulhu or a leprechaun in a Manhattan bar. What there is no arguing about is that Patrick is the award-winning author of fifty-plus books, including the beloved fantasy humor *Murphy's Lore* series, the darkly hilarious *Dear Cthulhu* advice empire, as well as the *Bikini Jones* adventure books. Patrick pens the *Hexcraft* and *Terrorbelle* urban fantasy series, co-writes the *Mystic Investigators* paranormal mystery series, and is the creator of the *Agents of the Abyss*.

Dear Cthulhu has expanded from magazines and books to broadcast monthly on the radio show *Destinies: The Voice of Science Fiction*. Over 100 of his stories have been published in magazines and anthologies. A number of his books were part of the props department of the *CSI* television show and *Nightcaps* was even thrown at a suspect's head. His urban fantasy *Fairy with A Gun* at one point had been optioned for film and TV by Laurence

Fishburne's Cinema Gypsy Productions. Top Men Productions turned his Soul For Hire Story, *Act of Contrition*, into a short film. DPH Games is releasing a card game based on his *142nd Starborne* military SF stories.

As Patrick T. Fibbs, he writes kids' books including the *Babe B. Bear Mysteries*, *The Undead Kid Diaries*, *Joy Reaper Checks Out*, *Emotional Support Nightmare*, and the *Fushia The Mermaid* and the *Ughabooz* picture books for younger kids.

Visit him at www.patthomas.net and www.patricktfibbs.com.

Michael A. Ventrella writes witty adventures such as the Teddy Roosevelt steampunk novel *Big Stick* and the Terin Ostler fantasy series. He has edited more than a dozen anthologies, including *Release the Virgins!*, *Three Time Travelers Walk Into...*, and (with Jonathan Maberry) the *Baker Street Irregulars* series. His nonfiction books include *How to Argue the Constitution with a Conservative* as well as books on the music of The Beatles and The Monkees. In his spare time, he is a lawyer. Find him online at MichaelAVentrella.com.

Dayton Ward is a *New York Times* bestselling author or co-author of more than forty novels and novellas, often working with his best friend, Kevin Dilmore. His short fiction has appeared in more than thirty anthologies, and he's written for magazines such as *NCO Journal, Kansas City Voices, Famous Monsters of Filmland, Star Trek,* and *Star Trek Communicator* as well as the websites Tor.com, StarTrek.com, and Syfy.com. You can find him at daytonward.com.

THE ACKNOWLEDGMENTS
OF THE APOCALYPSE

The editors would like to thank Danielle Ackley-McPhail, GraceAnne Andreassi DeCandido, the late Jay Lake, Mike McPhail, Lori Perkins, and Aaron Rosenberg for tremendous aid and assistance.

In addition, without the following, *The Four ???? of the Apocalypse* simply would *not* have happened. Our eternal gratitude to:

Benjamin Adler
Ross Aitken
Jeremy Alldredge
James Allen
Felicity Alma
Alex "KB" Altman
Sina Maria Alvarado
Lorraine Anderson
Peter Anderson
Peter J. Anderson
Karl Ansell
Austin Appleby
Blake Arledge
James Arrowood
Matej Artac
Eric Avedissian
Ian B.
Emily Baisch
Stephen Ballentine
Paul Balze
Howard Bamptom
Matthew Barr
Steven Bartels
Fred Bauer
Bonnie Beck
Cricket Bel
Sam Bertolami
Hal Bichel

Christopher A. Bier
Bill
Ultra Bilthalver
Kathryn Black
Nate Blanchard
Sarah Blanset
Sharon Bliss
Jeremy Bottroff
Chris Bower
Paul Boyle
Alan J. Brava
Morgan Brilliant
Tom Brincefield
Shay Brodbeck
Rachel Brune
Bryan
Wayne Budgen
Rose Marie Caratozzolo
Andrew Cardinale
Danny Chamberlin
Beatrice Chan-Smith
Owais Chaudhri
Chickadee
Harold L. Christensen III
Kelly J. Cooper
Andrew Corvin
Michael Costello
Mike Crate

Scott Crick
Jared Cross
Dagmar
Danielle
Alan Danziger
Mike Dean
Barbara deBary-Kesner
Glenn Dekhayser
Marti Dickinson
Elizabeth Donald
Len Dvorkin
Kath Eierman
Ross Emery
Jessica Enfante
Mario Escamilla
Joshua Evans
Jonathan Ezor
Bruce Fenton
Lynda Ferrell
Sondra Fielder
Richard Fine
Sebastian Finsel
Katie Fouks
Ashley Funkhouser
Dominic Galliano
David Gian-Cursio
Allyn Gibson
Barbara Goetz
Marian Goldeen
Amy Goldschlager
David Goldstein
Tina Good
Cathy Green
Alyx Griffen
Carol Guess
Jessica Guinness
Stuart Hall
James Hallam
Rebecca Hamilton
Roger Hammons
Russell J. Handelman
Kathleen Hannon
Jeffrey Harlan
Shael Hawman
Melissa Healer

Maggi Heffler
Tara Henderson
Sarah Hertz
Mary Jane Hetzlein
Lukas Heuel
Bryan Hill
Grey Hodge
RJ Hopkinson
Tony Hsieh
Caitlin Jane Hughes
Andrew Hunter
Elizabeth Inglee-Richards
Rowan Irelia
Tony Isabella
Saul Jaffe
James
Justin James
Jen1701D
Jessica
JMocha
Kaci Johnston
Carol Jones
Fowler Jones
Kyle Jones
Michael M. Jones
Mike Jones
Simon Jones
Andreas Kaluza
Kat Kan
Cheri Kannarr
Andrew Kaplan
Mary Kay Kare
Christina Karl
Katherine
Lesley Keech
John Keegan
Peggy Kimbell
Matt Knepper
Sergey Kochergan
Daniel Korn
Sonia Koval
Kerry Kuhn
Kate Kulig
Richard Kvale
Heidi Lambert

Lesley Landry
Courtland LaVallee
Kevin Lawrence
Lisa Leaheey
Bair Learn
Tracie Lee
Thomas Legg
Bill Leisner
Luke Leveque
Kimberly Lingley
Corey Liss
Rebecca Jane Lockley
Giusepee Lo Turco
Louise Löwenspets
Eric Lowmiller
James Lucas
Stephanie Lucas
Mark Lukens
Zan Lynx
maau
John MacLean
Rachel Machinton
Bert Maes
Shawn Marier
ToniAnn Marini &
Kyle McCraw
John Markley
William Martin
Karl "Thrillseeker" Maurer
Joshua McGinnis
Robin McKean
Deidre McLeod
Jerry McMullen
Mdtommyd
Jeff Metzner
Edgar Middel
Mihai
Stuart Moore
Brooks Moses
Randi Moulton
mouselet
Sarah Muck
Ty Myrick
Sasquatch N.
Jon Nepsha

Juanita Nesbitt
Mark Newman
Hung Nguyen
Michael Nichols
Dianne Nicholson
Amanda Nixon
Raven Oak
Christopher Ochs
Richard O'Shea
David Phillip Oster
Jennifer "Bildingmeyer"
 Osterman
Xana Ouellette
Jeffrey Palmer
Bells Parlato
Joseph D. Payne
Scott Pearson
Mary P. Perez
Meredith PeruzziMichael Pescuma
Pierre Pettinger
Jakob Pfafferdodt
Brian David Phillips
Jennifer L. Pierce
John M. Portley
Jennifer Postley
Craig Poth
Aaron Pound
Kal Powell
Ryan Power
Joe Pranevich
Simon Prior
Joshua L. Pritchett Jr.
Chelsea Nicole Provencher
Miranda Prowell
Karen Purcell
Arne Radtke
Rachael Raffensperger
Ed Read
Aysha Rehm
Jack Reichert
Alison Richards
Christopher Riley
Rivka
Chuck Robinson
Zan Rosin

THE ACKNOWLEDGMENTS OF THE APOCALYPSE

Claire Rosser
Dale Russell
David Salmansohn
Scantrontb
Jack Scheer
William Schulz
Sarah Sexton
Catherine Sharp
Wendy Sheridan
Jay Shull
Silent Parade Press
Linda Silverman
Jeff Singer
Subrata Sircar
Katiana Slaton
Koyeli Solanki
Raequel Solomon
Jacob Sommer
Tina Sorrentino
Mary Spila
William Spratt
S. Springate
Mark Squire
Rich Steeves
Tami Stone
Anthea Strezze
Brian Strezze
Mark Strock
Dan Styer
Raphael Sutton
Christine Swendseid
Corey T.
Raja Thiagarajan
Sven Thiede
Arthur Thomas
Pekka Timonen
Susan Tomaski
Edward Trayford
U.C.J.
Ricardo Valencia
Vijay Varman
Vulpecula
Judith Waidlich
Kathleen Walker
Tara Walsh

Josh Ward
Jim Westbrook
Sidney H. Whitaker
David White
WildCard
J. Lynn Williams
Phaedra Winters
Joanna Ka Wai Wong
Write or Die,
 writing and critique group
Allison M. Yambor
David Zicherman
Mike Zipser

Oh NO! You've Finished the Book!

Don't worry, it's not the end of the world!

Find your next favorite read at eSpec Books, an independent press specializing in quality speculative fiction, both long and short.

www.especbooks.com

TALES OF STEM-SAVVY GIRLS
IN SCI-FI WORLDS

DIVE INTO THESE COLLECTIONS OF SHORT
STORIES FEATURING BRAINY HEROINES WHO USE
THEIR SMARTS TO SAVE THE DAY. (AGES 10+)

PROCEEDS ARE DONATED TO THE
SOCIETY OF WOMEN ENGINEERS
SCHOLARSHIP FUND.

HTTP://BRAVENEWGIRLS.WEEBLY.COM/

GREAT BOOKS BY GREAT AUTHORS
DIRECT TO READERS

WHY?
BECAUSE WE'RE CRAZY!!!

www.crazy8press.com